IN THE FIELD OF FIRE

IN THE FIELD OF FIRE

Edited by
Jeanne Van Buren Dann
and Jack Dann

TOR

This is a work of fiction. All the characters and events portrayed in this book are fictional, and any resemblance to real people or incidents is purely coincidental.

IN THE FIELD OF FIRE

First printing: February 1987

A TOR Book

Published by Tom Doherty Associates, Inc.
49 West 24 Street
New York, N.Y. 10010

Hardcover ISBN: 0-312-93000-3
Paperback ISBN: 0-312-93008-9

Library of Congress Catalog Card Number: 86-50955

Printed in the United States of America

0 9 8 7 6 5 4 3 2 1

For Our Son Jody

Acknowledgments

The editors would like to thank the following people for their help and support:

Stephanie Hoffman, George Yonemura, Mara Peter-Raoul, James Dean, Suzanne Feehan, Tom Williams, Patrick Delahunt, Tappan King, Barry Malzberg, Lucius Shepard, Mike Peter, Trina King, Robert Lenham, Katherine Combellick, Gardner Dozois, Susan Casper, John Kessel, Annette Casparis, Terence M. Keane, Stanley Scobie, Bruce McAllister, Brian Aldiss, Kirby McCauley, Shawna McCarthy, Harvey Van Buren, Harvey Van Buren, Jr., Jeanne Van Buren, Murray I. Dann, Edith N. Dann, Lorne Dann, Dennis Etchison, John Douglas, Stu Schiff, William Ryan, Kim Stanley Robinson, Joe and Gay Haldeman, Brian Perry and Tawna Lewis of Fat Cat Books (263 Main Street, Johnson City, New York 13790).

A special thanks to our own editor, Beth Meacham.

Contents

Introduction
by
Jeanne Van Buren Dann
and Jack Dann

The time has come when Americans are reexamining what happened to us during the Vietnam War. It was the war that we, as a nation, repressed; and the veterans were the warriors we forgot. Only now, after what seems to have been over ten years of collective amnesia, are we trying to come to terms with what many consider to be an American tragedy. Witness the PBS thirteen-hour documentary *Vietnam: A Television History*, General Westmoreland's suit against CBS, and the large number of books now seeing print on the subject, books such as *Vietnam Voices: Perspectives on the War Years*, compiled by John Clark Pratt, *Everything We Had* by Al Santoli, *Long Time Passing: Vietnam and the Haunted Generation* by Myra MacPherson, *Charlie Company: What Vietnam Did to Us* by Peter Goldman and Tony Fuller, and *Dear America: Letters Home From Vietnam*, edited by Bernard Edelman. Novels that came and went during the 1960s and 1970s are being published again, thanks in part to Avon's reprint program that had brought back novels by Joe Haldeman, William Pelfrey, Philip Smith, Charles Durden, Smith Hempstone, and others.

Vietnam has once again become a compelling issue. Perhaps it's because we feel that the war has finally evaporated into history. We feel safe enough now to talk about it, to explore and examine it, and, unfortunately, to romanticize it.

But the war is *far* from being over, even though we pulled our troops out of Vietnam over ten years ago. In fact, we are in what might be called the second stage of the war. The first stage was the actual fighting, the mass demonstrations, the draft-card burnings. We were a country divided. It was the first war that we watched on television as if it were some kind of prime-time adventure rerun that had been worked up in Hollywood. It was the time of the living-room war, when we watched our men fighting and dying in the fields and paddies and mountains of Indochina while we sipped coffee. It was the time of the 1968 National Democratic Convention and the Tet offensive and My Lai. A time when antiwar activists poured gasoline over themselves and burned in the streets. A time of protest songs and Kent State. A time of SDS and Weathermen.

And it was a war fought by teenagers.

Many of those soldiers are still fighting the war, which continues to haunt the lives of Vietnam vets and their families. This is the second stage of the war that we had almost convinced ourselves was history.

It is estimated that 500,000 to 700,000 of our 1.2 million Vietnam War combat veterans suffer from Post-traumatic Stress Disorder,[1] of what the *Diagnostic and Statistical Manual III*, which is published by the American Psychiatric Association, terms PTSD.[2]

Some of the symptoms of PTSD are recurrent and intrusive recollections of a traumatic event, recurrent dreams of the event, sudden acting or feeling as if the traumatic event were recurring because of an association with an environmental or ideational stimulus, markedly diminished interest in one or more significant activities, feelings of detachment or estrangement from others, hyperalertness or exaggerated startle responses, sleep disturbances, survivor guilt, memory impariment, or trouble concentrating.[2]

PTSD can be acute, delayed, or chronic. Acute PTSD was formerly known as common stress response, shell shock, or combat fatigue, and was recognized among soldiers of World War II and Korea. Because of the nature of the Vietnam War, many of its veterans did not experience these symptoms until six months to ten years after their homecoming; they suffered or continue to suffer from delayed PTSD, and from chronic PTSD. Some researchers believe that the Vietnam veterans were in fact predisposed by the nature of the war to the development of delayed and/or chronic PTSD.[3–6]

The twelve-month rotation tour system, which, ironically,

was instituted to *alleviate* combat fatigue, was introduced during the Vietnam War. It was known by military planners that the highest incidence of breakdowns was suffered by those who were exposed to long periods of combat, and by the time of the Korean War the U.S. military was already using a point system of rotation, whereby a soldier who had accumulated a certain number of points would be sent home. Contrast this with World War II, when the soldier's only hope to return home safely was an end to the war. In a misguided attempt to reduce stress further, the DEROS system was instituted during the Vietnam War (DEROS stands for "date of expected return from overseas"). The idea was that a shorter period of time—twelve to thirteen months—would decrease the incidence of neuropsychological casualties.[4]

The system didn't work as expected. Rather, the DEROS system—combined with the traumatic reentry of vets rotated back into "the World," as the United States was called—interfered with the normal process of psychological recovery from combat stress.[5]

This process involves the symptoms listed for PTSD, particularly intrusion, characterized by flashbacks, nightmares, and recollections of traumatic events. It also includes a period of denial and what is called shock or psychological numbing. It is believed that Vietnam veterans spent long periods of time in denial, which was reinforced by the DEROS system. They knew that they would be out of danger within twelve or thirteen months, and thus were able to inhibit intrusive thoughts and images and remain in denial, which masked the symptoms of common stress response.[3–6]

Because of the rotation system, the vets felt no continuity with those who were there before them or those who would arrive after them; even their buddies would be rotated home at different times. New men, referred to as "fucking new guys," would be rotated into the unit as their buddies rotated out. These new men had no combat experience and were therefore considered by many soldiers to be dangerous and unreliable. They were usually avoided until, and if, they could survive to become experienced combat soldiers or grunts. The Vietnam War was a lonely, isolated war, a private, personal war for survival in a country where ally and enemy looked alike, where women and children could kill you as effectively as a mine in the brush. Vietnam itself became the enemy of the short-timer. The calendar replaced the *esprit de corps* of older, more popular wars. Counting down the calendar became a ritual; it was how they held on until their time was up. They fantasized how life would be back in "the World," and counted the days.[5,7,13]

Drug and alcohol use among our soldiers is also believed to have inhibited intrusive thoughts or dreams because of their psychological numbing effects.[8] Drugs were readily available and affordable. The heroin in Vietnam was 96 percent pure (heroin in the United States is usually 3–10 percent pure), and a multidose vial could be purchased for about $2.00.[9]

A study done to compare and contrast World War II, Korean, and Vietnam veterans revealed that Vietnam-era veterans manifested more symptoms of PTSD. It was also found that they drank significantly more alcohol.[10] There are other factors that researchers believe play a role in the development of delayed PTSD. Many returned home within seventy-two hours or less after being in Vietnam, with barely any interlude from their war experience to the time when they were faced with routine daily activities. They experienced culture shock, and the normalcy of being home again only further prolonged their denial. It only took them hours to leave a country where, as Frances FitzGerald wrote, "All the laws of civilization were suspended."[11] This experience was especially traumatic for the Vietnam veterans who went to war as teenagers and were at a particularly vulnerable age socially and psychologically. Not only may age play a role in predisposing a vet to PTSD, but research has demonstrated that Vietnam veterans whose fathers were in combat during World War II may be more prone to suffer a severe form of PTSD known as malignant post-Vietnam stress syndrome, which is life-threatening. This may happen to soldiers who went to Vietnam identifying with their "war hero" fathers, and upon their return found that their relationship with their fathers became strained.[12] Many Vietnam veterans grew up listening to their fathers' World War II victory stories, which were reinforced by old war films and shows such as *Combat* that were popular television fare. They went to war with visions of becoming American heroes, only to return home to mass demonstrations—or cold, silent indifference, which was even more devastating. There were no victory parades for them, as there were for their fathers. Instead of wearing their uniforms proudly, as their fathers had done, they quickly put them away and pretended to be civilians, lest they be called "baby killers" by those who were protesting what they believed to be an unjust war. Many were in a state of denial, still numbed by what they had seen and done in Vietnam, unable to share the common experience of being warriors with their fathers, as the generation of World War I had done with their sons. Instead, the bond between father and son was weakened by an ambiguous war, for self-loathing, bitterness, and hopelessness had replaced the Vietnam veterans' feelings of patriotism and heroism.

Symptoms of PTSD can also be severe when the disorder is delayed, and/or chronic if left untreated. A lack of understanding of this condition can lead to misdiagnosis and inappropriate treatment. Veterans who resent authority or who think their symptoms are abnormal may be reluctant to seek help. Many do not realize that the symptoms are *normal* reactions when stress of this magnitude is experienced.

Vietnam veterans with PTSD do not suffer from a hopeless disorder. The Disabled American Vietnam Veteran Outreach Program is providing educational material and services regarding the diagnosis and treatment of PTSD, and group and individual therapeutic techniques have been developed specifically for Vietnam veterans and have proven to be beneficial. At last these men have an opportunity to be gently guided through the normal process of recovery within a safe environment, where they can unlock their feelings and examine their fear, guilt, anger, and tremendous sense of personal loss.

We have, in effect, been sitting on a time bomb. It is only now that we are becoming aware of a war that never ended. It has been repressed, only to manifest itself in the violence and anxieties and sweat-soaked nightmares of a generation of veterans still suffering from the war. Vietnam-era veterans are 65 percent more likely to die from suicide as compared to those who avoided this war.[14]

None of us are exempt from questions and guilt. While veterans question why they had to fight a politically and morally ambiguous war, former protesters wonder if they chose the best method of responding to it. Many nonveterans feel guilty because they did not serve with their friends and neighbors who were killed or wounded.

The Vietnam War still goes on. . . .

Vietnam veterans don orange T-shirts that read SPRAYED AND BETRAYED, while their wives wonder if their children will be born with birth defects or be predisposed to serious illnesses due to their husbands' exposures to Agent Orange. Families wait for loved ones who they believe are still prisoners of war, while remains of MIAs are returned, a few at a time. Refugees leave their ruined homeland and immigrate to areas like Arlington, Virginia, known as "Little Saigon."

Studies have indicated that the dreams of Vietnam combat veterans can in some cases reveal entirely different and more accurate accounts of this war than the dreamer's waking memories. Also, these recurring dreams change over time, taking the form of "therapeutic drama."[15]

Fiction itself is a kind of waking dream, an exploration of our fears and nightmares, and at its best it dips into our unconscious to grab at our demons and bring them screaming and bleeding into the light. It, too, can be a "therapeutic drama" that transforms the terrifying chaos of war into meaning.

The Vietnam War was so psychologically cyclonic and horrific in its effect on individuals that perhaps the dark personal "truth" of their experience can best be reflected through the devices of metaphor and fantasy.

Science fiction and fantasy specialize in the creation of worlds and dreams. We think that these dreams, written by the best in these genres, bring another level of meaning and truth to the war that we have all—in our own ways—experienced.

Notes

1. Stephen B. Levenberg, "Vietnam Combat Veterans: From Perpetrator to Victim," *Family and Community Health*, vol. 5, no. 4 (February 1983), pp. 69–76.
2. American Psychiatric Association, *Diagnostic and Statistical Manual of Mental Disorders, Third Edition* (Washington, D.C.: American Psychiatric Association, 1980).
3. C. R. Figley, Introduction I, ed. C. R. Figley, *Stress Disorders Among Vietnam Veterans: Theory, Research, and Treatment* (New York: Brunner/Mazel, 1978).
4. H. R. Kormos, "The Nature of Combat Stress," ed. C. R. Figley, *Stress Disorders Among Vietnam Veterans: Theory, Research, and Treatment* (New York: Brunner/Mazel, 1978), as cited by Jim Goodwin, Psy.D., "Post-traumatic Stress Disorders of the Vietnam Veteran," Tom Williams, Psy.D., D.A.V., 1980, p. 6.
5. Jim Goodwin, Psy.D., "Post-traumatic Stress Disorders of the Vietnam Veteran," Tom Williams, Psy.D., DAV., 1980, pp. 6-7.
6. Mard J. Horowitz and George F. Solomon, "A Prediction of Delayed Stress Response Syndromes in Vietnam Veterans," *Journal of Psychological Issues*, vol. 31, no. 4 (1975), pp. 67–79.
7. Bourne, *Men, Stress and Vietnam* (Boston: Little, Brown, 1970), pp. 12–42. Cited by Jim Goodwin, Psy.D., "Post-traumatic Stress Disorders of the Vietnam Veteran," Tom Williams, Psy. D., DAV., 1980, p. 6.
8. Horowitz and Solomon, pp. 67–79.
9. Paul Starr, *The Discarded Army* (New York: Charterhouse, 1973), p. 116.
10. Mirian D. Blum *et al.*, "An Assessment of the Treatment Needs of Vietnam-era Veterans," *Hospital and Community Psychiatry*, vol. 35, no. 7 (July 1984), pp. 691–696.

11. Frances FitzGerald, *Fire in the Lake* (Boston: Little, Brown, 1972), p. 371.
12. Robert Rosenheck, "Father-Son Relationships in Malignant-Post-Vietnam Stress Syndrome," *American Journal of Social Psychiatry*, vol. 5, no. 1 (Winter 1985), pp. 19–23.
13. C. C. Moskos, "The American Combat Soldier in Vietnam." In D.M. Mantell & Pilisuk (Eds.), *Journal of Social Issues: Soldiers In and After Vietnam*, 1975, 31(4):25–37, as cited by Jim Goodwin, Psy.D., "Posttraumatic Stress Disorders of the Vietnam Veteran," Tom Williams, Psy.D., D.A.V., 1980, p. 7.
14. Norman Hearst, M.D., M.P.H., Thomas B. Neuman, M.D., M.P.H., and Stephen B. Hulley, M.D., M.P.H., "Delayed Effects of the Military Draft on Mortality," *The New England Journal of Medicine*, March 6, 1986, pp. 620–624.
15. Harry A. Wilmer, "Vietnam and Madness: Dreams of Schizophrenic Veterans," *Journal of the American Academy of Psychoanalysis*, vol. 10, no. 1 (January 1982), pp. 47–65.

"And it's 1, 2, 3, what are we fighting for?
Don't ask me I don't give a damn
Next stop is Vietnam."

Kim Stanley Robinson

Over the past decade, Kim Stanley Robinson has established himself as one of the most respected "new" writers in the genre. A Clarion Writers' Workshop graduate, he sold his first story to Damon Knight's *Orbit* anthology series in 1976 and continued to sell stories to Knight and other markets, such as Terry Carr's *Universe* and *The Magazine of Fantasy & Science Fiction*. His story "Venice Drowned" drew considerable critical attention in 1981—it is an evocative, haunting tale of the surreal goings-on in a submerged Venice after a Second Deluge—but Robinson came to full prominence in 1984 with the publication of his absolutely brilliant story "Black Air" and his first novel, *The Wild Shore*. "Black Air" is a masterwork, a deeply symbolic tour de force about a boy impressed into service aboard an ill-fated galleon sailing with the Spanish Armada. That story deservedly won the prestigious World Fantasy Award, and *The Wild Shore* went on to garner the Philip K. Dick Memorial Special Award. In the same year, he published *Icehenge*, his second novel, and a critical book entitled *The Novels of Philip K. Dick*. His most recent books are *The Memory of Whiteness*, a novel, and *The Planet on the Table*, a collection. Forthcoming is *The Blind Geometer*. Robinson holds a Ph.D. in literature and has taught writing at the University of California, Davis. He and his wife, Lisa Nowell, are currently living in Zürich, Switzerland.

The Memorial

by
Kim Stanley Robinson

I'm sitting here in Washington, D.C., on the grass under some trees, facing the Vietnam Memorial. It's August 1985. I'm sitting here with my notebook opened, trying to do something for Jack and Jeannie Dann, who are building a memorial of a different sort. I doodle inky black sketches of the thing: black wings on the lined page. Sue Hall would do a better job. It's hot and I have nothing to say. My mind, the black monument: two blanks facing each other.

Try. The monument, as everyone probably knows, is cut into a hillside—the hill has been given a black marble side, in the shape of a broad, deep V. From where I sit the fifty thousand names are just tiny white lines, evenly marking the black. People walk down a sidewalk placed beside the wall. At first they look down at small panels, then in the middle they look up at big panels. They pass little American flags and baskets of plastic flowers left at the foot of the wall. They talk, point, some touch the wall. They stop talking, they walk silently away.

Several of them are clustered around a man in a park service cap, listening to him talk. A tour guide at the Vietnam Memorial! I have to laugh. America, my country: you are crazy. Curiosity prods me and I leave my notebook to see what a tour guide can possibly say.

When I get there he is finishing his talk. His cap says VOLUNTEER. "There is significance in all aspects of the monument. For instance, this side marks a direct line to the Lincoln Memorial. And the other side marks a direct line to the Capitol.'' Strange, I think, that it should have come to this—that two such vectors of America would have intersected here, in Vietnam. Is it really true?

He guides us up one side of the thing as he talks. Facts, figures, stories. They say the human mind cannot truly imagine any number over a hundred. I look at the fifty thousand names and wonder about that. Dodger Stadium, full of fans. Imagine all of them dead. One big car crash. I remember the car crashes I have seen, the metal twisted as if it were flesh, the flesh—too horribly fragile to contemplate. Flesh broken as if it were only an idea. Then I try to imagine walking through a landscape of car crashes, one every few minutes going off to left and right of me, as in a Ballard nightmare, for day after day. My stunted version of the war. Fifty thousand car crashes.

The guide helps an elderly couple to do a rubbing. When he is done I approach him. ''Why do you do this?'' He walks me down toward the middle. ''My son died in Vietnam in 1968. That's his name up there, near the top. See it?'' I nod. ''It's important to show people what happened, to explain to them so they won't forget.'' He is calm as he tells me this, even serene.

Amazing, the power of the idea! Here this man's son was killed at age twenty, in a war whose meaning some how escapes everyone, and because of that this man would never see his son marry, have children, work through a career; a lifetime's casual, superficial American family get-togethers, so dumb individually, so precious taken as a whole—all gone. And now he faces that bitter fact, he lives with it and renders it meaningful, all by his own efforts talking and talking, all with the help of the monument, a work of art, an idea made into black marble.

I don't know anything about this war. My friend Dave Osborn had a high school rival—in a friendly way they competed in everything. Killed in Vietnam. Dave looked for his name once, didn't find it. Or I know Joe Haldeman, who sets off airport metal detectors when he walks through them.

Or the "James P. Kelly" that Kessel and I saw on the black marble once—an odd feeling, that: it could have been us, we were the right age. Or all the Robinsons up there.

Or my friend Dick's roommate Herbie. Dick told us stories about Herbie I could scarcely believe. And then one day I was in the gym after swimming and Herbie came in from tennis. We said hi. He stripped down for the shower and there on the side of his thigh and butt was a scar so deep and broad and S-shaped . . . no neat mark of surgery, that. He walked off to the showers (two or three deep puckers in his flank) with his shoulders thrown back proudly. Like a soldier.

Or another story told me, by my friend Ward. There is a one-quarter-sized model of the memorial that tours the country so that people who can't get to Washington can still get an idea of it. Don't ask me how it works. Do they dig a hole in the ground for it, or fit it against a hillside? I don't know. Anyway, my friend's father drove up with his wife to see it. He had been an Air Force pilot, and had flown soldiers in and out of Vietnam hundreds of times. And so he drove up to see the thing. "And my mom said, 'We stayed three times longer than we had planned to. He just kept walking back and forth, looking at it. And when we drove home he didn't say a single word.' "

So I sit on the grass before the Memorial, and try to understand. I try to *feel* it, you see, try to feel something so huge and nebulous and distant as a national grief. . . . Dismal failure. In the heat and the calm, the grass's smell and the buzzing of flies, I fall asleep.

And in my sleep I have a dream. The monument becomes a big black bird—see how its wings are spread against the hillside? A black swan carrying me off against my will, over the nation and across the wide ocean, to Vietnam. And we glide together over the green jungles and the white beaches, and we look down and see all that I have been unable to forget: jiggling TV images of rat-a-tat combat, the *Life* magazine faces, the Vietnamese with the pistol to his head, Haldeman's explosion, the scene in Michael Herr's book where the new arrivals watch the full body bags dumped from a hovering copter, the nurse's account of her hospital work, the cover of Paul Fussell's book, with the soldier boy's face emptied by horror, collapsed, the ultimate witness of what war does to us. . . . What that boy looks at none of us can see, thank God. But we can see him. And the swan turns its neck to look back at me—

It dumps me on the grass and soars back into the side of the hill, wings extended. Black marble, scored with white lines. Each white line, each wasted life, begins to talk, begins to tell its story, in tiny whispers so that in the aggregate they sound like crickets and the humming of flies. I wake up.

The guide walks back and forth, explaining and explaining. People pass by slowly in the heat, looking solemn, even stunned. And suddenly I see that we all feel it, everyone there, and that therefore it must indeed mean something to be part of a nation. The power of the idea to render reality: *national grief*. It's a strange thought. But here we are.

When all our years have passed and the monument remains, without parents to finger a name and ask for rubbings, without lovers to leave ID bracelets and baskets of plastic flowers, without even the many citizens like me who know that a friend's friend is up there—what will the monument say to those who come after? Black sink in the ground, mark of losses almost beyond bearing. . . . Remember the small-town World War I memorials, the score of forgotten names on a plaque. When has one meant anything to you? These huge black plates will be filled with names that no one will know, names that might as well have been computer-generated for all that they will mean to those who will look at them. What will it say then? What can it say?

Tiny voices in the white lines, like the humming of flies. We fought because America told us to. We died. Remember.

Lucius Shepard

In the three years since Lucius Shepard sold his first story to Terry Carr's *Universe,* he has won the John W. Campbell Award for best new writer and has been a Nebula finalist four times, a Hugo award and a World Fantasy Award finalist twice, and a finalist for the British Fantasy Award, the British Science Fiction Award, the John W. Campbell Memorial Award, and the Philip K. Dick Award—an impressive and perhaps unprecedented debut. His work is evocative and disturbing, and if stories such as "Salvador," "The Man Who Painted the Dragon Griaule," "A Traveler's Tale," "The Jaguar Hunter," "A Spanish Lesson," "Firezone Emerald," and "R & R" are any indication, Shepard may be one of the most important talents ever to come into the field. He has sold over thirty stories to magazines and anthologies, such as *Playboy, Isaac Asimov's Science Fiction Magazine, The Magazine of Fantasy & Science Fiction, Universe,* and *Omni.* His first novel, *Green Eyes,* was met with critical acclaim. Forthcoming are two novels—*The Man Who Painted the Dragon Griaule* and *Life During Wartime* —and the short story collection *The Jaguar Hunter.* Shepard lives in Staten Island, N.Y., and has a son named Gullivar.

Delta Sly Honey

by
Lucius Shepard

There was this guy I knew at Noc Linh, worked the corpse detail, guy name of Randall J. Willingham, a skinny red-haired Southern boy with a plague of freckles and eyes blue as poker chips, and sometimes when he got high, he'd wander up to the operations bunker and start spouting all kinds of shit over the radio, telling about his hometown and his dog, his opinion of the war (he was against it), and what it was like making love to his girlfriend, talking real pretty and wistful about her ways, the things she'd whisper and how she'd draw her knees up tight to her chest to let him go in deep. There was something pure and peaceful in his voice, his phrasing, and listening to him, you could feel the war draining out of you, and soon you'd be remembering your own girl, your own dog and hometown, not with heartsick longing but with joy in knowing you'd had at least that much sweetness of life. For many of us, his voice came to be the oracle of our luck, our survival, and even the brass who tried to stop his broadcasts finally realized he was doing a damn sight more good than any morale officer, and it got to where anytime the war was going slow and there was some free air, they'd call Randall up and ask if he felt in the mood to do a little talking.

The funny thing was that except for when he had a mike in his hand, you could hardly drag a word out of Randall. He had been a loner from day one of his tour, limiting his conversation to "Hey" and "How you?" and such, and his celebrity status caused him to become even less talkative. This was best explained by what he told us once over the air: "You meet ol' Randall J. on the street, and you gonna say, 'Why that can't be Randall J.! That dumb-lookin' hillbilly couldn't recite the swearin'-in-oath, let alone be the hottest damn radio personality in South Vietnam!' And you'd be right on the money, 'cause Randall J. don't go more'n double figures for IQ, and he ain't got the imagination of a stump, and if you stopped him to say 'Howdy,' chances are he'd be stuck for a response. But lemme tell ya, when he puts his voice into a mike, ol' Randall J. becomes one with the airwaves, and the light that's been dark inside him goes bright, and his spirit streams out along Thunder Road and past the Napalm Coast, mixin' with the ozone and changin' into Randall J. Willingham, the High Priest of the Soulful Truth and the Holy Ghost of the Sixty-Cycle Hum."

The base was situated on a gently inclined hill set among other hills, all of which had once been part of the Michelin rubber plantation, but now were almost completely defoliated, transformed into dusty brown lumps. Nearly seven thousand men were stationed there, living in bunkers and tents dotting the slopes, and the only building with any degree of permanence was an outsized Quonset hut that housed the PX; it stood just inside the wire at the base of the hill. I was part of the MP contingent, and I guess I was the closest thing Randall had to a friend. We weren't really tight, but being from a small Southern town myself, the son of gentry, I was familiar with his type—fey, quiet farmboys whose vulnerabilities run deep—and I felt both sympathy and responsibility for him. My sympathy wasn't misplaced: nobody could have had a worse job, especially when you took into account the fact that his top sergeant, a beady-eyed, brush-cut, tackle-sized Army lifer named Andrew Moon, had chosen him for his whipping boy. Every morning I'd pass the tin-roofed shed where the corpses were off-loaded (it, too, was just inside the wire, but on the opposite side of the hill from the PX), and there Randall would be, laboring among body bags that were piled around like huge black fruit, with Moon hovering in the background and scowling. I always made it a point to stop and talk to Randall in order to give him a break from Moon's tyranny, and though he never expressed his gratitude or said very much about anything, soon he began to call me by my Christian name, Curt, instead of by my rank. Each time I made to leave, I would see the strain come back into his face, and before I had gone beyond earshot, I would hear Moon reviling him. I believe it was those days of staring into stomach cavities, into charred hearts and brains, and Moon all the while screaming at him . . . I believe that was what had squeezed the poetry out of Randall and birthed his radio soul.

I tried to get Moon to lighten up. One afternoon I bearded him in his tent and asked why he was mistreating Randall. Of course I knew the answer. Men like Moon, men who have secured a little power and grown bloated from its use, they don't need an excuse for brutality; there's so much meanness inside them, it's bound to slop over onto somebody. But—thinking I could handle him better than Randall—I planned to divert his meanness, set myself up as his target, and this seemed a good way to open.

He didn't bite, however; he just lay on his cot, squinting up at me and nodding sagely, as if he saw through my charade. His jowls were speckled with a few days' growth of stubble, hairs sparse and black as pig bristles. "Y'know," he said, "I couldn't figure why you were buddyin' up to that fool, so I had a look at your records." He grunted laughter. "Now I got it."

"Oh?" I said, maintaining my cool.

"You got quite a heritage, son! All that noble Southern blood, all them dead generals and senators. When I seen that, I said to myself, 'Don't get on this boy's case too heavy, Andy. He's just tryin' to be like his great-grandaddy, doin' a kindness now and then for the darkies and the poor white trash.' Ain't that right?"

I couldn't deny that a shadow of the truth attached to what he had said, but I refused to let him rankle me. "My motives aren't in question here," I told him.

"Well, neither are mine . . . 'least not by anyone who counts." He swung his legs off the cot and sat up, glowering at me. "You got some nice duty here, son. But you go fuckin' with me, I'll have your ass walkin' point in Quanh Tri 'fore you can blink. Understand?"

I felt as if I had been dipped in ice water. I knew he could do as he threatened—any man who's made top sergeant has also made some powerful friends—and I wanted no part of Quanh Tri.

He saw my fear and laughed. "Go on, get out!" he said,

and as I stepped through the door, he added, "Come round the shed anytime, son. I ain't got nothin' against *noblesse oblige*. Fact is, I love to watch."

And I walked away, knowing that Randall was lost.

In retrospect, it's clear that Randall had broken under Moon's whip early on, that his drifty radio spiels were symptomatic of his dissolution. In another time and place, someone might have noticed his condition; but in Vietnam everything he did seemed a normal reaction to the craziness of the war, perhaps even a bit more restrained than normal, and we would have thought him really nuts if he hadn't acted weird. As it was, we considered him a flake, but not wrapped so tight that you couldn't poke fun at him, and I believe it was this misconception that brought matters to a head. . . .

Yet I'm not absolutely certain of that.

Several nights after my talk with Moon, I was on duty in the operations bunker when Randall did his broadcast. He always signed off in the same distinctive fashion, trying to contact the patrols of ghosts he claimed were haunting the free-fire zones. Instead of using ordinary call signs like Charlie Baker Able, he would invent others that suited the country lyricism of his style, names such as Lobo Angel Silver and Prairie Dawn Omega.

"Delta Sly Honey," he said that night. "Do you read? Over."

He sat a moment, listening to static filling in from nowhere.

"I know you're out there, Delta Sly Honey," he went on. "I can see you clear, walkin' the high country near Black Virgin Mountain, movin' through twists of fog like battle smoke and feelin' a little afraid, 'cause though you gone from the world, there's a world of fear 'tween here and the hereafter. Come back at me, Delta Sly Honey, and tell me how it's goin'." He stopped sending for a bit, and when he received no reply, he spoke again. "Maybe you don't think I'd understand your troubles, brothers. But I truly do. I know your hopes and fears, and how the spell of too much poison and fire and flyin' steel warped the chemistry of fate and made you wander off into the wars of the spirit 'stead of findin' rest beyond the grave. My soul's trackin' you as you move higher and higher toward the peace at the end of everything, passin' through mortar bursts throwin' up thick gouts of silence, with angels like tracers leadin' you on, listenin' to the cold white song of incoming stars. . . . Come on back at me, Delta Sly Honey. This here's your good buddy Randall J., earthbound at Noc Linh. Do you read?"

There was a wild burst of static, and then a voice answered, saying, "Randall J., Randall J.! This is Delta Sly Honey. Readin' you loud and clear."

I let out a laugh, and the officers sitting at the far end of the bunker turned their heads, grinning. But Randall stared in horror at the radio, as if it were leaking blood, not static. He thumbed the switch and said shakily, "What's your position, Delta Sly Honey? I repeat. What's your position?"

"Guess you might say our position's kinda relative," came the reply. "But far as you concerned, man, we just down the road. There's a place for you with us, Randall J. We waitin' for you."

Randall's Adam's apple worked, and he wetted his lips. Under the hot bunker lights, his freckles stood out sharply.

"Y'know how it is when you're pinned down by fire?" the voice continued. "Lyin' flat with the flow of bullets passin' inches over your head? And you start thinkin' how easy it'd be just to raise up and get it over with. . . . You ever feel like that, Randall J.? Most times you keep flat, 'cause things ain't bad enough to make you go that route. But the way things been goin' for you, man, what with stickin' your hands into dead meat night and day—"

"Shut up," said Randall, his voice tight and small.

"—and that asshole Moon fuckin' with your mind, maybe it's time to consider your options."

"Shut up!" Randall screamed it, and I grabbed him by the shoulders. "Take it easy," I told him. "It's just some jerk-off puttin' you on." He shook me off; the vein in his temple was throbbing.

"I ain't tryin' to mess with you, man," said the voice. "I'm just layin' it out, showin' you there ain't no real options here. I know all them crazy thoughts that been flappin' round in your head, and I know how hard you been tryin' to control 'em. Ain't no point in controllin' 'em anymore, Randall J. You belong to us now. All you gotta do is to take a little walk down the road, and we be waitin'. We got some serious humpin' ahead of us, man. Out past the Napalm Coast, up beyond the high country . . ."

Randall bolted for the door, but I caught him and spun him around. He was breathing rapidly through his mouth, and his eyes seemed to be shining too brightly—like the way an old light bulb will flare up right before it goes dark for good. "Lemme go!" he said. "I gotta find 'em! I gotta tell 'em it ain't my time!"

"It's just someone playin' a goddamn joke," I said, and then it dawned on me. "It's Moon, Randall! You know it's him puttin' somebody up to this."

"I gotta find 'em!" he repeated, and with more strength than I would have given him credit for, he pushed me away and ran off into the dark.

He didn't return, not that night, not the next morning, and we reported him AWOL. We searched the base and the nearby villes to no avail, and since the countryside was rife with NLF patrols and VC, it was logical to assume he had been killed or captured. Over the next couple of days, Moon made frequent public denials of his complicity in the joke, but no one bought it. He took to walking around with his holster unlatched, a wary expression on his face. Though Randall hadn't had any real friends, many of us had been devoted to his broadcasts, and among those devotees were a number of men who . . . well, a civilian psychiatrist might have called them unstable, but in truth they were men who had chosen to exalt instability, to ritualize insanity as a means of maintaining their equilibrium in an unstable medium: it was likely some of them would attempt reprisals. Moon's best hope was that something would divert their attention, but three days after Randall's disappearance, a peculiar transmission came into operations; like all Randall's broadcasts, it was piped over the PA, and thus Moon's fate was sealed.

"Howdy, Noc Linh," said Randall or someone who sounded identical to him. "This here's Randall J. Willingham on patrol with Delta Sly Honey, speakin' to you from beyond the Napalm Coast. We been humpin' through rain and fog most of the day, with no sign of the enemy, just a few demons twistin' up from the gray and fadin' when we come near, and now we all hunkered down by the radio, restin' for tomorrow. Y'know, brothers, I used to be scared shitless of wakin' up here in the big nothin', but now it's gone and happened, I'm findin' it ain't so bad. 'Least I got the feelin' I'm headed someplace, whereas back at Noc Linh I was just spinnin' round and round, and close to losin' my mind. I hated ol' Sergeant Moon, and I hated him worse after he put someone up to hasslin' me on the radio. But now, though I reckon he's still pretty hateful, I can see he was actin' under the influence of a higher agency, one who was tryin' to help me get clear of Noc Linh . . . which was somethin' that had to be, no matter if I had to die to do it. Seems to me that's the nature of war, that all the violence has the effect of lettin' a little magic seep into the world by way of compensation. . . .''

To most of us, this broadcast signaled that Randall was alive, but we also knew what it portended for Moon. And therefore I wasn't terribly surprised when he summoned me to his tent the next morning. At first he tried to play sergeant, ordering me to ally myself with him; but seeing that this didn't work, he begged for my help. He was a mess: red-eyed, unshaven, an eyelid twitching.

''I can't do a thing,'' I told him.

''You're his friend!'' he said. ''If you tell 'em I didn't have nothin' to do with it, they'll believe you.''

''The hell they will! They'll think I helped you.'' I studied him a second, enjoying his anxiety. ''Who did help you?''

''I didn't do it, goddammit!'' His voice had risen to a shout, and he had to struggle to keep calm. ''I swear! It wasn't me!''

It was strange, my mental set at that moment. I found I believed him—I didn't think him capable of manufacturing sincerity—and yet I suddenly believed everything: that Randall was somehow both dead and alive, that Delta Sly Honey both did and did not exist, that whatever was happening was an event in which all possibility was manifest, in which truth and falsity had the same valence, in which the real and the illusory were undifferentiated. And at the center of this complex circumstance—a bulky, sweating monster—stood Moon. Innocent, perhaps. But guilty of a seminal crime.

''I can make it good for you,'' he said. ''Hawaii . . . you

want duty in Hawaii, I can arrange it. Hell, I can get you shipped Stateside.''

He struck me then as a hideous genie offering three wishes, and the fact that he had the power to make his offer infuriated me. ''If you can do all that,'' I said, ''you ain't got a worry in the world.'' And I strode off, feeling righteous in my judgment.

Two nights later while returning to my hooch, I spotted a couple of men wearing tiger shorts dragging a large and apparently unconscious someone toward the barrier of concertina wire beside the PX—I knew it had to be Moon. I drew my pistol, sneaked along the back wall of the PX, and when they came abreast I stepped out and told them to put their burden down. They stopped but didn't turn loose of Moon. Both had blackened their faces with greasepaint, and to this had added fanciful designs in crimson, blue, and yellow that gave them the look of savages. They carried combat knives, and their eyes were pointed with the reflected brilliance of the perimeter lights. It was a hot night, but it seemed hotter there beside them, as if their craziness had a radiant value. ''This ain't none of your affair, Curt,'' said the tallest of the two; despite his bad grammar, he had a soft, well-modulated voice, and I thought I heard a trace of amusement in it.

I peered at him, but was unable to recognize him beneath the paint. Again I told them to put Moon down.

''Sorry,'' said the tall guy. ''Man's gotta pay for his crimes.''

''He didn't do anything,'' I said. ''You know damn well Randall's just AWOL.''

The tall guy chuckled, and the other guy said, ''Naw, we don't know that a-tall.''

Moon groaned, tried to lift his head, then slumped back.

''No matter what he did or didn't do,'' said the tall guy, ''the man deserves what's comin'.''

''Yeah,'' said his pal. ''And if it ain't us what does it, it'll be somebody else.''

I knew he was right, and the idea of killing two men to save a third who was doomed in any event just didn't stack up. But though my sense of duty was weak where Moon was concerned, it hadn't entirely dissipated. "Let him go," I said.

The tall guy grinned, and the other one shook his head as if dismayed by my stubbornness. They appeared wholly untroubled by the pistol, possessed of an irrational confidence. "Be reasonable, Curt," said the tall guy. "This ain't gettin' you nowhere."

I couldn't believe his foolhardiness. "You see this?" I said, flourishing the pistol. "Gun, y'know? I'm gonna fuckin' shoot you with it, you don't let him go."

Moon let out another groan, and the tall guy rapped him hard on the back of the head with the hilt of his knife.

"Hey!" I said, training the pistol on his chest.

"Look here, Curt . . ." he began.

"Who the hell are you?" I stepped closer, but was still unable to identify him. "I don't know you."

"Randall told us 'bout you, Curt. He's a buddy of ours, ol' Randall is. We're with Delta Sly Honey."

I believed him for that first split second. My mouth grew cottony, and my hand trembled. But then I essayed a laugh. "Sure you are! Now put his ass down!"

"That's what you really want, huh?"

"Damn right!" I said. "Now!"

"Okay," he said. "You got it." And with a fluid stroke, he cut Moon's throat.

Moon's eyes popped open as the knife sliced through his tissues, and that—not the blood spilling onto the dust—was the thing that froze me: those bugged eyes in which an awful realization dawned and faded. They let him fall face downward. His legs spasmed, his right hand jittered. For a long moment, stunned, I stared at him, at the blood puddling beneath his head, and when I looked up I found that the two men were sprinting away, about to round the curve of the hill. I couldn't bring myself to fire. Mixed in my thoughts were the knowledge that killing them served no purpose and the fear that my bullets would have no effect. I glanced left and right, behind me, making sure that no one was watching, and then ran up the slope to my hooch.

Under my cot was a bottle of sour mash. I pulled it out and had a couple of drinks to steady myself; but steadiness was beyond me. I switched on a battery lamp and sat cross-legged, listening to the snores of my bunkmate. Lying on my duffel bag was an unfinished letter home, one I had begun nearly two weeks before; I doubted now I'd ever finish it. What would I tell my folks? That I had more or less sanctioned an execution? That I was losing my fucking mind? Usually I told them everything was fine, but after the scene I had just witnessed, I felt I was forever past that sort of blithe invention. I switched off the lamp and lay in the dark, the bottle resting on my chest. I had a third drink, a fourth, and gradually lost both count and consciousness.

I had a week's R & R coming and I took it, hoping debauch would shore me up. But I spent much of that week attempting to justify my inaction in terms of the inevitable and the supernatural, and failing in that attempt. You see, now as then, if pressed for an opinion, I would tell you that what happened at Noc Linh was the sad consequence of a joke gone sour, of a war twisted into a demonic exercise. Everything was explicable in that wise. And yet it's conceivable that the supernatural was involved, that—as Randall had suggested—a little magic had seeped into the world. In Vietnam, with all its horror and strangeness, it was difficult to distinguish between the magical and the mundane, and it's possible that thousands of supernatural events went unnoticed as such, obscured by the poignancies of death and fear, becoming quirky memories that years later might pass through your mind while you were washing the dishes or walking the dog, and give you a moment's pause, an eerie feeling that would almost instantly be ground away by the mills of the ordinary. But I'm certain that my qualification is due to the fact that I want there to have been some magic involved, anything to lessen my culpability, to shed a less damning light on the perversity and viciousness of my brothers-in-arms.

On returning to Noc Linh, I found that Randall had also returned. He claimed to be suffering from amnesia and would not admit to having made the broadcast that had triggered Moon's murder. The shrinks had decided that he was bucking for a Section Eight, had ordered him put back on the corpse detail, and as before, Randall could be seen laboring beneath the tin-roofed shed, transferring the contents of body bags into aluminum coffins. On the surface, little appeared to have changed. But Randall had become a pariah. He was insulted and whispered about and shunned. Whenever he came near, necks would stiffen and conversations die. If he had offed Moon himself, he would have been cheered; but the notion that he had used his influence to have his dirty work jobbed out didn't accord with the prevailing concept of honorable vengeance. Though I tried not to, I couldn't help feeling badly toward him myself. It was weird. I would approach with the best of intentions, but by the time I reached him, my hackles would have risen and I would walk on in hostile silence, as if he were exuding a chemical that had evoked my contempt. I did get close enough to him, however, to see that the mad brightness was missing from his eyes; I had the feeling that all his brightness was missing, that whatever quality had enabled him to do his broadcasts had been sucked dry.

One morning as I was passing the PX, whose shiny surfaces reflected a dynamited white glare of sun, I noticed a crowd of men pressing through the front door, apparently trying to catch sight of something inside. I pushed through them and found one of the canteen clerks—a lean kid with black hair and a wolfish face—engaged in beating Randall to a pulp. I pulled him off, threw him into a table, and kneeled beside Randall, who had collapsed to the floor. His cheekbones were lumped and discolored; blood poured from his nose, trickled from his mouth. His eyes met mine, and I felt nothing from him: he seemed muffled, vibeless, as if heavily sedated.

"They out to get me, Curt," he mumbled.

All my sympathy for him was suddenly resurrected. "It's okay, man," I said. "Sooner or later, it'll blow over." I handed him my bandanna, and he dabbed ineffectually at the flow from his nose. Watching him, I recalled Moon's categorization of my motives for befriending him, and I understood now that my true motives had less to do with our relative social status than with my belief that he could be saved, that—after months of standing by helplessly while the unsalvageable marched to their fates—I thought I might be able to effect some small good work. This may seem altruistic to the point of naïveté, and perhaps it was, perhaps the brimstone oppressiveness of the war had from the residue of old sermons heard and disregarded provoked some vain Christian reflex; but the need was strong in me, nonetheless, and I realized that I had fixed on it as a prerequisite to my own salvation.

Randall handed back the bandanna. "Ain't gonna blow over," he said. "Not with these guys."

I grabbed his elbow and hauled him to his feet. "What guys?"

He looked around as if afraid of eavesdroppers. "Delta Sly Honey!"

"Christ, Randall! Come on." I tried to guide him toward the door, but he wrenched free.

"They out to get me! They say I crossed over and they took care of Moon for me . . . and then I got away from 'em." He dug his fingers into my arm. "But I can't remember, Curt! I can't remember nothin'!"

My first impulse was to tell him to drop the amnesia act, but then I thought about the painted men who had scragged Moon: if they were after Randall, he was in big trouble. "Let's get you patched up," I said. "We'll talk about this later."

He gazed at me, dull and uncomprehending. "You gonna help me?" he asked in a tone of disbelief.

I doubted anyone could help him now, and maybe, I thought, that was also part of my motivation—the desire to know the good sin of honest failure. "Sure," I told him. "We'll figure out somethin'."

We started for the door, but on seeing the men gathered there, Randall balked. "What you want from me?" he shouted, giving a flailing, awkward wave with his left arm as if to make them vanish. "What the fuck you want?"

They stared coldly at him, and those stares were like bad answers. He hung his head and kept it hung all the way to the infirmary.

That night I set out to visit Randall, intending to advise him to confess, a tactic I perceived as his one hope of survival. I'd planned to see him early in the evening, but was called back on duty and didn't get clear until well after midnight. The base was quiet and deserted-feeling. Only a few lights picked out the darkened slopes, and had it not been for the heat and stench, it would have been easy to believe that the hill with its illuminated caves was a place of mild enchantment, inhabited by elves and not frightened men. The moon was almost full, and beneath it the PX shone like an immense silver lozenge. Though it had closed an hour before, its windows were lit, and—MP instincts engaged—I peered inside. Randall was backed against the bar, holding a knife to the neck of the wolfish clerk who had beaten him, and ranged in a loose circle around him, standing among the tables, were five men wearing tiger shorts, their faces painted with savage designs. I drew my pistol, eased around to the front and—wanting my entrance to have shock value—kicked the door open.

The five men turned their heads to me, but appeared not at all disconcerted. "How's she goin', Curt?" said one, and by his soft voice I recognized the tall guy who had slit Moon's throat.

"Tell 'em to leave me be!" Randall shrilled.

I fixed my gaze on the tall guy and with gunslinger menace said, "I'm not messin' with you tonight. Get out now or I'll take you down."

"You can't hurt me, Curt," he said.

"Don't gimme that ghost shit! Fuck with me, and you'll be humpin' with Delta Sly Honey for real."

"Even if you were right 'bout me, Curt, I wouldn't be scared of dyin'. I was dead where it counts halfway through my tour."

A scuffling at the bar, and I saw that Randall had wrestled the clerk to the floor. He wrapped his legs around the clerk's waist in a scissors and yanked his head back by the hair to expose his throat. "Leave me be," he said. Every nerve in his face was jumping.

"Let him go, Randall," said the tall guy. "We ain't after no innocent blood. We just want you to take a little walk . . . to cross back over."

"Get out!" I told him.

"You're workin' yourself in real deep, man," he said.

"This ain't no bullshit!" I said. "I *will* shoot."

"Look here, Curt," he said. "S'pose we're just plain ol' ordinary grunts. You gonna shoot us all? And if you do, don't you think we'd have friends who'd take it hard? Any way you slice it, you bookin' yourself a silver box and air freight home."

He came a step toward me, and I said, "Watch it, man!" He came another step, his devil mask split by a fierce grin. My heart felt hot and solid in my chest, no beats, and I thought, He's a ghost, his flesh is smoke, the paint a color in my eye. "Keep back!" I warned.

"Gonna kill me?" Again he grinned. "Go ahead." He lunged, a feint only, and I squeezed the trigger.

The gun jammed.

When I think now how this astounded me, I wonder at my idiocy. The gun jammed frequently. It was an absolute piece of shit, that weapon. But at the time its failure seemed a magical coincidence, a denial of the laws of chance. And adding to my astonishment was the reaction of the other men: they made no move toward Randall, as if no opportunity had been provided, no danger passed. Yet the tall guy looked somewhat shaken to me.

Randall let out a mewling noise, and that sound enlisted my competence. I edged between the tables and took a stand next to him. "Let me get the knife from him," I said. "No point in both of 'em dyin'."

The tall guy drew a deep breath as if to settle himself. "You reckon you can do that, Curt?"

"Maybe. If you guys wait outside, he won't be as scared and maybe I can get it."

They stared at me, unreadable.

"Gimme a chance."

"We ain't after no innocent blood." The tall guy's tone was firm, as if this were policy. "But . . ."

"Just a coupla minutes," I said. "That's all I'm askin'."

I could almost hear the tick of the tall guy's judgment. "Okay," he said at last. "But don't you go tryin' nothin' hinkey, Curt." Then, to Randall. "We be waitin', Randall J."

As soon as they were out the door, I kneeled beside Randall. Spittle flecked the clerk's lips, and when Randall shifted the knife a tad, his eyes rolled up into heaven. "Leave me be," said Randall. He might have been talking to the air, the walls, the world.

"Give it up," I said.

He just blinked.

"Let him go and I'll help you," I said. "But if you cut him, you on your own. That how you want it?"

"Un-unh."

"Well, turn him loose."

"I can't," he said, a catch in his voice. "I'm all froze up. If I move, I'll cut him." Sweat dripped into his eyes, and he blinked some more.

"How 'bout I take it from you? If you keep real still, if you lemme ease it outta your hand, maybe we can work it that way."

"I don't know. . . . I might mess up."

The clerk gave a long shuddery sigh and squeezed his eyes shut.

"You gonna be fine," I said to Randall. "Just keep your eyes on me, and you gonna be fine."

I stretched out my hand. The clerk was trembling, Randall was trembling, and when I touched the blade it was so full of vibration, it felt alive, as if all the energy in the room had been concentrated there. I tried pulling it away from the clerk's neck, but it wouldn't budge.

"You gotta loosen up, Randall," I said.

I tried again and, gripping the blade between my forefinger and thumb, managed to pry it an inch or so away from the line of blood it had drawn. My fingers were sweaty, the metal slick, and the blade felt like it was connected to a spring, that any second it would snap back and bite deep.

"My fingers are slippin'," I said, and the clerk whimpered.

"Ain't my fault if they do." Randall said this pleadingly, as if testing the waters, the potentials of his guilt and innocence, and I realized he was setting me up the way he had Moon's killers. It was a childlike attempt compared to the other, but I knew to his mind it would work out the same.

"The hell it ain't!" I said. "Don't do it, man!"

"It ain't my fault!" he insisted.

"Randall!"

I could feel his intent in the quiver of the blade. With my free hand, I grabbed the clerk's upper arm, and as the knife slipped, I jerked him to the side. The blade sliced his jaw, and he screeched; but the wound wasn't mortal.

I plucked the knife from Randall's hand, wanting to kill

him myself. But I had invested too much in his salvation. I hauled him erect and over to the window; I smashed out the glass with a chair and pushed him through. Then I jumped after him. As I came to my feet, I saw the painted men closing in from the front of the PX and—still towing Randall along—I sprinted around the corner of the building and up the slope, calling for help. Lights flicked on, and heads popped from tent flaps. But when they spotted Randall, they ducked back inside.

I was afraid, but Randall's abject helplessness—his eyes rolling like a freaked calf's, his hands clawing at me for support—helped to steady me. The painted men seemed to be everywhere. They would materialize from behind tents, out of bunker mouths, grinning madly and waving moonstruck knives, and send us veering off in another direction, back and forth across the hill. Time and again, I thought they had us, and on several occasions, it was only by a hairsbreadth that I eluded the slash of a blade that looked to be bearing a charge of winking silver energy on its tip. I was wearing down, stumbling, gasping, and I was certain we couldn't last much longer. But we continued to evade them, and I began to sense that they were in no hurry to conclude the hunt; their pursuit had less an air of frenzy than of a ritual harassment, and eventually, as we staggered up to the mouth of the operations bunker and—I believed—safety, I realized that they had been herding us. I pushed Randall inside and glanced back from the sandbagged entrance. The five men stood motionless a second, perhaps fifty feet away, then melted into the darkness.

I explained what had happened to the MP on duty in the bunker—a heavyset guy named Cousins—and though he had no love for Randall, he was a dutiful sort and gave us permission to wait out the night inside. Randall slumped down against the wall, resting his head on his knees, the picture of despair. But I believed that his survival was assured. With the testimony of the clerk, I thought the shrinks would have no choice but to send him elsewhere for examination and possible institutionalization. I felt good, accomplished, and passed the night chain-smoking, bullshitting with Cousins.

Then, toward dawn, a voice issued from the radio. It was greatly distorted, but it sounded very much like Randall's.

"Randall J.," it said. "This here's Delta Sly Honey. Do you read? Over."

Randall looked up, hearkening to the spit and fizzle of the static.

"I know you out there, Randall J.," the voice went on. "I can see you clear, sitting with the shadows of the bars upon your soul and blood on your hands. Ain't no virtuous blood, that's true. But it stains you alla same. Come back at me, Randall J. We gotta talk, you and me."

Randall let his head fall; with a finger, he traced a line in the dust.

"What's the point in keepin' this up, Randall J.?" said the voice. "You left the best part of you over here, the soulful part, and you can't go on much longer without it. Time to take that little walk for real, man. Time to get clear of what you done and pass on to what must be. We waitin' for you just north of base, Randall J. Don't make us come for you."

It was in my mind to say something to Randall, to break the disconsolate spell the voice appeared to be casting over him; but I found I had nothing left to give him, that I had spent my fund of altruism and was mostly weary of the whole business . . . as he must have been.

"Ain't nothin' to be 'fraid of out here," said the voice. "Only the wind and the gray whispers of phantom Charlie and the trail leadin' away from the world. There's good company for you, Randall J. Gotta man here used to be a poet, and he'll tell you stories 'bout the Wild North King and the Woman of Crystal. Got another fella, guy used to live in Indonesia, and he's fulla tales 'bout watchin' tigers come out on the highways to shit and cities of men dressed like women and islands where dragons still live. Then there's this kid from Opelika, claims to know some of your people down that way, and when he talks, you can just see that ol' farmboy moon heavin' up big and yellow over the barns, shinin' the blacktop so it looks like polished jet, and you can hear crazy music leakin' from the Dixieland café and smell the perfumed heat steamin' off the young girls' breasts. Don't make us wait no more, Randall J. We got work to do. Maybe it ain't much, just breakin' trail and walkin' point and keepin' a sharp eye out for demons . . . but it sure as hell beats shepherdin' the dead, now don't it?'' A long pause. ''You come on and take that walk, Randall J. We'll make you welcome, I promise. This here's Delta Sly Honey. Over and out.''

Randall pulled himself to his feet and took a faltering few steps toward the mouth of the bunker. I blocked his path and he said, ''Lemme go, Curt.''

''Look here, Randall,'' I said. ''I might can get you home if you just hang on.''

''Home.'' The concept seemed to amuse him, as if it were something with the dubious reality of heaven or hell. ''Lemme go.''

In his eyes, then, I thought I could see all his broken parts, a disjointed shifting of lights and darks, and when I spoke I felt I was giving tongue to a vast consensus, one arrived at without either ballots or reasonable discourse. ''If I let you go,'' I said, ''be best you don't come back this time.''

He stared at me, his face gone slack, and nodded.

Hardly anybody was outside, yet I had the idea everyone was watching us as we walked down the hill; under a leaden overcast, the base had a tense, muted atmosphere such as must have attended rainy dawns beneath the guillotine. The sentries at the main gate passed Randall through without question. He went a few paces along the road, then turned back, his face pale as a star in the half-light, and I wondered if he thought we were driving him off or if he believed he was being called to a better world. In my heart I knew which was the case. At last he set out again, quickly becoming a shadow, then the rumor of a shadow, then gone.

Walking back up the hill, I tried to sort out my thoughts, to determine what I was feeling, and it may be a testament to how crazy I was, how crazy we all were, that I felt less regret for a man lost than satisfaction in knowing that some perverted justice had been served, that the world of the war—tipped off-center by this unmilitary engagement and our focus upon it—could now go back to spinning true.

That night there was fried chicken in the mess, and vanilla ice cream, and afterward a movie about a more reasonable war, full of villainous Germans with Dracula accents and heroic grunts who took nothing but flesh wounds. When it was done, I walked back to my hooch and stood out front and had a smoke. In the northern sky was a flickering orange glow, one accompanied by the rumble of artillery. It was, I realized, just about this time of night that Randall had customarily begun his broadcasts. Somebody else must have realized this, because at that moment the PA was switched on. I half expected to hear Randall giving the news of Delta Sly Honey, but there was only static, sounding like the crackling of enormous flames. Listening to it, I felt disoriented, completely vulnerable, as if some huge black presence were on the verge of swallowing me up. And then a voice did speak. It wasn't Randall's, yet it had a similar countrified accent, and though the words weren't quite as fluent, they were redolent of his old raps, lending a folksy comprehensibility to the vastness of the cosmos, the strangeness of the war. I had no idea whether or not it was the voice that had summoned Randall to take his walk, no longer effecting an imitation, and I thought I recognized its soft well-modulated tones. But none of that mattered. I was so grateful, so relieved by this end to silence, that I went into my hooch and—armed with lies—sat down to finish my interrupted letter home.

Craig Kee Strete

Craig Kee Strete seems to be a genre unto himself. Like R. A. Lafferty and the brilliant Jorge Luis Borges, he can influence other writers, but can't, in turn, be imitated. In the introduction to Strete's short story collection *If All Else Fails, We Can Whip the Horse's Eyes and Make Him Cry and Sleep,* Borges has written: "With this book, we risk the dangerous power of genius, of one who can construct a universe within the skull to rival the real." Strete's stories can also be found in his collections *The Bleeding Man and Other Science Fiction Stories* and *Sleep.* He has been a finalist for the Nebula and Hugo awards.

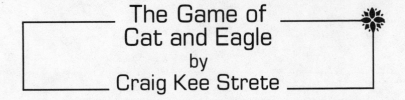

The Game of Cat and Eagle

by

Craig Kee Strete

The Marine band played the Air Force hymn loud enough to scare the eagle.

He wasn't happy in the cage anyway—no eagle ever is.

When I stepped off the chopper at Cam Ranh Bay, the caged eagle under my arm made me conspicuous.

Colonel Ranklin, a very correct soldier, impeccably starched, met me with a jeep at the end of the pier. The smell of the harbor, a heavy tang of oil and salt water mingled with sewage, struck my nostrils.

"I have orders to take you to your next transport," said Colonel Ranklin, saluting smartly.

There was a look of displeasure on his face. He expected possibly high brass, or somebody with a high covert status, anything but a long-haired Indian with a caged eagle.

I got into the jeep, glad to drop the cage. I had a couple of wounds where the eagle had got at me through the bars.

"You are the Mystery Guest?"

"I guess so. I've got a name, too—call me Lookseeker. You can't blame the code name on me. They always make a game out of everything."

"Right," said Colonel Ranklin, climbing into the jeep. He threw the jeep into gear and we were off. He never looked back, driving at a half slow and very cautious pace through the dock area. We threaded our way through what seemed like millions of tons of military cargo, awaiting transshipment.

He kept his back straight; perhaps he had been born with a back like that, formed to fit against the wall.

There was a coldness about him I didn't like, and he hadn't asked for proper identification or shown his own either.

They had issued me a standard sidearm but I had turned it in. Where the eagle and I were going, guns wouldn't help. But now, pondering the silent figure driving the jeep, I felt threatened and wished I had a weapon.

We went past a large storage shed and he turned the wheel abruptly to the right.

Two men lounging beside the shed sprang into action. They jerked on ropes and a steel shuttered door slid up. The jeep slewed, righted itself, and we shot into the open doorway.

As soon as we had made it inside, the heavy doors clanged shut behind us with a bang.

The lights went on, flooding the dimly lit interior with blazing light.

A tall man in a business suit sat on a chair, flanked by heavily armed men of the 315th Air Commando Group.

My driver got out of the jeep and walked away, not looking back. He lit a cigarette and strolled behind a stack of ammo cases.

"Don't bother getting out of the jeep, Lookseeker," said the man in civilian clothes. "I won't keep you very long."

"Who are you? Why am I being detained?"

The man winced. "Hardly detained. Let us say, momentarily delayed. I'm Hightower. I'm with the CIA."

"Somehow, I'm not surprised," I said.

"You know, this is a war we could win. I want you to know that I honestly believe that. I don't think I would like to see it end prematurely. We still need more time."

I studied him. He had a lean face, a killer's face, but a kind of sadness suffused his features. He projected a fatherly aura, radiating charm and warmth that probably did not exist.

"What does this have to do with me?" I asked. The eagle shrieked and flung itself at the bars of its cage as it had done many times before.

He smiled and I felt a cold wind, as if something had stirred the air above a grave. "Let us say that civilized as we may seem, America is no more civilized than we choose to be. Do we make war with logic and precision and science? The Pentagon would have us believe so. But you and I, Lookseeker, we know differently. Hitler had his astrologers. Eisenhower had a rabbit-foot in his pocket throughout the war. War brings out the mystic need for answers in the most civilized men."

"I am surprised. You seem to know what my mission is. I was told that no one would know," I said and I knew this was truly a dangerous man. And a dying man as well. I could feel it, almost see it glowing beneath his skin, an unstoppable cancer, a shadow riotously burgeoning with dark unlife.

"How I know is unimportant. But make no mistake about it, my friend, I am deeply concerned by what you are about to do. I don't like it. I detest it just as I detest all of the tired old mystical, religious mumbo jumbo of the past. I am an irreligious man. Winning is my religion."

"If you were to ask me, I would say you are a very religious man," I said, borrowing some of the eagle's wisdom. "If you were not, you would not so deeply fear what I am about to do."

The man jerked as if struck. His face greyed and he looked down at his hands. They were white, long and pale, like blind worms from a subterranean cave. There was a pallor about the man that suggested that he seldom saw the sun, sitting like a spider in his dark web, spinning dark nets to entrap his prey.

"Perhaps you are right," he said and he looked at me strangely. "You are not what I expected."

He looked at me carefully, as if trying to figure out just how dangerous I was by the way I looked.

I did not make an intimidating figure. I have long black very unmilitary hair. I am not tall, neither am I particularly handsome. My face is too thin, my eyes are too large with things that walk through the thousand thousand dark nights of man. The military uniform I wore was much too big for me. Hollywood would never have cast me as a warrior or a medicine man. In my own way though, I was both.

"I think you expected to see an old man, rattling skulls and waving feathers and chanting mysterious chants. Something like that."

"Yes." His smile was almost real now. "Perhaps, if you looked like a fake, I might be more inclined to dismiss you as a childish whim on his part."

"What do you want with me? I don't think you have the authority to stop me, if that's what you've got in mind."

"I could kill you," he said smoothly, his tone devoid of menace. "A sniper. This area is hit so often with snipers, we call them duty snipers. I could arrange it."

Colonel Ranklin had returned. He seemed nervous, a cigarette burning in the corner of his mouth. I noticed he had one hand on the butt of his sidearm.

"I'm sure you could," I said and then I lost all fear of Hightower, suddenly knowing he was just scared. Terrified. Of me, of what I stood for.

I motioned to Colonel Ranklin. "Let's go, driver. We've wasted enough time here."

Hightower stood up, moving angrily toward the jeep. He put his hand on the door of the jeep, his mouth set in a grim line.

"I haven't said you could go yet. I haven't decided if you'll ever go."

"Yes, you have." I felt sorry for him. "Because you want to know the answer as badly as the man who sent me. You'd kill me because you wanted to change the answer, that I believe, but you'd never kill me knowing that I may be the only one who can reveal the answer. You are more afraid of not knowing than knowing."

Colonel Ranklin now had his weapon out.

Hightower turned and looked back at him. Ranklin waited for an order.

"Drive him," said Hightower.

Ranklin looked disappointed as he reholstered his gun. The heavy doors went up and Ranklin got back into the jeep.

Hightower put his hand on my arm, like a supplicant seeking favor from the gods. "Don't tell anyone I talked to you. I'd appreciate it." The sadness was on his face again.

"Who would I tell," I said as the jeep began backing out of the shed. "I never met you, and if anyone asks why we're late, I'll tell them Colonel Ranklin stopped to pay a visit to a whorehouse to pick up his laundry and have his back ironed straight in the usual military fashion."

I heard Hightower laughing as we drove away. Even laughing, the man sounded scared.

Ranklin never spoke again. I knew he was a skilled assassin, and looking at him, I looked to see how he would die. The great lizard spoke to me and I saw Ranklin in a bar, drinking with a Vietnamese whore. He thought she loved him.

I looked up and saw a Vietnamese woman pull the pin from a grenade and toss it into the club. To save the girl, Ranklin fell on the grenade. It was a good death for an assassin. A little honor for a man who had none.

I made my next transport in time. Another chopper. On board, I fed the eagle another chunk of raw meet. Ungrateful, the eagle expressed a preference for my fingers as I tried to thrust the meat through the bars of the cage.

The eagle and I are not friends. My totem and my vision ally is a lizard, the Ancient of Reptiles, the eagle's enemy. Perhaps the eagle senses this and regards me as its enemy, perhaps I am simply contaminated with too much contact with men.

The unrelenting heat seemed to strike against us as the chopper sped toward my next jumping-off place.

The chopper pilot noticed my discomfort. "Welcome to Sauna City," he said, waving his thumb to the left toward Da

Nang as we passed near it. "At noon, you can fry rice in your helmet while you're wearing it."

"Any advice for a new recruit?" I asked. The chopper pilot looked at my dark skin, dark eyes, and slightly built body in the uniform at least a size too big for me.

"You'll pardon me saying so," he said in a lazy Texas drawl, "but you ain't exactly sporting a military look with the hair there, sport. Now I see lots of long hair, after you've parked here for a while, but you're the first greenie to arrive with it. You must be an Indian or a Mexican."

"I could plead guilty to one of those," I said, looking back to see how the eagle was taking to the chopper ride. He seemed fairly quiet. I found that strapping his cage near an open door seemed to make him content. The air rushing in must have made him think he was flying. "So what?"

"If I were you, Tonto or Pronto or whichever you are, I'd practice looking as white as possible. Over here the weirdness swallows you. It's best to look like just one side, not two."

We had arrived at our destination. I meant to ask him what he meant by that statement but he got busy landing us, so I let it ride. He hunched forward over the controls as he brought the chopper in. I saw the spot on his back where the flak would catch him and tear his insides out.

I jumped out the door of the chopper as soon as we touched down.

"Eagle for eating or do you ride it around?" said the pilot as he began handing down the cage to me.

"This not eagle, white boy, this is Texas chicken," I said with a grin.

The pilot touched the doorframe of the chopper. "Hell, boy, you just rode in a Texas chicken! That scrawny thing . . ." The eagle got him by the hand and bit down hard. "Christ! He cut me to the bone!" moaned the pilot, holding his bloody hand. "Good luck, Chief, and thanks for the Purple Heart!"

"First blood," I said under my breath to the eagle with a smile on my face and turned to look around at my surroundings. Behind me, the chopper lifted off, driving the eagle in the cage wild again.

I was on the helipad at Tan Son Nhut Air Base, temporarily assigned as a door gunner to the 145th. At least, that was the paperwork designation that hid my real mission there.

I heard a high-pitched whine and turned to see an F-100 taxi by on an adjacent runway. I wondered what the hell the chopper pilot had meant by what he had said. The weirdness swallows you? How does one look like one side and not two? I hadn't spoken it aloud, just thought it, but a voice answered, "He meant you look too Vietnamese." This came from a pilot sitting in the cockpit of a blunt-nosed Supersabre. "And you can bet your brown rear end, that's no real asset here. Sure as hell some trigger-happy cowboy is going to nail your ass thinking you're a VC infiltrator in a good-guy suit. Maybe you ought to curl your hair. Maybe they'll think you're a Jew with a severe tan." The pilot laughed. "Christ, I'm getting almost too funny to live!"

"How could you have heard what the chopper pilot said to me over the whine of the rotors? And how did you know I didn't understand what he meant?"

"Welcome to Vietnam. It ain't what people say that you got to hear, it's what they don't say that counts," said the pilot, giving me a double thumbs up and a wink.

I spotted the chopper that was to take me to Bien Hoa.

I turned to say thanks for the advice, lame as it was, to the pilot in the Supersabre, but the plane was gone. Where it had stood was a burned hulk of a jet in a mortar crater. The wreckage was at least six months old.

In spirit quests, by the Sacred Lake of my people, after long fasts and much suffering, I have seen animal spirits that were not there, and sometimes the dead spoke to me. But never in the real world have the dead spoken to me.

I looked all around me then and I saw that I was in a place that was unlike itself. I looked in the old ways of my people, where a tree stood I saw not the tree but its shadow. This was a shadow world, half robed in the strange clothes of the dead, and alive only with things of another world.

I approached the chopper I had been ordered to report to, staggering under the weight of cage and eagle. A line of bullet holes ran across the middle of the craft. Somebody had stuck plastic roses in the holes.

I knew the pilot, by name at least.

I saluted stiffly.

Lieutenant Colonel J. N. Howton regarded me with a strange look on his face. "Can the salute, pinhead! You must be Lieutenant Lookseeker. What the hell is it you do, boy? The brass said you were a very hush-hush secret weapon."

"I'm sorry. I have been instructed to say that the information you have requested is classified."

Howton jumped out of his craft, circling it. "OK, high-hat me, I don't give a shit. Just get your classified ass in the chopper. I'm preflighting it. It won't take long—just a few extra minutes of insurance. You a weapons specialist?"

"I have been instructed to say . . ." I began.

"Aw, shut the hell up with that crap, will ya," he growled. "Stow your equipment on board. If you don't know much about choppers, climb topside with me and I'll fill you in. Also, you can count the bullet holes on your side. If we come up with the magic number, we win a magic elephant, personally autographed by General Westmoreland himself."

I stowed the cage in the back and then I climbed up after him. He pointed out the rotor head, and then indicated a large retaining nut which holds the rotors to the mast.

"Just thought I'd tell you, this dingus keeps it flying. If this whatsis comes off, we lose the blades and we take on the aerodynamic capabilities of a pregnant rock. We call the dingus the Jesus nut."

"It won't come off," I said. "A Russian surface-to-air missile will down this chopper and fuse it in place."

"What did you say?" Howton had a strange look on his face.

I turned away. I had spoken before I thought. So often with me, I say things that I wish I could keep inside. But as these things so easily spring to my mind, also so easily do they spring to my lips.

"You're a strange one, Lookseeker," said Howton. "How many bullet holes on your side?"

"I count ten, eleven, uh, fourteen," I said.

"Damn, there's only twenty-two on my side. Never going to break no damn records this way," said Howton with a good-natured curse.

We climbed down and entered into the chopper.

I was already wearing a flak vest, but once inside the chopper, Howton insisted that I put on a fifteen-pound chest protector of laminated steel and plastic.

"Bet you never thought you'd ever be wearing an iron

brassiere,'' said Howton as he buckled himself in at the controls. The crew chief and door gunner fitted ammo belts into their M-60 machine guns. I was given a flight helmet and settled it on my head. I adjusted my headset so I could hear the radio transmission between our craft and Saigon ground control.

''Helicopter Nine Nine Four. Departure from Hotel Three. East departure midfield crossing.'' That was what Howton said into the radio. What I heard was Howton's life twisting in the dark like a lost white bird. I heard his heart stop in the crash that was yet to be and almost cried out because though Howton's heart died with no pain, it caused a hole between the two worlds of home and here, and the hole let the dark wind in.

All my life, I have feared the dark winds.

In a strongly Vietnamese-accented voice, Saigon control replied, ''Roger, Nine Nine Four. Takeoff approved. We have you for a cross at five hundred feet.''

We lifted with a thump, hovered over the adjoining runway, our nose tilted down, and then there was a larger thump as we went through transitional lift and soared up and away.

''Your first eyeball of the terrain?'' asked Howton over the roar of the blades. ''Or did you scope it on the flight in?''

I looked down at the land which I knew I would leave my bones in. I did not see what Howton saw. I saw the flat tabletop lands of my people, the great stone mesas, the pueblos gleaming in the shimmering heat.

I didn't speak. Howton dropped the chopper until we were flying just above the treetops. ''Why are we flying so low?''

''Heavy VC batteries in this section. I'm not cleared for the upper lane, so if I can't go high, I go as low as I can get it. Harder to hit us. Our exposure time is shorter this way.''

The UH-1D chopper vibrated a lot as we skirted the treetops. Two gunships joined up with us, taking up position on each side of us.

The radio crackled, giving off a brief series of orders in code which I did not recognize. It was half in code, half in slang.

Howton spoke into his headset. ''This is Hownow Howton. Nine Nine Four. I'd like permission to divert to extradite ARVNs at Phu Loi.''

"Negative. Continue with mission," was the immediate reply.

Howton regarded me sourly. He glanced upward—the sky was filling with jets, F-100s.

He began a rapid upward climb.

"Your nursemaids are here. Time to take the high road."

"Wish I knew what the hell it is you do," said Howton. "You're becoming an itch I can't scratch."

We gained a fairly high altitude, paced by the gunships on each side and the ever present jets.

"You're a short-timer," I said to Howton. "Your wife, Annie, loves you very much."

"Don't recall mentioning her name, Chief. Somebody brief you on me or what? Maybe you're one of those psychic types?" Howton regarded me with cynical distrust.

"I just know things," I said.

"Not in this case, partner," said Howton, hunched over the controls. "I've got a big four hundred and thirty-eight days to go. A long hard winter and a long hard summer and another goddamn winter to boot. Sort of like a two-for-one sale."

At times like this, when I know too much, I find myself growing quiet and cold and remote from life. Remote and cold because there is nothing I can do for those around me. Knowledge of what is yet to be is not always a way to change what is about to become.

I knew in less than ten days Lieutenant Colonel J. N. Howton would die in a fiery helicopter crash. I knew his wife, Annie, who hated war, would slowly drink herself to death and would know no other men in her life. And so, two lives would burn in the crash of a helicopter in this place of shadows.

Howton spoke into his headset, talking to the bay-door gunner. "What's the good word from the back of the bus?"

"This is Doctor Death, in basic black, here, talking the stuff at you, big pilot. I got zero unfriendlies. I got Rattlers on my sleeves and we is A-fine and Butt Ugly." Doctor Death was a huge black with gold teeth. Huge muscles threatened to burst the shoulders out of his olive-drab T-shirt. He wore a baseball cap decorated with chicken feathers and a huge button that said, I LIKE IKE. HE'S DEAD.

"That's the meanest son of a bitch who ever squatted over a quad 7.62 machine gun. They tell me he shot his mother. Claimed she was a VC infiltrator."

"He'll survive the war but not the heroin," I said and then wished I hadn't said it. I hadn't meant to.

Howton shook his head. "You are a little too weird to live, if you ask me, Big Chief. How about you do me and mine a favor and lay off the heavy gloom and doom."

"Sure." I grinned at him. "Maybe it's just Indians are naturally pessimistic. Probably has something to do with losing a whole continent."

"Hey! How come I gots to ride shotgun on this here wild-ass chicken? The damn thing just bit the hell out of me!" said Doctor Death.

"That's an eagle, numb butt! It's on the cargo manifest and it's classified top secret, so keep your paws off it! It's worth more than you are on this mission," snapped Howton.

I could tell Howton wanted to ask me about the eagle but perhaps he knew I couldn't tell him anything.

"Listen, since I am going to be the last to know, maybe you can tell me what kind of traffic we're heading for?" asked Howton.

"I know even less than you do. All I know is, I'm to join up with a unit called the 145th, at a place called Phu Loi."

"You ain't been out to fight no war yet, Big Chief. You smell green to me. So where do they get off calling you a secret weapon. You some kind of superskunk? Is that it, Big Chief—you lift your legs and squirt smell juice on old Uncle Ho Chi Minh?"

"I've donated blood on a battlefield on another world," I said, but I knew it was not something I could explain.

"Yeah, well you're a freaking Martian and I'm Doctor Death's toothless old mother," said Howton, scanning the horizon. "This is it. Our landing zone."

"Where are we exactly?"

"As the cootie flies, we're northwest of Saigon, near the Michelin Rubber Plantation, if that tells you anything."

We landed on the helipad. Howton turned in his seat, looked at me expectantly. "Now what?"

The radio kicked in. "Nine Nine Four. This is Gunship Tiger Fifty Seven Seven. Stand by for new orders."

"Ask and you shall receive," said Howton. "Got your ass covered back there, Doctor Death?"

"Wrapped in a pimp Cadillac, you limp-ass white boy. What's the poop?" sang out Doctor Death.

"No poop. We hang onto our mystery guest and wait for the sun to shine."

"I'm getting restless back here, boss. I ain't killed nothing all goddamn morning and I am getting a considerable mad on."

"How is the war going? Are we winning?" I asked Howton, although that was what I myself was here to find out and I knew Howton had no answers.

"War can't take you no place but cold and old. You ask me how the war's going, I'll tell you I miss the hell out of my wife and I don't think I'm ever going to be young again. You ought to be asking Doctor Death," suggested Howton. "If he don't exactly know the answer, he's sure-ass good at making up one that sounds good."

"Doctor Death?"

"Who that yammering in my ear?" said the big black with a wide grin splitting his face. "Is that the baby we want to throw out with the bathwater?"

"Affirmative."

"Welcome aboard, Chief. You out here trying to do to Vietnam what your folks done did to Custer?"

"Something like that," I said. "How do you think the war is going?"

"Just like a waitress with her legs crossed and her arms folded. The frigging service here is terrible."

Howton smiled and jerked his thumb back at Doctor Death. "His name is actually Jackson Jackson, but Doctor Death suits him better. Unwise to try to unconnect him with his own label. Ain't saying he's mean, but his pockets are full of teeth donated by second place in arguments with him."

"Sounds mean," I said. I spoke into the headset. "Once a tribesman, Elk Shoulder, fought many enemies single-handed, as many as the bar could hold I guess. He said he didn't like the damn white man music on the jukebox. Survived the fight without a scratch. He grabbed some guy's head, tore the legs off a bar stool, and beat on his head right along with the music, singing he don't know exactly what because he don't speak any English, but no matter 'cause he's got the rhythm down, that's for sure. And he walked off, where somebody else would have died. If you get the rhythm, it is said you can walk off. When you talk, I hear the same rhythm."

"That's me to a T. I am the King of Walking It Off," said Doctor Death. "I am so goddamn mean I am going to survive Vietnam. Man, you can't get no meaner than that."

Another chopper, a gunship, joined us on the helipad.

It discharged several men, two guns at ready, obviously guards, with a prisoner between them, and a man walking like an architect's idea of what a human would walk like if he were a high rise.

"Big lettuce coming, massa," said Doctor Death. "Look like to me we done getting the head dude."

Howton snapped a crisp salute, his face blanking, becoming an expressionless mask. Even Doctor Death stopped smiling as General W. approached the craft.

The general spotted me, smiled warily and gave a brisk salute. I did not return it. He did not seem surprised by my lapse.

"You're Lieutenant Lookspeaker? You know who I am. Let me make this perfectly clear. I have no part of this project other than arranging its final implementation. I decidedly do not approve of your mission. Is that understood, soldier?" The general's face was red, his voice clipped mean like overmown grass.

"I understand, General."

"I don't think you do," snapped the general. "In any case, I am delivering for interrogation purposes, or rather for what I assume is interrogation purposes, the highest-ranking VC prisoner we've got. His name and rank is—"

"I don't need to know that."

"Will you need an interpreter?" asked the general. "It wasn't mentioned but I have prepared for the contingency."

"That won't be necessary."

"You speak Vietnamese then," said the general, looking surprised.

I shook my head no. "I'll find out what I want to know from him anyway. It doesn't matter if I can't understand his language. What's important is that I understand his dreams."

The general contained his fury but it was an effort.

Through clenched teeth, he said, "I have been instructed to make a chopper and crew available to you with unrestricted flight plans. I have also been instructed to provide you with anything, in the way of hardware, ordnance or men, to accomplish your mission."

"I have what I need. Unhandcuff the prisoner and we'll be off."

"Would it be out of line to ask where the hell you intend to go?"

"Probably not, but I don't know where we're going, so I can't tell you."

The general looked troubled. "Is it true, the rumors, what they say about you?"

I smiled. "I don't know what you're talking about, sir." I gave him a sloppily executed salute, my hand coming off my nose like an inept karate chop.

That seemed to be the final straw for the general. He barked commands at the guards, who unhandcuffed the prisoner and helped him up into the bay door of the chopper.

The general spun on his heel and marched stiffly off like a man going to his own execution.

Howton shook his head. "Bloody m. f-ing Christ! I don't know what you're up to, Chief, but anyone who can twist the Old Man's mammaries in the wringer has sure got my vote."

Doctor Death regarded the prisoner balefully. "Hey, do I got to baby-sit and protect our ass, too?"

Howton turned to me. "He ought to be tied up. You can't trust the bastards any farther than you can. . . ."

"No need." I smiled at the prisoner. He seemed relaxed and cheerful. Undoubtedly, he already sensed that I would be setting him free. I send a lot when I begin receiving.

"He'll be OK. Give him a cigarette, if you have any," I said into the headset.

Doctor Death looked disgusted at the idea of sharing with the prisoner. "Man, I got bullets extra I could spare, but smokes, you must be funning!"

"Where to?" asked Howton, cranking the chopper up for flight.

"North, I think. For a while anyway. I'll tell you when to change direction as soon as I know."

"Are we heading for some real deep stuff. I mean, give

me some kind of idea what to expect. North to what, over what?''

''Don't expect anything,'' I said. ''That's probably the best way. I'd like to fly slow and fairly low. We'll be in the mountains mostly, is my best guess.''

''Guess!'' Howton lifted us off. ''It don't sound like you know what the hell you're doing! This ain't no place to be guessing about anything! Just thinking about it makes my BVDs want to seize up!''

''You copying this, Doctor Death?'' said Howton into the headset.

''Somebody better tell this dude that low and slow is full of lead and dead! Lordy, massa, this fool Indian keep pulling our tail with this kind of thing, I am going to frag his act right where it live.''

''He ain't happy,'' said Howton as the chopper began flying over low-lying mountain ranges. ''And I ain't getting ready to write you no love poems either. You're beginning to sound like a raffle ticket for buying the farm.''

I pointed. ''Go in that direction. Toward the highest mountain peak.''

Howton looked at me like I was crazy. The chopper responded to his touch on the controls, tilting to go in the direction I had pointed.

''I think that mountain is where we're going,'' I said, not knowing it for sure until I had said it. Once spoken, it sounded strangely right.

From somewhere to the left of and a little behind the chopper, antiaircraft guns began rattling at us.

Doctor Death leaned out the door, at the ready. He turned and looked back at us. ''Unfriendlies, a day late and a dollar short.''

In front of us, a jet dropped down at us seemingly from out of nowhere.

Howton grabbed the controls, ready to jerk us into an evasive pattern, expecting a missile launch.

''Relax,'' I said. ''The sun is in front of us and a little to the right. If this were noon, we might be in a lot of trouble but it's late enough we . . .''

Howton knew then that I was crazy. I could see it in his face.

The jet roared down out of the sky, a missile was launched. It screamed by us, close but striking to the left and behind us.

The jet flipped over, pulling out of the dive, and put itself into a pattern for another pass.

"I'm going down," said Howton. "I haven't got enough gojuice to beat the . . ."

The next missile was launched. It followed the same pattern as the last missile, exploding harmlessly against the lower slopes of the mountain.

"They can only see our shadow," I said, looking back at the rising mushroom of smoke from the missile. "Trust me. They can't see us."

As if to further prove my point, the jet returned on a strafing run. It streaked down beside us and laid a perfectly executed fire pattern across our moving shadow.

Howton muttered something under his breath and made the sign of the cross. "I don't understand it. I must be stoned on my f-ing ass."

"There!" I said, pointing at the horizon. "You'll have to go up a couple thousand feet. Where we're going is just beyond that mountain peak. There should be a valley there."

"I don't see any mountain!" Howton had a haunted look on his face. "What goddamn mountain! All I see is jungle! Goddamn jungle!"

I spoke into the headset. "You see the mountain, Doctor Death?"

"You order me to see a mountain, I'll see a frigging mountain, but you ask me, I see only ugly goddamn jungle, is all." The big black had a firm grip on his machine gun, as if its proximity gave him security of some kind.

"Take my word for it, there's a mountain there. If your prisoner could speak English, he could tell you he sees it, too. He saw it first actually."

I didn't tell them that I saw only jungle, too, when I looked out the window of the cockpit. The eyes can lie, in a world of shadows.

When I looked into the Vietnamese prisoner's dreams, I saw the mountain. No jungle, just a single great mountain shining in the sun. I knew what I had come to find was on the mountain I could not see.

We gained altitude until I felt we must be well clear of the highest reach of the mountain peaks.

We spiraled in for a landing.

"Better slow your descent," I said. "And go a little to the left. There's a flat place where we can land just a little beyond the ridge."

"I don't know what you're smoking, Tonto," snapped Howton. "I don't see a ridge. I don't see anything except jungle."

I had my eyes closed, my eyes going inward. I could see the mountain as clear as I could see my hands.

"Just humor me," I said. "Make a descent slow and gradual. Just kind of drift down. I'll tell you when we're on the ground."

Howton complied with murder in his heart.

There was a soft thump and our descent halted.

"Hey, what was that?" said Howton. "We've stopped moving."

"I know it looks like the ground is still a long way down but we've actually landed. Turn the engine off. Once you step outside, everything should be all right."

Doctor Death leaned out the bay door, looking down. "Hey, Hownow, my underwear is seizing up on me back here! Tell me you ain't going to shut the engine off!"

I opened the door and jumped out of the chopper. Doctor Death shrieked. "Howton! The man done killed himself!"

As I stepped out, I saw only the ground thousands of feet below me, but once my feet hit, I saw the mountain.

Howton stared at me, his face showing a considerable strain.

"I'm standing on the mountain," I shouted over the roar of the blades. "Shut the engine off."

Howton shut it down.

Doctor Death stared down at the ground, a look of absolute terror on his face.

"Everybody out," I said as the whine of the blades subsided. "You can only see the mountain when you're on it."

The Vietnamese general smiled and walked calmly past Doctor Death. The black pivoted, brought his gun up to cover him. With a smile, the general stepped out of the bay door and dropped down.

He fell a few feet and stopped.

Doctor Death shook his head, rubbed his jaw once as if trying to erase the whole crazy thing, then said, "Ah, what the hell, you only live once."

He jumped out of the chopper.

He nearly dropped his weapon. "Christ on crutches! I'm on a goddamn mountain!"

Howton climbed out slowly, hesitated a second or two before putting his foot down on what seemed like air. He, too, saw the mountain. "I don't understand it. There's no mountain here! It's not on any of my maps! There's not supposed to be anything here but jungle and swamp! Where the hell are we?" said Howton. "If this mountain has never been mapped, somebody has really screwed the pooch! It doesn't make sense to me; somebody has to have seen it before! It's too big to damn well miss!"

"No American has ever been here before. We are the first and maybe the last," I said, reaching through the back door and dragging out the eagle cage.

"But what is this? How come we couldn't see it until we stepped out on it?" asked Howton.

"Vietnam is a land of shadows. America is fighting a war against something it cannot feel, cannot see or sense."

"What we doing here, Chief?" said Doctor Death. "This place gives me the shrieking freakings."

"I have been sent to find out if America can win this war. Now that I've found this mountain, I think I'll soon know the answer."

"That where the eagle comes in?" asked Doctor Death. "Everything is so messed up here, the craziest answer got to be the most logical one."

"Yes. That's why the eagle is here. That's why we're all here. We've come all this way just to play the ancient game of Cat and Eagle."

The VC general turned and spoke to me. I nodded and pointed up the slope of the mountain, then smiled at him.

"What did he say?" asked Howton. "I thought you didn't understand his lingo?"

"I don't know the words, but I understand the sense of it. We've got some climbing to do. The general has graciously agreed to lead the way."

"He'll lead us right into an ambush," snarled Doctor Death. "No way I'm going to follow him. I want him walking ahead of me but just so I can keep my gun aimed at his goddamm—"

"He is free to go at any time," I said. "And he knows that."

"Are you authorized to let him go?" asked Howton. "Or shouldn't I be asking?"

"I have no choice. This is a strange place we are in. You'll see what I mean. For one thing, I don't think your weapons will work here."

"Say what?" said Doctor Death. "What kind of craziness are you talking about, boy. If I aim at something, it's dead!"

"Not here. Hand me your weapon. I'll demonstrate."

"You find yourself your own weapon, boy. This one is done occupied."

Howton reached into his flak jacket and started to pull out a .45 pistol.

I waved the pistol away. "OK, if you don't believe me, try to shoot me."

Doctor Death looked at Howton. Howton shrugged.

"Just aim at me and fire."

Doctor Death just stared at me. I looked at Howton and nodded.

Howton took the pistol, extended it two-handed until it was pointed at my head. "You get what you ask for in this man's . . ." He pulled the trigger. Nothing happened.

Howton dropped the pistol. "OK, you're proved your point. Where do we go from here?"

"We leave the weapons behind. We've got a bit of a climb ahead of us. I don't know how far we've got to go or what's waiting for us when we get there. I don't think the general knows either. He's never been here awake before. So most of what he knows of this place is only half remembered or very hazy."

"I don't go nowhere without my weapon," said Doctor Death.

"The eagle is our only weapon, and if you don't believe in the strength of the eagle's heart, this last part of the journey may not be for you. There is no dishonor in not going."

"Man, you have got to be kidding. You can't kill no VC with a frigging eagle! I don't want no part of this action!"

"Then stay with the chopper," I said. "You can stay, too, Howton, if you want to. There's really no need for you to go."

Howton scowled, straightened his shoulders and looked up at the ridge ahead of us. "I'm going to see what's on the other side."

I nodded approvingly. Howton was a brave man. But if I were going into combat, I would rather have had Doctor Death at my back. Howton would walk into the unknown, pretending not to be afraid. Only Doctor Death, who believed only in his weapons, had enough fear to be truly brave. He fought scared and therefore more truly alive than Howton, who tried to bury his fear.

He set off at a brisk pace until the going got rough.

"There should be a trail here somewhere, but the general doesn't remember where it is."

Howton looked uneasy. "Sounds weird, but since you mentioned it, I think the trail is to the left about a hundred feet. Don't ask me how I know, it just seemed to pop into my head."

I turned and walked in the direction Howton had indicated. I saw the trail.

"Glad you came along," I said. "This will save us hours."

The general walked up the trail ahead of us. He acted like a man in a dream, eyes nearly closed in sleep, stumbling like a robot up the path. He had the look of a sleepwalker.

The path came to a fork. The general stopped and looked back at us. He motioned first to the left and then pointed his finger at his chest. He pointed to the right fork, then signaled that we were to go in that direction.

I nodded. The general waved slowly as if we were already far away and then turned and stumbled off to the left.

"He's escaping!" said Howton. "And we just let him, right?"

"Yes. But it's more than that. Try to walk down the path he's taking."

Howton moved to the intersection of the two paths. He eyed me strangely for a few seconds then tried to follow the general. He seemed to freeze in midair.

"Just like the weapons, right?"

"And the general couldn't have gone down the path we're going to take. I knew something like this would happen. Didn't know how or in what way, but it's what I meant when I said we had no choice but to let him go."

"I think I can say, with a hundred-percent accuracy, that I am scared out of my freaking gourd!" said Howton. "I'm not that far away from the screaming—"

I interrupted. "I feel worse than you. If it helps any, you're going to come out of this alive. You'll make it back to the chopper and you'll make it back to base. So will Doctor Death." I didn't tell him that I would die here on this mountain even though I was as sure of it as I was of anything. It surprised me that Howton was admitting he was afraid. Maybe he had passed his limit.

We topped a rise and stood in a small clearing. Below us, we saw a valley, lush with vegetation. I knew we must be nearing the end of our journey. My arms were aching with the strain of carrying the heavy cage. I had a couple more scratches where the eagle had got at me again through the bars.

The trail led downward.

We began our descent.

I watched Howton now as much as I watched my footing on the path. My blindness was growing as his own vision grew.

He stopped suddenly, staring at something I could not see.

"What is it?" I asked, and stared in the direction Howton was looking. I saw nothing but trees and vegetation.

"I see people. At least, I think it's people. And a village, but it doesn't look like a Montagnard camp."

"I can't see it, but let's leave the path and walk toward the village," I said and the Ancient of Lizards moved in the desert of my memory, seeking a distant sun.

"What do you mean you don't see it?"

"You knew where the trail was and I didn't, neither did the general. Now you see the village and I can't. Like I said, this is a strange place and things happen here I can't explain."

We left the path and moved farther down into the valley. It was a rough descent for a while and then suddenly it was much easier.

"We're on another path," said Howton. "It seems to lead directly into the center of the village. Did you see it?"

I shook my head no. My blindness was growing. I looked back the way we had come. The trail and the mountain behind me seemed to vanish in the distance. Perhaps I was near my own death now. I could not tell.

We walked on, Howton leading, me stumbling along in the growing dark behind him. Howton stopped.

"Where are we?"

Howton turned and looked at me. "Either I'm having the granddaddy of granddaddy hallucinations or we're standing in the center of a village and we're surrounded by the entire tribe it looks like."

"What do they look like?"

"Like something out of a bad trip. Their eyes are strange. Like they are looking at things I can't see. They don't look like they ever laughed. This will really freak you, Chief. I think they got too many fingers on each hand. You suppose they are cannibals? I don't like the way they're looking at us."

"Describe how they are dressed," I said, cursing my blindness.

"In all the colors of the rainbow," said Howton, awed.

"Can you hear them speaking? If so, how does it sound?"

"It sounds like wild animals talking," said Howton. "You ask me, I'd say they are definitely hostile!"

"Look carefully. Are you sure they are not Montagnards?"

He shook his head. "They're like no Montagnards I ever saw. They're taller, and they've got—"

"I have to try to see them. I want you to close your eyes and keep them closed."

"You sure that's a good idea, Chief? They're brandishing weapons and they look downright hostile."

"They can't hurt you," I said and I closed my eyes.

When I was a young man climbing the lodge pole into manhood, I sought visions of power and wisdom. I chose the road of the shaman, and my vision ally was the spirit of a Great Snake. I called upon the Great Snake to make my eyes unblinking and terrible like his. I called upon him so that I might see into the shadows of this place that is the heart of Vietnam which no white man had ever seen before. If the

Ancient of Lizards was my ally, far greater was my Nightfather, the Great Ancient of Snakes, whose tail was wrapped around the center of the earth. In him, terrible and grim, lie all the truths of man.

I felt the presence of the Great Snake, and the blindness, which was the blindness of the white man, dropped from me.

In my vision, I stood alone on the mountain. The white man with closed eyes was gone. Then my aloneness was pierced by the war cry of the people of Vietnam's hidden heart. They attacked. They were strong, clean-limbed people, tall and golden in color. They killed me and cut my head off.

My head was on a spear made of gold, carved in the shape of an entwined snake. The eyes of the snake were red gems, gleaming in the hot sun.

My eyes were still open and I still saw. I saw what the white man could not see.

Beneath the shadows and smoke lived another Vietnam. These were the unseen ones, the ancestors of the people yet to be.

In the center of their village was a not alive, not dead statue of the Great Cat of Death. It was the one true symbol of this world the white man could not see.

This was a village that had been here since the beginning of beginnings and would exist long after the white man was gone.

An old man came and sat beside my disembodied head. "Why have you come so far to die?"

"I have come to play the game of Cat and Eagle," I said from my ghost mouth.

"No man has ever played it before. Already you are dead and have nothing left to win. Would you still play?"

"You know in your heart why I must play. Dead I may be, but I yet clearly see."

"If the eagle wins, I will give you back your life, your head back to its body. But know you that the Great Cat is strong and clever. He fights in his own land, where none but he is kin and king. Does your eagle see, heart true, so far from home, dead man, this is what I ask you?" said the old man.

"Only by playing the game will we know."

"Let it be so then," said the old man. He took the cage of

the eagle and held it out in front of him at eye level, as if it weighed nothing. Carefully, he opened the cage door and reached in with one hand and took hold of the eagle. The great bird tried to attack him but the old man seemed made of granite, not even flinching as the bird tried to sink its talons in the old man's arm.

The old one held the bird aloft, firmly holding it by the legs. "Great Bird, you see before you your enemy, the Great Cat. I make ready to send you to him."

My ghost eyes saw the living, not living statue of the Great Cat twist and arch its back, rising up off the great block of mountain stone. It snarled, its eyes coming open and seeing its enemy preparing to meet it in combat.

"Go, Eagle! May you fight well and find a good wind!" The old man released the bird.

The bird shot up like an arrow into the sky, thrusting up on wings of death. Beneath it, the Great Cat crouched, its eyes turned skyward, seeking the enemy.

The Great Eagle rose up so high it was almost invisible. Then it dived down, in its long, graceful killing swoop, claws flashing, eyes burning with great hunting wisdom.

The Great Cat seemed to stand helplessly in its path, making no move to avert the Great Eagle's killing plunge.

The Great Cat screamed. The Great Eagle struck, winged lightning falling upon its intended prey.

The Great Eagle's talons closed on air.

Unseen, the cat came up underneath him, and in one murderous lunge, seized the great bird and defeated him.

The Great Eagle's skull was crushed in the unseen jaws of the Great Cat of Death.

"The stranger is dead and the Great Cat has triumphed," said the old man. "So do the dreams of men die when they are not alive in the world they belong in. You have come from a great farness to see my people and our ways. Your people long ago walked in the same path as we once walked. The white man is not of your way or of ours. They come upon our path, but the way is forever barred to them. So it is with your people and ours."

I spoke from my dead mouth. "I knew that my bones would dwell among your people. The white men sent me to find out if they could win the war."

"They seek and we hide," said the old man. "So shall it always be. The white man cannot defeat what he cannot see, cannot conquer a land he cannot find. That is your answer."

"I wish to go home and be among my people."

"Leave your body with us and go back in the mind of the white man," said the old man. "We shall grind up your bones and flesh and eat of them, so then shall your ancestors join us in the flesh and blood of our children yet to be."

I closed my eyes for the last time. I had died.

Lieutenant Colonel J. N. Howton sat in the cockpit of his chopper. Doctor Death stared at the body of the Vietnamese general.

His gun was still smoking.

Howton turned in his seat, startled by the sudden burst of gunfire. "What happened?"

"I don't rightly know. One minute I'm watching his ass and the next minute he's charging down my gun trying to push me out the door. He just freaked out!"

"We'll probably get our noses ripped off for losing him," said Howton with a scowl.

"And Jesus, the bastard must have killed the eagle! I don't know how because I had my eye on him all the time, but this damn bird is sure dead. Ripped to shreds! How do you figure it, Hownow?" said Doctor Death.

A sudden burst of flak from the ground caused Howton to veer sharply to the right. "Big unfriendlies with nasty stuff!" said Howton. "We're going up and away."

He turned to me with an apologetic grin. "Sorry about your prisoner. Guess he did in your eagle, too. I said you can't trust the—"

He stopped talking when he realized I had been hit.

I could feel blood running down my neck. I didn't feel any pain, just a great coldness from my shoulders on down.

"Oh, Christ! Doctor Death, we got a casualty up here! The Chief picked up a package!"

"Head for home, Hownow! We got us a blown gig for damn sure!" cursed Doctor Death, leaning out the bay door, his heavy machine gun spitting angry death at the jungle below.

Howton increased the chopper's speed as he spun in a wide turn, heading back for base.

Howton spoke into the radio. "This is Nine Nine Four on the LOOKSEEK run. We've got one dead VC and Mystery Guest wounded. We must abort. Requesting medical assistance."

"How bad Mystery Guest?" I heard the radio immediately reply. It was the voice of General W. himself. I motioned weakly with my hand at Howton, but he didn't see me. I wanted to tell the general something but my mouth couldn't form the words.

"Very bad," said Howton, staring at me. "Head wounds at the base of the skull. Don't know if he'll make it."

"Get back as quick as you can," said the general. "And I'll want a full report of just how this thing got screwed up. You did your best, men, considering the assignment," said the general, signing off.

"I expected you to get your ears pasted back," said Doctor Death. "The Man sounds like he's glad the whole thing went into the toilet!"

I was beginning to lose consciousness. I knew I was dying. "Tell the general we can't . . ." I couldn't get the words out. Seemed so tired, so cold.

"Take it easy," said Howton. "We'll be home soon."

"No," I said and the pain began and almost obliterated me. "War . . . can't win . . . white men . . . in wrong Vietnam . . ."

I died in the cockpit of the UH-1D. At the moment of death, in the village on the mountain which the white man could not see, the women ground up my bones and flesh in a stone bowl.

The old man, the World Knower, came to sit beside the statue of the Great Death Cat. When the women had finished their task, they brought the stone bowl to him and he offered some of it to the Great Cat.

Then the people of the village came with bowls of food, and in each bowl, he put a small ancestral piece of me.

They ate of me and I became one with their children to be, one with the children that would live on in that world long after the white man was gone.

In a vision, in a rapidly moving helicopter, somewhere above a Vietnam the white man couldn't see, a Great Eagle died in the unsensed jaws of a Great Cat.

Karen Joy Fowler

Karen Joy Fowler studied writing with Kim Stanley Robinson and sold her first story in 1984 to *Isaac Asimov's Science Fiction Magazine*. She sold her second story to *Writers of the Future* two weeks later, and since then has been a frequent contributor to *IASFM* and *The Magazine of Fantasy & Science Fiction*. Her poetry has appeared in *The Ohio Journal* and the *California Quarterly*, as well as other journals. She has sold a collection of her stories entitled *Artificial Things* to Bantam. Fowler has two children and lives in Davis, California. She writes: "I consider this story to be a gesture of reconciliation—a love letter. I will never think that going to fight in Vietnam was the right thing to do, but I have reached a point in my life where I do want to listen. I do think those of us around my own age were defined by Vietnam in ways those much older and much younger will never understand. Which leaves us only each other to turn to for understanding."

Letters From Home

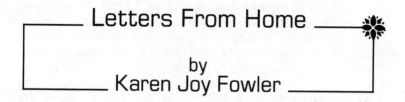

by
Karen Joy Fowler

You want to end the war and stuff,
you got to sing loud.
—Arlo Guthrie*

I wish you could see me now. You would laugh. I have a husband. I have children. Yes. I drive a station wagon. I would laugh, too. Our turn to be the big kids, the grown-ups. Our turn to be over thirty. It astonishes me whenever I stop and think about it. It has to be a joke.

I miss you. I've always missed you. I want us to understand each other. I want to tell you what I did after you left. I want to tell you what I did during the war. Most of all, I want to tell you the truth. This is what makes it so difficult. I have learned to distrust words, even my own. Words can be made to say anything. I know this. Do you?

Much of what I will tell you actually happened. You will be able to identify these parts, or you can ask me. This does not mean, of course, that any of it is true. Even among the people who were there with me are some who remember it differently. Gretchen said something once which echoed my own feelings. "We were happy, weren't we?" she said. "In spite of everything. We made each other happy. Ill-advised, really, this putting your happiness into other people's hands. I've tried it several times since and it's never worked again."

But when I repeated this to Julie she was amazed. "Happy?" she asked. "How can you say that? I was so fat. I was being

*Alice's Restaurant by Arlo Guthrie © copyright 1966, 1967 by Appleseed Music Inc. All rights reserved. Used by permission.

screwed by that teaching assistant. And 'screwed' is the only word that applies. There was a *war*. Don't you remember?''

Can I tell you what I remember about the war? I remember the words. Vietnam was the language we spoke—secret bombings, the lottery, Vietnamization, self-immolation, Ho-Ho-Ho Chi Minh, peace with honor, peace at any price, peace, peace, peace. Somewhere, I imagine, on the other side of the world, these words meant something. Somewhere they had physical counterparts. Except for the last set, of course. If peace has ever had a physical value anywhere, none of us has been able to find it. But the other words corresponded to something. There was a *real* war going on and in many ways we were untouched by it. This is what I'm trying to say: if the words alone were powerful enough to shape us and our lives as they did, what kind of an impact must the real war have had on *its* people?

I remember sitting on our sofa watching television. Julie is on the floor at my feet. She's the red-haired Jewish one. She's studying set design and is busy gluing together a tiny throne, part of a mock-up for the set of *Saint Joan*. ''Women have fought in wars before,'' she reminds us. ''But only when God tells them to.''

Lauren is next to me. She's black, though rather light-skinned and freckled. Her dog is on her lap, giving the television the same studied attention the rest of us are. Gretchen is standing in the doorway to the kitchen drinking a diet soda. She has short brown hair and heavy bangs, a white Catholic though not a practicing one. She clings to Catholicism because it protects her from being a WASP. This unpleasant designation is applicable only to me. You know me. I'm the plain white one on the end there with my legs drawn up to my chest and my arms around them. And that ten-inch figure on the screen with his hands in motion before him and the map of Cambodia behind him—that's President Nixon. The Quaker. He is busy redrawing the Cambodian border and explaining to us that we are not really invading Cambodia, because the border is not where we have always thought it was. Gretchen swallows the last of her soda. ''My God,'' she says. ''The man may be right. Just now, just out of the corner of my eye, I saw the border jump.''

Nixon is impervious to our criticism. He is content;

he feels it is enough merely to have found something to say.

I am twenty years old. I believe nothing I hear.

I was not always like that. Here is an earlier memory. We are standing on my parents' front porch and you have your arms around me. You have driven all the way down from San Francisco to tell me you have been drafted. I find this incomprehensible. I know you could have avoided it. Isn't Allen in Manhattan Beach getting braces put on his teeth? Hasn't Greg moved three times in three months, burying his induction notice in the U.S. mails? Hasn't Jim joined VISTA, taking advantage of the unspoken agreement that if you are reluctant to burn villages and bomb children, your country will accept two years of urban volunteerism instead?

You are so thin I feel your bones inside your arms. If you fasted, you could fall below the required weight. Why will you do none of these things? I can't help feeling betrayed.

You try to explain and I try to listen. You tell me that the draft is unfair because you *could* evade it. You say if you don't go, they will just send someone else. (Yes, I say. Yes.) You say that perhaps you can have some impact from within. That an evasion won't realistically affect the war effort at all, but maybe if you were actually there . . . "Hey." You are holding your arms about me so tightly, helping me to hold myself so tightly inside. "Don't cry. I'm going to subvert every soldier I meet. The war will be over by Christmas." And I don't cry. Remember? I don't cry.

You disappeared into the real war and you never got one word back out to me. I never heard from you or of you again. So that is what I remember about the war. The words over here. The war over there. And increasingly little connection between the two.

You are put on a bus and sent to basic training. You take the last possible seat, left rear corner. The bus fills with young men, their white necks exposed by new haircuts, their ears open and vulnerable.

It reminds you of going to camp. You suggest a game of telephone. You whisper into the ear closest to you. You whisper, "The Geneva Accords." The man next to you leans across the aisle. The message travels over thc backs of the seats and crisscrosses the bus. When it comes out at the front, it is "the domino theory."

You try again. "Buddhist bar-b-cues," you whisper. You think the man next to you has it right, repeats it just the way you said it. You can hear the "b's" and the "s's" even over the bus motor. But the large man at the front of the bus, the one whose pink scalp is so vivid you can't even guess what color the fuzz of his hair might be, claims to have heard "strategic hamlets." Someone is changing the words.

"Body bags!" You have shouted it accidentally. Everyone turns to look at you. Fifty faces. Fifty selected faces. Already these men are different from the men they were yesterday, a difference of appearance, perhaps, and nothing else. It may stay this way. It may be the first hint of the evolution of an entirely new person. You turn to the tinted window, surprised by your own face staring at you.

The other men think you have said, "Operation Rolling Thunder." Even so, nobody smiles.

When you leave the bus, you leave the face in the window. You go and it stays. So it cannot have been *your* face after all.

After you left I went to Berkeley. I lived in the student dorms for a year, where I met Gretchen and Julie. When we moved out, we moved out together, into a fairly typical student apartment. It had a long shag carpet—even the rugs were hairy then—of a particularly putrid green and the appliances were avocado. The furniture had been stapled together. There were four beds and the rent clearly had been selected with four in mind. We advertised for a roommate in the *Daily Cal*. Although taking a stranger into our home entailed a definite risk, it seemed preferable to inviting anyone we actually knew.

I remember that we flipped a coin to see which of us would have to share the bedroom with the newcomer and Julie lost. She had some procedural objection she felt was sufficiently serious to require a second toss, but Gretchen and I refused. The new roommate hadn't even appeared and was already making things sticky.

Lauren was the first respondent to our ad—a beautiful, thin curly-haired girl with an elegant white curly-haired dog. They made a striking pair. Julie showed Lauren the apartment; the conversation was brisk and businesslike. Gretchen and I petted the dog. When Lauren left, Julie had said we would take her.

I was unsettled by the speed of the decision and said so. I had no objections to Lauren, but I'd envisioned interviewing several candidates before making a selection.

"I'm the one who has to room with her. I should get to choose." Julie held out one long strand of her own red hair and began methodically to split the end. Julie was artistic and found the drab apartment painful. Initially, I believe she wanted Lauren mostly for decor. Lauren moved in the next day.

Immediately objectionable characteristics began to surface. If I'd had your address, I would have written long complaints. "She dresses with such taste," I would have said. "Who would have guessed she'd be such a slob?" Lauren's messiness was epic in its proportions. Her bed could hardly be seen under the pile of books, shoes, combs, and dirty dishes she left on it. She had to enter it gingerly at night, finding small empty spaces where she might fit an arm or a leg. She would sleep without moving, an entire night spent in the only position possible.

"She's late wherever she goes," I would have written, "not by minutes or quarter hours, but by afternoons. On her night to cook, we eat in front of Johnny Carson."

Then I would have divulged the worst complaint of all. "She talks baby talk, to the dog, which is tolerable, to her boyfriend, which is not." Lauren's boyfriend was a law student at Boalt. He was older than us, big, and wore his hair slicked back along his head. Of course, *no one* wore their hair like that then. There was a sort of Mafioso cut to his clothes, an intensity in his eyes. I never liked being alone with him, but Lauren called him Owlie and he called her his Sugarbear. "It is absolutely sickening the way you two go on," I told her and she was completely unabashed. She suggested that, although we didn't have the guts to be as up front about it as she was, we probably all talked baby talk to our boyfriends, an accusation we strenuously denied. We had no boyfriends, so the point was academic. Owlie studied judo as well as the law, and there was always a risk, opening some door, that you might find him demonstrating some hold to Lauren. Sickening, like I said.

I would have finished my letter by telling you, if you could only meet her, you would love her. Well, we all did. She was vivacious, imaginative, courageous. She removed some previously unnoticed tensions from our relationships—somehow with four the balance was better. By the spring of 1970, when the war of the words achieved its most intense pitch ever, this balance had become intricate and effortless.

I had gone out to protest the Cambodian invasion and come home in a cast. The police had removed their badges, donned their gas masks and chased us down, catching me just outside Computer Sciences. They had broken my ankle. Owlie was gone. His birthday had been drawn seventeenth in the lottery and he'd relocated to a small town in Oregon rumored to have a lenient draft board. Gretchen had acquired a boyfriend whose back had been injured in a high school wrestling match, rendering him 4-F with no tricks. He went off to Europe and was, consequently, very little trouble. Julie had switched her major from set design to Chicano studies. We heard that the National Guard was killing people on the campus of Kent State. I heard nothing from you.

You are in a small room, a cell. It is cold and the walls are damp stone. You sit cross-legged like a monk on the thin mattress and face the wall. There is so much moisture you can imprint your hand in it. By 10 A.M. the prints disappear. The sun has reached the wall, but it still is not warm. If you were sure no one would come to look, you would levitate yourself into the sunshine. You are thinking of me.

How much I expected of you. How stupid I am. I probably believed you could end the war by Christmas. You can imagine me believing that. Even now I am probably working out long chain-letter calculations—if you subvert four soldiers every day and they subvert four soldiers and *they* subvert four soldiers, how many days will the war last? When will you come home?

Do I expect miracles from a prison cell? Why should you provide them? You make a decision. You decide to be warm. You exhale your warmth into the air. It rises to the ceiling, it seems to disappear, but as you repeat this, over and over, the layers eventually drop to where they surround you.

When you leave the cell, you will leave it filled with your heat.

It is a small room. Any man can accomplish a small task.

In response to the invasion of Cambodia and the deaths at Kent State (Can I say murders? Will you object? Will you compare those four deaths to the body count in Vietnam on any single day or on May 4 itself and believe you have made some point?) U.C. Berkeley suspended classes. When they recommenced, they had been reconstituted; they were now supposed to be directly relevant to the single task of ending the war in Southeast Asia. I will not pretend to you that there was no opposition within the university to this. But a large segment of the campus made this commitment together—we would not continue with our lives until the war was over.

At the same time Nixon made his own pledge to the American people. He promised them that nothing, *nothing* we could do would affect policy in any way.

The war of the words took on a character which was at once desperate and futile, a soul-dampening combination we never shook free of. We did the work because it seemed right to us. We had no illusions of its potency. It began to feel like a game.

Julie and I had volunteered for a large committee whose purpose was to compile a list of war profiteers so that their products could be boycotted. We researched mergers and parent companies; this list grew like a chain letter. It would have been quicker to list those companies not turning a profit in Vietnam. I remember Lauren perusing our list one day with great dissatisfaction. "The counterculture makes roach clips," she said. "It makes liquid sculptures you can plug in and they change shape."

"Lava lamps," I told her.

"Whatever. It makes hash pipes. I need a raincoat. What am I supposed to do?"

"Get wet," Julie suggested.

"Get stoned," said Gretchen. "And then get wet. You'll hardly notice."

Lauren had volunteered herself for the university's media watchdog committee. Her job was to monitor three news shows daily and report on the coverage they gave to the war and to the student movement. The idea was that we would apply whatever pressure we could on those stations whose coverage seemed slanted in favor of the Administration. The fallacy was that we had any meaningful pressure which could be brought to bear. We wrote letters. We added their sponsors to the boycott. Nobody cared.

I know that Nixon felt undermined and attacked by the media. We did not see it this way. None of the major networks met with our approval. Only the local public station reported the news in Berkeley the way we saw it happening. One of their reporters was a young man who covered those stories felt to be of particular interest to the black community. He was handsome, moustached, broad-shouldered. He had the same dark, melting eyes as Lauren's dog. His name was Poncho Taylor. Lauren fell in love with him.

Well, you didn't expect us to give up love, did you? Just because there was a war on? I never expected you to.

Poncho was politically impeccable. He was passionate, he was committed. He was gorgeous. Any one of us could have fallen in love with him. But Lauren was the first to announce her passion and we were content to provide support. We took turns with her transcribing duties during his airtime so she wouldn't miss a moment of his face. We listened patiently while she droned on about his cheekbones, his hair, the sexy tremor in his voice when a story had an unhappy conclusion, and we agreed. We saw it all. He was wonderful.

I remember a night when we made chocolate chip cookies and ate the dough. Nestlé had just made the boycott list, but the chips were old. "The sooner we eat them, the better," Julie had suggested.

Gretchen had just returned from an organizational meeting with new instructions for us. We had been told to band together into small groups like the revolutionaries in *The Battle of Algiers*. These were to be called affinity groups and we were to select for them people we trusted absolutely. We were to choose those people we would trust with our lives. We smiled at one another over the bowl of dough as it suddenly occurred to us that, for us, this choice had already been made. Just as Gretchen said, when we could find our happiness nowhere else, we were able to put it into each other's hands and hold it there.

"There's more," Gretchen continued. "We're supposed to arm ourselves." Julie took another spoonful of dough, heavy on the chips. I used the handle of my spoon to reach inside my cast and scratch myself. Nobody said anything for a long time.

Finally Julie indicated the boycott list. "The pen is mightier than the sword," she suggested. She didn't sound sure.

Gretchen did. "The boycott is liberal bullshit," she said. "It's too easy. What good will it possibly do?"

Lauren cleared her throat and tapped the air with the back of her spoon. "It's a capitalist country. Money matters."

"You can't destroy the system from within the system." Gretchen was very unhappy. "We're too safe."

We sent Nixon a telegram. Gretchen composed it. "End this obscene war at once Stop Pull out the way your father should have Stop." It didn't make us feel better.

We should have done more. I look back on those years and it's clear to me that we should have done more. It's just not clear to me *what* more we should have done.

Perhaps we lacked imagination. Perhaps we lacked physical courage. Perhaps our personal stakes were just not high enough. We were women. We were not going to Vietnam. We were privileged. Our brothers, our lovers were not going to Vietnam. But you do us an injustice if you doubt our sincerity. Remember that we watched the news three times a day. Three times a day we read the body count in the upper right-hand corner of the screen like the score of a football game. This is how many of them we killed today. They killed this many of us. Subtract one figure from the other. Are we winning?

Could anyone be indifferent to this? Always, I added the two numbers together. My God, I would think. Dear God. Look how many people died today! (What if one of them was you?)

You are on a plane, an ordinary plane. You could be en route to Denver from Chicago or going home for Christmas if you just close your eyes and believe only your ears. But you are really between Japan and Vietnam. The plane has a stewardess dressed in a bathing suit like Miss America. This is designed as a consolation for you. If you are very, very frightened, she may agree to wear rabbit ears and a tail when she brings you your drink. But you must not touch her. She is a white woman and looks familiar to you—her height, her build quite ordinary. This will change. When you remember her later she will seem exotic. It will seem odd to you that a woman should be so big. You will remember that she came and tightened your seat belt as if she were your mother. What was she keeping you safe for? Whose body is it anyway? You look at your legs, at your hands, and wonder what your body will be like when it is returned to you. You wonder who will want it then.

The immediate threat is the plane's descent. You make a sudden decision not to descend with it. You spread your arms to hold yourself aloft. You hover near the top of the plane. But it is hopeless. If they have to shoot you down, they will. Friendly fire. You return to your seat. The plane carries your body down into Vietnam.

You think of me. How I will hate you if you don't live through this. How you must protect me. And during your whole tour, every time you meet someone returning home, you will give him a message for me. You will write your message on the casts of the wounded. You will print it on the foreheads of those who return walking, on the teeth of those who return bagged. *I am here, I am here, I am here.* So many messages. How are you to know that none will get through?

My affinity group was very kind about you. I would tell them frequently how the war would be over by Christmas, how you were responsible for the growing dissatisfaction among servicemen. Vets against the war, I said to them, was probably one of your ideas. They never mentioned how you never wrote. Neither did I. You were my wound. I had my broken ankle and I had you. It was so much more than they had. It made them protective of me.

They didn't want me at any more demonstrations. ''When you *could* run,'' Lauren pointed out, ''look what happened to you.'' But I was there with them when the police cordoned off Sproul Plaza, trapping us inside, and gassed us from the air. You don't want to believe this. Governor Ronald Reagan and all the major networks assured you that we had been asked to disperse, but had refused. Only Poncho Taylor told the truth. We had not been allowed to leave. Anyone who had tried to leave was clubbed. A helicopter flew over the area and dropped teargas on us. The gas went into the hospital and into the neighboring residential areas. When the police asked the city to buy them a second helicopter so that they could enlarge operations, many people not of the radical persuasion objected. A committee was formed to prevent this purchase, a committee headed by an old Bay Area activist. She happened to be Poncho Taylor's grandmother. Lauren took it as a sign from God.

Lauren's passion for Poncho had continued to grow and we had continued to feed it. It's difficult to explain why Poncho had become so important to us. Partly it was just that Lauren loved him and we loved Lauren. Whatever Lauren wanted she should have. But partly it was the futility of our political work. We continued to do it but without energy, without hope. Poncho began to seem attainable when peace was not. Poncho began to represent the *rest* of our lives, outside the words.

Lauren told everyone how she felt. Our friends all knew and soon their friends knew and then the friends of their friends. It was like a message Lauren was sending to Poncho. And if it didn't reach him, then Lauren could combine useful political effort with another conduit. She called Poncho's grandmother and volunteered us all for the Stop the Helicopter campaign.

We went to an evening organizational meeting. (We did more organizing than anything else.) Though now I remember that Julie did not come with us, but stayed at home to rendezvous in the empty apartment with her teaching assistant.

The meeting was crowded, but eventually we verified Poncho's absence. After interminable discussion we were told to organize phone trees, circulate petitions, see that the city council meeting, scheduled for the end of the month, was packed with vocal opponents. Lauren couldn't even get close to Poncho's grandmother.

When we returned home, Julie was drunk. Her lover had failed to show, but Mike, a friend of mine, had come by with a bottle of wine. Julie had never known Mike very well or liked him very much, but he had stayed the whole evening and they had gotten along wonderfully. Julie had a large collection of Barbra Streisand records we refused to let her play. Mike had not only put them on but actually cried over them. "He's a lot more sensitive than I thought," Julie told me.

Mike denied it all. He was so drunk he wove from side to side even sitting down. He tried to kiss me and landed on my shoulder. "How did the meeting go?" he asked and snorted when we told him. "Phone trees." He lifted his head to grin at me, red-faced, unshaven, wine-soaked breath. "The old radicals are even less ballsy than the young ones."

I picked up one of his hands. "Do you think it's possible," I asked him, "for a revolution to be entirely personal? Suppose we all concentrated on our own lives, filled them with revolutionary moments, revolutionary relationships. When we had enough of them, it would be a revolution."

"No." Mike removed his hand from mine. "It wouldn't. That's cowardice talking. That's you being liberal. That's you saying, let's make a revolution, but let's be nice about it. People are dying. There's a real war going on. We can't be incremental."

"Exactly," said Gretchen. "Exactly. Time is as much the issue as anything else."

"Then we should all be carrying guns," said Julie. "We should be planning political assassinations."

"We should be robbing banks," said Mike. "Or printing phony bills." Mike had been known to pass a bad check or two. Though he never needed the money. He was an auto mechanic by day, a dope dealer by night. He was the richest person we knew. "Lauren," he called and Lauren appeared in the doorway to the kitchen. "I came here tonight because I have a surprise for you." He was grinning.

"If it's dope, I'm not interested," said Lauren. "Nor am I solvent."

"What would you say," Mike asked, "if I told you that right now, right at this very moment, I have Poncho Taylor's car sitting in my garage waiting for repairs?" Lauren said we would go right over.

Poncho had a white convertible. Lauren loved it. She sat in the driver's seat, because Poncho had sat there. She sat on the passenger side, because that was where she would be sitting herself. I discovered an old Valentine in the glove compartment. Lauren was torn between the despair of thinking he already had a girlfriend and the thrill of finally discovering something personal. She opened it.

" 'Love and a hundred smooches, Deborah.' " Lauren read it aloud disapprovingly. "This Deborah sounds like a real sap."

"Poncho seems more and more to be the perfect match for you," I added. The Valentine had one feature of incontrovertible value. It had Poncho's address on it. Lauren began to copy it, then looked at us.

"What the hell," she said and put the whole thing in her purse.

I had no address for you, you know. I mean, in the beginning I did and I probably should have written you first. Since I hardly talked to you when you came to say good-bye. Since I didn't cry. I *did* miss you. I kept thinking *you* would write *me*. And then later, when I saw you wouldn't, it was too late. Then I had no address. I couldn't believe you would *never* write me. What happened to you?

Even our senators sent me form letters. More than I got from you.

Dear (fill in name),

Well, here I am in Vietnam! The people are little and the bugs are big, but the food is Army and that means American. As far as I can see, Saigon has been turned into one large brothel. I go there as often as I can. It beats my other way of interacting with the locals, which is to go up in planes and drop "Willie Peter" on them. Man, those suckers burn forever!

I made my first ground kill yesterday. Little guy in a whole lot of pieces. You have to bring the body for the body count and the arm came off right in my hand. We were able to count him six times, which everyone said was really beautiful. Hey, he's in so many pieces he's never going to need any company but his own again. The dope is really heavy-duty here, too. I've lost my mind.

Listen, I got to go. We're due out tonight on a walk-through with ARVN support and you know what they say here about the ARVN—with friends like thesc . . . Ugly little buggers.

Dust off the women. I'll be home by Christmas. Love you all,

(Fill in name)

Now you're angry. I hope. Who am I to condemn you? What do I know about the real war? Absolutely nothing. Gretchen says you're a running-dog imperialist. She thinks she met you once before you left, before she knew me, at a party at Barbara Meyer's. In Sausalito? I don't think it was you. She waited a long time to tell me about it. I was married before she told me. I don't think it was you. So . . .

So, it took Lauren two days to formalize her final plan. It was audacious. It was daring. It had Lauren's stamp all over it. Mike called when Poncho came in and picked up his car. This was our signal to start.

It was Lauren's night to cook dinner and she saw no reason to change this. She had bought the ingredients for cannelloni, a spectacular treat she made entirely from scratch. It required long intervals, she claimed, when the dough must be allowed to rest. During one of these rest periods, she fixed herself up and Julie drove her to San Francisco, where Poncho lived. Julie returned in forty minutes. She had only stayed long enough to see Lauren safely inside.

Lauren came home perhaps a half an hour later. She changed her clothes again, dropping the discarded ones onto the living room floor, and went into the kitchen to roll out the cannelloni dough. We sat around her at the kitchen table, chopping the onions, mixing the filling, stuffing the rolls while she talked. She was very high, very excited.

"I knocked on the door," she said. "Poncho's roommate let me in. Poncho was lying on the couch, reading. Poncho Taylor! He was there!"

"Can I come in?" Lauren had asked. She made her voice wobble. She showed us how. "A man in a car is following me."

"What was the roommate like?" Julie asked hopefully. "Pretty cute?"

"No. He wears big glasses and his hair is very short.

James. His name is James. He asked me why I came to their apartment since they live on the second floor."

"Good question," I admitted. "What did you say?"

"I said I saw their Bobby Seale poster and I thought they might be black."

"Good *answer*," said Julie. "Lauren thinks on her feet. All right!"

"There's nothing wrong with glasses," Gretchen objected. "Lots of attractive people wear glasses." She cut into an onion with determined zeal. "Maybe he's gay," she said.

"No," said Lauren. "He's not. And it wasn't the glasses. It was the competition. Poncho is *so* . . ." We waited while she searched for the word worthy of Poncho. "Magnetic," she concluded.

Well, who could compete with Poncho? Gretchen let the issue drop.

Lauren had entered the apartment and James and Poncho had gone to the window. "What make was the car?" James had asked. "I don't see anybody."

"Green VW bug," said Lauren.

"*My* car," said Julie. "Great."

"They wanted me to call the police," Lauren said. "But I was too upset. I didn't even get the license."

"Lauren," said Gretchen disapprovingly. Gretchen hated women to look helpless. Lauren looked back at her.

"I was distraught," she said evenly. She began picking up the finished cannelloni and lining the pan with neat rows. Little blankets. Little corpses. (No. I am being honest. Of course I didn't think this.)

Poncho had returned immediately to the couch and his book. "Chicks shouldn't wander around the city alone at night," he commented briefly. Lauren loved his protectiveness. Gretchen was silent.

"Then I asked to use the phone," Lauren said. She wiped her forehead with her upper arm since her hands were covered with flour. She took the pan to the stove and ladled tomato sauce into it. "The phone was in the kitchen. James took me in, then he went back. I put my keys on the floor, very quietly, and I kicked them under the table. Then I pretended to phone you."

"All your keys?" Julie asked in dismay.

Lauren ignored her. "I told them no one was home. I told them I'd been planning to take the bus, but by now, of course, I'd missed it."

"All your keys?" I asked pointedly.

"James drove me home. Damn! If he hadn't been there . . ." Lauren slammed the oven door on our dinner and came to sit with us. "What do you think?" she asked. "Is he interested?"

"Sounds like James was interested," said Gretchen.

"You left your name with your keys?" I said.

"Name, address, phone number. Now we wait."

We waited. For two days the phone never rang. Not even our parents wanted to talk to us. In the interests of verisimilitude Lauren had left all her keys on the chain. She couldn't get into the apartment unless one of us had arranged to be home and let her in. She couldn't drive, which was just as well since every gas company had made the boycott list but Shell. Shell was not an American company, but we were still investigating. It seemed likely there was war profiteering there *somewhere*. And, if not, then we'd heard rumors of South African holdings. We were looking into it. But in the meantime we could still drive.

"The counterculture is going to make gas from chicken shit," said Julie.

"Too bad they can't make it from bullshit," Lauren said. "We got plenty of that."

Demonstrators had gone out and stopped the morning commute traffic to protest the war. It had not been appreciated. It drove something of a wedge between us and the working class. Not that the proletariat had ever liked us much. I told our postman that more than two hundred colleges had closed. "BFD," he said, handing me the mail. Nothing for me.

You are on the surface of the moon and the air itself is a poison. Nothing moves, nothing grows, there is nothing, but ash. A helicopter has left you here and the air from its lift-off made the ash fly and then resettle into definite shapes, like waves. You don't move for fear of disturbing these patterns, which make you think of snow, of children lying on their backs in the snow until their arms turn into wings. You can see the shadows of winged people in the ash.

Nothing is alive here, so you are not here, after all, on this man-made moon where nothing can breathe. You are home and have been home for months. Your tour lasted just over a year and you only missed one Christmas. You have a job and a wife and you eat at restaurants, go to baseball games, commute on the bus. The war is over and there is nothing behind you but the bodies of angels flying on their backs in the ash.

Poncho never called. We went to the city meeting on the helicopter, all four of us, to help the city make this decision. The helicopter was item seven on the agenda. We never got to it. Child care had been promised, but not provided. Angry parents dumped their children on the stage of the Berkeley Community Theater to sit with the council members. A small girl with a sun painted on her forehead knocked over a microphone. The conservative council members went home. Berkeley.

Lauren found Poncho and James in the dress circle. Poncho was covering the meeting. Lauren introduced us all. "By the way," she said carefully, "you didn't find a set of keys at your house, did you? I lost mine and that night is the last I remember having them."

"Keys?" asked Poncho. "No." Something in his smile told me Lauren must have overplayed herself that evening. He knew exactly what was going on.

"If you do find them, you will call me?"

"Of course."

Julie drove us home and I made Lauren a cup of tea. She held my hand for a moment as she took it from me. Then she smiled. "I thought we were boycotting Lipton's," she said.

"It's a British tea." I stirred some milk into my own cup. "That should be all right, shouldn't it?"

"Have you ever heard of Bernadette Devlin?" Gretchen asked.

We never saw Poncho again except on TV. On June 29 he told us all American forces had been withdrawn from Cambodia. Your birthday, so I remember the date. Not a bad lottery number either. So I always wondered. Were you really drafted? Did you enlist?

Poncho lost his job about the same time Nixon lost his.

Some network executive decided blacks didn't need special news so they didn't need special reporters to give it to them. Let them watch the same news as the rest of us. And apparently Poncho's ability to handle generic news was doubtful. The network let him go. Politically we regretted this decision. Privately we thought he had it coming.

God, it was years ago. Years and years ago. I got married. Lauren went to Los Angeles and then to Paris and now she's in Washington writing speeches for some senator. Hey, we emerged from the war of the words with *some* expertise. Gretchen and Julie had a falling-out and hardly speak to each other now. Only when I'm there. They make a special effort for me.

Julie asked me recently why I was so sure there ever had been a real war. What proof did I have, she asked, that it wasn't a TV movie of the decade? A miniseries? A maxiseries?

It outraged Gretchen. "Don't do that," she snapped. "Keep it real." She turned to me. She said she saw you about a month ago at Fisherman's Wharf in San Francisco. She said you had no legs.

It doesn't alarm me as much as you might think. I see you all the time, too. You're in the park, pushing your kids on the swings and you've got one hand and one hook. Or you're sitting in a wheelchair in the aisle of the movie theater watching *The Deer Hunter*. Or you're weighing vegetables at the supermarket and you're fine, you're just fine, only it's never really you. Not any of them.

So what do you think of my war? At the worst I imagine you're a little angry. "My God," I can imagine you saying. "You managed a clean escape. You had your friends, you had your games. You were quite happy." Well, I promised you the truth. And the truth is that some of us went to jail. (Damn few. I know.) Some of us were killed. (And the numbers are irrelevant.) Some of us went to Canada and to Sweden. And some of us had a great time. But it wasn't a clean escape, really, for any of us.

Look at me. I'm operating all alone here with no affinity group and it seems unnatural to me. It seems to me that I should be surrounded by people I'd trust with my life. Always. It makes me cling to people, even people I don't care for all that much. It makes me panic when people leave. I'm sure they're not coming back. The war did this to me. Or you did. Same thing. What did the war do to you?

Look how much we have in common, after all. We both lost. I lost my war. You lost your war. I look today at Vietnam and Cambodia and Laos and I feel sick inside. Do you ever ask yourself who won? Who the hell won?

Your war. I made it up, of course. It was nothing, *nothing* like that. Write me. Tell me about it. Please. If I have not heard from you by Christmas, I have decided to ask Lauren to go to the monument and look for your name. *I don't want to do this*. Don't make me do this. Just send me some word.

I am thirty-five years old. I am ready to believe anything you say.

Robert Frazier

Robert Frazier is well known in science fiction circles as a poet. After attending the Iowa Writers' Workshop in Iowa City, he began publishing his poetry, and his work can be found in *Galaxy, Amazing, Isaac Asimov's Science Fiction Magazine, Analog, The Magazine of Fantasy & Science Fiction, Light Years and Dark, A Spadeful of Space Time, Science 86, Portland Review,* and *Pacific Quarterly*. His first collection, *Peregrine*, was published in 1978. Forthcoming are two collections of poetry, *Perception Barriers* and *Co-Orbital Moons*. Winner of the Rhysling Award in 1980 for his poem "Encased in the Amber of Eternity," Frazier was the longtime editor of *Star * Line* and the *Speculative Poetry Review* and is the editor of the collection *Burning With a Vision: Poetry of Science and the Fantastic*. He lives in Nantucket, Massachusetts.

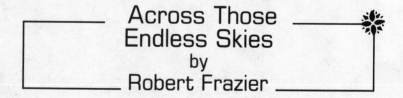

Across Those Endless Skies

by

Robert Frazier

Cowboy was all hopped up and "fried to the gills on them little white pills," as he often put it, the first time he saw the big choppers.

Near Da Lat his patrol had stopped on a ridgeback haloed with defoliated trees that looked for all the world like a twisted mass of cables and brake lines, so Cowboy propped his gaunt wiry body against a hunk of standing deadwood, pulled his helmet down over his bat ears and peach-fuzz black hair, and buzzed off into space. As he traced a yellowed fingernail along the trigger on his M-16, and along the fine pinstripes he'd applied to the stock with painstaking care, the choppers plowed over the next hill and hovered above the shimmering rice paddies and the nameless villes between. There were four in a diamond formation, sausage-shaped Chinook-47s with bloodred running lights. A dark, mica-flecked haze of purple exhaust surrounded them like a ragged cloak. And the low moan that accompanied them, like that of some unearthly herd rumbling across a celestial highway, sent a lightning bolt of fear spiking down his spine.

Cowboy shook his head "to clear out the cobs." When he looked back they were gone. He popped a couple more dexies from a useless gunmetal lighter he kept stashed in the recesses of his baggy fatigues and went back to fingering his M-16.

You see, pills were a way of life for him; they made the extraordinary seem ordinary. He'd started with painkillers back in Fitchburg when Pa beat him at night, and twice on Sundays. Then he'd used speedballs a few times for racing his '69 Chevy—all that sweet chrome down to the heads and the Hurst on the floor—in the streets from Leominster to Concord to Boston. In 'Nam they became a necessity. They began to shape a dreamland for him there, a haven apart from which he'd steer clear one day, tack some Purple Heart or somesuch thing to the mantle next to the old man's bowling trophies, and blow his past off in a cloud of monoxide. He'd sure be happy to dust off his mechanic's tools. Maybe he'd even follow up that lead on an assembly-line job in Detroit. Settle and start a family.

So what was one hallucination or another to him? What was required was an icy cool and a purpose in life. Survival.

He saw the choppers again during a recon with Chin into a village near the company outpost. They'd been losing men to snipers and trip traps, and the captain figured there was a VC tunnel—maybe a complex—somewhere in the area. Chin was a local: a grinning madman, a storyteller who favored folk ditties about dragons eating children, and the best intelligence source the battalion could find.

Chin singled out a small crude hamlet with a half-dozen hooches about fifteen kilometers south of the outpost; it was smack in the middle of the trouble area. Stalking through the farm town like Gary Cooper at high noon, Chin made one villager, a barefoot teenager actually, nervous enough to warrant interrogation. Most of the patrol milled about with the captain at one end of the village while Chin and Cowboy worked. Chin's signature and specialty was the cheap cigar he kept burning at one corner of his mouth. The questioning got rough for Cowboy, for no matter how hardened he had become, no matter how thick a wall the drugs placed between him and his actions, the duty of holding a twitching, screaming boy brought back memories. Bad memories.

Sensing this, perhaps, Chin broke out a pipe after it was over, and he passed it to Cowboy with a moist brown lump of what Cowboy called ''temple ball'' hash. The smoke rolled through Cowboy's head, blocking out the hot day and the sting of the biting insects. It calmed Cowboy's shakes.

''So, did ya get anything?'' he asked.

Chin smiled and nodded, the smoke trickling from his small nostrils and curling around his floppy green jungle hat. ''There is tunnel, yes,'' he said in slow, imprecise English.

''Where?''

''Cowboy''—Chin laughed—''you are standing right over it.''

Cowboy stiffened. Nobody taunted him or pushed him about anymore. He towered over the Vietnamese agent for a moment.

''Don't worry, Cowboy. There is only a few gooks. They stay quiet until we flush them.''

Chin passed the pipe and more smoke rolled through him. He was ''stoked fine,'' he told Chin. That is, he was until he had to shade his eyes from a sudden brilliance from above.

The choppers hung over them like a string of hypnotist's jewels swaying in undulous motions, and the glare that blinded him issued from large red searchlights mounted under their black noses. At their tails the fins were shiny as chrome. Between noses and tails, flame decals licked along their bellies like iridescent blue and yellow leeches. The searchlights blinked, great reptilian eyes peering into his soul. He thought he heard muffled voices.

Cowboy freaked and hit the dirt gut first, head down. Chin did not. You see, Chin didn't see anything. Just the crazed look in a soldier's face, which he didn't care to see ever again. After Chin reported the VC hideout and they cleaned it out for the tunnel rats with a few thermite grenades, Chin personally drove Cowboy back to his outpost.

For a while, Cowboy cut out the drugs. He seemed genuinely shaken by the return of the choppers. Also, word had leaked around about his "bad trip in the field," later just a bad "field trip." He felt the eyes watching him. So he listened to old rock and roll on the reel-to-reel wired by his bunk. Ritchie Valens. Eddie Cochran. Link Wray and the Wray Men. But after the Tet offensive pushed down on them from the North, and Chin and several of his company buddies were KIA, Cowboy began all over again. This time with heavy painkillers. In a particularly grueling mop-up of an enemy ville, he caught some explosive flak in his shoulder and doubled up on his barbiturates.

Working closely with forward observers and an Air Force controller circling overhead, Cowboy's company advanced through the houses and fields behind a wall of howitzer fire and the suppressive fire of their own 81-mm mortars. The company was laden with thermite grenades as well as flamethrowers, so the timing was critical. One round short of the mark, or one man too close to the phase line of exploding rounds, and a chain explosion might level the ranks that were as closely packed as race cars at a starting line. Nursing his shoulder, Cowboy hung back a few steps. "Cooled his everlovin' jets," as he'd called it at the strip back home in Massachusetts.

A cry of "short round" came from someone ahead as the ground shook and a spidery column of thin smoke drifted onto the advancing men. Cowboy tried to yell, to warn them that it was an enemy round—characteristically weak, you see—and meant to panic them. It wasn't their own support fire falling short after all. But they panicked anyway. Someone must have run right into the phase line, because later

Cowboy was flat in the mud, bleeding like a stuck pig, caught in a shower of raining debris.

Almost immediately, he could hear the gunships descend to rake the village ahead with rockets and allow medical ships to evacuate the wounded. He felt the hot breath of their rotors whipping the smoke into a froth about him. But they weren't gunships, at least not ones from Air Cav. Their black noses peeked out of the brown haze above him. Searchlights blinked wildly. He could make out the pilots' faces streaked like stock-car drivers' with dirt and sweat. Men with the hollow eyes and the blurred expressions of the shell-shocked. Or the KIA.

God, he didn't want to think about that.

One pilot looked very much like Chin. He had a dragon-jowled grin and smoke curling from his flared nose. He called down to him. It was his father's voice, filled with Catholic wrath.

"Cowboy. Change your ways."

Cowboy gulped down all the barbs in his cigarette lighter, squeezed his eyes shut, and waited for them to fade away as they had before. But, you see, they did not. Chin's angry cry turned into an engine screaming through the wind tunnel inside his head. He looked up again and pissed himself when he saw their red searchlights crossing to form a pentagram. Their exhaust grilles gleaming like the needle-toothed mouths that snapped up babies in Vietnamese folktales. Slowly, ever so orderly and without mishap, the choppers—edged in foxfire—landed at the five points around him with stretcher-bearing zombies waiting in the open bays. Waiting to take him under their wings of smoke and away across those endless skies.

Waiting to take him into a war zone where fighting continued without a break or a leave or a discharge; and where death and rebirth were in constant flux, a dark high that he could ride, as he once said in a wishful yet absurd complaint about the quality of Vietnamese dope, "without ever having to turn off the ignition."

Charles L. Grant

Charles L. Grant began his career as a science fiction writer, winning two Nebula awards, for his stories "A Crowd of Shadows" and "A Glow of Candles," but then turned to the horror genre, where he has exerted considerable influence, both as a writer and an anthologist. He created and edits the popular *Greystone Bay* series of chronicle novels, and his continuing anthology *Shadows* is easily one of the most important forums for the best work being produced in the genre. Grant won a World Fantasy Award as editor of the original *Shadows* collection and also won two more for his novella "Confess the Seasons" and his short story collection *Nightmare Seasons*. Stephen King has called him "one of the premier fantasists of our time." His stories have appeared in *The Magazine of Fantasy & Science Fiction, Analog, Amazing, Fantastic, Orbit, Dark Forces, The Arbor House Treasury of Horror and the Supernatural,* and many other magazines and anthologies. Some of these stories are collected in *Nightmare Seasons* and *Tales From the Nightside*. His novels include the *Oxrun* series, *Tea Party, Nightsongs, The Pet,* and the best-selling *The Nestling*. He has also edited the anthologies *Terrors, Nightmares*, and *Fears*, among others. Grant lives in New Jersey with his wife, the writer Kathryn Ptacek.

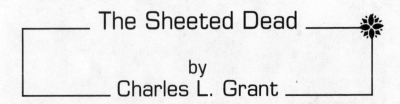

The Sheeted Dead

by
Charles L. Grant

The overcast lay in grey strips over the valley—pale where the sun nearly broke through the clouds, darker where the rain clung in ragged stubborn patches, and bulges so dark they could have been black, hanging low and rolling, spun and flayed by a wind that carried with it a charge of lightning. It permitted no shadows, only a darkening of color; it made the green hills taller because it drifted so low; and each morning it murdered hope that the chill would be gone, the chill that had no business in the valley, in June.

And on the sixth day of the overcast Gregory walked the road toward town, down the broken white line without checking behind him, because there was no fear of traffic, no need to watch for trucks, no caution necessary—he wasn't going to die.

He kicked a large chunk of gravel over to the shoulder, followed it with his gaze and looked into a field beyond a barbed-wire fence rusted and sagging. No cows grazed. No horses walked. No plow; no tractor. A lone crow lifted from the newly green, weedy furrows and circled a few times before settling again. Not a cry, not a warning, not a snap of a wing. Black feathers and black eyes, feeding on the dead.

On the other side it was the same, the quiet intensified by the sight of a small farmhouse surrounded by small trees. Nothing moved there either, inside or out.

Silence.

Nothing moved *on the hillside where he knew they were waiting, weapons aimed, sights trained, and when he turned to look for help he was alone on the road, in the heat, in the open, no one left to watch him but the watchers on the hill.*

He cleared his throat and pulled his hands from his pockets, let his arms swing until he found himself marching. A lop-sided smile broke the rhythm, slowed it, and he kicked another stone, spinning around as he did to walk backward to be sure he was really alone.

Where is everybody?

Not that it mattered, but where the hell are they?

The smile snapped off as he snapped a salute to the crow and the farmhouse and broke into a trot that brought him to another house ten minutes later. Freshly painted, empty, a fern in a hanging pot twisting in the wind.

And silence.

He listened, and he ran. Easily, though he felt a sharp pain in his side and heard as if muffled in a pair of cupped hands the slap of his soles, the touch of his heels, the rasp and wheeze of his breath when his lungs finally protested, and finally he slowed, and slowed further, to walk with a trembling hand pressed hard to his waist and stare at the wooden bones of a scarecrow with nothing left to guard.

A breeze rippled its tattered sleeves, shivered the brim of its floppy hat, and Greg saw a corncob still pinned to the cloth, a rifle at the ready, and he closed his eyes against the sound when the wind shook the cob free and the cob fell to the ground and there was nothing the thing could do but stand there, limp and dark.

Another half mile and the houses began to cluster, most of them white, all of them old, the fields yielding to front yards and backyards and high trees that lined winter-split side-walks, the road finally interrupted by intersections and amber lights, curbs rising from the tarmac and cars parked at the curbs, storefronts and dead neon and wire-cage litter bins empty even of dust.

Display windows that reflected his passing against shelves of shoes and mannequins in swimsuits and posters for new albums and menus the sun had faded . . . when the sun used to shine and the grill was still hot and the salt was kept from hardening by grains of rice in the shaker.

A sigh. Wind-sigh. Heart-sigh.

He paused for a long moment in front of the red-brick post office, wondering when it was he'd last had a letter, or a piece of junk mail, or a bill, or a card, or a letter to tell him where the hell they all were. His fingers snapped nervously, barely making a sound. Never, he decided; he'd never had any of it because he wasn't the same now as he had been before.

Then, back then, years ago then when the overcast was still coming, when rain meant green and winter meant white, he'd been a teacher of students who only wanted to go to college in order to beat the draft, who wanted their diplomas so they could get a decent job, who wanted to get the hell out of school so they could start living.

Then, back then, he had faculty friends, and faculty acquaintances, and waited for the right woman to come along and share his bed; he went bowling alone and driving alone and went to the lounges to dream of the women in their silver cages, in phosphorescent bathing suits, dancing alone, to music no one heard because they were watching the women, in silver cages, dancing alone.

Then. And now.

Now there was no mail because now he was alone.

He moved on toward the other side of town, past the last intersection before the fields began again, and turned through a gap in a low picket fence, the gate long since fallen off and nearly submerged in the grass. The flagstone walk had been repaired that spring, the flanking cherry trees trimmed, the trim around the porch scraped and repainted. It had taken him months, and while none of it was perfect, it was suitable, and pleasing, and when he sat wearily on the top step he could admit a bit of pride in doing something like this, something he'd never done before, something he may never do again.

He closed his eyes and tried to pick out the smells of the town he had left over a decade ago. But there were none. He couldn't smell the grass, or the roses on the trellis, or the new leaves on the sapling he was nurturing by the steps; there was no scent of rain, or of animals in the adjoining yard, or cooking in someone's oven, or even gasoline from passing cars; no odors, no aromas, no perfumes on the air.

He was frightened.

And didn't move *until he heard someone crying, heard someone screaming, heard someone telling the rest of them to shut up and get to their feet and get to their weapons and sonofabitch if he couldn't remember what the hell had happened.*

And the ghost of the sun set behind the hills, and the crow circled the house, and he went into the front room and turned on the lamps. And the light in the dining room, the light in the kitchen, over the landing on the stairs, in his bedroom, the bathroom, the unshaded bulb in the attic. He turned on the radio sitting black on the nightstand, the television by his chair, the radio by the refrigerator that gave him nothing but static. He pulled the shades, and drew the curtains, and locked all of the doors.

He made a supper of cold sandwiches and lay down on his bed and stared at the ceiling and wished for blue skies until he finally fell asleep and dreamed about a rifle that was aimed at his head.

On the eighth day of the overcast, somewhat darker, somewhat colder, he moved a pile of old bricks from alongside the garage to alongside the house, near the slanted cellar doors he hadn't used since he returned. It took him over an hour. A handful at a time. Then an hour more while he arranged them in stacks so they didn't look so much like a crypt waiting to be built.

When he was finished, he dusted his hands on his jeans and went inside, had a glass of water at the kitchen sink, splashed water on his face, and stood there while the water dripped on the counter from his chin.

A sigh. Heart-sigh. Dead-sigh.

He changed his clothes, made himself a quick lunch of sandwiches and milk, and went to the porch, where he looked at the blacktop, and the sidewalks, and the fading red house that faced his, across the street.

Julie Miller.

Dark hair and dark eyes and, though he didn't know it at the time, Jewish enough to resist his flirtations because he was worse than gentile—he was atheist and proud of it. It hadn't made sense then, and it didn't make sense now, and he blew the red house a kiss before heading into town.

Where he checked the post office for mail, and the luncheonette for a new menu, and stood in front of the movie theater and willed a title to appear on the dead lights of the dead and blind marquee.

He couldn't read it.

It didn't matter.

He didn't go to the movies anymore, hadn't gone for years. No loss, he thought; he didn't know they were gone, and they hadn't noticed he'd come back.

Dust devils in the gutters. A yellowed newspaper on a bench by the bus stop near the church. A faded candy wrapper stuck in the cyclone fence that surrounded the schoolyard. A broken window in the town hall. A broken bottle in the weeds. Dust devils in the gutters, slowly turning red.

And dancing alone.

He thought of a tune and whistled, and stopped after the fifth note; he pulled his hands out of his pockets and found himself marching, and stopped after the fifth step; he looked down at his wrinkled white shirt and wondered why he hadn't put on a tie this morning.

He shivered, and headed back home.

He paused in front of Julie Miller's house and wondered if he dared go in, walk up the steps and into her room, to see what she'd been like when she wouldn't let him kiss her. He changed his mind when he saw the dust devil on the porch. It didn't matter. She was gone. Like the women in their glittering gold cages, she was gone with the music no one remembered anymore.

That night he turned on all the lights, and all the radios, and the television, and he went to bed with his clothes on and stared at the ceiling.

His left hand gripped the edge of the mattress so he wouldn't fall off; his right lay across his middle, covering the scar that burrowed wormlike to his stomach.

He dreamed of a rifle that was held to his head, and of a band that marched through every street in his hometown.

On the tenth day of the overcast he finished bricking up the cellar door, the kitchen door, and the kitchen windows.

Darker in the house then, and he wandered about in the twilight, touching the walls, the backs of the chairs, opened the door and stood in the twilight, clinging to the porch post, staring over at the Millers' yard, then rubbing his eyes with the back of one hand and returning inside, where he nodded at the new darkness settled in the kitchen. It was cool, not at all stifling, and he figured he ought to be able to finish the rest of the first floor in two days, no more.

And when he slept, he slept badly.

The marching band passed his house—cornets and trumpets and trombones and drums and sousaphones and glockenspiels and a majorette in a white skirt that barely reached her knees and a whistle that shrilled the change in music and a car driving behind with the top down and the driver grinning and the corpse in the backseat waving an American flag.

He woke covered in perspiration, grimaced at his sour smell, and took a long cold shower. He paid no attention to the scar on his stomach. He was used to it. It had been there for a decade, and a few years more, and once in a while a woman saw it, and asked him how he got it, and he would tell her he'd been in a knife fight when he was a child.

Cold porcelain, cold water *pounding the hell out of his shoulders, echoing through his helmet, spraying from the wheels of the jeep in a continuous outward wave, making the steering wheel slippery because the top wasn't up, making visibility impossible because the sun hadn't shone in over a week; cold water, cold food, cold noise of a convoy slipping between the hills that should have been green because of the season and were grey in the fog that the rain carried with it; trucks and jeeps and troopers and ammunition and food and clothing and the flash of orange on the hill and on the road ahead and just behind his eyes*

when the light bulb finally blew and the bathroom went to twilight, and he grabbed the edge of the sink, jaw tight, lips back, knees locked, stomach rolling.

He went downstairs and had breakfast, and halfway through a barely scrambled egg he heard the horn. A car horn. And the chair toppled to the floor when he jumped to his feet, stared toward the front, stared at the bricked-up door and windows.

Jesus Christ, he thought, and ran out to the porch.

Mr. Miller was raking up the leaves in his yard, a pile in the gutter smoldering and smoking. When he saw Greg he waved, and Greg waved back, slipped his hands into his pockets, and went out to the sidewalk.

"How's it going?" he called.

"I could be younger," the old man said with a laugh.

"Julie around?"

The old man—white shirt, suspenders, baggy brown trousers, battered sneakers on his feet—shrugged elaborately. "Who's to know, huh? She's a big girl, she tells me." He shrugged again, a little faster, then grinned and waved the rake. "Save me, Greg! Save me, for god's sake! Marry her—please!—and get her the hell out of my house."

They laughed, and he decided it would be a good time to pick up some milk, some bread, a few more cans, before he finished working on the house.

He walked, then, and winced at the traffic that filled the downtown streets. There were so many people, he thought; god, where the hell'd they all come from?

After struggling with two housewives he didn't know for possession of the last cans of soup on the corner market shelf, he found a few more things he thought he'd need, paid for them, hefted the bag, and crossed over to the post office.

His box was empty.

As he walked down to check on what was playing at the theater tonight, he was nearly knocked over by two kids on skateboards, one of them plugged against the world by earphones and a hip radio, the other laughing an apology that sounded more like a sneer. Greg held his breath, the sure cure for his temper, then moved on, shaking his head and wondering what the little bastards would be like when they grew up.

Chuck Pringle was on the ladder switching the titles on the marquee when Greg walked up.

"Hey, Chuck, when you gonna show *Gone With the Wind*?"

Pringle, his stomach resting against the grid to keep him from falling, didn't laugh. He looked down, and scowled. "You college guys are all alike, you know it? You think a little class will make me a fortune." He dipped into the tray of letters, pulled one out, and shook it at him. "You gotta have tits, Goodman, don't you know that by now? Tits for the guys, a little cock for the broads. I show anything else I go broke, right?"

Greg nodded, and listened for five more minutes, learning as he did every time he asked the question about the hardships of running a theater that didn't belong to a national chain, of the state of the film industry from the managerial point of view, and the state of the country's teenagers.

"On the other hand," Pringle said, "your *Gone With the Wind* didn't have any tits, y'know? And a man my age, man, he can't get enough of that."

"Right," Greg said, turned around and walked away.

There were no newspapers at the luncheonette or the drugstore, so he brought his groceries home, put them away, and went out to the garage to get more bricks for the windows. When he was finished, there was only the front door left, and he had to save that until the upstairs was done.

He showered.

He ate dinner.

He sat on the front porch drinking a beer and watching the sun set, and didn't move at all when he saw the lion in Miller's yard.

He blinked, put the beer can down on the top step, and looked again. Over there. In Julie Miller's yard. Frowning, because if it was there, he still ought to be able to see it. It had been big enough—teeth, mane, tufted tail, muscles working in a lean frame that would worry an elephant to death if the lion were hungry enough.

But it was gone now, or it had never been, and he couldn't explain to himself why he just didn't get his butt in gear and walk over there. It wasn't that he was afraid he might find prints in the dry grass, that he might smell something, or hear something.

He was afraid. Of not knowing, and of knowing too much.

He stood, slowly, and walked slowly into the house, into the new twilight where the windows reflected nothing but the ghost of his passing.

The telephone rang just before he went to bed. When he answered it, positive it was only an electrical storm in the area that had found him and was taunting him, he heard someone breathing and asked who it was.

"Me," said Julie. "I was wondering if you wanted to go to the movies tonight?"

His arms ached from lifting and holding the bricks; there was mortar under his fingernails, and dust in his hair despite the shower he'd taken.

"I'm beat," he said, smiling at the wall. "I won't be much company."

"If I wanted company," she said, "I would've asked one of Father's friends. You going or not?"

"Give me ten minutes to clean up."

"Five," she said. "It's almost time."

"Aw, Jesus, Julie, give me a break."

"Men," she said, laughing, and rang off.

He couldn't remember ever moving so damned fast in his life, it was almost as if he were *flying across the road and into the ditch, listening to the mortars, to the trucks blowing up, to the guns, to the shouting, to the whistles, to the wind, to the rain that blinded him because his goggles had been knocked off when the shell knocked him from the jeep. Then he felt dizzy, too dizzy just from running so hard, and he looked down*

and realized he still had his stupid slippers on. He slapped himself across the cheek, changed into his shoes and ran outside, just in time to see a meteor shower turn the sky green. He stood on the walk, openmouthed, moaning his pleasure now and then, grunting when one seemed to be heading straight for him. He almost ducked, explained to himself how ridiculous that was going to look, and hurried to the curb when the light show was over.

The windows in the Miller house were dark.

None of the streetlights worked.

A single streak of green flew over the house, over the hill behind, and left the stars to themselves, pallid and unwinking.

"Damn," he said, picking up a pebble and throwing it across the street. "Damn. You should've just gone, you stupid jackass."

And saw the lion again.

Maybe, he thought, Julie's got herself a new pet, and laughed aloud at the preposterous notion that her father would let anything larger than his old Skye terrier through the front door.

The lion turned the corner of the house and vanished in the high weeds that grew and tangled with the hedge.

Dust devils in the street, borne on the night wind.

"Where are you?" he asked softly. "Where did you go?"

* * *

On the fourteenth day of the overcast, he decided to go to the school, just to see how things were going. He looked in at his old classroom, walked through the principal's office, sat in the auditorium for nearly an hour, and listened to the seniors practicing their graduation speeches. In the gym he watched a ragged, good-natured game of basketball between the male and female faculty, in the cafeteria he swiped an ice cream bar from the freezer beside the cash register, and in the teachers' lounge he saw a man he knew vaguely, from the Math Department maybe, who grabbed his hand and grinned.

"Jesus H., it's Greg Goodman. Christ, man, where the hell have you been?"

"Away," he said, and left through the shattered side door, walked slowly across the football field, and stood on the top row in the wooden visitors' bleachers.

"Where are you?" he asked, as if speaking to an old friend. "Please. Where are you?"

And didn't wait for the answer. He ran down the seats, ran across the field, didn't stop until he'd reached the main street and saw the parade.

The band—horns and drums.

The marchers—young and smiling.

A cage on a flatbed pulled by a silent tractor—the lion standing, unmoving, its mane falling in clouds.

The car with the honored guest—rusted and wheezing.

He ran out in front of them and held up his hands, and took a deep breath when they marched right through him, turned the corner, and vanished, like shadows in sunlight, like pebbles thrown in a pond.

When the car came abreast, he didn't recognize the guest. He only knew it wasn't him.

And it hadn't been, back then, when the menus were changed daily in the luncheonette window and the newspapers were placed on the bench by the drugstore and the theater was open at six-thirty every Friday and that sonofabitch in the Math Department hadn't remembered his name, and hadn't known where he'd been.

He watched the car drive out of town, watched the crow circle over it, before he walked back home and picked up the first brick to be placed in the front door.

Behind him he could hear Julie Miller singing.

To either side he could hear the other guys shouting, calling, asking where the medics were, jesus god wasn't anybody there?

And in front of him the light burned in the kitchen, and static snapped from the radio, and shadows walked through the halls. Shadows in white, in featureless winding sheets that whispered over the floors, that whispered against the walls, that whispered "Here we are" as he bent down for the mortar.

Richard Paul Russo

Richard Paul Russo has a B.A. in psychology, has done graduate work in creative writing, and is a graduate of the 1983 Clarion Writers' Workshop. Although he has published little science fiction up to now, his non-science fiction stories have appeared in literary magazines. He has won three literary awards for his mainstream work: two for short stories and one for a play. He has recently turned to writing science fiction almost exclusively and has just sold his first novel to Tor Books on the strength of the fine story that follows.

In the Season of the Rains

by

Richard Paul Russo

I still search the night skies when it rains, hoping to see. . . .

It's been a lot of years since my tour ended. Most of them have been all right. But there are times when I think about Scolini, and wonder where he is. And there are times when I wish I'd gone with him.

* * *

First there was the heat, wet and heavy and solid around us. Then there was the stifling, lush growth of the jungle, choking the air with its humid breath. And finally, there was the rain. Monsoon season had just begun. The rains came, and did not seem to leave. Even though they stopped during the day, the air was so humid, and we sweated so heavily, we hardly noticed the difference.

Scolini was reading a novel then, *Lord of Light,* by Roger Zelazny. " 'It was in the season of the rains . . . It was well into the time of the great wetness . . .' " That's how the book started, and that's how it was in the jungle. Scolini used to quote those lines over and over at us as we humped through the paddies and over the dikes and into the dense trees and brush and tall grass, weapons turning hot and slick in our hands, the heat leaching water and energy and life from us.

"Fuck you, Scolini," Spider called. "No more."

" 'It was well into the time of the great *wetness'!*" Scolini yelled back.

"I'm gonna pound your face into the fucking great wetness you don't shut the fuck up." That was the Wizard, grumbling at Scolini's back.

I said nothing. I didn't care, and neither did anyone else, really. It had been a bad week, and we'd been out in the bush too long. Bitching was a way to stay awake, stay alert, and stay alive.

" 'It was in the days of the rains that their prayers went up,' " Scolini intoned. He paused, gazed up through the dense foliage as though searching for something. "Except there's nothing to pray to." He spat violently, and lapsed into silence.

It didn't rain all afternoon, but we never dried out, and the sun boiled up a constant, steamy heat from the jungle. We found the mines and the booby traps on the trails, though, and no one was killed or injured that day—just miserable. Near dusk we came across a silent, deserted village, half a dozen empty, rotting hooches, a ville that wasn't even on the maps. No signs of locals, no signs of VC. Relief and disappointment collided. We were sick of being shot at, picked off by mines, with no way to strike back.

We dug in for the night. Scolini and I carved our foxhole

deep in the grass and mud and clay, then ate C rations as the rain started in again with the falling darkness. The wind kicked up, whipped the rain in under our ponchos.

"I want out of this hellhole," Scolini said.

I didn't answer. What was I supposed to say? Most of us wanted out. But there was a desperate intensity to his voice, and a strange distance, as if he was already partially gone. Still, I thought, he was new, just two months in-country, and I'd probably been the same myself, once.

He went on guard, leaving me alone in the darkness. I sat in the wet foxhole, unable to sleep. Waking dreams came and went, mingling with the reality around me until I couldn't distinguish between the two. It didn't matter. I was used to it now, and it no longer bothered me much.

What still bothered me, though, was that I could not remember what Megan looked like. We were the same age when I left, talking about marriage, but now I felt I must be at least ten, fifteen years older than she, and I could not call up the image of her face. I thought she had light brown hair, but was it long or short, straight or curly or wavy? Hazel eyes, probably, but that's what my own were, and maybe I was confusing hers with mine. Her mouth, her nose and chin, all the rest was a blank.

I was still trying to call up a picture of her face, and still failing, when Scolini slid down into the foxhole, scattering mud everywhere.

"Fuckin' *a*, Sahara, you're not gonna believe what I saw out there!" His voice was a hissed whisper, broken by heavy panting.

"Try me."

"I don't know, man, a flying saucer, a spaceship, something like that."

"You've been reading too much of that science fiction."

"No, no, I *saw* it, man, a fucking spaceship. Just above the trees, kind of silent and shimmering, a weird shape, a blue-green glowing, and pulsing into black, like it was shifting in and out of existence."

"You drop that acid you've been saving?"

"No, goddammit! I'm telling you, Sahara, it's for real." He grabbed his helmet with both hands and slammed it into the mud. "Shit, I saw the fuckin' thing, I *saw* it."

"Basketball ship," I tried. "Maybe something doing recon, I don't know."

Scolini didn't answer. He picked up his helmet, dumped out the mud and water, then held it out to let the rain wash it clean. Distant mortar fire was barely audible, muffled by the rain. Scolini stood and put on his helmet. He was the only one who wore the damn thing.

"Gotta get back out," he finally said. "I'm still supposed to be on watch."

"Hey, Scolini . . ." I started. But he was already climbing out of the foxhole, and a moment later he was gone.

We were supposed to check out a ville the next afternoon, but we had to get through the morning first. The rain stopped just after sunrise, and damp, sweltering heat rode in on us again. The clay trail was slick and littered with mines, which we located and exploded, one after another. All morning we were harassed by sniper fire. No one was hit, but nerves were shot.

Just after midday, during a lull, we stopped to eat, and Scolini pulled out *Lord of Light* again. It was his second or third time through, and the book was falling apart in the dampness. He read silently for a few minutes, then quoted to us again: " 'A light rain was falling upon the building, the lotus and the jungle at the foot of the mountains. For six days he had offered many kilowatts of prayer, but the static kept him from being heard On High.' "

"Ain't that the fucking truth," said Fishbone. Scolini nodded, then resumed reading to himself.

"Hey, Rocket Man," Wizard said.

Scolini looked up. "Who, me?"

Wizard grinned. "Yeah, you with the outer-space books. You want to keep reading that stuff out loud, that's just fine. Maybe the dinks'll shoot at you instead of me."

We all laughed, and Scolini smiled. He put the book away, and we started back onto the trail.

The afternoon was worse than the morning. The heat baked us, and sniper fire was continuous. Fishbone missed a trip wire, triggered a booby-trapped grenade. Somehow he saw it, or heard it roll out into the trail, yelled, and everyone dove for cover. Fishbone got a footful of metal, but it wasn't going to kill him, and he grinned and laughed waiting for the dustoff, knowing he was going home.

"Hey, Scolini," I said. "There's your way out." I pointed at Fishbone's foot.

"I've thought about it," he said, serious. "Too goddamn risky. End up like Bristol." He shook his head and gazed into the sky, far away again.

As we neared the ville, the jungle went silent on us. Spider was on point, and slowed us to a crawl. We waited for the ambush, and were surprised when it didn't come. Hot and tense, we crept forward.

The ville was quiet in the heat. Pigs snuffled through the mud, and a dog whined. Old women chewed betel nut, squatting in the shade of the hooches, and grinned at us with dark, red-stained teeth. A baby cried, and we marched in.

The village search was rapid and thorough. We cleared out the hooches, herded all the old men, the women and children into a clearing. Interrogations were brief, repetitive, and fruitless.

We found tunnels. The lieutenant was talking with two sergeants, trying to decide whether to search or blow. Someone else made the decision for them.

"Fire in the hole!" a voice cried out. A few seconds later, two muffled explosions shook the air, then two more. "Fire in the hole!" again, and two more paired explosions.

When the lieutenant walked over to the tunnel mouths to see who'd dropped the grenades, there was no one around. He stood in silence, staring at the ground.

Three men dragged a young woman into an empty hooch, and I walked away so I wouldn't hear it, so I wouldn't see them when they came out.

We continued to search the hooches, tearing baskets apart, smashing pottery, knocking over rice-filled urns and spilling the rice out through the doorways. A dog yelped when somebody kicked it, and someone else knifed a squealing pig. Chickens squawked, and I thought I could hear the cries of a woman.

Crazy Carl was with the villagers; he started slapping the old men with his open palm, and screamed into their faces. Wizard marched a pig past them, then blew it away with his shotgun. Two old women started to laugh, thinking it was supposed to be funny, but when they saw the look on Wizard's face, they stopped. The lieutenant huddled in conference with the two sergeants, standing in the shade, letting things go, trying not to notice, which was fine with everyone.

I spotted Scolini in the brush, squatting with his back against a tree. He'd covered his ears with his hands, and his eyes were closed. I walked over to him, knelt at his side. Behind me, the noise continued unabated—the splintering of wood, the smashing of crockery, the smacking of Crazy Carl's hands, the grunting and squealing and whining and crying of people and animals, one indistinguishable from the other.

I tapped Scolini on the shoulder, and he jerked back, grabbing for his rifle, eyes snapping open. When he saw it was me, he settled back with a long, drawn-out shudder.

"I've had it," he said.

We shared a cigarette and listened to the operation winding down. As the noise level dropped, the heat seemed to grow, the air became thick, stagnant and hard to breathe. Before long, we were ready to move out. Incredibly, the Zippo lighters did not appear, and the thatched roofs did not go up in flames.

But as we marched out of the ville, someone took out two of the hooches with a white phosphorous grenade. I stood at the edge of the jungle, Scolini at my side, the sudden heat sucking our breath away, and we watched the hooches burn to the ground in beautiful, delicate flames and clouds of white smoke.

We marched on for another hour, up and down the lower mountain slopes, and finally dug in for the night. An atmosphere of peace hung in the air, and no one seemed to mind the rain that started falling at dusk. I gave in to a watering mouth and aching cheeks, and opened my last can of peaches. I offered some to Scolini, but he silently refused. He fixed himself a cup of coffee instead, smoked a final cigarette for the day.

We huddled together in the rain, keeping each other warm, not talking. Just after dark I went out on guard, but when I came back, Scolini was gone. The foxhole was cold, and I sat under the poncho, wet and shivering, wondering where the hell he'd gone, and wondering if he'd ever come back. The rain continued, the night went on, and I could not sleep.

When Scolini dropped into the foxhole long after midnight, I knew there would be another story. He was breathing heavily, and even in the darkness I could see a flush to his skin.

"Christ," he said after a few minutes, then nothing more.

"Don't tell me you saw flying saucers again."

"No. I mean yes, but more than that. Sahara, I saw them, Jesus Christ, they were . . . they were *aliens*. It *is* a spaceship, they're from another goddamn world."

"Scolini, it's probably a trick, a helicopter disguised as a—"

He shook his head vigorously, cutting me off. "They weren't human, Sahara, they weren't human. No fucking way it was a disguise, man, they were . . ." He shuddered, and shook his head. "It was weird, Sahara. I'm telling you, it was too fuckin' weird."

"So tell me, Scolini."

We crouched under our ponchos, the rain still falling, and he started. "I'm sitting here, watching and listening, I get these funny feelings. Like some kind of strange vibrations going through me. I know it sounds crazy, but they were there, shaking inside me, telling me things."

"Like what?"

"Like I had to go back to the ville, the one we hit."

"You didn't."

"I did. I crawled out of this damn hole and started back along the trail. I don't know, somehow I knew it'd be clear, nothing new planted—I could just head on down it and I'd be okay. And I was. Made my way mostly by feel. The vibes were still inside me, and I felt like I was in tune with the jungle, with whatever was out there."

He paused, and blew into his hands a few times. I wanted to tell him he was losing his goddamn mind, but I couldn't. I said nothing, and he went on.

"The village was silent, not even the animals made a sound. Spooky, Sahara, real spooky. So I didn't go in. I stayed in the trees, and I circled the ville, watching for movement, listening hard. Nothing except the rain. No fires. Everyone asleep or dead. Then I saw them.

"Four of them came out from between the huts, glowing like the ship I saw last night. They were taller than anyone I've ever seen—seven, seven and a half feet—and thin, like they had no meat on their bones. Two legs, and I guess two arms, long rubbery things with something like hands attached. They were pale, with dark spots and patches of hair all over their bodies, and long heads with huge dark eyes, but I couldn't tell if there was any mouth or nose or ears, only more of the splotches and chunks of hair. There was the blue-green glow around them, just like the ship, and it pulsed, sometimes going into black so that for a second they would disappear, then shift back. The rain didn't seem to touch them.

"It was only after a couple of minutes I realized they weren't alone. Three of the villagers were with them, walking just behind them as they moved away from the ville. One, I think, was the woman those shits took into the hut today, and the other two were old men. They seemed so casual about it, as if they were just out for a walk, going along willingly, and they just followed the aliens into the jungle.

"I stayed back a ways, hoping they wouldn't see me, and kept pace. Most of the time it was easy. I couldn't see the villagers, but I could keep that glow in sight, even in the thickest parts of the trees.

"I don't know how long I followed them. No one noticed me. Finally the glow stopped moving, and I edged in closer. A clearing had been burned out of the jungle, probably by the ship. I could still smell smoke, and the rain made a hissing sound. The ship was on the ground, shimmering and glowing, the same one, or the same kind. Big, like twenty feet high, fifty or sixty feet across. It glowed so much I couldn't really see its shape. I don't know, kind of like a giant claymore mine.

"The four aliens and the villagers stood next to it without moving. All of a sudden a hole sort of melted away in the side of the ship, then pop! pop! pop!, the aliens and villagers were just sucked inside, pop! pop! pop! Instantaneous. Then the hole closed. A minute later the ship started up, the ground shook a little, and I heard the hollowest sound, more popping in my ears, and the ship rose, pulsing in and out, color into black into color.

"I don't know what happened. Next thing I knew I was out in the clearing, under the ship and yelling up at it, screaming at them to come back, yelling and waving. But the ship didn't stop, it kept going up, and up, and when it got above the trees, it hung there for a minute, then shot forward and disappeared."

Scolini stopped, and was quiet for a long time. The rain became heavier, blew in under the ponchos, but it didn't seem to bother him. Finally he spoke again. "Shit, Sahara, I wanted to go with them. I wanted them to come back, and take me away."

In the morning, the heat returned. The peace of the night before had become exhaustion, bodies trying desperately to shut down. We slogged through the jungle, and took sporadic sniper fire, but no one seemed to care. The lieutenant was trying to get us a resupply, but got no promises.

Scolini was distant, preoccupied all morning. He didn't read, he didn't quote anything to us, he didn't say a word. His movements were lethargic and careless, and he kept gazing up at the sky and into the treetops, paying no attention to the trail. I tried talking to him, told him he'd get killed that way, but he didn't answer me.

Midday, Spider was on point as usual, and he brought us to a halt. Word came down the line that there was a clearing ahead, and bodies. Word came down it was bad. Bad was not the right word.

One by one we entered the clearing, and there was no way not to see them. Hanging from the trees, facing us as we emerged from the jungle, were the half-dressed, mutilated corpses of three Marines.

They had been dead a long time, and the worst was the most visible—their sexual organs had been cut off and stuffed into their mouths.

That was the first thing we all saw, the one thing none of us could ignore. Much more had been done to them, and the evidence was there if you could keep looking. I couldn't, and I turned away, seeing nothing more. But it was too late, I'd already seen them, and that first image has never left me. It's usually what brings on the nightmares.

Watson was on his hands and knees, retching. The Wizard

and Spider stood side by side in front of the limp bodies, their gazes to the ground. Spider had his knife out, as though preparing to cut them down. Crazy Carl had wandered to the edge of the clearing and stared into the jungle, cursing. "Jesus Christ, they're fucking animals, Jesus Christ, they're fucking animals, Jesus Christ . . . !" It was a litany he kept repeating without pause, louder each time until he was screaming it at the sky. The lieutenant started yelling at him, telling him to can it, ordering him to help Spider cut down the bodies.

And Scolini . . . Scolini was the only one who looked at them without turning away. He stood in the center of the clearing, his stare fixed on the three bodies. His face was dead, without expression. He didn't blink. When he finally moved, he walked slowly to the trees, climbed up into them, and out along the thick branches, and cut down the bodies without a word.

So we got our resupply after all. The helicopters brought in beer, Coke, and ice, food and cigarettes, ammunition and mail, and they took what was left of the bodies back with them. We were through for the day.

I sat with Scolini in the shade of a tall, thick bush. I was on my third cigarette and my second Coke, rereading the one piece of mail I'd received—a letter from Megan. The words in her letter carried no meaning. There was no picture enclosed, and her face became even less distinct. Scolini was sucking on ice, staring into the trees. He hadn't opened any of his mail.

"Sahara, what would you do if some alien beings offered to take you away in their ship?"

"Run like hell," I said. "Call in the gunships." I tried laughing, didn't quite make it. I'd hoped he wouldn't mention the aliens again.

"It would be a way out of here," he said.

"I've got a way out. A nice safe airplane back to the World."

"If you make it till then."

"I've only got a month and a half. Forty-six days. I'll make it."

"I won't." He bit down on the ice, cracking it. "I've got

ten fucking months. No way I'll make it out of here with my body and mind both intact.'' He shook his head. ''Look at you. Your heart's dead. You don't feel a fuckin' thing anymore.'' He sighed. ''I'm sorry.'' For a minute he seemed very far away. ''After today, you know what's going to happen in the next ville we hit? It's going to make yesterday look like a picnic.''

I couldn't argue with him, but I didn't really want to think about it.

''I'm going after them,'' Scolini said.

''Who?''

''The aliens.''

''They're not real, Scolini.''

''They're real. And I'm going to find them. I'm going to find them and make them take me away from here. I'm leaving this goddamn war, Sahara, and I'm not coming back.''

I knew he would go, and I knew I couldn't stop him, so when night fell and Scolini headed silently back down the trail, I went along. I didn't believe we'd find anything, but I wanted to be with him when he realized that, with him when he lost it all and freaked. I wanted to bring him back alive. And—I don't know—maybe I wanted to believe there *was* something out there that would take us away from the war.

The rain was light, but the darkness was complete. Scolini took us off the trails almost immediately, and we forced our way slowly through the lush jungle growth. It was crazy, two idiots wandering aimlessly through the jungle at night, but I couldn't say anything to him. Somehow we were quiet enough so we didn't get shot at by anyone. Maybe the rain helped. Maybe it was Scolini's vibes.

''Where the hell we going?'' I asked.

''I'm tracking,'' he said. ''I can hear them, just a taste. We're doing all right.''

I could hear nothing but the rain above, water dripping from the leaves, animal noises, and my heartbeat. I could see nothing but Scolini's dark form just in front of me.

''We're going to get wasted,'' I said.

''By who?''

''VC. Booby traps. Our own guys. The jungle. Maybe even your goddamn aliens.''

Scolini laughed. "Shit, not a chance." Then, "There! See it? Now it's gone."

"See what?"

"The flash. The glow."

I'd seen nothing, and I didn't answer. We pushed on. My eyes adjusted to the darkness, and now I could see the leaves and branches ahead of me, and the ground at my feet. The moon was nearly full, and once in a while there'd be a break in the clouds and dull silver light would trickle down through the canopy for a brief moment before the darkness returned.

Every few minutes Scolini would hiss "There!" or "Hear that?" and follow with "We're getting closer, Sahara. I'm beginning to feel them." Each time I saw and heard nothing, and before long I was convinced Scolini had gone completely mad.

We moved through areas where mosquitos overwhelmed us, pockets of jungle so thick we had to crawl. We waded through a river that might have been the one we'd forded that morning. We waded through other rivers of wet, chest-high grass. Several times we crossed trails that would have made the going easier, but Scolini ignored them and pushed back into the jungle.

Hours passed, felt like days. Exhaustion pressed in on me along with the trees and the rain and the darkness, and I just wanted to sleep. I itched everywhere, and I felt as if my flesh was dotted with tiny burning wounds. My clothes were soaked with sweat and rain, clinging to me. My breath came in hard, aching gasps, but Scolini pressed on, stronger and confident, seeing flashes and glows more often as we continued, homing in on inaudible sounds.

After a while, though, I was beginning to see the flashes myself. "There," Scolini would say, and just in the corner of my vision I'd spot a shimmer of color. Sometimes I caught a glimpse before he said a word. When I told him I was seeing the flashes, he picked up the pace, rejuvenated. Soon I even began to hear what Scolini heard: a brief, hollow vibration, a fluttering in my ears.

But what was it we were seeing? Glimpses of a spaceship somewhere deep in the jungle, or groups of aliens moving through the trees? And the sounds—were they the result of alien machines and technology? Or was it all hallucination? I thought of Wizard, who had once said the entire war was a consensus hallucination. I was beginning to think Scolini wasn't so crazy, and that it didn't matter what was real.

Sometime after midnight, Scolini stopped, and pointed through the dense foliage. In the distance shimmered a dim, blue-green glow, fragmented by leaves and branches and tree trunks. It was more than a flash, more than an uncertain glimpse, and it remained in sight, motionless.

"There it is." Scolini's voice was a hushed whisper. "Our way out."

"You're serious," I said. "About going away with them, whatever they are."

"Of course. Aren't you?"

"I didn't even believe in the goddamn things." I still didn't know what I was seeing, but I was certain it was, in some sense, real.

"Then why the hell are you here?"

"I don't know."

Scolini started to laugh. "Oh, shit, man." He grabbed my arm. "Hey, it doesn't matter. You're here now, and there they are. Let's go." He pulled at me and headed for the shimmering glow.

The timing was too damn good. They must have sensed us coming. As Scolini pushed through the trees, and I followed, a heavier vibration shook the jungle floor.

"Christ, Sahara, they're leaving!" He surged forward, crashing through the trees and grass and bushes. I followed, but couldn't match his pace, and he emerged into the clearing before I did.

The ship lifted slowly from the ground, and Scolini staggered toward it, arms outstretched. "Don't go!" he shouted. "Take us with you, goddammit!"

I reached the edge of the clearing and stopped, watching him, staring at the ship, which rose only an inch every few seconds. As big as Scolini had said, it was encased in a blurred, blue-green shell of light that pulsed regularly. Its outline was indistinct, fuzzy with the glow.

The ship rose to chest level and stopped, silently vibrating the air around us. Scolini yelled, leaped upward, and tried to grab onto it. His hands disappeared within the glow for a moment, he hung a foot or two above the earth, then a dark, swirling hole opened in the side of the ship, and Scolini was sucked inside. His helmet flew off, ejected away from the ship, and tumbled to the ground. The hole collapsed, the ship's glow solidified, and Scolini was gone.

I stepped out of the trees and approached the ship. It hovered, still not rising, as if waiting for me. I stared at it, watched it pulse as it loomed above. Scolini was inside, and I felt certain if I jumped at the ship, it would take me as well. But what were they doing to him? What would they do to me?

I took two, three steps back, afraid another hole would open in the side of the ship. I wanted out, just like everyone else, but not this way. This was crazy, wasn't it?

I didn't move, and the ship remained motionless, nearly silent. Every ten or fifteen seconds it flickered to black for just an instant, then the color returned. I felt my heartbeat slow to match the rhythm of the colored pulse, felt it hesitate each time the ship went to black. I didn't know what to do; I could not approach the ship, and I could not back away. Once I leaned slightly forward, and a spot of black started to form within the glow, but I jerked backward and the spot disappeared. Finally, after what seemed like more than an hour, I took two more steps back, and the ship began to rise once more.

I watched, unmoving, as the huge, glowing craft rose above the treetops and hovered for several moments. It shifted colors, tailing momentarily to indigo, then slipped back to blue-green and shot forward, vanishing into the west.

The rain had stopped. I picked up Scolini's helmet, put it on, and gazed up into the cloud-covered sky. I waited a long time, watching for colored glows, listening for the hollow vibrations in my ears, but there was nothing. The ship did not return. The wind picked up, cold and damp, and once again it began to rain.

I never saw him again. Nor did anyone else. He was listed MIA, a status that never changed.

Maybe the aliens took Scolini for a long ride, then dropped him off somewhere else in the jungle, where he later died. Maybe they kept him, studied and experimented on him, tortured and killed him. But maybe he found a way to talk with the aliens, explained to them what he wanted, and they took him away to a better place.

It's been a lot of years since my tour ended. Most of them have been all right. But there are times that haven't been. Scolini was wrong about one thing. My heart isn't dead; it is just encased in a protective shell, preserving what still survives. Sometimes that shell cracks, or begins to melt away, and then come the bad times—when hallucinations overwhelm me and I see rice paddies in my bathtub and body bags in mail trucks; when I get the shakes and can't hold down any food; and when the nightmares start with the three dead Marines, and get so bad I wake up screaming in the hot darkness, afraid to go back to sleep.

Times when I think about Scolini, and wonder where he is.

Times when I wish I'd gone with him.

And when it rains, I still search the night skies, hoping to see . . .

Lucius Shepard

Here's another story by Lucius Shepard.

Shades

by
Lucius Shepard

This little gook cadre with a pitted complexion drove me through the heart of Saigon—I couldn't relate to it as Ho Chi Minh City—and checked me into the Hotel Heroes of Tet, a place that must have been quietly elegant and very French back in the days when philosophy was discussed over Cointreau rather than practiced in the streets, but now was filled with cheap production-line furniture and tinted photographs of Uncle Ho. Glaring at me, the cadre suggested I would be advised to keep to my room until I left for Cam Le; to annoy him I strolled into the bar, where a couple of Americans—reporters, their table laden with notebooks and tape cassettes—were drinking shots from a bottle of George Dickel. "How's it goin'?" I said, ambling over. "Name's Tom Puleo. I'm doin' a piece on Stoner for *Esquire*."

The bigger of them—chubby, red-faced guy about my age, maybe thirty-five, thirty-six—returned a fishy stare; but the younger one, who was thin and tanned and weaselly handsome, perked up and said, "Hey, you're the guy was in Stoner's outfit, right?" I admitted it, and the chubby guy changed his attitude. He put on a welcome-to-the-lodge smile, stuck out a hand and introduced himself as Ed Fierman, *Chicago Sun-Times*. His pal, he said, was Ken Witcover, CNN.

They tried to draw me out about Stoner, but I told them maybe later, that I wanted to unwind from the airplane ride, and we proceeded to do damage to the whiskey. By the time we'd sucked down three drinks, Fierman and I were into some heavy reminiscence. Turned out he had covered the war during my tour and knew my old top. Witcover was cherry in Vietnam, so he just tried to look wise and to laugh in the right spots. It got pretty drunk at that table. A security cadre—fortyish, cadaverous gook in yellow fatigues—sat nearby, cocking an ear toward us, and we pretended to be engaged in subversive activity, whispering and drawing maps on napkins. But it was Stoner who was really on all our minds, and Fierman—the drunkest of us—finally broached the subject, saying, "A machine that traps ghosts! It's just like the gooks to come up with something that goddamn worthless!"

Witcover shushed him, glancing nervously at the security cadre, but Fierman was beyond caution. "They coulda done humanity a service," he said, chuckling. "Turned alla Russians into women or something. But, nah! The gooks get behind worthlessness. They may claim to be Marxists, but at heart they still wanna be inscrutable."

"So," said Witcover to me, ignoring Fierman, "when you gonna fill us in on Stoner?"

I didn't care much for Witcover. It wasn't anything personal; I simply wasn't fond of his breed: compulsively neat (pencils lined up, name inscribed on every possession), edgy, on the make. I dislike him the way some people dislike yappy little dogs. But I couldn't argue with his desire to change the subject. "He was a good soldier," I said.

Fierman let out a mulish guffaw. "Now that," he said, "that's what I call in-depth analysis."

Witcover snickered.

"Tell you the truth"—I scowled at him, freighting my words with malice—"I hated the son of a bitch. He had this young-professor air, this way of lookin' at you as if you were an interestin' specimen. And he came across pure phony. Y'know, the kind who's always talkin' like a black dude, sayin' 'right on' and shit, and sayin' it all wrong."

"Doesn't seem much reason for hating him," said Witcover, and by his injured tone, I judged I had touched a nerve. Most likely he had once entertained soul-brother pretensions.

"Maybe not. Maybe if I'd met him back home, I'd have passed him off as a creep and gone about my business. But in combat situations, you don't have the energy to maintain that sort of neutrality. It's easier to hate. And anyway, Stoner could be a genuine pain in the ass."

"How's that?" Fierman asked, getting interested.

"It was never anything unforgivable; he just never let up with it. Like one time a bunch of us were in this guy Gurney's hooch, and he was tellin' 'bout this badass he'd known in Detroit. The cops had been chasin' this guy across the rooftops, and he'd missed a jump. Fell seven floors and emptied his gun at the cops on the way down. Reaction was typical. Guys sayin' 'Wow' and tryin' to think of a story to top it. But Stoner he nods sagely and says, 'Yeah, there's a lot of that goin' around.' As if this was a syndrome to which he's devoted years of study. But you knew he didn't have a clue, that he was too upscale to have met anybody like Gurney's badass." I had a slug of whiskey. " 'There's a lot of that goin' around' was a totally inept comment. All it did was to bring everyone down from a nice buzz and make us aware of the shithole where we lived."

Witcover looked puzzled but Fierman made a noise that seemed to imply comprehension. "How'd he die?" he asked. "The handout says he was KIA, but it doesn't say what kind of action."

"The fuck-up kind," I said. I didn't want to tell them. The closer I came to seeing Stoner, the leerier I got about the topic. Until this business had begun, I thought I'd buried all the death-tripping weirdness of Vietnam; now Stoner had unearthed it and I was having dreams again and I hated him for that worse than I ever had in life. What was I supposed to do? Feel sorry for him? Maybe ghosts didn't have bad dreams. Maybe it was terrific being a ghost, like with Casper. . . . Anyway, I did tell them. How we had entered Cam Le, what was left of the patrol. How we had lined up the villagers, interrogated them, hit them, and God knows we might have killed them—we were freaked, bone-weary, an atrocity waiting to happen—if Stoner hadn't distracted us. He'd been wandering around, poking at stuff with his rifle, and then, with this ferocious expression on his face, he'd fired into one of the huts. The hut had been empty, but there must have been explosives hidden inside, because after a few rounds the whole damn thing had blown and taken Stoner with it.

Talking about him soured me on company, and shortly afterward I broke it off with Fierman and Witcover, and walked out into the city. The security cadre tagged along, his hand resting on the butt of his sidearm. I had a real load on and barely noticed my surroundings. The only salient points of difference between Saigon today and fifteen years before were the ubiquitous representations of Uncle Ho that covered the facades of many of the buildings, and the absence of motor scooters: the traffic consisted mainly of bicycles. I went a dozen blocks or so and stopped at a sidewalk café beneath sun-browned tamarinds, where I paid two dong for food tickets, my first experience with what the Communists called "goods exchange"—a system they hoped would undermine the concept of monetary trade; I handed the tickets to the waitress and she gave me a bottle of beer and a dish of fried peanuts. The security cadre, who had taken a table opposite mine, seemed no more impressed with the system than was I; he chided the waitress for her slowness and acted perturbed by the complexity accruing to his order of tea and cakes.

I sat and sipped and stared, thoughtless and unfocused. The bicyclists zipping past were bright blurs with jingling bells, and the light was that heavy leaded-gold light that occurs when a tropical sun has broken free of an overcast. Smells of charcoal, fish sauce, grease. The heat squeezed sweat from my every pore. I was brought back to alertness by angry voices. The security cadre was arguing with the waitress, insisting that the recorded music be turned on, and she was explaining that there weren't enough customers to warrant turning it on. He began to offer formal "constructive criticism," making clear that he considered her refusal both a breach of party ethics and the code of honorable service.

About then, I realized I had begun to cry. Not sobs, just tears leaking. The tears had nothing to do with the argument or the depersonalized ugliness it signaled. I believe that the heat and the light and the smells had seeped into me, triggering a recognition of an awful familiarity that my mind had thus far rejected. I wiped my face and tried to suck it up before anyone could notice my emotionality; but a teenage boy on a bicycle slowed and gazed at me with an amused expression. To show my contempt, I spat on the sidewalk. Almost instantly, I felt much better.

Early the next day, thirty of us—all journalists—were bussed north to Cam Le. Mist still wreathed the paddies, the light had a yellowish green cast, and along the road women in black dresses were waiting for a southbound bus, with rumpled sacks of produce like sleepy brown animals at their feet. I sat beside Fierman, who, being as hung over as I was, made no effort at conversation; however, Witcover—sitting across the aisle—peppered me with inane questions until I told him to leave me alone. Just before we turned onto the dirt road that led to Cam Le, an information cadre boarded the bus and for the duration proceeded to fill us in on everything we already knew. Stuff about the machine, how its fields were generated, and so forth. Technical jargon gives me a pain, and I tried hard not to listen. But then he got off onto a tack that caught my interest. "Since the machine has been in operation," he said, "the apparition seems to have grown more vital."

"What's that mean?" I asked, waving my hand to attract his attention. "Is he coming back to life?"

My colleagues laughed.

The cadre pondered this. "It simply means that his effect has become more observable," he said at last. And beyond that he would not specify.

Cam Le had been evacuated, its population shifted to temporary housing three miles east. The village itself was nothing like the place I had entered fifteen years before. Gone were the thatched huts, and in their stead were about two dozen small houses of concrete block painted a quarantine yellow, with banana trees set between them. All this encircled by thick jungle. Standing on the far side of the road from the group of houses was the long tin-roofed building that contained the machine. Two soldiers were lounging in front of it, and as the bus pulled up, they snapped to attention; a clutch of officers came out the door, followed by a portly, white-haired gook: Phan Thnah Tuu, the machine's inventor. I disembarked and studied him while he shook hands with the other journalists; it wasn't every day that I met someone who claimed to be both Marxist and mystic, and had gone more than the required mile in establishing the validity of each. His hair was as fine as cornsilk, a fat black mole punctuated one cheek, and his benign smile was unflagging, seeming a fixture of some deeply held good opinion attaching to everything he saw. Maybe, I thought, Fierman was right. In-fucking-scrutable.

"Ah," he said, coming up, enveloping me in a cloud of perfumy cologne. "Mr. Puleo. I hope this won't be painful for you."

"Really," I said. "You hope that, do you?"

"I beg your pardon," he said, taken aback.

"It's okay." I grinned. "You're forgiven."

An unsmiling major led him away to press more flesh, and he glanced back at me, perplexed. I was mildly ashamed of having fucked with him, but unlike Cassius Clay, I had plenty against them Viet Congs. Besides, my wiseass front was helping to stave off the yips.

After a brief welcome-to-the-wonderful-wacky-world-of-the-Commie-techno-paradise speech given by the major, Tuu delivered an oration upon the nature of ghosts, worthy of mention only in that it rehashed every crackpot notion I'd ever heard: apparently Stoner hadn't yielded much in the way of hard data. He then warned us to keep our distance from the village. The fields would not harm us; they were currently in operation, undetectable to our senses and needing but a slight manipulation to "focus" Stoner. But if we were to pass inside the fields, it was possible that Stoner himself might be able to cause us injury. With that, Tuu bowed and reentered the building.

We stood facing the village, which—with its red dirt and yellow houses and green banana leaves—looked elementary and innocent under the leaden sky. Some of my colleagues whispered together, others checked their cameras. I felt numb and shaky, prepared to turn away quickly, much the way I once had felt when forced to identify the body of a chance acquaintance at a police morgue. Several minutes after Tuu had left us, there was a disturbance in the air at the center of the village. Similar to heat haze, but the ripples were slower. And then, with the suddenness of a slide shunted into a projector, Stoner appeared.

I think I had been expecting something bloody and ghoulish, or perhaps a gauzy, insubstantial form; but he looked no different than he had on the day he died. Haggard; wearing sweat-stained fatigues; his face half-obscured by a week's growth of stubble. On his helmet were painted the words *Didi Mao* (''Fuck Off'' in Vietnamese), and I could make out the yellowing photograph of his girl that he'd taped to his rifle stock. He didn't act startled by our presence; on the contrary, his attitude was nonchalant. He shouldered his rifle, tipped back his helmet and sauntered toward us. He seemed to be recessed into the backdrop: it was as if reality were two-dimensional and he was a cutout held behind it to give the illusion of depth. At least that's how it was one moment. The next, he would appear to be set forward of the backdrop like a pop-up figure in a fancy greeting card. Watching him shift between these modes was unsettling . . . more than unsettling. My heart hammered, my mouth was cottony. I bumped into someone and realized that I had been backing away, that I was making a scratchy noise deep in my throat. Stoner's eyes, those eyes that had looked dead even in life, pupils about .45 caliber and hardly any iris showing, they were locked onto mine and the pressure of his stare was like two black bolts punching through into my skull.

''Puleo,'' he said.

I couldn't hear him, but I saw his lips shape the name. With a mixture of longing and hopelessness harrowing his features, he kept on repeating it. And then I noticed something else. The closer he drew to me, the more in focus he became. It wasn't just a matter of the shortening distance; his stubble and sweat stains, the frays in his fatigues, his worry lines—all these were sharpening the way details become fixed in a developing photograph. But none of that disturbed me half as much as did the fact of a dead man calling my name. I couldn't handle that. I began to hyperventilate, to get dizzy, and I believe I might have blacked out; but before that could happen, Stoner reached the edge of the fields, the barrier beyond which he could not pass.

Had I had more mental distance from the event, I might have enjoyed the sound-and-light that ensued: it was spectacular. The instant Stoner hit the end of his tether, there was an ear-splitting shriek of the kind metal emits under immense stress; it seemed to issue from the air, the trees, the earth, as if some ironclad physical constant had been breached. Stoner was frozen midstep, his mouth open, and opaque lightnings were forking away from him, taking on a violet tinge as they vanished, their passage illuminating the curvature of the fields. I heard a scream and assumed it must be Stoner. But somebody grabbed me, shook me, and I understood that I was the one screaming, screaming with throat-tearing abandon because his eyes were boring into me and I could have sworn that his thoughts, his sensations, were flowing to me along the track of his vision. I knew what he was feeling: not pain, not desperation, but emptiness. An emptiness made unbearable by his proximity to life, to fullness. It was the worst thing I'd ever felt, worse than grief and bullet wounds, and it had to be worse than dying—dying, you see, had an end, whereas this went on and on, and every time you thought you had adapted to it, it grew worse yet. I wanted it to stop. That was all I wanted. Ever. Just for it to stop.

Then, with the same abruptness that he had appeared, Stoner winked out of existence and the feeling of emptiness faded.

People pressed in, asking questions. I shouldered them aside and walked off a few paces. My hands were shaking, my eyes weepy. I stared at the ground. It looked blurred, an undifferentiated smear of green with a brown clot in the middle: this gradually resolved into grass and my left shoe. Ants were crawling over the laces, poking their heads into the eyelets. The sight was strengthening, a reassurance of the ordinary.

"Hey, man." Witcover hove up beside me. "You okay?" He rested a hand on my shoulder. I kept my eyes on the ants, saying nothing. If it had been anyone else, I might have responded to his solicitude; but I knew he was only sucking up to me, hoping to score some human interest for his satellite report. I glanced at him. He was wearing a pair of mirrored sunglasses, and that consolidated my anger. Why is it, I ask you, that every measly little wimp in the universe thinks he can put on a pair of mirrored sunglasses and instantly acquire magical hipness and cool, rather than—as is the case—looking like an asshole with reflecting eyes?

"Fuck off," I told him in a tone that implied dire consequences were I not humored. He started to talk back, but thought better of it and stalked off. I returned to watching the ants; they were caravanning up inside my trousers and onto my calf. I would become a legend among them: The Human Who Stood Still for Biting.

From behind me came the sound of peremptory gook voices, angry American voices. I paid them no heed, content with my insect pals and the comforting state of thoughtlessness that watching them induced. A minute or so later, someone else moved up beside me and stood without speaking. I recognized Tuu's cologne and looked up. "Mr. Puleo," he said. "I'd like to offer you an exclusive on this story." Over his shoulder, I saw my colleagues staring at us through the windows of the bus, as wistful and forlorn as kids who have been denied Disneyland: they, like me, knew that big bucks were to be had from exploiting Stoner's plight.

"Why?" I asked.

"We want your help in conducting an experiment."

I waited for him to continue.

"Did you notice," he said, "that after Stoner identified you, his image grew sharper?"

I nodded.

"We're interested in observing the two of you in close proximity. His reaction to you was unique."

"You mean go in there?" I pointed to the village. "You said it was dangerous."

"Other subjects have entered the fields and shown no ill effects. But Stoner was not as intrigued by them as he was with you." Tuu brushed a lock of hair back from his forehead. "We have no idea of Stoner's capabilities, Mr. Puleo. It *is* a risk. But since you served in the Army, I assume you are accustomed to risk."

I let him try to persuade me—the longer I held out, the stronger my bargaining position—but I had already decided to accept the offer. Though I wasn't eager to feel that emptiness again, I had convinced myself that it had been a product of nerves and an overactive imagination; now that I had confronted Stoner, I believed I would be able to control my reactions. Tuu said that he would have the others driven back to Saigon, but I balked at that. I was not sufficiently secure to savor the prospect of being alone among the gooks, and I told Tuu I wanted Fierman and Witcover to stay. Why Witcover? At the time I might have said it was because he and Fierman were the only two of my colleagues whom I knew; but in retrospect, I think I may have anticipated the need for a whipping boy.

We were quartered in a house at the eastern edge of the village, one that the fields did not enclose. Three cots were set up inside, along with a table and chairs; the yellow walls were brocaded with mildew, and weeds grew sideways from chinks in the concrete blocks. Light was provided by an oil lamp that—as darkness fell—sent an inconstant glow lapping over the walls, making it appear that the room was filled with dirty orange water.

After dinner Fierman produced a bottle of whiskey—his briefcase contained three more—and a deck of cards, and we sat down to while away the evening. The one game we all knew was Hearts, and we each played according to the dictates of our personalities. Fierman became quickly drunk and attempted to Shoot the Moon on every hand, no matter how bad his cards; he seemed to be asking fate to pity a fool. I paid little attention to the game, my ears tuned to the night sounds, half expecting to hear the sputter of small-arms fire, the rumor of some ghostly engagement; it was by dint of luck alone that I maintained second place. Witcover played conservatively, building his score through our mistakes, and though we were only betting a nickel a point, to watch him sweat out every trick you would have thought a fortune hung in the balance; he chortled over our pitiful fuck-ups, rolling his eyes and shaking his head in delight, and whistled as he totaled up his winnings. The self-importance he derived from winning fouled the atmosphere, and the room acquired the staleness of a cell where we had been incarcerated for years.

Finally, after a particularly childish display of glee, I pushed back my chair and stood.

"Where you going?" asked Witcover. "Let's play."

"No, thanks," I said.

"Christ!" He picked up the discards and muttered something about sore losers.

"It's not that," I told him. "I'm worried if you win another hand, you're gonna come all over the fuckin' table. I don't wanna watch."

Fierman snorted laughter.

Witcover shot me an aggrieved look. "What's with you, man? You been on my case ever since the hotel."

I shrugged and headed for the door.

"Asshole," he said half under his breath.

"What?" An angry flush numbed my face as I turned back.

He tried to project an expression of manly belligerence, but his eyes darted from side to side.

"Asshole?" I said. "Is that right?" I took a step toward him.

Fierman scrambled up, knocking over his chair, and began pushing me away. "C'mon," he said. "It's not worth it. Cool out." His boozy sincerity acted to diminish my anger, and I let him urge me out the door.

The night was moonless, with a few stars showing low on the horizon; the spiky crowns of the palms ringing the village were silhouettes pinned onto a lesser blackness. It was so humid, it felt like you could spoon in the air. I crossed the dirt road, found a patch of grass near the tin-roofed building and sat down. The door to the building was cracked, spilling a diagonal of white radiance onto the ground, and I had the notion that there was no machine inside, only a mystic boil of whiteness emanating from Tuu's silky hair. A couple of soldiers walked past and nodded to me; they paused a few feet farther along to light cigarettes, which proceeded to brighten and fade with the regularity of tiny beacons.

Crickets sawed, frogs chirred, and listening to them, smelling the odor of sweet rot from the jungle, I thought about a similar night when I'd been stationed at Phnoc Vinh, about a party we'd had with a company of artillery. There had been a barbecue pit and iced beer and our CO had given special permission for whores to come on the base. It had been a great party; in fact, those days at Phnoc Vinh had been the best time of the war for me. The artillery company had had this terrific cook, and on movie nights he'd make doughnuts. Jesus, I'd loved those doughnuts! They'd tasted like home, like peace. I'd kick back and munch a doughnut and watch the bullshit movie, and it was almost like being in my own living room, watching the tube. Trouble was, Phnoc Vinh had softened me up, and after three weeks, when we'd been airlifted to Quan Loi, which was constantly under mortar and rocket fire, I'd nearly gotten my ass blown off.

Footsteps behind me. Startled, I turned and saw what looked to be a disembodied white shirt floating toward me. I came to one knee, convinced for the moment that some other ghost had been lured to the machine; but a second later a complete figure emerged from the dark: Tuu. Without a word, he sat cross-legged beside me. He was smoking a cigarette . . . or so I thought until I caught a whiff of marijuana. He took a deep drag, the coal illuminating his placid features, and offered me the joint. I hesitated, not wanting to be pals; but tempted by the smell, I accepted it, biting back a smartass remark about Marxist permissiveness. It was good shit. I could feel the smoke twisting through me, finding out all my hollow places. I handed it back, but he made a gesture of warding it off and after a brief silence, he said, "What do you think about all this, Mr. Puleo?"

"About Stoner?"

"Yes."

"I think"—I jetted smoke from my nostrils—"it's crap that you've got him penned up in that astral tiger cage."

"Had this discovery been made in the United States," he said, "the circumstances would be no different. Humane considerations—if, indeed, they apply—would have low priority."

"Maybe," I said. "It's still crap."

"Why? Do you believe Stoner is unhappy?"

"Don't you?" I had another hit. It was *very* good shit. The ground seemed to have a pulse. "Ghosts are by nature unhappy."

"Then you know what a ghost is?"

"Not hardly. But I figure unhappy's part of it." The roach was getting too hot; I took a final hit and flipped it away.

"How 'bout you? You believe that garbage you preached this mornin'?"

His laugh was soft and cultivated. "That was a press release. However, my actual opinion is neither less absurd-sounding nor more verifiable."

"And what's that?"

He plucked a blade of grass, twiddled it. "I believe a ghost is a quality that dies in a man long before he experiences physical death. Something that has grown acclimated to death and thus survives the body. It might be love or an ambition. An element of character . . . Anything." He regarded me with his lips pursed. "I have such a ghost within me. As do you, Mr. Puleo. My ghost senses yours."

The theory was as harebrained as his others, but I wasn't able to deny it. I knew he was partly right, that a moral filament had snapped inside me during the war and since that time I had lacked the ingredient necessary to the development of a generous soul. Now it seemed that I could feel that lack as a restless presence straining against my flesh. The sawing of the crickets intensified, and I had a rush of paranoia, wondering if Tuu was fucking with my head. Then, moods shifting at the chemical mercies of the dope, my paranoia eroded and Tuu snapped into focus for me . . . or at least his ghost did. He had, I recalled, written poetry prior to the war, and I thought I saw the features of that lost poet melting up from his face: a dreamy fellow given to watching petals fall and contemplating the moon's reflection. I closed my eyes, trying to get a grip. This was the best dope I'd ever smoked. Commie Pink, pure buds of the revolution.

"Are you worried about tomorrow?" Tuu asked.

"Should I be?"

"I can only tell you what I did before—no one has been harmed."

"What happened during those other experiments?" I asked.

"Very little, really. Stoner approached each subject, spoke to them. Then he lost interest and wandered off."

"Spoke to them? Could they hear him?"

"Faintly. However, considering his reaction to you, I wouldn't be surprised if you could hear him quite well."

I wasn't thrilled by that prospect. Having to look at Stoner was bad enough. I thought about the eerie shit he might say:

admonitory pronouncements, sad questions, windy vowels gusting from his strange depths. Tuu said something and had to repeat it to snap me out of my reverie. He asked how it felt to be back in Vietnam, and without forethought, I said it wasn't a problem.

"And the first time you were here," he said, an edge to his voice. "Was that a problem?"

"What are you gettin' at?"

"I noticed in your records that you were awarded a Silver Star."

"Yeah?"

"You must have been a good soldier. I wondered if you might not have found a calling in war."

"If you're askin' what I think about the war," I said, getting pissed, "I don't make judgments about it. It was a torment for me, nothing more. Its geopolitical consequences, cultural effects, they're irrelevant to me . . . maybe they're ultimately irrelevant. Though I doubt you'd agree."

"We may agree more than you suspect." He sighed pensively. "For both of us, apparently, the war was a passion. In your case, an agonizing one. In mine, while there was also agony, it was essentially a love affair with revolution, with the idea of revolution. And as with all great passions, what was most alluring was not the object of passion but the new depth of my own feelings. Thus I was blind to the realities underlying it. Now"—he waved at the sky, the trees—"now I inhabit those realities and I am not as much in love as once I was. Yet no matter how extreme my disillusionment, the passion continues. I want it to continue. I need the significance with which it imbues my past actions." He studied me. "Isn't that how it is for you? You say war was a torment, but don't you find those days empowering?"

Just as when he had offered me the joint, I realized that I didn't want this sort of peaceful intimacy with him; I preferred him to be my inscrutable enemy. Maybe he was right, maybe—like him—I needed this passion to continue in order to give significance to my past. Whatever, I felt vulnerable to him, to my perception of his humanity. "Good-night," I said, getting to my feet. My ass was numb from sitting and soaked with dew.

He gazed up at me, unreadable, and fingered something

from his shirt pocket. Another joint. He lit up, exhaling a billow of smoke. ''Good-night,'' he said coldly.

The next morning—sunny, cloudless—I staked myself out on the red dirt of Cam Le to wait for Stoner. Nervous, I paced back and forth until the air began to ripple and he materialized less than thirty feet away. He walked slowly toward me, his rifle dangling; a drop of sweat carved a cold groove across my rib cage. ''Puleo,'' he said, and this time I heard him. His voice was faint, but it shook me.

Looking into his blown-out pupils, I was reminded of a day not long before he had died. We had been hunkered down together after a firefight, and our eyes had met, had locked as if sealed by a vacuum: like two senile old men, incapable of any communication aside from a recognition of the other's vacancy. As I remembered this, it hit home to me that though he hadn't been a friend, he *was* my brother-in-arms, and that as such, I owed him more than journalistic interest.

''Stoner!'' I hadn't intended to shout, but in that outcry was a wealth of repressed emotion, of regret and guilt and anguish at not being able to help him elude the fate by which he had been overtaken.

He stopped short; for an instant the hopelessness drained from his face. His image was undergoing that uncanny sharpening of focus: sweat beads popping from his brow, a scab appearing on his chin. The lines of strain around his mouth and eyes were etched deep, filled in with grime, like cracks in his tan.

Tides of emotion were washing over me, and irrational though it seemed, I knew that some of these emotions—the fierce hunger for life in particular—were Stoner's. I believe we had made some sort of connection, and all our thoughts were in flux between us. He moved toward me again. My hands trembled, my knees buckled, and I had to sit down, overwhelmed not by fear but by the combination of his familiarity and utter strangeness. ''Jesus, Stoner,'' I said. ''Jesus.''

He stood gazing dully down at me. ''My sending,'' he said, his voice louder and with a pronounced resonance. ''Did you get it?''

A chill articulated my spine, but I forced myself to ignore it. "Sending?" I said.

"Yesterday," he said, "I sent you what I was feeling. What it's like for me here."

"How?" I asked, recalling the feeling of emptiness. "How'd you do that?"

"It's easy, Puleo," he said. "All you have to do is die, and thoughts . . . dreams, they'll flake off you like old paint. But believe me, it's hardly adequate compensation." He sat beside me, resting the rifle across his knees. This was no ordinary sequence of movements. His outline wavered, and his limbs appeared to drift apart: I might have been watching the collapse of a lifelike statue through a volume of disturbed water. It took all my self-control to keep from flinging myself away. His image steadied, and he stared at me. "Last person I was this close to ran like hell," he said. "You always were a tough motherfucker, Puleo. I used to envy you that."

If I hadn't believed before that he was Stoner, the way he spoke the word "motherfucker" would have cinched it for me: it had the stiffness of a practiced vernacular, a mode of expression that he hadn't mastered. This and his pathetic manner made him seem less menacing. "You were tough, too," I said glibly.

"I tried to be," he said. "I tried to copy you guys. But it was an act, a veneer. And when we hit Cam Le, the veneer cracked."

"You remember . . ." I broke off because it didn't feel right, my asking him questions; the idea of translating his blood and bones into a best-seller was no longer acceptable.

"Dying?" His lips thinned. "Oh, yeah. Every detail. You guys were hassling the villagers, and I thought, Christ, they're going to kill them. I didn't want to be involved, and . . . I was so tired, you know, so tired in my head, and I figured if I walked off a little ways, I wouldn't be part of it. I'd be innocent. So I did. I moved a ways off, and the wails, the shouts, they weren't real anymore. Then I came to this hut. I'd lost track of what was happening by that time. In my mind I was sure you'd already started shooting, and I said to myself, I'll show them I'm doing my bit, put a few rounds into this hut. Maybe"—his Adam's apple worked—"maybe they'll think I killed somebody. Maybe that'll satisfy them."

I looked down at the dirt, troubled by what I now understood to be my complicity in his death, and troubled also by a new understanding of the events surrounding the death. I realized that if anyone else had gotten himself blown up, the rest of us would have flipped out and likely have wasted the villagers. But since it had been Stoner, the explosion had had almost a calming effect: Cam Le had rid us of a nuisance.

Stoner reached out his hand to me. I was too mesmerized by the gesture, which left afterimages in the air, to recoil from it, and I watched horrified as his fingers gripped my upper arm, pressing wrinkles in my shirtsleeve. His touch was light and transmitted a dry coolness, and with it came a sensation of weakness. By all appearances, it was a normal hand, yet I kept expecting it to become translucent and merge with my flesh.

"It's going to be okay," said Stoner.

His tone, though bemused, was confident, and I thought I detected a change in his face, but I couldn't put my finger on what the change was. "Why's it gonna be okay?" I asked, my voice more frail and ghostly-sounding than his. "It doesn't seem okay to me."

"Because you're part of my process, my circuitry. Understand?"

"No," I said. I had identified what had changed about him. Whereas a few moments before he had looked real, now he looked more than real, ultra-real; his features had acquired the kind of gloss found in airbrushed photographs, and for a split second his eyes were cored with points of glitter as if reflecting a camera flash . . . except these points were bluish white not red. There was a coarseness to his face that hadn't been previously evident, and in contrast to my earlier perception of him, he now struck me as dangerous, malevolent.

He squinted and cocked his head. "What's wrong, man? You scared of me?" He gave an amused sniff. "Hang in there, Puleo. Tough guy like you, you'll make an adjustment." My feeling of weakness had intensified: it was as if blood or some even more vital essence were trickling out of me. "Come on, Puleo," he said mockingly. "Ask me some questions? That's what you're here for, isn't it? I mean this must be the goddamn scoop of the century. Good News From Beyond the Grave! Of course''—he pitched his voice low and sepulchral—''the news isn't all that good.''

Those glittering cores resurfaced in his pupils, and I wanted to wrench free; but I felt helpless, wholly in his thrall.

''You see,'' he went on, ''when I appeared in the village, when I walked around and''—he chuckled—''haunted the place, those times were like sleepwalking. I barely knew what was happening. But the rest of the time, I was somewhere else. Somewhere really fucking weird.''

My weakness was bordering on vertigo, but I mustered my strength and croaked, ''Where?''

''The Land of Shades,'' he said. ''That's what I call it, anyway. You wouldn't like it, Puleo. It wouldn't fit your idea of order.''

The lights burned in his eyes, winking bright, and—as if in correspondence to their brightness—my dizziness increased. ''Tell me about it,'' I said, trying to take my mind off the discomfort.

''I'd be delighted!'' He grinned nastily. ''But not now. It's too complicated. Tonight, man. I'll send you a dream tonight. A bad dream. That'll satisfy your curiosity.''

My head was spinning, my stomach abubble with nausea. ''Lemme go, Stoner,'' I said.

''Isn't this good for you, man? It's very good for me.'' With a flick of his hand, he released my wrist.

I braced myself to keep from falling over, drew a deep breath and gradually my strength returned. Stoner's eyes continued to burn, and his features maintained their coarsened appearance. The difference between the way he looked now and the lost soul I had first seen was like that between night and day, and I began to wonder whether or not his touching me and my resultant weakness had anything to do with the transformation. ''Part of your process,'' I said. ''Does that . . .''

He looked me straight in the eyes, and I had the impression he was cautioning me to silence. It was more than a caution: a wordless command, a sending. ''Let me explain something,'' he said. ''A ghost is merely a stage of growth. He walks because he grows strong by walking. The more he walks, the less he's bound to the world. When he's strong enough''—he made a planing gesture with his hand—''he goes away.''

He seemed to be expecting a response. ''Where's he go?'' I asked.

''Where he belongs,'' he said. ''And if he's prevented from walking, from growing strong, he's doomed.''

''You mean he'll die?''

''Or worse.''

''And there's no other way out for him?''

''No.''

He was lying—I was sure of it. Somehow I posed for him a way out of Cam Le. ''Well . . . so,'' I said, flustered, uncertain of what to do and at the same time pleased with the prospect of conspiring against Tuu.

''Just sit with me a while,'' he said, easing his left foot forward to touch my right ankle.

Once again I experienced weakness, and over the next seven or eight hours, he would alternately move his foot away, allowing me to recover, and then bring it back into contact with me. I'm not certain what was happening. One logic dictates that since I had been peripherally involved in his death—''part of his process''—he was therefore able to draw strength from me. Likely as not, this was the case. Yet I've never been convinced that ordinary logic applied to our circumstance: it may be that we were governed by an arcane rationality to which we both were blind. Though his outward aspect did not appear to undergo further changes, his strength became tangible, a cold radiation that pulsed with the steadiness of an icy heart. I came to feel that the image I was seeing was the tip of an iceberg, the perceptible extremity of a huge power cell that existed mainly in dimensions beyond the range of mortal vision. I tried to give the impression of an interview to our observers by continuing to ask questions; but Stoner sat with his head down, his face hidden, and gave terse, disinterested replies.

The sun declined to the tops of the palms, the yellow paint of the houses took on a tawny hue, and—drained by the day-long alternation of weakness and recovery—I told Stoner I needed to rest. ''Tomorrow,'' he said without looking up. ''Come back tomorrow.''

''All right.'' I had no doubt that Tuu would be eager to go

on with the experiment. I stood and turned to leave; but then another question, a pertinent one, occurred to me. "If a ghost is a stage of growth," I said, "what's he grow into?"

He lifted his head, and I staggered back, terrified. His eyes were ablaze, even the whites winking with cold fire, as if nuggets of phosphorus were embedded in his skull.

"Tomorrow," he said again.

During the debriefing that followed, I developed a bad case of the shakes and experienced a number of other, equally unpleasant reactions; the places where Stoner had touched me seemed to have retained a chill, and the thought of that dead hand leeching me of energy was in retrospect thoroughly repellent. A good many of Tuu's subordinates, alarmed by Stoner's transformation, lobbied to break off the experiment. I did my best to soothe them, but I wasn't at all sure I wanted to return to the village. I couldn't tell whether Tuu noticed either my trepidation or the fact that I was being less than candid; he was too busy bringing his subordinates in line to question me in depth.

That night, when Fierman broke out his whiskey, I swilled it down as if it were an antidote to poison. To put it bluntly, I got shit-faced. Both Fierman and Witcover seemed warm human beings, old buddies, and our filthy yellow room with its flickering lamp took on the coziness of a cottage and hearth. The first stage of my drunk was maudlin, filled with self-recriminations over my past treatment of Stoner: I vowed not to shrink from helping him. The second stage . . . Well, once I caught Fierman gazing at me askance and registered that my behavior was verging on the manic. Laughing hysterically, talking like a speed freak. We talked about everything except Stoner, and I suppose it was inevitable that the conversation work itself around to the war and its aftermath. Dimly, I heard myself pontificating on a variety of related subjects. At one point Fierman asked what I thought of the Vietnam Memorial, and I told him I had mixed emotions.

"Why?" he asked.

"I go to the Memorial, man," I said, standing up from the table where we had all been sitting. "And I cry. You can't help but cryin', 'cause that"—I hunted for an appropriate image—"that black dividin' line between nowheres, that says it just right 'bout the war. It feels good to cry, to go public with grief and take your place with all the vets of the truly outstandin' wars.'' I swayed, righted myself. ''But the Memorial, the Unknown, the parades . . . basically they're bullshit.'' I started to wander around the room, realized that I had forgotten why I had stood and leaned against the wall.

''How you mean?'' asked Witcover, who was nearly as drunk as I was.

''Man,'' I said, ''it's a shuck! I mean ten goddamn years go by, and alla sudden there's this blast of media warmth and government-sponsored emotion. 'Welcome home, guys,' ever'body's sayin'. 'We're sorry we treated you so bad. Next time it's gonna be different. You wait and see.' '' I went back to the table and braced myself on it with both hands, staring blearily at Witcover: his tan looked blotchy. ''Hear that, man? 'Next time.' That's all it is. Nobody really gives a shit 'bout the vets. They're just pavin' the way for the next time.''

''I don't know,'' said Witcover. ''Seems to—''

''Right!'' I spanked the table with the flat of my hand. ''You don't know. You don't know shit 'bout it, so shut the fuck up!''

''Be cool,'' advised Fierman. ''Man's entitled to his 'pinion.''

I looked at him, saw a flushed, fat face with bloodshot eyes and a stupid reproving frown. ''Fuck you,'' I said. ''And fuck his 'pinion.'' I turned back to Witcover. ''Whaddya think, man? That there's this genuine breath of conscience sweepin' the land? Open your goddamn eyes! You been to the movies lately? Jesus Christ! Courageous grunts strikin' fear into the heart of the Red Menace! Miraculous one-man missions to save our honor. Huh! Honor!'' I took a long pull from the bottle. ''Those movies, they make war seem like a mystical opportunity. Well, man, when I was here it wasn't quite that way, y'know. It was leeches, fungus, the shits. It was searchin' in the weeds for your buddy's arm. It was lookin' into the snaky eyes of some whore you were bangin' and feelin' weird shit crawl along your spine and expectin' her head to do a Linda Blair three-sixty spin.'' I slumped into a chair and leaned close to Witcover. ''It was Mordor, man. Stephen King land. Horror. And now, now I look around at all these movies and monuments and crap, and it makes me wanna fuckin' puke to see what a noble hell it's turnin' out to be!"

I felt pleased with myself, having said this, and I leaned back, basking in a righteous glow. But Witcover was unimpressed. His face cinched into a scowl, and he said in a tight voice, "You're startin' to really piss me off, y'know."

"Yeah?" I said, and grinned. "How 'bout that?"

"Yeah, all you war-torn creeps, you think you got papers sayin' you can make an ass outta yourself and everybody else gotta say, 'Oh, you poor fucker! Give us more of your tortured wisdom!' "

Fierman muffled a laugh, and—rankled—I said, "That so?"

Witcover hunched his shoulders as if preparing for an off-tackle plunge. "I been listenin' to you guys for years, and you're alla goddamn same. You think you're owed something 'cause you got ground around in the political mill. Shit! I been in Salvador, Nicaragua, Afghanistan. Compared to those people, you didn't go through diddley. But you use what happened as an excuse for fuckin' up your lives . . . or for being assholes. Like you, man." He affected a macho-sounding bass voice. " 'I been in a war. I am an expert on reality.' You don't know how ridiculous you are."

"Am I?" I was shaking again, but with adrenaline not fear, and I knew I was going to hit Witcover. He didn't know it—he was smirking, his eyes flicking toward Fierman, seeking approval—and that in itself was a sufficient reason to hit him, purely for educational purposes: I had, you see, reached the level of drunkenness at which an amoral man such as myself understands his whimsies to be moral imperatives. But the real reason, the one that had begun to rumble inside me, was Stoner. All my fear, all my reactions thus far, had merely been tremors signaling an imminent explosion, and now, thinking about him nearby, old horrors were stirred up, and I saw myself walking in a napalmed ville rife with dead VC, crispy critters, and beside me this weird little guy named Fellowes who claimed he could read the future from their scorched remains and would point at a hexagramlike structure of charred bone and gristle and say, "That there means a bad moon on Wednesday," and claimed, too, that he could read the past from the blood of head wounds, and then I was leaning over this Canadian nurse, beautiful blond girl, disemboweled by a mine and somehow still alive, her organs dark and wet and pulsing, and somebody giggling, whispering about what he'd like to do, and then another scene that was whirled away so quickly, I could only make out the color of blood, and Witcover said something else, and a dead man was stretching out his hand to me and . . .

I nailed Witcover, and he flew sideways off the chair and rolled on the floor. I got to my feet, and Fierman grabbed me, trying to wrangle me away; but that was unnecessary, because all my craziness had been dissipated. "I'm okay now," I said, slurring the words, pushing him aside. He threw a looping punch that glanced off my neck, not even staggering me. Then Witcover yelled. He had pulled himself erect and was weaving toward me; an egg-shaped lump was swelling on his cheekbone. I laughed—he looked so puffed up with rage—and started for the door. As I went through it, he hit me on the back of the head. The blow stunned me a bit, but I was more amused than hurt; his fist had made a funny *bonk* sound on my skull, and that set me to laughing harder.

I stumbled between the houses, bouncing off walls, reeling out of control, and heard shouts . . . Vietnamese shouts. By the time I had regained my balance, I had reached the center of the village. The moon was almost full, pale yellow, its craters showing: a pitted eye in the black air. It kept shrinking and expanding, and—as it seemed to lurch farther off—I realized I had fallen and was lying flat on my back. More shouts. They sounded distant, a world away, and the moon had begun to spiral, to dwindle, like water being sucked down a drain. Jesus, I remember thinking just before I passed out, Jesus, how'd I get so drunk?

I'd forgotten Stoner's promise to tell me about the Land of Shades, but apparently he had not, for that night I had a dream in which I was Stoner. It was not that I thought I was him: I *was* him, prone to all his twitches, all his moods. I was walking in a pitch-dark void, possessed by a great hunger. Once this hunger might have been characterized as a yearning for the life I had lost, but it had been transformed into a lust for the life I might someday attain if I proved equal to the tests with which I was presented. That was all I knew of the Land of Shades—that it was a testing ground, less a place than a sequence of events. It was up to me to gain strength from the tests, to ease my hunger as best I could. I was ruled by this hunger, and it was my only wish to ease it.

Soon I spotted an island of brightness floating in the dark, and as I drew near, the brightness resolved into an old French plantation house fronted by tamarinds and rubber trees; sections of white stucco wall and a verandah and a red tile roof were visible between the trunks. Patterns of soft radiance overlaid the grounds, yet there were neither stars nor moon nor any source of light I could discern. I was not alarmed by this—such discrepancies were typical of the Land of Shades.

When I reached the trees, I paused, steeling myself for whatever lay ahead. Breezes sprang up to stir the leaves, and a sizzling chorus of crickets faded in from nowhere as if a recording of sensory detail had been switched on. Alert to every shift of shadow, I moved cautiously through the trees and up the verandah steps. Broken roof tiles crunched beneath my feet. Beside the door stood a bottom-out cane chair; the rooms, however, were devoid of furnishings, the floors dusty, the whitewash flaking from the walls. The house appeared to be deserted, but I knew I was not alone. There was a hush in the air, the sort that arises from a secretive presence. Even had I failed to notice this, I could scarcely have missed the scent of perfume. I had never tested against a woman before, and, excited by the prospect, I was tempted to run through the house and ferret her out. But this would have been foolhardy, and I continued at a measured pace.

At the center of the house lay a courtyard, a rectangular space choked with waist-high growths of jungle plants, dominated by a stone fountain in the shape of a stylized orchid. The woman was leaning against the fountain, and despite the grayish-green half-light—a light that seemed to arise from the plants—I could see she was beautiful. Slim and honey-colored, with falls of black hair spilling over the shoulders of her *ao dai*. She did not move or speak, but the casualness of her pose was an invitation. I felt drawn to her, and as I pushed through the foliage, the fleshy leaves clung to my thighs and groin, touches that seemed designed to provoke arousal. I stopped an arm's length away and studied her. Her features were of a feline delicacy, and in the fullness of her lower lip, the petulant set of her mouth, I detected a trace of French breeding. She stared at me with palpable sexual interest. It had not occurred to me that the confrontation might take place on a sexual level, yet now I was certain this would be the case. I had to restrain myself from initiating the contact: there are rigorous formalities that must be observed prior to each test. And besides, I wanted to savor the experience.

"I am Tuyet," she said in a voice that seemed to combine the qualities of smoke and music.

"Stoner," I said.

The names hung in the air like the echoes of two gongs.

She lifted her hand as if to touch me, but lowered it: she, too, was practicing restraint. "I was a prostitute," she said. "My home was Lai Khe, but I was an outcast. I worked the water points along Highway Thirteen."

It was conceivable, I thought, that I may have known her. While I had been laid up in An Loc, I'd frequented those water points: bomb craters that had been turned into miniature lakes by the rains and served as filling stations for the water trucks attached to the First Infantry. Every morning the whores and their mama sans would drive out to the water points in three-wheeled motorcycle trucks; with them would be vendors selling combs and pushbutton knives and rubbers that came wrapped in gold foil, making them look like those disks of chocolate you can buy in the States. Most of these girls were more friendly than the city girls, and knowing that Tuyet had been one of them caused me to feel an affinity with her.

She went on to tell me that she had gone into the jungle with an American soldier and had been killed by a sniper. I told her my story in brief and then asked what she had learned of the Land of Shades. This is the most rigorous formality: I had never met anyone with whom I had failed to exchange information.

"Once," Tuyet said, "I met an old man, a Cao Dai medium from Black Virgin Mountain, who told me he had been to a place where a pillar of whirling light and dust joined earth to sky. Voices spoke from the pillar, sometimes many at once, and from them he understood that all wars are merely reflections of a deeper struggle, of a demon breaking free. The demon freed by our war, he said, was very strong, very dangerous. We the dead had been recruited to wage war against him.''

I had been told a similar story by an NLF captain, and once, while crawling through a tunnel system, I myself had heard voices speaking from a skull half buried in the earth. But I had been too frightened to stay and listen. I related all this to Tuyet, and her response was to trail her fingers across my arm. My restraint, too, had frayed. I dragged her down into the thick foliage. It was as if we had been submerged in a sea of green light and fleshy stalks, as if the plantation house had vanished and we were adrift in an infinite vegetable depth where gravity had been replaced by some buoyant principle. I tore at her clothes, she at mine. Her *ao dai* shredded like crepe, and my fatigues came away in ribbons that dangled from her hooked fingers. Greedy for her, I pressed my mouth to her breasts. Her nipples looked black in contrast to her skin, and it seemed I could taste their blackness, tart and sour. Our breathing was hoarse, urgent, and the only other sound was the soft mulching of the leaves. With surprising strength, she pushed me onto my back and straddled my hips, guiding me inside her, sinking down until her buttocks were grinding against my thighs.

Her head flung back, she lifted and lowered herself. The leaves and stalks churned and intertwined around us as if they, too, were copulating. For a few moments my hunger was assuaged, but soon I noticed that the harder I thrust, the more fiercely she plunged, the less intense the sensations became. Though she gripped me tightly, the friction seemed to have been reduced. Frustrated, I dug my fingers into her plump hips and battered at her, trying to drive myself deeper. Then I squeezed one of her breasts and felt a searing pain in my palm. I snatched back my hand and saw that her nipple, both nipples, were twisting, elongating; I realized that they had been transformed into the heads of two black centipedes, and the artful movements of her internal muscles . . . they were too artful, too disconnectedly in motion. An instant later I felt that same searing pain in my cock and knew I was screwing myself into a nest of creatures like those protruding from her breasts. All her skin was rippling, reflecting the humping of thousands of centipedes beneath.

The pain was enormous, so much so that I thought my entire body must be glowing with it. But I did not dare fail this test, and I continued pumping into her, thrusting harder than ever. The leaves thrashed, the stalks thrashed as in a gale, and the green light grew livid. Tuyet began to scream—God knows what manner of pain I was causing her—and her screams completed a perverse circuit within me. I found I could channel my own pain into those shrill sounds. Still joined to her, I rolled atop her, clamped her wrists together and pinned them above her head. Her screams rang louder, inspiring me to greater efforts yet. Despite the centipedes tipping her breasts, or perhaps because of them, because of the grotesque juxtaposition of the sensual and the horrid, her beauty seemed to have been enhanced, and my mastery over her actually provided me a modicum of pleasure.

The light began to whiten, and looking off, I saw that we were being borne by an invisible current through—as I had imagined—an infinite depth of stalks and leaves. The stalks that lashed around us thickened far below into huge pale trunks with circular ribbing. I could not make out where they met the earth—if, indeed, they did—and they appeared to rise an equal height above. The light brightened further, casting the distant stalks in silhouette, and I realized we were drifting toward the source of the whiteness, beyond which would lie another test, another confrontation. I glanced at Tuyet. Her skin no longer displayed that obscene rippling, her nipples had reverted to normal. Pain was evolving into pleasure, but I knew it would be short-lived, and I tried to resist the current, to hold onto pain, because even pain was preferable to the hunger I would soon experience. Tuyet clawed my back, and I felt the first dissolute rush of my orgasm. The current was irresistible. It flowed through my blood, my cells. It was part of me, or rather I was part of it. I let it move me, bringing me to completion.

Gradually the whipping of the stalks subsided to a pliant swaying motion. They parted for us, and we drifted through their interstices as serenely as a barge carved to resemble a coupling of two naked figures. I found I could not disengage from Tuyet, that the current enforced our union, and resigned to this, I gazed around, marveling at the vastness of this vegetable labyrinth and the strangeness of our fates. Beams of white light shined through the stalks, the brightness growing so profound that I thought I heard in it a roaring; and as my consciousness frayed, I saw myself reflected in Tuyet's eyes—a ragged dark creature wholly unlike my own self-image—and wondered for the thousandth time who had placed us in this world, who had placed these worlds in us.

Other dreams followed, but they were ordinary, the dreams of an ordinarily anxious, ordinarily drunken man, and it was the memory of this first dream that dominated my waking moments. I didn't want to wake because—along with a headache and other symptoms of hangover—I felt incredibly weak, incapable of standing and facing the world. Muzzy-headed, I ignored the reddish light prying under my eyelids and tried to remember more of the dream. Despite Stoner's attempts to appear streetwise, despite the changes I had observed in him, he had been at heart an innocent and it was difficult to accept that the oddly formal, brutally sexual protagonist of the dream had been in any way akin to him. Maybe, I thought, recalling Tuu's theory of ghosts, maybe that was the quality that had died in Stoner: his innocence. I began once again to suffer guilt feelings over my hatred of him, and, preferring a hangover to that, I propped myself on one elbow and opened my eyes.

I doubt more than a second or two passed before I sprang to my feet, hangover forgotten, electrified with fear; but in that brief span the reason for my weakness was made plain. Stoner was sitting close to where I had been lying, his hand outstretched to touch me, head down . . . exactly as he had sat the previous day. Aside from his pose, however, very little about him was the same.

The scene was of such complexity that now, thinking back on it, it strikes me as implausible that I could have noticed its every detail; yet I suppose that its power was equal to its complexity and thus I did not so much see it as it was imprinted on my eyes. Dawn was a crimson smear fanning across the lower sky, and the palms stood out blackly against it, their fronds twitching in the breeze like spiders impaled on pins. The ruddy light gave the rutted dirt of the street the look of a trough full of congealed blood. Stoner was motionless—that is to say, he didn't move his limbs, his head, or shift his position; but his image was pulsing, swelling to half again its normal size and then deflating, all with the rhythm of steady breathing. As he expanded, the cold white fire blazing from his eyes would spread in cracks that veined his entire form; as he contracted, the cracks would disappear and for a moment he would be—except for his eyes—the familiar figure I had known. It seemed that his outward appearance—his fatigues and helmet, his skin—was a shell from which some glowing inner man was attempting to break free. Grains of dust were whirling up from the ground beside him, more and more all the time: a miniature cyclone wherein he sat calm and ultimately distracted, the likeness of a warrior monk whose meditations had borne fruit.

Shouts behind me. I turned and saw Fierman, Tuu, Witcover, and various of the gooks standing at the edge of the village. Tuu beckoned to me, and I wanted to comply, to run, but I wasn't sure I had the strength. And, too, I didn't think Stoner would let me. His power surged around me, a cold windy voltage that whipped my clothes and set static charges crackling in my hair. "Turn it off!" I shouted, pointing at the tin-roofed building. They shook their heads, shouting in return. ". . . can't," I heard, and something about ". . . feedback."

Then Stoner spoke. "Puleo," he said. His voice wasn't loud but it was all-encompassing. I seemed to be inside it, balanced on a tongue of red dirt, within a throat of sky and jungle and yellow stone. I turned back to him. Looked into his eyes . . . fell into them, into a world of cold brilliance where a thousand fiery forms were materialized and dispersed every second, forms both of such beauty and hideousness that their effect on me, their beholder, was identical, a confusion of terror and exaltation. Whatever they were, the forms of Stoner's spirit, his potentials, or even of his thoughts, they were in their momentary life more vital and consequential than I could ever hope to be. Compelled by them, I walked over to him. I must have been afraid—I could feel wetness on my thighs and realized that my bladder had emptied—but he so dominated me that I knew only the need to obey. He did not stand, yet with each expansion his image would loom up before my eyes and I would stare into that dead face seamed by rivulets of molten diamond, its expression losing coherence, features splitting apart. Then he would shrink, leaving me gazing dumbly down at the top of his helmet. Dust stung my eyelids, my cheeks.

"What . . ." I began, intending to ask what he wanted; but before I could finish, he seized my wrist. Ice flowed up my arm, shocking my heart, and I heard myself . . . not screaming. No, this was the sound life makes leaving the body, like the squealing of gas released from a balloon that's half pinched shut.

Within seconds, drained of strength, I slumped to the ground, my vision reduced to a darkening fog. If he had maintained his hold much longer, I'm sure I would have died . . . and I was resigned to the idea. I had no weapon with which to fight him. But then I realized that the cold had receded from my limbs. Dazed, I looked around, and when I spotted him, I tried to stand, to run. Neither my arms nor legs would support me, and—desperate—I flopped on the red dirt, trying to crawl to safety; but after that initial burst of panic, the gland that governed my reactions must have overloaded, because I stopped crawling, rolled onto my back and stayed put, feeling stunned, weak, transfixed by what I saw. Yet not in the least afraid.

Stoner's inner man, now twice human-size, had broken free and was standing at the center of the village, some twenty feet off: a bipedal silhouette through which it seemed you could look forever into a dimension of fire and crystal, like a hole burned in the fabric of the world. His movements were slow, tentative, as if he hadn't quite adapted to his new form, and penetrating him, arcing through the air from the tin-roofed building, their substance flowing toward him, were what appeared to be thousands of translucent wires, the structures of the fields. As I watched, they began to glow with Stoner's blue-white-diamond color, their substance to reverse its flow and pour back toward the building, and to emit a bass hum. Dents popped in the tin roof, the walls bulged inward, and with a grinding noise, a narrow fissure forked open in the earth beside it. The glowing wires grew brighter and brighter, and the building started to crumple, never collapsing, but—as if giant hands were pushing at it from every direction—compacting with terrible slowness until it had been squashed to perhaps a quarter of its original height. The hum died away. A fire broke out in the wreckage, pale flames leaping high and winnowing into black smoke.

Somebody clutched my shoulder, hands hauled me to my feet. It was Tuu and one of his soldiers. Their faces were knitted by lines of concern, and that concern rekindled my fear. I clawed at them, full of gratitude, and let them hustle me away. We took our places among the other observers, the smoking building at our backs, all gazing at the yellow houses and the burning giant in their midst.

The air around Stoner had become murky, turbulent, and this turbulence spread to obscure the center of the village. He stood unmoving, while small dust devils kicked up at his heels and went zipping about like a god's zany pets. One of the houses caved in with a *whump,* and pieces of yellow concrete began to lift from the ruins, to float toward Stoner; drawing near him, they acquired some of his brightness, glowing in their own right, and then vanished into the turbulence. Another house imploded, and the same process was initiated. The fact that all this was happening in dead silence—except for the caving in of the houses—made it seem even more eerie and menacing than if there had been sound.

The turbulence eddied faster and faster, thickening, and at last a strange vista faded in from the dark air, taking its place the way the picture melts up from the screen of an old television set. Four or five minutes must have passed before it became completely clear, and then it seemed sharper and more in focus than did the jungle and the houses, more even than the blazing figure who had summoned it: an acre-sized patch of hell or heaven or something in between, shining through the dilapidated structures and shabby colors of the ordinary, paling them. Beyond Stoner lay a vast forested plain dotted with fires . . . or maybe they weren't fires but some less chaotic form of energy, for though they gave off smoke, the flames maintained rigorous, stylized shapes, showing like red fountains and poinsettias and other shapes yet against the poisonous green of the trees. Smoke hung like a gray pall over the plain, and now and again beams of radiance—all so complexly figured, they appeared to be pillars of crystal—would shoot up from the forest into the grayness and resolve into a burst of light; and at the far limit of the plain, beyond a string of ragged hills, the dark sky would intermittently flash reddish orange as if great batteries of artillery were homing in upon some target there.

I had thought that Stoner would set forth at once into this other world, but instead he backed a step away and I felt despair for him, fear that he wouldn't seize his opportunity to escape. It may seem odd that I still thought of him as Stoner, and it may be that prior to that moment I had forgotten his human past; but now, sensing his trepidation, I understood that what enlivened this awesome figure was some scrap of soul belonging to the man-child I once had known. Silently, I urged him on. Yet he continued to hesitate.

It wasn't until someone tried to pull me back that I realized I was moving toward Stoner. I shook off whomever it was, walked to the edge of the village and called Stoner's name. I didn't really expect him to acknowledge me, and I'm not clear as to what my motivations were: maybe it was just that since I had come this far with him, I didn't want my efforts wasted. But I think it was something more, some old loyalty resurrected, one I had denied while he was alive.

"Get outta here!" I shouted. "Go on! Get out!"

He turned that blind, fiery face toward me, and despite its featurelessness, I could read therein the record of his solitude, his fears concerning its resolution. It was, I knew, a final sending. I sensed again his emptiness, but it wasn't so harrowing and hopeless as before; in it there was a measure of determination, of purpose, and, too, a kind of . . . I'm tempted to say gratitude, but in truth it was more a simple acknowledgment, like the wave of a hand given by one workman to another after the completion of a difficult task.

"Go." I said it softly, the way you'd speak when urging a child to take his first step, and Stoner walked away.

For a few moments, though his legs moved, he didn't appear to be making any headway; his figure remained undiminished by distance. There was a tension in the air, an almost impalpable disturbance that quickly evolved into a heated pulse. One of the banana trees burst into flames, its leaves shriveling; a second tree ignited, a third, and soon all those trees close to the demarcation of that other world were burning like green ceremonial candles. The heat intensified, and the veils of dust that blew toward me carried a stinging residue of that heat; the sky for hundreds of feet above rippled as with the effects of an immense conflagration.

I stumbled back, tripped and fell heavily. When I recovered I saw that Stoner was receding, that the world into which he was traveling was receding with him, or rather seeming to fold, to bisect and collapse around him: it looked as if that plain dotted with fires were painted on a curtain, and as he pushed forward, the fabric was drawn with him, its painted distances becoming foreshortened, its perspectives exaggerated and surreal, molding into a tunnel that conformed to his shape. His figure shrank to half its previous size, and then—some limit reached, some barrier penetrated—the heat died away, its dissipation accompanied by a seething hiss, and Stoner's white fire began to shine brighter and brighter, his form eroding in brightness. I had to shield my eyes, then shut them; but even so, I could see the soundless explosion that followed through my lids, and for several minutes I could make out its vague afterimage. A blast of wind pressed me flat, hot at first, but blowing colder and colder, setting my teeth to chattering. At last this subsided, and on opening my eyes, I found that Stoner had vanished, and where the plain had been now lay a wreckage of yellow stone and seared banana trees, ringed by a few undamaged houses on the perimeter.

The only sound was the crackle of flames from the tin-roofed building. Moments later, however, I heard a patter of applause. I looked behind me: the gooks were all applauding Tuu, who was smiling and bowing like the author of a successful play. I was shocked at their reaction. How could they be concerned with accolades? Hadn't they been dazzled, as I had, their humanity diminished by the mystery and power of Stoner's metamorphosis? I went over to them, and drawing near, I overheard an officer congratulate Tuu on "another triumph." It took me a while to register the significance of those words, and when I did I pushed through the group and confronted Tuu.

" 'Another triumph'?" I said.

He met my eyes, imperturbable. "I wasn't aware you spoke our language, Mr. Puleo."

"You've done this before," I said, getting angry. "Haven't you?"

"Twice before." He tapped a cigarette from a pack of Marlboros; an officer rushed to light it. "But never with an American spirit."

"You coulda killed me!" I shouted, lunging for him. Two soldiers came between us, menacing me with their rifles.

Tuu blew out a plume of smoke that seemed to give visible evidence of his self-satisfaction. "I told you it was a risk," he said. "Does it matter that I knew the extent of the risk and you did not? You were in no greater danger because of that. We were prepared to take steps if the situation warranted."

"Don't bullshit me! You couldn't have done nothin' with Stoner!"

He let a smile nick the corners of his mouth.

"You had no right," I said. "You—"

Tuu's face hardened. "We had no right to mislead you? Please, Mr. Puleo. Between our peoples, deception is a tradition."

I fumed, wanting to get at him. Frustrated, I slugged my thigh with my fist, spun on my heel and walked off. The two soldiers caught up with me and blocked my path. Furious, I swatted at their rifles; they disengaged their safeties and aimed at my stomach.

"If you wish to be alone," Tuu called, "I have no objection to you taking a walk. We have tests to complete. But please keep to the road. A car will come for you."

Before the soldiers could step aside, I pushed past them.

"Keep to the road, Mr. Puleo!" In Tuu's voice was more than a touch of amusement. "If you recall, we're quite adept at tracking."

Anger was good for me; it kept my mind off what I had seen. I wasn't ready to deal with Stoner's evolution. I wanted to consider things in simple terms: a man I had hated had died to the world a second time and I had played a part in his release, a part in which I had no reason to take pride or bear shame, because I had been manipulated every step of the way. I was so full of anger, I must have done the first mile in under fifteen minutes, the next in not much more. By then the sun had risen above the treeline and I had worked up a sweat. Insects buzzed; monkeys screamed. I slowed my pace and turned my head from side to side as I went, as if I were walking point again. I had the idea my own ghost was walking with me, shifting around inside and burning to get out on its own.

After an hour or so I came to the temporary housing that had been erected for the populace of Cam Le: thatched huts; scrawny dogs slinking and chickens pecking; orange peels, palm litter, and piles of shit in the streets. Some old men smoking pipes by a cookfire blinked at me. Three girls carrying plastic jugs giggled, ran off behind a hut and peeked back around the corner.

Vietnam.

I thought about the way I'd used to sneer the word. 'Nam, I'd say. Viet-fucking-nam! Now it was spoken proudly, printed in Twentieth Century-Fox monolithic capitals, brazen with hype. Perhaps between those two extremes was a mode of expression that captured the ordinary reality of the place, the poverty and peacefulness of this village; but if so, it wasn't accessible to me.

Some of the villagers were coming out of their doors to have a look at the stranger. I wondered if any of them recognized me. Maybe, I thought, chuckling madly, maybe if I bashed a couple on the head and screamed "Number Ten VC!" maybe then they'd remember.

I suddenly felt tired and empty, and I sat down by the road to wait. I was so distracted, I didn't notice at first that a number of flies had mistaken me for a new and bigger piece of shit and were orbiting me, crawling over my knuckles. I flicked them away, watched them spiral off and land on other parts of my body. I got into controlling their patterns of flight, seeing if I could make them all congregate on my left hand, which I kept still. Weird shudders began passing through my chest, and the vacuum inside my head filled with memories of Stoner, his bizarre dream, his terrible Valhalla. I tried to banish them, but they stuck there, replaying themselves over and over. I couldn't order them, couldn't derive any satisfaction from them. Like the passage of a comet, Stoner's escape from Cam Le had been a trivial cosmic event, causing momentary awe and providing a few more worthless clues to the nature of the absolute, but offering no human solutions.

Nothing consequential had changed for me: I was as fucked up as ever, as hard-core disoriented. The buzzing sunlight grew hotter and hotter; the flies' dance quickened in the rippling air.

At long last a dusty car with a gook corporal at the wheel pulled up beside me. Fierman and Witcover were in back, and Witcover's eye was discolored, swollen shut. I went around to the passenger side, opened the front door and heard behind me a spit-filled, explosive sound. Turning, I saw that a kid of about eight or nine had jumped out of hiding to ambush me. He had a dirt-smeared belly that popped from the waist of his ragged shorts, and he was aiming a toy rifle made of sticks. He shot me again, jiggling the gun to simulate automatic fire. Little monster with slit black eyes. Staring daggers at me, thinking I'd killed his daddy. He probably would have loved it if I had keeled over, clutching my chest; but I wasn't in the mood. I pointed my finger, cocked the thumb and shot him down like a dog.

He stared meanly and fired a third time: this was serious business, and he wanted me to die. "Row-nal Ray-gun," he said, and pretended to spit.

I just laughed and climbed into the car. The gook corporal engaged the gears and we sped off into a boil of dust and light, as if—like Stoner—we were passing through a metaphysical barrier between worlds. My head bounced against the back of the seat, and with each impact I felt that my thoughts were clearing, that a poisonous sediment was being jolted loose and flushed from my bloodstream. Thick silence welled from the rear of the car, and not wanting to ride with hostiles all the way to Saigon, I turned to Witcover and apologized for having hit him. Pressure had done it to me, I told him. That, and bad memories of a bad time. His features tightened into a sour knot and he looked out the window, wholly unforgiving. But I refused to allow his response to disturb me—let him have his petty hate, his grudge, for whatever good it would do him—and I turned away to face the violent green sweep of the jungle, the great troubled rush of the world ahead, with a heart that seemed lighter by an ounce of anger, by one bitterness removed. To the end of that passion, at least, I had become reconciled.

Kate Wilhelm

Kate Wilhelm came to prominence in the late 1960s and early 1970s with brilliant, psychologically probing stories, such as "Somerset Dreams," "The Chosen," "The Fusion Bomb," "On the Road to Honeyville," "The Encounter," "The Infinity Box," "The Funeral," and "The Planners," for which she won a Nebula award in 1968. She won another Nebula for her novel *Where Late the Sweet Birds Sang.* She has also won the Hugo award and the Jupiter Award. Her stories, many of which appeared in Damon Knight's influential *Orbit* series, have been compared with the best short fiction of Shirley Jackson and Katherine Anne Porter. Wilhelm is also a consummate novelist, and her novels—like many of her stories—merge the concerns of science fiction and mainstream fiction. They include *Let the Fire Fall, Margaret and I, The Clewiston Test, Welcome Chaos, Juniper Time, More Bitter Than Death, City of Cain, Fault Lines,* and *Huysman's Pets.* Many of her short stories have been collected in *The Mile Long Space Ship, The Downstairs Room, The Infinity Box,* and *Somerset Dreams and Other Fiction.* She is also the editor of the anthologies *Nebula Award Stories 9* and *Clarion SF.* Wilhelm was co-director of the Milford Science Fiction Writers' Conference from 1963 to 1972 and has lectured at Tulane University and the Clarion Science Fiction Writers' Conference.

The Village

by Kate Wilhelm

Mildred Carey decided to walk to the post office early, before the sun turned the two blocks into a furnace. "They've done something to the weather," she said to her husband, packing his three sandwiches and thermos of lemonade. "Never used to be this hot this early."

"It'll get cooler again. Always does."

She followed him to the door and waved as he backed out of the drive. The tomato plants she had set out the day before were wilted. She watered them, then started to walk slowly to town. With a feeling of satisfaction she noticed that Mrs. Mareno's roses had black spot. Forcing the blooms with too much fertilizer just wasn't good for them.

Mike Donatti dozed as he awaited orders to regroup and start the search-and-clear maneuver. Stilwell nudged him. "Hey, Mike, you been over here before?"

"Nope. One fuckin' village is just like the others. Mud or dust. That's the only fuckin' difference."

Stilwell was so new that he was sunburned red. Everyone else in the company was burned black. "Man, could we pass," they liked to say to Latimore, who couldn't.

Mr. Peters was sweeping the sidewalk before the market. "Got some good fresh salami," he said. "Ed made it over the weekend."

"You sure Ed made it, not Buz? When Buz makes it, he uses too much garlic. What's he covering up is what I want to know."

"Now, Miz Carey, you know he's not covering up. Some folks like it hot and strong."

"I'll stop back by after I get the mail."

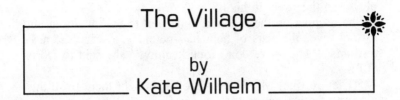

The four Henry children were already out in the street,

filthy, chasing each other randomly. Their mother was not in sight. Mildred Carey pursed her lips. Her Mark never had played in the street in his life.

She dropped in the five-and-dime, not to buy anything but to look over the flats of annuals—petunias, marigolds, nasturtiums. ''They sure don't look healthy,'' she said to Doris Offinger.

''They're fine, Miz Carey. Brother bought them fresh this morning from Connor's down at Midbury. You know Connor's has good stock.''

''How's Larry getting along? Still in the veterans' hospital at Lakeview?''

''Yes. He'll be out in a couple of weeks, I guess.'' Doris' pretty face remained untroubled. ''They've got such good doctors down there, I hate to see him get so far from them all, but he wants to come home.''

''How can these people stand this heat all the time?'' Stilwell said after a moment. The sun wasn't up yet, but it was eighty-six degrees, humidity near one hundred percent.

''People, he says. Boy, ain't you even been briefed? People can't stand it, that's the first clue.'' Mike sighed and sat up. He lighted a cigarette. ''Boy, back home in August. You know the hills where I come from are cold, even in August?''

''Where's that?''

''Vermont. I can remember plenty of times it snowed in August. Nights under a blanket.''

''Well, he can help out here in the store. With his pension and the store and all, the two of you are set, aren't you? Isn't that Tessie Hetherton going in Peters' market?''

''I didn't notice her. Did you want one of those flats, Miz Carey?''

''No. They aren't healthy. Connor's must have culled the runts and set *them* out.'' She stood in the doorway squinting to see across the way to Peters' market. ''I'm sure it was. And she told me she's too arthritic to do any more housework. I'll just go talk to her.''

''I don't think she will, though. Miz Avery wanted her on Wednesdays and she said no. You know Mr. Hetherton's got a job? With the paper mill.''

''Shtt. That won't last. They'll pay off a few of last winter's bills and then he'll start to complain about his liver or something and she'll be hustling for work. I know that man." She left the store without looking back, certain that Doris would be eyeing the price tags of the flats. "You take care of yourself, Doris. You're looking peaked. You should get out in the sun.

"Mrs. Hetherton, you're looking fit again," Mildred Carey said, cornering the woman as she emerged from the store.

"Warm weather's helped some."

"Look, can you possibly come over Thursday morning? You know the Garden Club meets this week, and I can't possibly get ready without some help."

"Well, I just don't know . . . Danny's dead set against my going out to work again."

"But they're going to have to close down the mill. And then where will he be?"

"Close it down? Why? Who says?"

"It's been in the papers for weeks now. All those dead fish, and the stink. You know that committee came up and took samples and said they're the ones responsible. And they can't afford to change over the whole process. They're going to move instead."

"Oh, that. Danny said don't hold your breath. They're making a study, and then they'll have to come up with a plan and have it studied, and all in all it's going to take five years or even more before it all comes to a head."

"Hm. Another big kill and the Department of Health . . ."

Mrs. Hetherton laughed and Mildred Carey had to smile too. "Well, anyway, can you come over just this time? For this one meeting?"

"Sure, Miz Carey. Thursday morning? But only half a day."

The school bus turned the corner and rolled noisily down the broad new street. The two women watched it out of sight. "Have you seen the Tomkins boys lately?" Mildred Carey asked. "Hair down to here."

"Winona says they're having someone in to talk about drugs. I asked her point blank if there are drugs around here and she said no, but you never can tell. The kids won't tell you nothing."

"Well, I just thank God that Mark is grown up and out of it all."

"He's due home soon now, isn't he?"

"Seven weeks. Then off to college in the fall. I told him that he's probably safer over there than at one of the universities right now." They laughed and moved apart. "See you Thursday."

"Listen, Mike, when you get back, you'll go through New York, won't you? Give my mother a call, will you? Just tell her . . ."

"What? That you got jungle rot the first time out and it's gone to your brain?"

"Just call her. Say I'm fine. That's all. She'll want to have you over for dinner, or take you to a good restaurant, something. Say you don't have time. But it'd mean a lot to her to have you call."

"Sure. Sure. Come on, we're moving."

They walked for two hours without making contact. The men were straggling along in two uneven columns at the sides of the road. The dirt road was covered with recent growth, no mines. The temperature was going to hit one hundred any second. Sweat and dirt mixed on faces, arms, muddy sweat trickled down shirts.

The concrete street was a glare now. Heat rose in patterns that shifted and vanished and rose again. Mildred Carey wondered if it hadn't been a mistake to rebuild the street, take out the maples and make it wide enough for the traffic that they predicted would be here in another year or two. She shrugged and walked more briskly toward the post office. That wasn't her affair. Her husband, who should know, said it was necessary for the town to grow. After being in road construction for twenty-five years, he should know. Fran Marple and Dodie Wilson waved to her from outside the coffee shop. Fran looked overdue and miserable. Last thing she needed was to go in the coffee shop and have pastry. Mildred Carey smiled at them and went on.

Claud Emerson was weighing a box for Bill Stokes. Bill leaned against the counter smoking, flicking ashes on the floor. "Don't like it here, get out, that's what I say. Goddamn kids with their filthy clothes and dirty feet. Bet they had marijuana up there. Should have called the troopers, that's what I should have done."

"They was on state land, Bill. You had no call to run them off."

"They didn't know that. You think I'm going to let them plop themselves down right outside my front door? Let 'em find somewhere else to muck about."

Claud Emerson stamped the box. "One seventy-two."

Stilwell and Mike were following Laski, Berat, and Humboldt. Berat was talking.

"You let it stick out, see, and come at them with your M-16 and you know what they watch! Man, they never seen nothing like it! Scared shitless by it. Tight! Whooee! Tight and hot!"

Stilwell looked as if he saw a green monster. Mike laughed and lit another cigarette. The sun was almost straight up when the lieutenant called for a break. He and Sergeant Durkins consulted a map and Humboldt swore at great length. "They've got us lost, the bastards. This fuckin' road ain't even on their fuckin' map."

Mildred Carey looked through the bills and advertising in her box, saving the letter from Mark for last. She always read them twice, once very quickly to be sure that he was all right, then again, word for word, pausing to pronounce the strange syllables aloud. She scanned the scrawled page, then replaced it in its envelope to be reread at home with coffee.

Bill Stokes' jeep roared outside the door, down the street to screech to a halt outside the feed store.

Mildred shook her head. "He's a mean man."

"Yep," Claud Emerson said. "Always was, always will be, I reckon. Wonder where them kids spent the night after he chased them."

Durkins sent out two scouts and the rest of them waited, cursing and sweating. A helicopter throbbed over them, drowned out their voices, vanished. The scouts returned.

Durkins stood up. "Okay. About four miles. The gooks are there, all right. Or will be again tonight. It's a free-fire zone, and our orders are to clean it out. Let's go."

Loud voices drifted across the street and they both looked toward the sound. "Old Dave's at it again," Claud Emerson said, frowning. "He'll have himself another heart attack, that's what."

"What good does arguing do anyway? Everybody around

here knows what everybody else thinks and nobody ever changes. Just what good does it do?'' She stuffed her mail into her purse. ''Just have to do the best you can. Do what's right and hope for the best.'' She waved good-bye.

She still had to pick up cottage cheese and milk. ''Maybe I'll try that new salami,'' she said to Peters. ''Just six slices. Don't like to keep it more than a day. Just look at those tomatoes! Sixty-nine a pound! Mr. Peters, that's a disgrace!''

''Field-grown, Miz Carey. Up from Georgia. Shipping costs go up and up, you know.'' He sliced the salami carefully, medium thick.

A new tension was in them now and the minesweepers walked gingerly on the road carpeted with green sprouts. Stilwell coughed again and again, a meaningless bark of nervousness. Durkins sent him to the rear, then sent Mike back with him. ''Keep an eye on the fuckin' bastard,'' he said. Mike nodded and waited for the rear to catch up with him. The two brothers from Alabama looked at him expressionlessly as they passed. They didn't mind the heat either, he thought, then spat. Stilwell looked sick.

''Is it a trap?'' he asked later.

''Who the fuck knows?''

''Company C walked into an ambush, didn't they?''

''They fucked up.''

Mildred Carey put her milk on the checkout counter alongside the cottage cheese. Her blue housedress was wet with perspiration under her arms and she could feel a spot of wetness on her back when her dress touched her skin. That Janice Samuels, she thought, catching a glimpse of the girl across the street, with those shorts and no bra, pretending she was dressing to be comfortable. Always asking about Mark. And him, asking about her in his letters.

''That's a dollar five,'' Peters said.

They halted again less than a mile from the village. The lieutenant called for the helicopters to give cover and to close off the area. Durkins sent men around the village to cover the road leading from it. There was no more they could do until the helicopters arrived. There were fields under cultivation off to the left.

''What if they're still there?'' Stilwell asked, waiting.

"You heard Durkins. This is a free-fire zone. They'll be gone."

"But what if they haven't?"

"We clear the area."

Stilwell wasn't satisfied, but he didn't want to ask the questions. He didn't want to hear the answers. Mike looked at him with hatred. Stilwell turned away and stared into the bushes at the side of the road.

"Let's go."

There was a deafening beating roar overhead and Mildred Carey and Peters went to the door to look. A green-and-brown helicopter hovered over the street, then moved down toward the post office, casting a grotesque shadow on the white concrete. Two more of the monstrous machines came over, making talk impossible. There was another helicopter to the north; their throb was everywhere, as if the clear blue sky had loosened a rain of them.

From the feed-store entrance Bill Stokes shouted something lost in the din. He raced to his jeep and fumbled for something under the seat. He straightened up holding binoculars and started to move to the center of the street, looking through them down the highway. One of the helicopters dipped, banked, and turned, and there was a spray of gunfire. Bill Stokes fell, jerked several times, then lay still. Now others began to run in the street, pointing and shouting and screaming. O'Neal and his hired hand ran to Bill Stokes and tried to lift him. Fran Marple and Dodie Wilson had left the coffee shop, were standing outside the door; they turned and ran back inside. A truck rounded the corner at the far end of the street and again the helicopter fired; the truck careened out of control into cars parked outside the bank. One of the cars was propelled through the bank windows. The thunder of the helicopters swallowed the sound of the crash and the breaking glass and the screams of the people who ran from the bank, some of them bleeding, clutching their heads or arms. Katharine Ormsby got to the side of the street, collapsed there. She crawled several more feet, then sprawled out and was still.

Mildred Carey backed into the store, her hands over her mouth. Suddenly she vomited. Peters was still on the sidewalk. She tried to close the door, but he flung it open, pushing her toward the rear of the store.

"Soldiers!" Peters yelled. "Soldiers coming!"

They went in low, on the sides of the road, ready for the explosion of gunfire, or the sudden eruption of a claymore. The helicopters' noise filled the world as they took up positions. The village was small, a hamlet. It had not been evacuated. The word passed through the company: slopes. They were there. A man ran into the street holding what could have been a grenade, or a bomb, or anything. One of the helicopters fired on him. There was a second burst of fire down the road and a vehicle burned. Now the company was entering the village warily. Mike cursed the slopes for their stupidity in staying.

Home was all Mildred Carey could think of. She had to get home. She ran to the back of the store and out to the alley that the delivery trucks used. She ran all the way home and, panting, with a pain in her chest, she rushed frantically through the house pulling down shades, locking doors. Then she went upstairs, where she could see the entire town. The soldiers were coming in crouched over, on both sides of the road, with their rifles out before them. She began to laugh suddenly; tears streaming, she ran downstairs again to fling open the door and shout.

"They're ours," she screamed toward the townspeople, laughing and crying all at once. "You fools, they're ours!"

Two of the khaki-clad GIs approached her, still pointing their guns at her. One of them said something, but she couldn't understand his words. "What are you doing here?" she cried. "You're American soldiers! What are you doing?"

The larger of the two grabbed her arm and twisted it behind her. She screamed and he pushed her toward the street. He spoke again, but the words were foreign to her. "I'm an American! For God's sake, this is America! What are you doing?" He hit her in the back with the rifle and she staggered and caught the fence to keep her balance. All down the street the people were being herded to the center of the highway. The soldier who had entered her house came out carrying her husband's hunting rifle, the shotgun, Mark's old .22. "Stop!" she shrieked at him. "Those are legal!" She was knocked down by the soldier behind her. He shouted at her and she opened her eyes to see him aiming the rifle at her head.

She scrambled to her feet and lurched forward to join the others in the street. She could taste blood and there was a stabbing pain in her jaw where teeth had been broken by her fall. A sergeant with a notebook was standing to one side. He kept making notations in it as more of the townspeople were forced from their houses and stores into the street.

Mike Donatti and Stilwell herded a raving old woman to the street; when she tried to grab a gun, Mike Donatti knocked her down and would have killed her then, but she was crying, obviously praying, and he simply motioned for her to join the others being rounded up.

The sun was high now, the heat relentless as the people were crowded closer together by each new addition. Some of the small children could be heard screaming even over the noise of the helicopters. Dodie Wilson ran past the crowd, naked from the waist down, naked and bleeding. A soldier caught her and he and another one carried her jerking and fighting into O'Neal's feed store. Her mouth was wide open in one long unheard scream. Old Dave ran toward the lieutenant, clutching at him, yelling at him in a high-pitched voice that it was the wrong town, damn fools, and other things that were lost. A smooth-faced boy hit him in the mouth, then again in the stomach, and when he fell moaning, he kicked him several times about the head. Then he shot him. Mildred Carey saw Janice Samuels being dragged by her wrists and she threw herself at the soldiers, who fought with her, their bodies hiding her from sight. They moved on, and she lay in a shining red pool that spread and spread. They tied Janice Samuels to the porch rail of Gordon's real-estate office, spread her legs open, and half a dozen men alternately raped and beat her. The sergeant yelled in the gibberish they spoke and the soldiers started to move the people as a lump toward the end of town.

Mike Donatti took up a post at the growing heap of weapons and watched the terrorized people. When the order came to move them out, he prodded and nudged, and when he had to, he clubbed them to make sure they moved as a unit. Some of them stumbled and fell, and if they didn't move again, they were shot where they lay.

The filthy Henry children were screaming for their mother. The biggest one, a girl with blond hair stringing down her back, darted away and ran down the empty street. The lieutenant motioned to the troops behind the group and after an appreciable pause there was a volley of shots and the child was lifted and for a moment flew. She rolled when she hit the ground again. Marjory Loomis threw herself down on top of her baby, and shots stilled both figures.

The people were driven to the edge of town, where the highway department had dug the ditch for a culvert that hadn't been laid yet. The sergeant closed his notebook and turned away. The firing started.

The men counted the weapons then, and searched the buildings methodically. Someone cut down a girl who had been tied to a rail. She fell in a heap. Fires were started. The lieutenant called for the helicopters to return to take them back to base camp.

Berat walked with his arm about Stilwell's shoulders, and they laughed a lot. Smoke from the fires began to spread horizontally, head high. Mike lighted another cigarette and thought about the cool green hills of Vermont and they waited to be picked up.

Dave Smeds

Before turning to writing, Dave Smeds made his living as a commercial artist. His first fiction sale was to Orson Scott Card's anthology *Dragons of Light* in 1980, and subsequently he has contributed stories to *Far Frontiers, Isaac Asimov's Science Fiction Magazine,* and various men's magazines. His first novel, *The Sorcery Within,* was published by Ace Books in 1985, and the sequel, entitled *The Talisman of Alemar,* has recently been sold. Smeds is currently working on a novel version of "Goats." He is married and lives in Cotati, California.

Goats

by
Dave Smeds

I

Even from the chopper, coming over from Maui, Kahoolawe looked dead. Rising low and squat across the Alalakeiki Channel, the island was eroding before our eyes, a brick-red plume streaming off the top of Mount Lua Makika, iron-oxide dust offered to the skies of the Pacific, a ghost of the eruptions that the volcano could no longer disgorge. For a few moments, I could see most of the island, from the steep cliffs along the eastern shore, over the central highland and its dramatic ravines, to the less rugged western peninsula, with its border of tide pools, beaches, and rocky islets. It was lifeless and stark—even the scattered masses that I knew to be vegetation seemed nothing more than blemishes on a cracked mound of clay. This was not Hawaii as mainlanders imagined it. Kahoolawe was a pockmark on the face of paradise: the island of Kanaloa, Brother Death.

I held my camera lens near the chopper window, trying to avoid the grease and dirt. "Ka-ho-o-LAH-vay," I said to myself. Like most of the place names in the islands, this one warped the lips of anyone accustomed to Indo-European languages. Sometimes I felt so inundated in vowels I thought my tongue would atrophy. I took three exposures.

Around me, the noise of the chopper was constant and inescapable. I scooted back into my place between cartons of C rations, trying to find that magic place that didn't make dents in my flesh or vibrate it off my bones. You could almost see the dust motes dance. I had finally, long miles from Kaneohe, realized what was wrong. It was the doors. Hueys weren't supposed to have doors—at least, not closed ones. I kept waiting for the belly-grabbing sensation of looking out over green waves of jungle, knowing nothing but atmosphere separated me from hillsides where the last slick through had taken unfriendly fire; and instead, all I saw was fuselage and cargo and two grunts in freshly laundered fatigues. This was the States, I reminded myself. Helicopters had doors here. Without them, Kahoolawe's winds would have blown us out in the first three minutes. The trades. Set out a sail and you'd end up in Tahiti, three thousand miles due south.

Beside me, Potter was turning green. I could just imagine hot, yellow puke rolling around under my boots, the smell in the enclosed space reaming my nostrils like oily fingers. Nothing can bring up my own stomach like the odor when somebody else loses it, just like a school-bus chain reaction. I took another hit off my joint: preventive measure.

Potter had one of those baby faces that made you wonder if he had really been old enough when the recruiter nabbed his ass. He was still soft-cheeked, still not quite in need of a razor daily, pimples on his face and neck—scrotum head, like a recruit, although in actual fact he was a lance corporal. Potter thought being an E-3 made him a man. He wouldn't admit the rough ride was getting to him. I'd given him some dimenhydrinate earlier, and practically had to open his jaw for him to get him to take it.

"We're almost there," I told him, squeaky-voiced from trying to keep in the marijuana. He didn't hear. You had to yell your lungs out to get above the racket. I held out the joint.

He shook his head. Automatic gesture. Get thee behind me Satan.

Jones accepted, though, reaching across Potter's lap, toking once, and transferring the remains to his roach clip. We shared a knowing smile. When Potter glanced at me I pretended I was tracking a butterfly up out of sight. Jones was one of the better breaks about this trip. He and I had been on the last excursion. He was big and black, with lips like Mick Jagger's—sheer joy watching him sucking a reefer—looking just as ugly, dumb, and mean as you'd expect of a Marine Corps private, but once you caught the twinkle in his eyes, you knew that was camouflage. He'd been around. Dumb he wasn't. He knew that the principal purpose for going to Kahoolawe was to fuck around.

It was my sixth trip. The others had been weekenders, routine training runs for the pilots out of Kaneohe. This time we had ships coming through. The other corpsmen at the base hospital felt sorry for me: no nice little brown Hawaiian pussy to chase during off-duty hours, no bars, no television. I was laughing behind my teeth the whole time. Kahoolawe was a whole different trip; a man couldn't beg, borrow, or steal the same experiences on Oahu.

We were part of an ANGLCO squad. Air and Naval Gunfire Liaison Company. Kahoolawe is one of the USA's biggest target ranges. Sooner or later, the gun crews on every ship headed for Vietnam, and every pilot stationed in the islands or on an aircraft carrier, would put a piece of this rock in their sights. Every year a third of the ship crews were green men barely out of basic training; every year pilots had to be recertified. No one who handles the big stuff wants a virgin next to him going into a war zone; this was where the boys lost their cherries. Kahoolawe was forty-five square miles of clay pigeon.

ANGLCOs are the forward observation teams that coordinate the bombing, shelling, and strafing of the island. Usually there were only five or six of us; this time, there were nine. Most of the added personnel were trainees learning how to be forward observers. The regulars included the head forward observer, one or two shit-detail men like Jones, a corpsman or medic like me, and the bomb disposal people.

That was the official story. It's true we had work to do. But the work didn't last forever. I was churning out the hormones so fast the joint didn't even cool me out. Vacation time. Disneyland.

Jones leaned over until his face was right next to Potter's—deep brown classic Negro features against freckled, crew-cut Kansas redneck. The lance corporal didn't notice at first; he was too busy growing pale and staring wanly in indeterminate directions. Jones hung there, smiling, teeth wide and brilliantly white, looking like a beast of prey waiting at its leisure for the moment to pounce. Finally Potter turned and their eyes locked. Jones still didn't say anything, just smiled. Suddenly, violently, Potter pushed him away.

"Get outta here, Jones!" he yelled.

Jones laughed. So did I. This was one of those times when I could see through his facade. Jones could play it to the hilt, right down to the black grammar and the jive. At times I had been convinced he was nothing more than an obnoxious nigger. Then he'd do something like this. Crazy-ass therapy, but it had worked. Potter was so red in the face that he wasn't remembering to be nauseated.

Soon the whine of the engine changed pitch. "What's that?" Potter shouted.

"Get ready," I said. "We're going in." We had to grab for handholds as we hit hard air. Our bellies suddenly dropped out. We heard a crunch from the back of the Huey. I could see the senior pilot jabbering instructions to his companion. We rose again, the floor tilting at an odd angle. Out the window, we caught glimpses of hillsides and billows of dust from the Huey's backwash. My knuckles were white where I gripped the safety strap.

This time the drop was smoother. We seemed to come to a stop, though the chopper's rotors were beating furiously and the whole craft shuddered with each gust of wind. Irregular thuds came from the rear, some not so gentle. The floor was slanted, pilots on the high side, tail section low.

It was time.

Jones grabbed the handle of one door; I got the other one. We slid them back simultaneously, opening up both sides of the Huey. Instantly dust enveloped us, sucked up by the rotors. Outside it seemed like the ground was alive, churned by our artificial whirlwind. It gave everything an eerie lack of solidity that made it hard just to keep our balance. The fuselage wobbled underneath us every moment. I knew that from the cockpit all the pilots could see was a whiteout.

We tossed our gear out first—packs, cartons, blankets, and three very heavy fifty-five-gallon drums. Once the cargo deck was clear, the pilots moved us a few yards to open ground. I joined Potter at the opening.

"Jump!" I yelled.

He stared at the rippling landscape underneath us. "But—"

I pushed. As soon as I could be sure where he was going to end up, I followed. The earth was deceptively hard under its blanket of dust. I was filthy in an instant, spitting out grit and trying to keep more of the same out of my eyes. The back-wash whipped my clothes until I thought it would raise bruises, bathing me in the sweet kerosene smell of turbine exhaust. In a few seconds, but seeming much longer, the chopper noise faded to a more tolerable, more distant *klap-klap-klap*.

The landing zone was a raked circle of dirt, marked by whitewashed chunks of rock. A road led off across stark, dry hills toward the tiny base camp. The ocean was to the west, several hundred yards away. This was it. LZ Kahoolawe. Follow the yellow lines to the baggage claim area, please.

The next chopper came in, and we headed for cover before the backwash began to get unpleasant. Moderately protected by the drums and cartons we'd brought, I could show Potter why our landing had been so unorthodox. The second Huey settled in as ours had, at an angle, forward end high. It couldn't land. The winds and the improper surface made it almost impossible to get the Hueys in the air again should they sacrifice their lift. With the tail section a few inches off the ground, the pilot tried to hold the chopper steady by banking against the wind. It was a good trick. They didn't send Mickey Mouse pilots to Kahoolawe.

This guy was hot. Must have been just back from his tour. He laid her down on the first try, and kept her there. We watched a repeat performance of our own show. It was surprising to realize how little time it actually took. The choppers weren't heavily loaded. The base camp, though uninhabited between trips, had an ample supply for most of our needs. We were bringing mainly what we would require in the next two weeks: drinking water, food, personal items, and ammunition.

Suddenly Potter pointed past the LZ. "What's that?"

He'd finally spotted the goat. It was less than a hundred yards away, perched on a boulder, as old, scraggly, and beat up as the brush that hid its bottom half. At first glance it was easy to take it for part of the shrubbery; it was motionless except when the breeze rustled its beard. It seemed to be watching the chopper.

"Oh, that," I said. "That's just Old Billy."

"Ol' Billy, he de welcomin' committee," Jones added.

Potter took another good look at the eyeless sockets and the stained horns. I don't know which ANGLCO had skinned the animal and left him to guard the LZ, but it had to have been within the year. Another few months in the weather and the thing would be so desiccated it would blow away.

"Sure is ugly," Potter commented.

I agreed and we turned to watch the third Huey settle in.

II

The sign in front of the barracks read:

SHERATON KAHOOLAWE

In front of the mess hall:

KAHOOLAWE COUNTRY CLUB
MEMBERS AND INVITED GUESTS ONLY

The signs were done by hand, and they'd been there for a while. That in itself was a proclamation: this was the real world. No curfew, no spit-shine boots. Kahoolawe was for working men. No one with enough rank to avoid it would be caught out here.

The buildings were small, joined by a short causeway. No air-conditioning. The light bulbs were bare, the walls painted the same drab olive green as half the military architecture on the planet. The radio shack and the shed for the jeeps were the only other structures. Kahoolawe's thriving community: Smuggler's Cove. The base camp. Permanent population: zero.

Jones and I were at the back door to the pantry, unloading the drums of beer that we'd hauled over from the LZ. We had just popped the lid on the first drum when Lieutenant Priest showed up.

"I understand you've been out here before, Corpsman."

"Yes, sir," I replied.

"Do you know where the magazine is? And the cap house?"

"As a matter of fact, I do."

He tossed me a set of keys. "As soon as you're done here, go show the EOD guys."

"Sure thing."

He nodded, turned to go. "Don't overload that refrigerator," he added. "If there's anything I hate worse than shook-up beer, it's *hot* shook-up beer."

Sayre and Lombard, the EOD men, were of a type. Both were in their forties, probably Spec-7, career men, Navy. They looked like their faces would crack into pieces if they tried to laugh. Sayre, in particular, had an air about him that made you give him a little extra space. It showed in the muscles, in the crew cut, in the burn scars on his cheeks. I'd seen that look before, on the face of a long-range reconnaissance patroller in II Corps. I suspect Lurps and bomb experts have something in common.

We took a jeep. Sayre drove. I made feeble attempts at small talk, to which neither man responded. By the time we reached the magazine, I was eager to hop out to open the padlock. Soon we were looking in at boxes and boxes of TNT, plastique, reel, wire, canvas bags—whatever the EOD men would require to fill out their demolition kits, minus the caps. The makings of one hell of a Fourth of July.

"Nice," Sayre said.

His voice was a Clint Eastwood rasp. I was just as glad he hadn't spoken earlier. They took what they needed, set it in the back of the jeep, and covered it with a tarp. We continued to the cap house. Like the magazine, it was out of sight of the base camp. The distance from the living quarters was intentional.

The walls of the structure were thick concrete, the door solid steel, designed to be both waterproof and peopleproof. The hinges groaned as it opened. Lombard went in alone, and soon returned with a box, which he placed in my lap.

"You hang onto that real good, now," he advised.

"What's in it?" I asked, though I already knew.

"Blasting caps. TNT in the back—this stays up front." As the sweat broke out on my palms, he climbed behind my seat and sat down on the tarp. Sayre drove us away, more slowly, I noticed, than he had driven on the way there.

"You see the crater?" Sayre inquired. He meant the depression in which Lombard was working. Sayre and I were behind a rock outcropping, observing as the other EOD man gingerly picked at a low mound, pulling away its mantle of grass almost blade by blade. "That's a giveaway of unexploded ordnance. A blast creates a circular crater. Impact alone makes a fan-shaped one."

Lombard used one hand strictly for support, never hurrying. He began to scoop away small handfuls of dirt, painstakingly revealing a rusted surface. The piece began to take on a distinctive shape.

"7.2 depth charge," he called to Sayre.

Sayre pursed his lips. "That's bad."

"What's a depth charge doing this far inland?" I asked.

"Guess they missed the ocean."

Lombard crawled away from the ordnance. Once clear, he rose and joined us.

"C-4 on this one?" he asked Sayre. The other nodded and Lombard opened one of their boxes, revealed a couple of dozen polyethylene bags of the plastique.

"You or me?"

Lombard shrugged. "I'll do it."

Sayre and I settled down behind the outcropping. We

shared a tense few moments. "What makes a depth charge so dangerous?" I asked, trying to cut the air.

"All ways acting fuse," he said.

"What's that?"

He smirked. "Means it'll kill you all sorts of different ways."

"Wonderful."

"Ain't so bad," he said. He seemed to be enjoying my anxiety. "Ain't no buildings or civilians out here to worry about. No problem to just blow the cocksuckers away. Beats *defusing* them."

Lombard was back with us within a few minutes. He pulled the galvanometer out of his bag. The needle jumped as he touched the lead wires to the terminals. With a satisfied nod he connected the wires to the blasting machine. He twisted the key without preamble.

The explosion made the ground shake. A wide cloud of dust rose over the crest of the hill.

The EOD men nodded to each other. "Still had some good shit in it," Sayre said.

The crater was deep, rather than wide. The freshly ruptured soil made the site look as if it had been sprinkled with paprika. It was still smoking.

"Good stuff, that Composition C-4," Sayre said. "If we'd used C-3, you wouldn't want to be smelling this hole."

I leaned down and felt the dirt near the rim. It was warm. Along the edge pebbles were still settling into the pit in miniature avalanches. I'd seen a hole like this before. Sayre was right. This one smelled better.

Sayre and Lombard stared when I announced that I was going to walk back to camp. "I'll be fine," I said, pointing to the west. "I'll stay in troop safety zone. It hasn't been shelled in years."

Sayre gave me a mock bow. "Whatever you say, Corpsman."

"I've hiked this side of the island before," I added.

He shrugged. "I'm sure you let us know if you find any bombs." He and Lombard chuckled and turned back toward their work. I self-consciously flicked a speck of grime off my sleeve and headed off.

The terrain wasn't exactly desolate. Deprived was more

the word. Whatever lived on Kahoolawe looked the same: haggard, malnourished, abused. Not that the ground was totally naked. Grass clustered where hillocks and dunes sheltered it from the wind. There were stands of brush—full of thorns, snarled into grotesque shapes—consisting mainly of kiawe, a low-lying, shrublike tree. What you wouldn't find was the tropical flora typical of the other Hawaiian Islands. Both the territorial government and the ranchers who had formerly caretaken Kahoolawe had tried to introduce more productive vegetation, but most of this had vanished, neglected under an indifferent military ownership. Little could thrive without maintenance. Kahoolawe is in the lee of Haleakala on Maui, and the volcano sucks the rain clouds dry before they make it to the smaller island.

The most striking sight, of course, was the shrapnel. In many places I couldn't walk two steps without tripping over a piece. I passed chunks of twisted, jagged, rusting steel as much as twenty or thirty inches long. One of the reasons the EOD men had to depend on visual cues such as the one Sayre had taught me was that metal detectors are useless on Kahoolawe—they give a constant indication. The island has been bombed steadily since World War II.

To be truthful, I enjoyed the scenery, knowing virtually no living person had put his feet where I was putting mine.

I found a familiar-looking track that cut through the underbrush in random directions. The edges of the vegetation had been nibbled at. Goat path. I noticed occasional tufts of hair caught on thorns. I sidestepped a decomposing turd, spotting it easily against the astoundingly red color of the soil.

I continued on into dense meshes of twigs and branches, thorns tearing at my clothing and skin as I tried to force my way through openings meant for much smaller creatures. In due time I found myself trudging along between the steep walls of a ravine. Rocks and roots and layers of strata had been exposed on either side, savaged by the island's exuberant erosion. It was easy to spot the object poking out of the ground about halfway up one of the banks.

Considering the types of things you can find in Kahoolawe's earth, I looked very carefully before deciding it was safe to touch. It came free with one tug, along with a lot of sand. Judging from the distance to the top of the gully, the thing must have been buried for a long time. It was choked with grit, so encrusted that it took me several seconds to realize that it was wooden. There were seven cylinders of proportionately greater length, fastened side by side, made of what looked like sections of bamboo or reed. Scarred as it was, it was still obvious it was a musical instrument.

I tucked it in a pocket of my fatigues and walked on.

When I got back to the base camp, I discovered that Jones, Potter, and PFC Melendez were hard at work burying the stacks of empty C ration tins that previous ANGLCOs had piled behind the mess hall. Not wishing to join them, I sneaked into the Sheraton Kahoolawe, changed into my cut-offs, and took a dip in the ocean to get rid of the blood, dust, and sweat of my hike. Then I spread Sea & Ski on my nose and took advantage of Smuggler's Cove's beautiful white beach.

When I wasn't just flaking out, enjoying the sunshine and listening to my radio, I was cleaning away the grit from the pipes, digging out the cracks with a dental pick. I had thought that the instrument was just a group of tubes, hollow all the way through, but once the filth was gone, I found that each pipe was closed off at one end. I scrubbed it with fluid and a rag until it practically gleamed.

Even clean, it was nondescript, and primitive. I pulled at it experimentally, and the smallest pipe broke off. Once free, I could see that some sort of wax held the pieces together. I'd fix it with model cement when I returned to the barracks.

I wondered how the instrument had ended up in the gully. Sure as hell no serviceman had brought it. I could only guess it to be a Hawaiian relic, or that some rancher's kid had dropped it a few decades back, before we started blowing Kahoolawe to bits.

I tried playing a scale. At first, it was dull and unmusical, but as I cleaned it more and adjusted my lip posture, it wasn't half bad. It had a captivating tone. I practiced until Melendez called chow time, then again that night, just before going to bed.

III

I walked, naked, along a stony path barely visible in the moonless night, not feeling the pebbles grind into my heels or the chill of the air. The hillside below was spotted with trees that resembled kiawe, but not quite like any I had seen before. In the gullies and on the knolls, the ground was rocky and scarred, as it should have been, but next to the path the grass was knee-deep, luxuriant, ungrazed. The trees ahead were not Hawaiian at all; they were large, healthy pines, firs, and oaks.

The spot was both familiar and alien, as if one world had supplanted parts of another. It was both a place I had been to many times before and one I had never known existed. There was a flavor in the atmosphere, one that both soothed me and, paradoxically, drove me to excitement. I knew that great rewards waited if only I could get past the next bend, or the next after that.

Who was I? I glanced at my hands, recognized the creases and calluses, and did not know whose hands they were. It was up to greater powers to name me, but they had not deigned to do so. At times it seemed my own feet trod the stones; at other times I was a detached observer, watching another man's strides.

The farther I went, the clearer I could hear music. It was the sound of many instruments, from all directions, instruments of reed and wood and string, and ram's horn. The notes wove together, rich with nuance, with suggestion, with allure, a haunting blend that could only come from the hands of individuals who have played the same song for time beyond reckoning. The melody was light, cheerful, yet exquisite in construction. Without conscious intent, my feet found the cadence and fell in step. I felt as if I would leave the ground, walk the air, a feathery, insubstantial being called into the clouds.

Female voices chanted in a language I did not recognize, a soprano wail suffused with eroticism, drawing me sirenlike to the top of a hill. I looked down into a small vale. Around a raging bonfire, twenty women—naked, dusky, dark-haired, young, and sprite of step—danced lithely on a ring of trampled earth. They ranged from slender to stocky, breasts delicate to heavy, but each pure vixen, undeniable. My tongue was heavy in my mouth, my breath quick and biting.

Their dance seemed effortless, yet the choreography was perfect. No individual made a move that failed to be reflected among the others. They danced apart; they joined in a circle; they split into several smaller rings, smiling as they continued to chant. Sweat streamed down their bodies, making breasts glisten, creating wet pops of noise as thigh rubbed thigh.

I was mesmerized, forced to look, until my erection was rigid and aching and I had to step toward them.

And they were gone.

They maintained their dance even as they departed, spiraling away from the flames, vanishing like elves into the foliage, so quickly that it seemed that they did not so much duck between the trees as into them, hiding more completely than seemed possible. I willed them to return, as if they were phantoms of my creation, mine to command, but they did not. I began to doubt they had ever been there, except that I could see the fire still blazing and the footprints in the soil and grass.

"Where are you?" I called, my voice seeming harsh and intrusive, threatening to break the spell of this enchanted place, like a wolf cry in the pasture.

A breath of air caressed my right ear. I turned to find another woman a few paces away. She was a slender nude, breasts taut and upturned, legs supple like a runner's. At first she seemed Caucasian, but her eyes were slanted slightly, her skin tanned deep brown; she could have been of almost any race. Her hair was black, cascading to her waist. At the hairline of each temple, tiny nubs of horn protruded from her scalp. Seeing them, I realized the women around the fire had also been horned.

"Who are you?" I asked, barely finding the breath to utter the question. The others had been merely erotic. This one was more.

"Who are you?" she repeated. I felt goose pimples rise on my scrotum. She had mimicked my voice exactly, retaining even the male pitch. She smiled at my shock.

"What are you doing here? How did you get on this island?" I demanded.

"What are you doing here? How did you get on this island?" Again, she returned every emphasis and hesitation, the words following a second behind my own. She smiled more widely. One hand threaded through her pubic hair. The fingers came away moist.

I wanted her more than I had ever wanted a woman. I reached forward.

She leaned back.

I stepped forward. She stepped back.

I leaped. Gracefully she pranced away, always just out of reach. I was startled at the ease with which she avoided me. Nor could I understand the lust in my body; it was as if she had reached inside and turned on a spigot. I was under her control, not my own. She giggled, turning her fanny toward me. She spread the cheeks and wiggled invitingly.

She was only one step away . . .

I bellowed as I charged her. She sidestepped, merrily echoing my roar. My momentum carried me tumbling past her. I skinned my knees on the gravel of the path, the pain only making my desire more intense. I stumbled to my feet. She laughed and fingered herself. I leapt again.

And tripped, breath knocked from my lungs as I belly-flopped into the grass. I gaped like a fish, waiting for air to enter me again, vaguely aware of the shell casing that I had caught my foot on. Uncontrollably, my pelvis pumped the roots and soil.

The woman straddled my prone figure. She extended a hand to me. I snatched for it. She scribed a circle around my jab and waved her hand still closer. I grabbed. She eluded me, three, four, five times. Eventually I stopped, waiting, licking my lips, watching her. I had rolled over during my struggles and waited now on one elbow, the other arm suspended in a ready position. When she waved her hand over my face again, instead of reaching for it, I lowered mine.

She raised an eyebrow. Smiling more widely, she brought her fingertips even closer to my lips. I simply watched. Soon she bent over me, waving her nipples in front of my eyes. They were delicately pink, slick, and erect. She squatted down, deluging my nostrils with the scent of her vulva.

I clutched for her with both arms, but somehow she was not there. I heard her land behind me.

I screamed in rage, whirling to face her.

She screamed back, and jumped away.

The chase began in earnest. I sprinted after her, while she loped ahead, always slightly out of reach. Her feet hardly seemed to land before she was in the air again, her speed unaffected by slopes or uneven ground. She deftly ducked under branches of kiawe without breaking her stride, while I tripped on their roots or stepped into shadowed potholes. She breathed smoothly, giggling all the while. My side was soon aching, a sharp knot under the rib cage, but I kept on, through a eucalyptus grove and a steep ravine, barely side-stepping a jagged projection of shrapnel at the bottom of the gully. The woman no longer hung back. She soon disappeared from sight, only to reappear when I had recovered my wind. She led me on again until exhaustion prevented me from continuing. After another rest, she appeared again. I wanted to stop, end the frustration, but one look at her made it impossible. I gave up only when my legs were nothing but useless muscle, and she not even a distant, whitish shape flitting through the brush.

I sagged to my knees. The music was gone, taking with it the euphoria and the heady sense of stamina and strength. My body was foul with perspiration, my diaphragm nearly paralyzed. My feet bled from contact with sharp rocks, my torso from scratches from the brush I had tumbled through. My throat was parched, my penis limp.

And still I wanted her.

On the top of a knoll barren of growth, the woman appeared, fondling her breasts, taunting me with her laughter. I sucked in a violent breath, and cried, "Goddamn you to hell!"

"Goddamn you to hell!" she shrieked jovially.

"Who are you?"

"Who are you?"

"Who are you?"

"Who are you? are you? are you? you? you? you? you?"

My eyes burst open, focusing on and not recognizing at first the rafters of the Sheraton Kahoolawe. The Elephant was on my chest. My heart felt like it was going to knock holes through my sternum.

Who are you? you? you?

Something near me was moving. I remained motionless on my cot, cautiously turning my head just enough to get a clear view. It was Jones. His big hulk was shuffling slowly by, eyes wide open and glazed. I identified the signs. My own sister had been a persistent sleepwalker.

The barracks were hushed in the pre-dawn. Even the snores had temporarily faded. It was warm despite the hour. I dripped. Jones was just passing the end of my cot, moving slowly, feeling his way with his feet. He was chewing his inner cheek as would a nervous kindergarten pupil.

He soon bumped into Lieutenant Priest's bed and stopped, shins against the cot frame. Priest mumbled incoherently and rolled over. I shrugged off my disorientation, sat up, and called quietly to Jones in an officer's tone of voice: "Going somewhere, Private?"

At first Jones merely continued to chew his cheek. He was deep in, really zombie. Eventually a tiny, incongruously childish voice answered, "I got to pee-pee, sir."

I got up and led him by the shoulders. Once out of the doorway, he moved as if awake. I had automatically been routing him toward the outhouse; instead, he crossed the porch and began pissing off the edge of the planks. I shrugged, and stepped to the opposite side to take care of my own bladder.

The smell of my urine brought up images of corpses being stuffed into body bags: the sphincters relax at the moment of death. Even today I can't abide unflushed toilets. This did nothing to quell my sense of unease. I quickly shook myself and turned back to Jones. He was still standing in the same spot, prick abandoned outside his skivvies, and was tapping his foot to a beat. His head bobbed in cadence. It was so stereotypically black that I would have smiled if I hadn't been so scared. There was something familiar to the rhythm of Jones's foot. His glazed eyes were staring toward the hills.

"Pretty ladies," he murmured, a dreamy smile on his face. He giggled, the embarrassed laugh of a toddler.

I felt a lizard crawl down my spine. "What ladies, Jones?"

He pointed to the desolate hillside directly in front of him. I followed the line of sight, but knew whatever he saw was internal. Eventually his eyes dropped and his cheek-chewing resumed. I tried to slow the pace of my thoughts, but they spouted out one after the other. I hardly controlled my distractedness long enough to tell Jones to get back to bed.

"Ummm," he answered, nodding his head in exaggerated motions. He walked back to his cot with the same measured pace he had shown before. Within moments he was under the sheet, zonked out like he'd never risen at all.

I sat on my cot, contemplating a knothole in the wall, trying to force my mind to be still. It was too hot. Every sound was amplified beyond perspective: the creaking of the building in the wind, the shifting of my companions' breathing, my own heartbeat.

Nymphs.

I reached under the bed, found my shirt, and withdrew the instrument I had found in the ravine. I knew now what I'd found. It wasn't Hawaiian. Nor had some rancher's kid lost it.

It was Greek.

IV

"You ever have funny dreams?" I asked Jones the next morning.

He picked his nose and shrugged. "Sure. Doesn't everybody?"

That was as close as I could come to talking about the night. Even if Jones had had a similar dream, he obviously didn't remember it. In daylight a fantasy of chasing nymphs through the brush seemed ludicrous. I certainly would not look for psychoanalysis from a grunt.

Jones, Potter, and I were down in the artillery range with a load of white paint, touching up the ship-to-shore bombardment targets before the destroyer arrived from Pearl Harbor. It looked like every war in history had been fought on the land around us. It was like the moon: cratered and devoid of life. Whole sections of the valley contained nothing but pulverized soil and a series of impact sites. In rare places, a bit of gnarled scrub brush poked surrealistically from the incredibly red earth, some of it unbelievably still alive. The ground was littered with rocket pods, shell casings, aircraft machine guns, napalm canisters, shrapnel—all in varying degrees of corrosion. Dirt roads crisscrossed the area, strung with convoys of derelict vehicles, both military and civilian: targets. Whitewashed tires had been piled in the shapes of aircraft or missile silos, and whitewashed rocks imitated runways and formed bull's-eyes. It was the latter we were working on.

"It don't have to be perfect, Pot," Jones said, as the lance corporal carefully covered each square inch of the rock he was painting.

"Lieutenant Priest said to do a good job."

Jones shook his head sadly. "Fuckin' officers."

"Aw, he ain't so bad," Potter said.

"Look—anybody who makes me paint rocks that's gonna get blowed up the same day is no friend of mine."

When we finished we wandered over to the convoy. I decided to play a tune.

"What's that?" Potter asked, pointing at the instrument.

"A syrinx," I replied. He frowned. "A panpipe," I added. "Found it on the island."

"I'll be damned. Sounds nice."

We came across a corroding wreck of an automobile, mired deep in the red silt. Nothing was left but the chassis, one front wheel, and half a radiator. The metal was riddled with bullet holes.

"Christ, do they shoot up gook country like this?" Jones asked.

He stirred up his paint and slapped a splotch on the radiator, while I mused on the emphasis he had put on the word *gook*. I looked at the desolation surrounding us, noting a rusting napalm canister, a shredded, half-buried tire, and a bleached goat skeleton.

"No," I answered honestly. "They don't." In spite of the Hobo Woods, in spite of all of Johnson's bombing of Hanoi and Haiphong, the amount of ordnance dropped on Vietnam was less than Kahoolawe had endured.

The sound from the destroyer's gun was impressive in spite of the distance. If we stood on the sandbags, we could see the ship out in the Kealaikahiki Channel, barrel smoking.

"All *right*," Potter yelled, and waved at it.

He, Jones, and I were in a slit trench at the edge of the troop safety zone, a mile inland. The rest of the squad was farther uphill, in the observation tower.

The shell landed, sending a geyser of dirt airward, far short of the rocks we'd just whitewashed. We heard a sharp report, like a shotgun blast.

"Shit, I thought it'd be better than that," Potter complained.

"Practice ordnance," I explained.

Lieutenant Priest's voice crackled over our PRC-10. "Texas Ten to Texas Twenty. How do you mark that round?"

"Fi-yuv zero zero meters short," I answered, calculating how badly they'd have to miss to hit us.

When the first live shell struck, I dived for the bottom of the trench. As the island shook, so did I.

"Direct hit!" Potter yelled. He stayed on his feet, switching rapidly between binoculars and straightforward viewing. Jones, the official spotter, just stared slack-jawed at the explosion—a sharp crack, very quick, felt more than seen. I stayed down in the trench. I'm safe, I'm safe, I told myself. The range is seven thousand acres in area; that bull's-eye is a long way off. As Jones informed the lieutenant of the accuracy, I lit up another joint.

"Hey, Short, you okay?" Potter asked.

I let the buzz settle in and cool me out. "Yeah, fine," I told him, and passed the joint to Jones.

"Smooth," Jones said after he had exhaled. "What is this?"

"Maui Wowee." I thought that was funny, since I'd actually picked it up on Maui.

"They say pot's real cheap in 'Nam."

I nodded. "Especially in the highlands. I once picked up a party pack for a dollar."

"A party pack?"

"Yeah. Ten big, *thick* reefers. Only takes one to get a guy wasted."

"Heaven."

"Local medicine," I declared. "It was my job to research it in depth." While I spoke, Jones handed the remainder to Potter.

"More? Already?" Potter puffed the joint like a cigarette.

"Naw, man," Jones chided. "Here, before you let it all burn away." He showed Potter the right way, but it was no use. No way was any white lance corporal going to compete with lips like that. "Can't waste it. Shit like this was hard to come by in my neighborhood."

"Your mama," I said.

"Didn't say you couldn't get pot. Jus' you had to have bread to get *good* pot."

"You must have had it real tight, Jones."

"Hell, we was so poor we put up tumbleweeds for Christmas trees."

"Is it true this stuff will destroy your brain cells?" Potter asked.

"Yes," I said.

Potter had all the requirements of a natural stoner. I was just helping fate. He was in midtoke when we heard the guns again. I thought I had been prepared, but once again I made love to the dirt. I found myself craving oxygen, like something had reached inside my lungs and taken it out.

Potter spat the roach out in surprise. "Damn!" This wasn't just one round. The ship had found the range. Lieutenant Priest had ordered them to fire for effect.

"Muthuh*fuck*," Jones whispered.

Despite their stunned postures, I would have traded places with Jones or Potter at the drop of a hat. It's one thing to see heavy ordnance; it's another to remember it raining down all around you. In an instant it was as if I'd never been stoned.

As my chest pressed against the ground, I felt something hard in my pocket. It was the syrinx. I pulled it out. I played. At first I couldn't hear it over the bells in my ears, but I kept playing, right through to the last salvo, keeping my mind on the placement of my lips, on my breathing, on the music itself, waiting for the helpless feeling to go away.

"Look at the goats," Sayre said.

I accepted his binoculars. Out in the valley, coats bright in the late afternoon sun, was a herd of about two hundred animals. I had seen groups like this on other ANGLCO excursions. They frequently came down from the eastern heights to find the rainwater that collected in the bomb craters.

I was once again in a slit trench, a different one this time. With me were Sayre and Sergeant Wall. Wall was a black in his late thirties, a lanky, balding man whose habitual expression had caused us to nickname him Stone Wall—not to his face, of course. Potter and Jones were now up in the tower with Lieutenant Priest. The ship was through with its test against known targets. Its crew now had to be tested against unknown targets, for which we in the trenches had to set up counterbatteries.

"Them things is right where the lieutenant wanted us to fire the first marking round," Sayre commented dryly. "Ain't that a shame."

"Suppose he'll give us new coordinates?" Stone Wall asked.

Sayre chuckled. I just continued setting up the mortar. Stone Wall hadn't been to Kahoolawe before. The odd thing was that Sayre hadn't, either.

"Bet you ten bucks you can't hit that black and white one with the broken horn," said the EOD man.

"Bet you're right," I said, seeing the old buck perched on a boulder. "Ain't no sights on this thing." We didn't need them for our kind of work.

"All right. Ten bucks if you make it anywhere in the main knot. But aim for old Charlie there."

"Deal."

It was only a few seconds later that we received the confirmation from Priest—time to start the exercises. I estimated the distance. Downslope—undershoot a little for that. I tilted the tube, removed one ring of powder bags, then hefted the shell. Sayre and Stone Wall shuffled a little farther away.

I eased the shell toward the tube's mouth, held my breath, let go, and fell back.

Flame belched out of the mortar. I could hear nothing but the ringing in my ears. Abruptly a splash of white phosphorous glare sprouted out on the valley floor, chain-reacting into tentacles.

After our eyes adjusted, we could see goats milling in confused patterns around the brilliant white smoke. I had struck the edge of the herd. Two ragged, bloodied shapes, small lumps of hair even to binocular view, lay limp as the cloud rose.

Sayre handed me a crumpled ten.

We could hear the bleating of the herd echoing across the landscape. Charlie seemed to be the leader. He ran to the edges of the herd, rounding up the kids that had scattered. Within a few seconds he was urging his charges toward the east side of the island. The retreat was efficient and organized. Kids and does first, spikes next, then bucks.

Too late.

The first round from the ship was live. It obliterated the boulder where Charlie had originally stood. Three goats went down. The herd panicked. The adult animals began overtaking the young, leaving them either to follow or to wander in disoriented circles, wailing for their mothers.

The ship gunners had managed to strike gold dirt on the first try. We didn't bother with another marking round. "Fire for effect," I murmured, pretending I was the forward observer. Within a few seconds we heard the guns pound, steady and loud.

That section of the valley went up in dust and smoke. One round landed immediately at the forefront of the biggest clump of goats. The herd staggered back, momentum stolen. Two groups split in opposite directions and hardly broke stride in their haste to get away; others paused, as if uncertain which way to run. I noticed a knot of about fifteen animals as they hopped over the rim of an old impact crater and disappeared into the depression, just before a shell landed there. I kept watching, but never saw any goats reappear above the rim.

As the smoke and dust rose, we spotted limp, hairy bodies scattered all over the target site. The herd had been broken into sparse clumps. The babies were still scurrying from place to place, bawling, totally confused, abandoned by their mothers. Only the largest group seemed to have a leader. Those goats were hurrying toward Mount Lua Makika in the east. I thought I saw Charlie at the rear, goading stragglers to greater speed.

I wasn't feeling quite so helpless anymore.

V

She was the same: almond eyes, brown skin, horns on the forehead. She was waiting for me, her laugh part of the wind.

Salt breezes stroked my uncovered body, though where and in what direction the ocean might be I could not tell. Lush grass grew to either side of the path. Shrubs and trees were lost into the darkness. The only light was from the stars, and from the woman, who seemed to glow.

She was naked and glorious, breasts ripe for the plucking. I could smell her siren fragrance, full and potent and female. It made my head swim. It was all I could do to keep the image in my mind of the night before, of frustration and aimless pursuit. I had to resist her lure. The way to her was indirect.

I brought my hand away from behind my back, and held up the yellow, weathered reed to her light. One of her eyebrows raised, her smile no longer temptress-coy, but intrigued. I raised the syrinx to my lips and played a single note.

The woman opened her mouth, her teeth a row of starlit white enamel, and the note returned out of her throat.

I played a measure.

And it was echoed.

She placed one foot in front of the other, a simple, graceful move that drew my attention immediately to her thighs and the perfect triangle of pubic hair between them. I almost forgot my plans, almost threw down the instrument, but I could tell from the tremble of her muscles what she was truly aching for. She had had the chase a thousand times. I could give her what would fulfill her.

I played, longer this time, with more confidence. She repeated the music a moment later with both voice and movement. It was a dance such as I had never seen before, only read hints of in old literature and heard in the dubious tales of drunk old men. Primitive. Erotic. Complete. It was her dance, only for her, and no one else could perform it like she even should they be able to mimic the choreography. It came from a deep, archetypal place. It defined her.

The song I was playing was the same. I didn't know where

the melody came from; it simply entered my lips and tongue and fingers, flowing out without my conscious direction. Should I have put my will to it, I could have stopped it, but I could not have changed it. It was her song, given to me so that I could help her give it form. I could do what she could not. I could originate the sounds.

All too soon, it was done. My breath rolled one last time down the reed, and to the end her voice was one instant behind. I stood, mesmerized by the gradual dying of her movements. She stopped in front of me.

She opened her arms. Beckoning.

This was not the temptation she had earlier thrust in my face. This was genuine welcome. She wanted me as I wanted her. The knowledge turned my legs to water. When I failed to approach her, she came to me, lifting a hand to caress my cheek, lifting lips toward mine. I could now see tiny white flowers in her hair, and smell their faint, meadowy fragrance. Her breath was sweet.

But as her hand and her lips reached me, they passed right through, without touch, and the vision of her itself became indistinct and faded into the wind, leaving a numbness, an unreal whisper of contact.

"Where are you?" I cried, but she was gone.

"You cannot touch her." The voice came from behind me. I whirled.

The speaker was only a few steps away, yet had given no sound of her coming. Like the first woman, she was beautiful, but without the painful perfection that had driven me to such extremes the night before. Her body was fuller—heavier breasts and thighs; wide, rich lips; horns slightly more prominent.

"She is Echo, bride of the wind and the cliffsides," said the woman. "No one may touch her, not even we, her sisters. She gave up that ability long ago. It was the only way she could avoid the pursuit of Great Pan himself."

"But she wanted to touch me," I said.

"Yes, she did," she said gently. "And so she has sent me. You reached her the only way you could have—with your music. It pleased her as nothing has in many an age." She kissed me firmly on the mouth, warmly, skillfully. "I am Aspasia. What the virgin cannot give, my sisters and I will provide."

She said her name as if it held a meaning of its own, and soon my mind brought it to consciousness: welcome.

She took my arm in hers. "They are waiting nearby. Join us."

We walked down the path. Almost as soon as we rounded the first bend, I could hear the crackle of a fire and sounds of revelry. The darkness was tempered on the horizon, throwing the knoll ahead of us into silhouette. I knew that when I reached the spot, all would be well.

That was when I felt the presence behind me. I stopped, cocking my ear. I heard a strange, feral grunting, the pounding of hooves, heavy, desperate breathing. It was coming nearer.

Aspasia tugged at my arm. "Hurry. We must get into the light."

Something shadowy and hairy was shambling our way. Suddenly the night turned cold. I began to shiver, but in spite of the horror, I felt rooted to the earth.

"What is that?" I asked.

"Another side of the Dream," Aspasia answered.

"I don't understand."

"All mortals dream the same Dream. But they choose their own parts to experience. You have all sides within you. Will you have that one tonight?"

I hesitated, trembling. The right decision seemed obvious, but I couldn't move. Despite the warmth of Aspasia's thigh against mine, there was something—some taste of excitement—waiting back along the trail. The fear, bitter on the surface, held hidden sweetness.

Aspasia tugged my arm again. "Choose—quickly."

Suddenly I tore my eyes away from the shadows and ran with her. In a few seconds we reached the top of the hill.

Below us was the amphitheater I had seen the previous night, with its floor of trampled grass, its cobble-ringed fire in the center. A dozen naked women shone in the light of the coals, some dancing, some drinking from earthenware mugs, some chanting in a language long dead. When Aspasia and I came into sight, they all rose and came toward us. They embraced me one by one. Few of the touches were chaste.

"I am Eulalia," the first one said. Her voice was clearer than any I had ever heard before, the diction and pitch hauntingly pretty. Next was one so beautiful she glowed as Echo had, but in a tangible, touchable way. "I am Ilona," she said, lifting her chin beside my head and giving me a carnal nibble on my ear.

Each one named herself. Althea, Zoe, Sybil—the names escaped me as I was caught up in the intoxication of their presence. It was almost orgasmic to look at them, even more so to feel their caresses.

For a brief moment I felt again the presence that had pursued me. I heard fevered piping in the distance, and once more the rumble of hooves. A figure crossed the hilltop, shrouded by the night, leaving me able to see only his half-man, half-animal outline, and the glint of horns on his head.

Then the nymphs took me, and there on a blanket of flattened grass, gave me sanctuary from the darkness.

VI

"Lemme get this straight. We're *supposed* to shoot the goats."

"That's right," Sergeant Richert told Stone Wall as we loaded more ammunition in the jeep. "Otherwise they'll eat everything on the island. Their hooves chew up the ground, too. They're the main cause of all this erosion."

"Makes sense," Stone Wall said, and shrugged. "Seems a shame to let all that chevon go to waste."

"These goats aren't livestock," Richert said. "They're just goddamned nuisances."

It wasn't exactly our duty to hunt the goats. That belonged to the Navy sharpshooters who periodically visited the island. But as long as we had a leisurely couple of days until the next ship was due, Lieutenant Priest saw nothing wrong with doing our part to help curb the problem, much as we had at the artillery range.

"You dudes all set?" Jones asked as he and Potter strode up, slapping the dirt off their hands. "Luau pit's dug."

The EOD guys were climbing into the other jeep. Everyone was present except Lieutenant Priest, who was staying in camp to clear up paperwork from the previous day's exercises.

"Let's go," Richert said.

"You'd think they'd find some way to get rid of all the goats," Potter said as we rolled through the troop safety zone. "Maybe let loose some tigers to hunt 'em down."

"Tigers attack human beings," I said.

"Oh. That's right." He blushed. "Well, what about poison, or traps?"

"They tried that," Richert said. "Never gets them all." He grabbed the side of the jeep as we hit a deep rut. "They breed like rabbits. Lieutenant says there might be four or five thousand goats on Kahoolawe right now. Navy's supposed to keep it down to two hundred or less."

Up ahead the jeep with the EOD men, Melendez, and Stone Wall rolled to a stop. Jones swung us up even with it and we piled out. I checked my rifle one final time. I noticed that Sayre's weapon was an M-1.

"Got something against M-16s?" I asked.

He nodded. "Pieces of shit."

"Goats won't know the difference."

"I will."

I got out some tape and began greasing my clips together. Potter watched, openmouthed.

"Never seen this before, eh?"

"No."

"Here," I said, placing the bottoms of two of his clips together and starting the tape around. I handed it to him to finish. "Little thing that might help you someday."

He slowly wound the rest of the tape, shaking his head. "You sure know a lot about this stuff, Short. I thought corpsmen didn't even carry weapons."

Sayre laughed. So did Richert, a vet.

I raised an eyebrow, and decided not to answer Pot. One of life's classic bad jokes had been played on me: I joined the medical corps to get out of the infantry and ended up in the single most dangerous occupation the infantry had.

Since Jones and I had been to Kahoolawe before, we were the guides. "Let's fan out," I said. "Remember. Nobody fires until we all do. Spook those goats and we'll have to chase them all the way to the cliffs to get another shot.'' We were going to the other side of the island eventually, but first we needed a goat that Melendez could take back to camp and roast while the rest of us continued to hunt.

We found a herd of about fifty animals grazing in a small valley. Some were enjoying the early morning sunshine; some were rubbing their scrawny bodies against the trunks of kiawe trees, which grew sparsely across most of the dell. One buck tucked his head under himself and urinated on his beard and forelegs. And people wonder why billy goats stink.

Chance brought me next to Sayre. ''Look,'' he whispered.

Following the line of his finger, I saw that the spotter for the herd was none other than Charlie. His broken horn and black and white coat left no doubt. He had his head up, alert, gazing from side to side as does near him blithely nibbled the grass.

''I want that goat,'' Sayre murmured.

''It's a long shot,'' I advised. ''Look at that nanny in the way. How about that little guy over there? He'd be nice and tender for the luau.''

Sayre stared fixedly at Charlie for several long moments. ''You shoot the kid. That fucker's mine.''

We'd agreed that Jones would be the first to shoot. He checked and saw that we were all ready, and took aim. I hoped someone else was also going to try for the kid. I wasn't a good marksman. That's why I preferred automatic weapons.

Jones fired.

Within two seconds all I could hear was gunfire. I emptied my clip in four long bursts. Every goat in the group containing the kid went down, heads and legs flailing. I suspect at least three other members of the squad had chosen the same general target. I flipped over the clip.

Most of the adult animals bolted toward the east. We tried to pick them off as they went, but running targets were much more of a challenge. I think I hit a doe.

As usual, there were several bewildered kids left to follow their elders as best they could. As the last of the main herd vanished, the babies were fodder. The last one standing must have been hit by twenty bullets in the same three seconds. The impacts actually kept it from falling for a moment.

"Goddamn it!" Sayre snapped. I realized Charlie was not among the dead.

Potter was yelping like a cowboy as he raced down the hill. The rest of us followed at a more dignified pace. Up close the goats were a pitiful lot—protruding ribs, distended bellies, fur infested with parasites. Another burst or two finished off any that hadn't been killed outright.

We were coming up on my kid. About five steps from it, it suddenly lifted its head and began screaming.

It was the most human cry I've ever heard from an animal's throat. I stopped.

Sayre stopped, too. Yet while I was covering my ears and jumping back in surprise, he just stared down, expressionless.

"Jesus Christ, kill that little bastard!" I shouted.

At first it was as if he hadn't heard me. He watched the kid bawl until its tongue hung out of its mouth and its lips were flecked with bloody foam. It didn't seem able to get to its feet, though its legs kicked frantically. Its dark eyes flashed at us with terror written deeply in their pupils.

Then Sayre moved, as fast as I've ever seen a man move, grabbing the kid by the ears and drawing his commando dagger across its neck. Blood spurted outward, staining his boots and pant cuffs. He held it at waist level, letting the blood drip from the wound. One last gurgle and the kid was quiet.

We chose another goat for the luau.

"Twenty-seven," Potter said.

"Hmmm?"

"Twenty-seven goats. That's how many I got so far," he told me. He was probably counting a few that other people had hit, but I'm sure he wasn't far off.

"Congratulations," I muttered. We had just arrived at our destination: the cliffs on the eastern side of the island. While Melendez had trekked back to Smuggler's Cove with our evening meal over his shoulders, the rest of us had hunted our way around the north side of the volcano. Here the land dropped sharply to surround Kanapou Bay, just broken enough that in one or two places a man could actually walk down to a tiny, driftwood-dotted beach. From our vantage point we could scan miles of near-vertical coastline.

And there were the goats.

The cliffs were the reason no one—not the ranchers, not the Hawaiian territorial government, not the U.S. military—had ever been able to clear the goats off Kahoolawe. Through my binoculars I could see some of the animals nonchalantly negotiating clefts, shelves, and washouts that no human being could have touched without climbing ropes. As one disappeared into a cave, another popped into view from behind a tiny shrub that I would have sworn it never could have hidden behind. If we'd had machine guns, napalm, choppers, and a month's time, we might have gotten every goat off those cliffs, but I doubt it.

The population on the heights had already been swelled by the goats we'd chased ahead of us. They were now scattered across the slope along paths we couldn't hope to follow. Not that we had any intention of doing so.

It was a bit like a shooting gallery at the fair. Spot a goat, aim, let off a few rounds, pause to see whether the shot had been good. I splintered a shrub next to my first one. The goat bleated, dropped to the next shelf down, and ran. I followed it with more rounds, making the dirt and grass fly behind it. Finally I struck the rubble underneath it and started a small avalanche. The goat lost its footing and tumbled out from the wall. It hit three or four times on the way down, finally plunging into the ocean. It surfaced a few seconds later, and tried to swim for the shore. Unfortunately for it, it faced a sheer rock wall with no place to climb out of the surf.

Naturally, we got the closest goats first. The easiest were the ones slowed down by difficult terrain. In most cases, however, they would sprint for cover as if running on level ground. All they needed was a tiny foothold. The lucky ones found boulders, caves, or crevices that would hide them. One young buck must have covered a hundred yards before a round split his skull; he caught on a piece of brush a few feet lower down and hung there for several minutes, until we ran out of easy targets and blasted the shrubbery off the cliff. Within fifteen minutes the ocean and beach were dotted with the bodies of goats that had fallen. Others lay limp where the bullets had found them.

When the nearby targets had been used up, we concentrated on long shots, aiming to the limit our 16s could fire. Most of the rounds missed, of course, but we had plenty of time. There was always a goat or two moving somewhere on the cliff. We scanned with binoculars to see if any of the ones already hit were still wiggling.

After forty-five minutes, we'd cleaned off the easy targets. We spent about five minutes watching and waiting for the occasional unwary goat to stick its head out from behind cover, then Sergeant Richert brought out his M-79 grenade launcher.

It must have been his personal piece. It had been cut down and fitted with a special stock, and you could tell the amount of care it had received from the way the sunlight blazed off the metal. He lifted the weapon, opened the breech, and dropped in one of its swollen rounds. Resting the barrel on top of his left arm, right hand relaxed near the trigger, he searched for a good target.

"Any choices?" he asked.

Potter piped up quickly. "I saw four or five goats duck into that little cave up there." He indicated a dent in the mountain only a few hundred feet away, slightly below our elevation.

Richert nodded and aimed. Abruptly there was a shower of orange sparks on the cliffside, a few feet to the right of the cave mouth. Clods of dirt and chunks of rock tumbled downward. Listening carefully over the sound of the wind and the *ka-chik* of the M-79 being opened, I could just hear the bleating of goats.

"Think I got the range now," Richert said. He reloaded and fired.

The cave mouth belched dirt, grass, and the bodies of two goats. They lay twitching in response-to-impact poses, perched precariously at the edge of the rock. Smoke and dust plumed out of the opening.

"There it is," Richert said.

We took turns with the grenade launcher. Naturally we killed a few more goats, but the best part was seeing how spectacularly we could chew up the mountain.

Eventually we decided to have lunch. A light one, in anticipation of the feast that night. I dug through my supply of C rations and took out a can of crackers and some Cheddar-cheese spread. I sat down and pulled my P-38 opener from my belt.

Sayre wandered off to take a leak. I noticed him giving his thousand-yard stare to the pile of rocks he was irrigating. Made curious, I examined it more thoroughly myself. Gradually I felt the hair on the nape of my neck begin to rise.

The rocks were not a natural formation. Though crude, eroded, and obviously long-abandoned, it was definitely human work. I recalled pictures I had seen in a museum on Oahu. The pile was a heiau. A shrine, left by fishermen to their gods.

I was thankful I was already sitting. My knees got the quiver so bad I dropped the opener.

Sayre turned away from it suddenly, and I, equally quick, focused my eyes once more at the sights. Out in the water I saw driftwood, coconuts, seaweed, and even goats, caught in the current that skims Kahoolawe and carries its flotsam and jetsam toward the shores of Maui, past the little half-ring islet of Molokini. I could also make out Lanai and Molokai toward the north.

Directly below, fins jutted up out of the water. The bodies of goats jerked. Soon more fins appeared. Suddenly the water thrashed and a goat disappeared completely, leaving only an upwelling of crimson and patches of hair.

Sayre was back, and was gazing with the rest of us down at the tableau.

"I don't like sharks," he said.

It was only then I noticed the quarter-pound block of TNT in his hand. He stroked it like a penis.

"I don't like sharks, either," Potter said loudly.

Shut up, Pot, I thought.

"You been carrying that stuff with you the whole time?" Stone Wall asked, nodding at the satchel at Sayre's waist. The zipper was open, revealing it to be full of the cylindrical blocks.

"Uh-huh. Never know when you might want to blow something up." Even as he said this he was capping the explosive.

In another few moments the block was sailing through the air. It hit the waves near one of the largest conglomerations of dead goats. A few seconds later the ocean geysered, spraying water, blood, goats—and part of a shark—into the air.

"There it is!" Potter shouted.

More sharks rushed in from the boundaries, attracted by the ruptured goats, drawn to the carcass of their own brother, their frenzied feeding rendering the ocean almost cauldronish. The Alalakeiki Channel is famous for its concentration of sharks. Sayre blew up two more of them with another quarter-pound block. He followed that with three more in rapid succession, until the ocean practically spat goat and shark flesh. The bodies of smaller fish, killed by the shock wave, welled to the surface.

I stopped watching. I know he threw in at least half a dozen more blocks. I listened to the bleating of goats trapped on the cliff and reached in my pocket, found the firm, smooth contours of the syrinx, and held on tight.

VII

The smoke inside the Kahoolawe Country Club was like an inversion layer, the scent of the tobacco tainted with the odors of beer and sweat. I leaned back in my folding chair and lowered my fork, too full to eat anymore. The goat Melendez had brought back had roasted in the pit for eight hours, and had been perfect.

Potter dropped his cards for the fourth time. Jones chuckled. "You little dudes got to learn how to hold yo' liquor. How'd they let a shrimp like you in the Marines, anyhow?"

"I ain't that little," Potter said, and burped.

"You is little for dat six-pack."

Melendez helped Potter put his cards back together. "Man, you won't last long in this game."

"I'm a good poker player," Pot retorted.

"Whatcha got?"

"Full house."

Jones leaned over and lowered Potter's hand, glancing at the contents. Potter snatched it back, too late. Melendez and Jones shook their heads and threw their own cards down.

"Aw, fuck you guys." Potter stood up, none too steadily.

His hair, short as it was, was mussed. ''I'm gonna go call my girlfriend.''

''You ain't big enough to have a girlfriend,'' Richert commented from the other side of the table.

''You bet your ass,'' Potter said. ''Got me a damn nice bitch.''

Jones started gathering the cards together. ''Be cool, Pot. We ain't got no telephones out here. How you gon' call yo' girlfriend?''

Potter hiccupped and stared at the floor, as if he didn't quite comprehend what Jones was saying. ''I'll . . . I'll call Kaneohe and have 'em hook me up.''

Little wrinkles grew on Jones's forehead. ''Shee-it. Look, junior, your chick prob'ly ain't even home, somethin' like dat. You get ev'body in a lotta trouble for nothin'.''

''She'll be home! She ain't got no other guy but me!''

Jones stood up, put his hands on Potter's shoulders, and said evenly, ''Aw right, aw right, she a good girl. But supposin' she ain't home? What if she be out with her girlfriend?''

''I don't care. I wanna call her anyway.'' He pulled free of Jones's grip and began wobbling toward the doorway on the side nearest the radio shack.

''Lance Corporal! Sit *down!*''

Potter stopped, turning back toward Lieutenant Priest. His lower lip trembled, but he couldn't quite get his glare high enough to meet that of our CO. Priest didn't bother to repeat himself. Finally Jones walked over and tugged Potter's arm.

''C'mon, Pot, we got a game goin' on here.''

Potter allowed himself to be led back to the table, scowling, and began picking up the cards Melendez was dealing. He grabbed another beer and sucked at it petulantly.

''What you got to tell your gal that so all fired important, anyhow?'' Jones asked.

Potter shrugged. ''I was gonna tell her how many goats I got today.''

Jones's expression lost the friendly, big brother mirth. He leaned forward, placing his deep brown, intimidating Negro features in front of Potter's ruddy white-boy cheeks, much as he had back in the chopper. He squeezed Potter's shoulder until the lance corporal winced.

"Nah, Pot. You ain't gon' tell your woman nothin' 'bout dat shit. You ain't never gon' tell her 'bout dat, not now, not after you get back to Kaneohe."

Potter sucked both his lips between his teeth and tried to keep his eyes dry. With one finger he tugged at the grip on his shoulder, ineffectually. I was grateful I wasn't the object of Jones's stare. The private's pupils were wide and incredibly dark, deep enough to completely swallow young lance corporals.

"Okay," Potter murmured. When Jones didn't move, he said it again.

Eventually Jones's expression lost its fire. He turned away and picked up his cards. "Hey, Short," he asked casually, "you done stuffin' your face? Get in the game so I can get some chips back, boy."

I shook my head.

He shrugged and they began to ante in. Potter, I noticed, did not join the table talk. By the time they had taken their additional cards, I had slipped outside.

My mood had been introspective ever since the scene at the cliff, mitigated by the excellence of the luau and the anesthetizing effect of the beer. Jones's words had turned it further inward. I needed to be alone.

I went down to the beach. At this tide it was little more than a sliver of white trim along the cove. I hunkered down on the sand, my back to the withered landscape surrounding the base camp.

It was deathly quiet. Not in the sense of noise, because there was the surf and the wind. No, it was the lack of human presence. It was all too easy to feel the fact that men had never domesticated Kahoolawe.

The starlight glinted off a still sea. Straight ahead, southwest, lay the islands of the Pacific. The ancient Hawaiians used to use this part of Kahoolawe as their departure point. They called the snout of land to my right Lae o Kealaikahiki, "The Carrying Away to Distant Lands." To the southwest, to Asia.

To Vietnam.

My tour had been over for months. But there, on that beach, I realized for the first time that when I kissed

II-Corps good-bye, a piece of me never left. It was still back at Dak To.

I reached into my pocket and pulled out my tobacco can. Filled, of course, with my stash. It contained enough marijuana, so I had calculated, to last me the whole two weeks. I sat down and began rolling a party pack. By the time I was done, I had eight monstrous reefers. I lit the first one and began smoking.

" 'Bout time you fucking got back, Corpsman," Lieutenant Priest said.

They were all on the knoll where we had been sleeping since that first, overly hot night in the barracks. The camp fire had faded, but no one was asleep. As I wobbled into the group and sat on my hammock, Lombard and Stone Wall arrived from another direction and set down two boxes of ammunition. Melendez was hastily reassembling his M-16. Sayre had out a .45, his M-1, his Fairbairn-Sykes dagger, and a row of quarter-pound blocks of TNT, caps ready. Richert's M-79 was out of its holster.

"There's . . . noises out there," I said, nodding at the shadowy landscape beyond the kerosene lanterns' glow.

"No shit," Priest said.

It was the sound of breaking twigs, the patter of feet, small moans, piping. Above that was a pasture stench that grew stronger with each flutter of the breeze.

"Here," Sayre said, and tossed me a rifle. "You'll need this."

"Why?" I asked, still groggy. Beside me, Potter, pale as a ghost, had broken out the new ammo, though there was already enough on the knoll to arm a company. Jones was scanning the brush to the east. Abruptly he stood up and fired a long burst, obliterating twigs and branches. When the noise quit ringing in our ears, we heard only the same low, ominous rumbles.

"They're out there—somewhere," Sayre said, stroking the barrel of his .45.

I got down—low, where corpsmen should be if they're smart. The clip was oily as I loaded it; it almost dropped from my hands.

"Point that motherfucker away from me!" Jones yelled at Potter, who jumped and redirected his rifle barrel.

"Hssst!" Sayre said, finger to his lips. Out in the dark the sounds had stopped.

The eyes appeared.

Hundreds of eyes. All around the camp. Lit with a feral glow.

My mouth went cotton dry. I couldn't swallow. Nearby Potter's fingers were trembling so badly he couldn't keep his trigger finger in the gap. Sayre picked up a block of TNT and armed it.

A tidal wave of goats charged us at a full run.

Our 16s mowed down the front row. Sayre's block of TNT and Richert's M-79 tore huge, bloody holes in their formation. But the second row simply jumped over the bodies of the first.

Their thin, ghastly bodies were no match for the power of close-range fire; the bullets passed right through and hit the goats behind. Hundreds died in the first five seconds. They didn't even slow down. Within moments the circle of carcasses was three or four deep. The living ones had to climb to get over the fallen. The ring grew tighter and tighter around us, the stack of corpses higher.

Somebody was whimpering; I don't know who. My throat was sore. Gore splattered on my face, flung from the impact of Richert's M-79 shells. The fighting was getting too close for him to use the weapon. The goats were higher than eye level now. Someone was praying; I don't know who.

My clip was empty. Was this the third, or the fourth? I jammed in another and shot—upward now, at a forty-five-degree angle. I didn't have many clips left. The heat of my rifle barrel singed hair off the back of my hand.

It was starting to rain pieces of goat.

Somewhere beyond the mountain, even above the thunder of the rifles, I could hear the frenzied music of pipes. It was then that I lost control of my bowels.

Melendez was the first one to die. A buck launched from the top of the crater and skewered him in the guts, in spite of the fact that he'd shot off its hind legs in midair.

Stone Wall was next, taken down by five or six does that bit off his nose, his ears, his fingers, his balls.

Lombard shot himself.

We were knee-deep in blood and severed limbs. The open air above had narrowed to a puny circle. The bottom layer of goats was leaking like a bin of overripe fruit. I had just enough time to see the corpsman killed before the walls collapsed in on me.

I was held immobile by the pressure of hot flesh. It was hard to inhale. One arm was above me, still holding my .45; I couldn't lower it. I could see a tiny section of sky directly above. The only sound was the gurgle of blood seeping, and intestines popping.

A shadow appeared in the opening above. A goat's head. It had a broken horn.

"I'll get you, you bastard!" I shouted. *"I've got you now! I've got you!"* I had just enough freedom of movement to aim my pistol. I grinned triumphantly and pulled the trigger.

Empty.

For some reason, I could see Charlie perfectly now, as if it were day. He was smiling. He stood, and suddenly he had the upper body of a man. The broken horn grew out, and both horns began to gleam as if made of gold. He had a pine wreath wrapped around his neck. He raised pipes to his lips and blew three piercing notes.

Then the mountain of goats collapsed completely.

"Corpsman! Corpsman!"

Priest was doing the shouting. I pulled the lead out of my heels and sprinted up the knoll. I could already hear Sayre whimpering. I was shaking so bad I wasn't sure I could control my bladder, but my head spun with one jubilant thought: *It wasn't me! He didn't get me!*

I bounded into the group. They were gathered around Sayre's sleeping bag. Priest and Richert were holding the EOD man by the arms. Sayre was shaking, sweat popping from his neck and forehead. I was finally close enough to hear what he was moaning.

"Goats . . . goats . . . goats . . ." It sounded as if he were begging.

"Where the fuck have you been?" Priest yelled at me. He and Richert were having a hard time of it. Sayre was rigid in their grip, left arm stiff like a man in cardiac arrest. Foam gushed over his lips, breath coming in staccato bursts.

"At the beach," I answered.

Jones was trying to put a stick between Sayre's teeth. I took it from him.

"Don't. It's not that kind of seizure." I knelt next to Sayre. "Just let him breathe."

I leaned down until I could stare Sayre in the eyes. He didn't focus on me. "Goats." He wept softly. "Goats."

"He was screaming that a couple of minutes ago. Woke us all up," Priest said.

"Somebody hand me a handkerchief, will you?"

Stone Wall held one out. I used it to wipe away the spittle from Sayre's lips and throat. His beard was like sandpaper. "Goats. Goats." I knew those hushed words were going to haunt me.

"Do you know if he was on any kind of medication?" I asked Lombard.

The other EOD man shook his head. "Never saw any." I had Potter check his gear. Just aspirin.

"Goats . . ."

Sayre was finally beginning to relax. Priest and Richert let him lay down on his pillow. His eyelids finally began to blink. He glanced at me, at Priest, at Jones.

"How are you, Sayre?" I asked.

He seemed startled by my voice. "Fine. I'm fine."

"Do you remember what happened to you just now?"

He began wiping away the traces of the spittle with the back of his hand. He didn't answer.

"How are you, Sayre?" I asked again.

"Fine. I'm fine," he said automatically, as if unaware that I had asked the question earlier.

I pursed my lips and glanced at my companions. "Just let him lay here. He doesn't need spectators."

Jones stood up, went to his hammock, and pulled a pair of trousers over his skivvies. Gradually each of the others left with him for the Sheraton Kahoolawe, except Melendez, whom I asked to stay.

"I'm tired," Sayre murmured. His eyelids were beginning to sag. "Long day . . ." Beside me Melendez made the sign of the cross.

* * *

The sweat on the back of my neck was cold as I stepped into the mess hall. Somebody had started coffee.

"How is he?" Priest asked.

"Asleep. I left Melendez with him just in case. Better call Kaneohe and have a medevac sent out here first thing in the morning."

"Right."

Déjà vu. How many times had I given advice to an officer about medevacs. They always accepted what I said without qualm. As if I ever knew what the fuck I was talking about.

For several seconds no one said anything. The sound of the coffee brewing was unusually loud. Then Jones glanced quickly from side to side and said, "Where's Pot?"

We stared at each other. Potter wasn't with us.

"He wasn't on the knoll, either, come to think of it," Richert said.

Priest jerked a thumb toward the door. Stone Wall and Jones went to check his gear.

"He's not there. His rifle's missing, too," Jones announced.

Lieutenant Priest sighed. "I'm going to ream that little faggot's ass."

"He's probably curled up in a gully somewhere, sleeping off his drunk," Richert said.

Priest nodded. "But he could also have tripped over a piece of shrapnel. We gotta go find him."

"Sir?" Richert asked.

Priest's voice sounded tired. "I'm responsible for every man on this goddamned island. Do it. I'll stay here with Melendez and Sayre."

We hesitated, but it was clear that however angry the lieutenant might be with Potter, he was serious about the search. Eventually Jones picked up a flashlight. "Can't sleep no mo' anyway," he muttered.

I told everyone not to bother with the beach, so the five of us headed inland, flashlights in one hand, rifles on the opposite shoulder. After a few hundred yards Lombard, Richert, and Stone Wall branched off to the left. Jones and I continued to walk together.

We saw no sign of Potter. Our beams flitted over pieces of

shrapnel, into thorn thickets, stopped on clods of clay. The lack of conversation was conspicuous. Finally we reached a fork in the path that would require us to separate. We stopped there.

"Well," Jones murmured, "what do you think it was?"

"Sayre?" I asked, as if it weren't obvious.

"That guy—he give me the motherfuckin' shakes first time I seen him. Never thought I see him crying like a babe. So what you think?"

I had, of course, thought of nothing else since I'd heard the incoherent screams on my way up from the beach. By this time I had a theory.

"Everything, Jones. It was just fucking *everything*."

I could barely see his expression in the moonlight, but I knew he read me right. "Ev'thing, huh? Ain't that the motherfucker."

"There it is," I said faintly.

He nodded slowly, taking a step forward, stopped again. "You done good back there, Short."

"Jim."

He didn't say it, but I saw his white teeth gleam. "See you back in camp. I'll take the left." Within a few moments we rounded opposite sides of a hillock and I was alone.

Everything. Everyone dreams the same dream. We just dream it differently.

A bat flew across my field of vision. I was still so stoned I saw winged afterimages hang in the air long after it had passed. I hadn't seen anything like that since Vietnam.

I hadn't gone far when I heard rocks slide to my right. I spun and had my M-16 aimed even before I got the flashlight up.

It was a goat.

It was old, skin hanging slack from its neck, horns fissured and stained. It waited in the beam of light, motionless on stiff legs. It was no more than twenty yards away.

I raised the barrel of my rifle. The goat still didn't move. Gradually I realized from the clouds in its rheumy eyes that it had cataracts. It was blind.

I stood there with my M-16. The goat just bleated.

I lowered the barrel. "Get out of here!" I yelled. "Go on! Get the fuck out of here!"

The animal just stared back. Gradually it hit me. The thing was deaf, too.

I picked up a rock and threw it. It landed near one of the goat's hooves. Startled, it finally scrambled into the kiawe. I followed it with my beam until it was thoroughly gone.

I slowly slung my rifle back on my shoulder, my hand slick against the stock. I turned to continue on, but I couldn't get my feet to move. What was I doing here anyway?

I was chasing a drunk, armed lance corporal over an island full of bombs.

I felt something hard in my shirt pocket, and pulled it out. It was the syrinx, the pale yellow reed almost luminescent in the dark. I ran my hands over its hard, ancient surface, and thought of Sayre.

I tucked the flashlight under an armpit to light the barren path back to the base camp, leaving both hands free to cup the panpipes to my lips. I played them the whole way, and prayed the gods would send me only pleasant dreams.

Ben Bova

Ben Bova has written nearly seventy books of science fiction and science journalism. He has been a science writer and marketing manager for Avco-Everett Research Labs, a technical editor for Project Vanguard, and a screenwriter for the Physical Science Study Committee at MIT. He is currently president of the National Space Society. In 1971 he became editor of *Analog* and breathed new life into the magazine by publishing innovative and important work by Joe Haldeman, George R. R. Martin, Spider Robinson, Orson Scott Card, Norman Spinrad, Roger Zelazny, Gene Wolfe, Vonda N. McIntyre, and others. He went on to become editor of *Omni* in 1978, and has received six Hugo awards for best editor. His own short stories and science articles have appeared in all the major science fiction magazines, as well as in *Smithsonian, The IEEE Spectrum, Psychology Today,* and many other periodicals and anthologies. Some of his short stories can be found in the collections *Forward in Time, Maxwell's Demons, The Astral Mirror,* and *Prometheans.* His novels include *The Exiles Trilogy, Colony, Privateers, Voyagers, Orion, The Dueling Machine, The Weathermakers, Star Watchman, Millennium, The Starcrossed, As on a Darkling Plain,* and his latest work, *Voyages II: The Alien Within.* He has also edited several anthologies, among them *The Best of Analog, The Best of Astounding, The Many Worlds of SF, The Analog Science Fact Reader,* and the giant two-book set *Science Fiction Hall of Fame, Vol-*

ume Two. His latest nonfiction book is *Star Peace: Assured Survival,* an exploration of the Strategic Defense Initiative. He is currently editing the *Ben Bova Discovery* series, a new line of novels, for Tor Books.

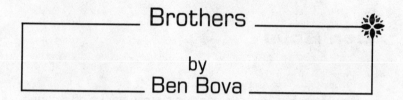

Brothers

by
Ben Bova

Command Module Saratoga, *in Lunar Orbit*

Alone now, Bill Carlton stopped straining his eyes and turned away from the tiny triangular window. The landing module was a dwindling speck against the gray pockmarked surface of the barren, alien moon.

He tried to lean his head back against the contour couch, remembered again that he was weightless, floating lightly against the restraining harness. All the old anger surged up in him again, knotting his neck with tension even in zero gravity.

Sitting here like a goddamned robot. Left here to mind the store like some goddamned kid while they go down to the surface and get their names in the history books. The also-ran. Sixty miles away from the moon, but I'll never set foot on it. Never.

The Apollo command module seemed almost large now that Wally and Dave were gone. The two empty couches looked huge, luxurious. The banks of instruments and controls hummed at him electrically. We can get along fine without you, they were saying. We're machines, we don't need an also-ran to make us work.

This tin can stinks, he said to himself. Three days cooped up in here, sitting inside these damned suits. *I* stink.

With a wordless growl, Bill turned up the gain on the radio. His earphones crackled for a moment, then the robotic voice of the Capcom came through.

"You're in the approach phase, *Yorktown*. Everything looking good."

Wally's voice answered, "Manual control okay. Altitude forty-three hundred."

Almost three seconds passed. "Forty-three, we copy." It was Shannon's voice from Houston. Capcom for the duration of the landing.

Bill sat alone in the command module and listened. His two teammates were about to land. He had traveled a quarter million miles, but would get no closer than fifty-eight miles to the moon.

U.S.S. Saratoga, *in the Tonkin Gulf*

Bob Carlton tapped the back of his helmet against the head knocker and held his gloved hands up against the canopy's clear plastic so the deck crew could see he was not touching any of the controls. The sky-blue paint had been scratched from the spot where the head knocker touched the helmet. Sixty missions will do that.

Sixty missions. It seemed more like six hundred. Or six thousand. It was endless. Every day, every day. The same thing. Endless.

The A-7 was being attached to the catapult now. It was the time when Bob always got just slightly queasy, staring out beyond the edge of the carrier's heaving deck into the gray mist of morning.

"Cleared for takeoff," said the launch director's voice in his earphones.

"Clear," Bob repeated.

He rammed the throttle forward and felt the bomber's jet engine howl and surge suddenly, straining, making the whole plane tremble like a hunting dog begging to be released from its leash.

"Three . . . two . . . one . . . GO!"

His head slammed back and his whole body seemed to flatten against itself, pressed into the seat as the A-7 leaped off the carrier's deck and into the misty air. The deep rolling swells of blue-green water slid by and then receded as he pulled the control column back slightly and the swept-wing plane angled up through the sullen, low-hanging clouds. Without even thinking consciously of it, he reached back and pushed the head knocker up into its locked position. Now he could fire the ejection seat if he had to.

In a moment the sun broke through and sparkled off the mirrors arrayed around the curve of the canopy. Bob saw the five other planes of his flight and formed up on the left end of their vee. The queasiness was gone now. He felt strong and good in the sunshine.

He looked up and saw the pale shadow of a half moon grinning lopsidedly at him. Bill's up there, he thought. Can you see me, Bill? Can you hear me calling you?

Then he looked away. A dark slice of land lay on the horizon, slim and silent as a dagger. Vietnam.

"Contact. All lights on. Engines stop. We're down." Bill heard Dave McDonald's laconic voice announce their landing on the moon.

"We copy, *Yorktown*. Good job. Fantastic." Shannon sounded excited. He was due to fly the next mission. "*Saratoga*, do you read?"

Bill was surprised that he had to swallow twice before his voice would work. "Copy. *Yorktown* in port. Good going, guys."

It was an all-Navy crew, so they had named their modules in honored Navy tradition. The lunar lander became *Yorktown*. Bill rode alone in the command module, *Saratoga*. The old men with gold braid on their sleeves and silver in their hair loved that. Good old Annapolis spirit.

"You are go for excursion," said Shannon, lapsing back into technical jargon.

"Roger." McDonald's voice was starting to fade out. "We'll take a little walk soon's we wiggle into these special suits."

And I'll sit here by myself, Bill thought. What would Shannon and the rest of those clowns at Houston do if I screwed my helmet on and took a walk on my own?

The fucking oxygen mask never fit right. It pressed across the bridge of Bob's nose and cut into his cheeks. And the stuff was almost too cold to breathe, it made his teeth ache. Bob felt his ears pop slightly as the formation of six attack bombers dove to treetop height and then streaked across the mottled green forest.

This was the part of the mission that he liked best, racing balls-out close enough to the goddamned trees to suck a monkey into your air intake. Everything a green blur outside the cockpit. Six hundred knots and the altimeter needle flopping around zero. The plane took it as smooth as a new Cadillac tooling up to the country club. Not a shake or a rattle in her. She merely rocked slightly in the invisible air currents bubbling up from the forest.

Christ, any lower and we'll come back smeared green. He laughed aloud.

Bob flew the bomb-laden plane with mere touches of his thumb against the button on the control column that moved the trim tabs. The A-7 responded like a thoroughbred, jumping smoothly over an upjutting tree, turning gracefully in formation with the five others.

Why don't we just fly like this forever? Bob wondered. Just keep on going and never, never stop.

But up ahead the land was rising, ridge after ridge of densely wooded hills. In a valley between one particular pair of ridges was an NVA ammunition dump, according to their preflight briefing. By the time they got there, Bob guessed, the North Vietnamese would have moved their ammo to someplace else. We'll wind up bombing the fucking empty jungle again.

But their antiaircraft guns will be there. Oh, yes indeed, the little brown bastards'll have everything from slingshots to radar-directed artillery to throw at us. They always do.

There was a whole checklist of chores for Bill to do as he waited alone in the command module. Photographic mapping. Heat sensors. Housekeeping checks on the life-support systems.

Busywork, Bill grumbled silently. He went through the checklist mechanically, doing even the tiniest task with the numb efficiency of a machine. Just a lot of crap to make me feel like I'm doing something. To make *them* feel like there's something for me to do.

The radio voices of Peters and McDonald were fading fast now. The command module was swinging around in its orbit toward the far side of the moon. Bill listened to Wally and Dave yahooing and joking with each other as they bounced and jogged on the moon's surface, stirring up dust that had waited four billion years for them to arrive.

"Wish you could be here, buddy!" sang Wally.

"Yeah, Bill. You'd love the scenery," Dave agreed happily.

Bill said into his radio microphone, "Thanks a lot, you guys." So what if they heard him in Houston. What more could they do to him?

"*Saratoga*, you are approaching radio cutoff," Shannon reminded him needlessly.

"Radio cutoff," Bill repeated to Houston. Then he counted silently, one thousand, two thousand, three . . .

"See you on the other side," said Shannon, his radio voice finally crossing the distance between them.

"That's a rog," Bill said.

The far side of the moon. Totally alone, separated from the entire human race by a quarter million miles of distance and two thousand miles of solid rock.

Bill stole one final glance at the earth as the spacecraft swung around in its orbit. It was blue and mottled with white swirling clouds, glowing like a solitary candle on a darkened altar. He could not see Vietnam. He did not even try to find it.

"Check guns." The flight leader's voice in his helmet earphones almost startled Bob.

The easy part of the flight was finished. The work was beginning. He thumbed the firing button on his control column, just the slightest tap. Below his feet he could feel a brief buzz, almost like a small vacuum cleaner or an electric shaver. Just for an instant.

"Corsair Six, guns clear." His microphone was built into the oxygen mask.

The flight leader kept an open mike. Bob could hear him breathing noisily inside his mask. The ground was rising now, still green and treacherous, but reaching up into the sky in steep ridges.

Their flight plan took advantage of the terrain. Come in low, skim the treetops, until the final ridge. Then zoom up over that last crest, dive flat out into the valley and plaster the joint with high-explosive bombs and napalm. Get in and get out before they know you're there.

Good plan. Except for tail-end Bobby. Four planes could get past the fucking slopes before they can react. Maybe five. But six was expecting too much. They'll have their radars tracking and their guns firing by the time I come through.

The only sound in the command module was the inevitable electrical hum of the equipment. Bill ignored it. It would make no impression on his conscious mind unless it stopped.

He floated gently against the light restraining harness of his couch and closed his eyes. This was the time he had waited for. His own time. They could pick him for the shit job of sitting here and waiting while Wally and Dave got all the glory, but they couldn't stop him from doing this one experiment, this test that nobody in the world knew about.

Nobody except Bobby and me, he thought.

Eyes closed, Bill tried to relax his body completely. Force the tension out of his muscles. Make those tendons ease their grip.

"Bobby," he whispered. "Bobby, can you hear me?"

They had agreed to the experiment a year earlier, the last time they had seen each other, at the lobby bar in the Saint Francis Hotel.

"What the hell are *you* doing here?" they had asked simultaneously.

"I'm rotating back to 'Nam," said Bob.

"I'm attending an engineering conference over at Ames."

They marveled at the coincidence. Neither of them had ever gone to the hotel bar before. And at four in the afternoon!

"For twin brothers, we sure don't see much of each other," Bill said, after the bartender had set up a pair of Jack Daniel's neat, water on the side, before them. "Takes a coincidence like this."

"This is more than a coincidence," said Bob.

"You think so?"

Bobby nodded, picked up his drink and sipped at it.

"I think you've been out in the mystic East too long, kid. You're going Asiatic."

"Maybe you've been hanging around with too many scientists," Bob countered. "You're starting to think like a machine."

"Come on, Bobby, you don't really believe—"

"What made you come in here this afternoon?"

Bill shrugged. "Damned if I know. What about you?"

A twin shrug. "Can't say it was a premonition. On the other hand, I usually don't even come to this part of town when I'm on leave in Frisco."

They drank for several hours, ignoring the bar girls who sauntered through looking for early action. They talked about family and old times. They avoided comparing their Navy duties. Bob was a frontline pilot in a carrier attack squadron. Bill was on detached duty with the astronaut corps. They had both made their decisions about that years earlier.

"You really believe this ESP stuff?" Bill asked as they fumbled in their pockets for money to pay the tab.

"I don't know." Then Bob looked directly into his brother's eyes. "Twins *ought* to be close."

"Yeah. I guess so."

"I'll be shipping out next week."

"They've scheduled me for a shot two months from now."

"Good! Good luck."

"Luck to you, kid." Bill got up from the barstool.

Bob did the same. "Stay in touch, huh? Wouldn't hurt you to write me a line now and then."

With a sudden grin, Bill said, "I'll do better than that. I'll give you a call from the moon."

"Sure," Bob replied.

"Why not? You think this ESP business is real, let's give it a test."

Bob put on the same frown he had worn as a child when his twin brother displeased him.

"I'm serious, Bobby. We can try it, at least." Bill hesitated, then added, "I dream about you, sometimes."

Bob's frown melted. "You dream about me?"

"Sometimes."

He grinned and clapped his brother on the shoulder. "Me, too," he said. "I dream about you, now and then."

"So let's see if we can make contact from the moon!" Bill insisted.

Bob shrugged, the way he always did when he gave in to his older brother. "Sure. Why not?"

But now as he sat alone in the silence of space, where he

could not even see the earth, Bill's call to his younger brother went unanswered.

"Bobby," he said aloud. It was almost a snarl, almost a plea. "Bobby, where in hell are you?"

The valley was long and narrow, that's why they had to go in Indian file. Bob saw the green ridges tilt and slide beneath him, then straighten out as he banked steeply and put the A-7 into a flat dive, following the plane ahead of him, sixth in the flight of six.

He felt a strange prickling at the back of his neck. Not fear. Something he had never felt before. As if someone far, far away was calling his name. No time for that now. He nosed the plane down and started the bomb run.

For once, intelligence had the right shit. The flight leader's cluster of bombs waggled down into the engulfing forest canopy, then all hell broke loose. The bombs and napalm went off, blowing big black clouds streaked with red flame up through the roof of the jungle. Before the next plane could drop its load, the secondary explosions started. Huge fireballs. Tracers whizzing out in every direction. Searing white magnesium flares.

The second plane released its bombs as Bob watched. Everything seemed to freeze in place for a moment that never ended, and then the plane, the bombs, the fireballs blowing away the jungle below all merged into one big mass of flame and the plane disappeared.

"Pull up, pull up!" Bob heard somebody screaming in his earphones. He had already yanked the control column back toward his crotch. Planes were scattering across the sky, jettisoning their bomb loads helter-skelter. Bob glanced at his left hand and was shocked to see that the bomb release switches next to it had already been tripped.

The valley was seething with explosions. The ammo dump was blowing itself to hell and anybody who was down there was going along for the ride. Including the flight leader's wingman. Who the hell was flying wing for him today? Bob wondered briefly.

"Form up on me," the voice in his earphones commanded. "Come on, dammit, stop gawking and form up."

Bob craned his neck to find where the other planes were.

He saw two, three . . . and another one pulling gees to catch up with them.

As he banked and started climbing to rejoin his group, he felt a stray tendril of thought, like the wispy memory of a tune that he could not fully recall.

"Bill?" he asked aloud.

Then something exploded and he was slammed back in his seat, pain flaming through his legs and groin.

The shock of contact was a double hammer blow. Bill's body went rigid with sudden pain.

Bobby! What happened? But he knew, immediately and fully, just as if he sat in the A-7's cockpit.

Flak, Bobby gasped. I'm hit.

Jesus Christ, the pain!

I'm bleeding bad, Billy. Both legs . . .

Can you work the controls?

It took an enormous effort to move his arms. Tabs and ailerons okay. Elevators. Another surge of agony, dizziness. Can't use my legs. Rudder pedals no go.

Radio's shot to hell, too.

They're leaving me behind, Billy. They're getting out of here and leaving me.

That's what they're supposed to do! We've got to gain altitude, Bob. Get away from their guns.

Yeah. We're climbing. Engine's running rough, though.

Never mind that. Grab altitude. Point her home.

Can't make the rudder work. Can't turn.

Use the trim tabs. Go easy. She'll steer okay. Like that time we broke the boom on the sailfish. We'll get back okay.

You see anything else out there? MiGs?

No, you're clear. Just concentrate on getting this bird out over the sea. You don't want to eject where they'll capture you.

Don't want to eject, period. Or ditch. Not in the shape I'm in.

We'll get back to the carrier, don't worry.

I won't be able to land it, Billy. I don't think I can last that long anyway.

We'll do it together. I'll help you.

You can't . . .

Who says I can't?

Yeah, but . . .

We'll do it together.

I don't think I'll make it. I'm . . .

Don't fade out on me! Bobby, stay awake! Here, let me get that damned oxygen mask off you; we're low enough to suck real air.

Bill, you shouldn't try this. I don't want us both to get killed.

I've got to, kid. Nothing else matters.

But . . .

Bobby, listen to me. I ought to be there with you. For real. I should've been on the line with you instead of playing around out here in space. I took the easy way out. The coward's way out. They gave me a chance to play astronaut and I took it. I jumped at it!

Who wouldn't?

You didn't. I owe you my life, Bobby. You're doing the fighting while I'm playing it safe a quarter million miles away from the real thing.

You're crazy! You think blasting off into space on top of some glorified skyrocket and riding to the fucking moon in a tin can is *safe?*

There's no Indians up here shooting at us, kid.

I'll take the Indians.

Bobby, I'm not kidding. I feel so goddamned ashamed. I've always grabbed the best piece of the pie away from you. All our lives. I ran out on you . . .

I always got the piece I wanted, big brother. You did what you had to do. And it's important work. I know that. We all know that. I'm doing what I want to do.

You're putting your life on the line.

So are you.

I shouldn't have run out on you. I should have helped you fight this war.

There's enough of us fighting this lousy war. Too many. It's all a wagonload of shit, Bill. Talk about feeling ashamed. Making war on goddamned farmers and blowing villages to hell isn't my idea of glory.

But how else . . .

You do what you have to do, brother. Doesn't make any

difference why. You and your teammates are locked into the job by the powers that be.

The gold braid.

The gods.

Whatever.

We're locked in, Billy. It's all a test, just like Father Gilhooley always told us. We do what we have to do, because if we do less than that, we let down the guys with us. Nobody flies alone, brother. We've got each other's lives in our hands.

You believe that?

I know it.

The pain was flowing over them both in waves now, like breakers at the beach. They could sense a new surge growing and gliding toward them and then engulfing them, drenching them until they finally broke out of it only to see a new wave heading their way.

I'm not going to make it, Bill.

Yes, you are. We can make it.

I don't think so.

Look! The carrier, Bob!

Where? Yeah. Looks damned small from up here.

You're almost home. I'll handle the rudder, you work the stick.

Yeah, okay. Maybe we can make it. Maybe . . .

No maybe about it! We're going to put this junk heap down right in front of the admiral's nose.

Sure.

Gear down?

Yeah. Indicator light says it's locked.

Thank god for small miracles.

LSO's waving us in.

They've cleared the deck for us.

Nice of them.

Easy now, easy on the throttle. Don't stall her!

Stop the backseat driving.

Deck's coming up too damned fast, Bobby!

Don't worry . . . I can . . . make it.

You did it! We're down!

We did it, brother. We did it together.

The deck team rushed to the battered plane. Fire fighters

doused the hot engine area and wings with foam. Plane handlers climbed up to the cockpit and slid the canopy back to find the pilot crumpled unconscious, his flight suit soaked with blood from the waist down. The medics lifted Bob Carlton from the cockpit tenderly and had whole blood flowing into his arm even while they wheeled him toward the sick bay.

"Look at his face," said one of the medics. "What the hell's he smiling about?"

It took thirty more orbits around the moon before Peters and McDonald left the surface to rendezvous with the command module and begin the flight back to earth. Thirty orbits while Bill Carlton sat totally alone. New attempts to contact his brother were fruitless. He knew that Bob was alive; that much he could sense. But there was no answer to his silent calls.

Wally Peters wormed through the airlock hatch first, a quizzical expression on his square-jawed face.

"How you doing, Billy boy?"

"Just fine. Glad to have you back."

Dave McDonald came through and floated to his couch on Bill's left. "Miss us?"

"Yeah, sure."

"Lonesome in here, all by yourself?" Wally grinned.

"Kind of." Bill grinned back.

Wally and Dave glanced at each other. Bill realized it had been a long time since either of them had seen him smile.

"Here," said Wally. "We brought you a present." He reached into the pouch in the leg of his suit and took out a slim flat dark piece of stone.

"Your very own moon rock," Dave said.

Bill took it from them wordlessly.

"We're sorry you couldn't have been down there with us, Bill. You would've enjoyed it."

"Yeah, we felt kind of bad leaving you here."

Bill laughed. "It's okay, guys. We all do what we have to do. We get the job done. Whatever it is. Wherever it is. We do what we've got to do, and we don't let our teammates down."

Dave and Wally stared at him for a moment.

"Come on," said Bill. "Let's get this tin can home."

Gardner Dozois

With stories such as "A Special Kind of Morning," "The Last Day of July," "Horse of Air," "Flash Point," "The Visible Man," "A Dream at Noonday," and "Chains of the Sea"—a hauntingly beautiful depiction of the alien strangeness and aching loneliness of childhood—Gardner Dozois firmly established himself as one of the leading prose stylists of the 1970s. These stories and others have been collected in *The Visible Man,* which the writer and critic Michael Bishop has called "a benchmark not only in Dozois's career but in the development of science fiction in the 1970's." Dozois's short fiction has appeared in *Playboy, Penthouse, Omni,* and most of the leading magazines and anthologies. He won two Nebula awards, for "The Peacemaker" and "Morning Child," and has been many times a finalist for other Nebulas and the Hugo awards. He is also the author of the novel *Strangers,* and a critical chapbook, *The Fiction of James Tiptree, Jr.*, as well as the editor of over twenty-five anthologies. These include the *Best Science Fiction of the Year* series, *The Year's Best Science Fiction* series, *A Day in the Life,* and *Another World.* He has also edited a number of anthologies with Jack Dann, including *Future Power, Aliens!, Unicorns!, Magicats!, Bestiary!, Mermaids!, Sorcerers!,* and *Demons!* In 1985 he became editor of *Isaac Asimov's Science Fiction Magazine.* He is currently at work on another novel, *Nottamun Town;* a new short story collection is forthcoming from Bluejay Books.

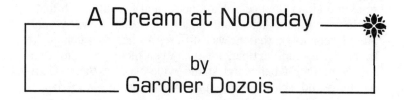

A Dream at Noonday

by
Gardner Dozois

I remember the sky, and the sun burning in the sky like a golden penny flicked into a deep blue pool, and the scuttling white clouds that changed into magic ships and whales and turreted castles as they drifted up across that bottomless ocean and swam the equally bottomless sea of my mind's eye. I remember the winds that skimmed the clouds, smoothing and rippling them into serene grandeur or boiling them into froth. I remember the same wind dipping low to caress the grass, making it sway and tremble, or whipping through the branches of the trees and making them sing with a wild, keening organ note. I remember the silence that was like a bronzen shout echoing among the hills.

—It is raining. The sky is slate-grey and grittily churning. It looks like a soggy dishrag being squeezed dry, and the moisture is dirty rain that falls in pounding sheets, pressing down the tall grass. The rain pocks the ground, and the loosely packed soil is slowly turning into mud and the rain spatters the mud, making it shimmer—

And I remember the trains. I remember lying in bed as a child, swathed in warm blankets, sniffing suspiciously and eagerly at the embryonic darkness of my room, and listening to the big trains wail and murmur in the freight yard beyond. I remember lying awake night after night, frightened and darkly fascinated, keeping very still so that the darkness wouldn't see me, and listening to the hollow booms and metallic moans as the train coupled and linked below my window. I remember that I thought the trains were alive, big dark beasts who came to dance and to hunt each other through the dappled moonlight of the world outside my room, and when I would listen to the whispering clatter of their passing and feel the room quiver ever so slightly in shy response, I would get a crawly feeling in my chest and a prickling along the back of my neck, and I would wish that I could watch them dance, although I knew that I never would. And I remember that it was different when I watched the trains during the daytime, for then even though I clung tight to my mother's hand and stared wide-eyed at their steam-belching and spark-spitting they were just big iron beasts putting on a show for me; they weren't magic then, they were hiding the magic inside them and pretending to be iron beasts and waiting for the darkness. I remember that I knew even then that trains are only magic in the night and only dance when no one can see them. And I remember that I couldn't go to sleep at night until I was soothed by the muttering lullaby of steel and the soft, rhythmical hiss-clatter of a train booming over a switch. And I remember that some nights the bellowing of a fast freight or the cruel, whistling shriek of a train's whistle would make me tremble and feel cold suddenly, even under my safe blanket-mountain, and I would find myself thinking about rain-soaked ground and blood and black cloth and half-understood references to my grandfather going away, and the darkness would suddenly seem to curl in upon itself and become diamond-hard and press down upon my straining eyes, and I would whimper and the fading whistle would snatch the sound from my mouth and trail it away into the night. And I remember that at times like that I would pretend that I had tiptoed to the window to watch the trains dance, which I never really dared to do because I knew I would die if I did, and then I would close my eyes and pretend that I was a train, and in my mind's eye I would be hanging disembodied in the darkness a few inches above the shining tracks, and then the track would begin to slip along under me, slowly at first then fast and smooth like flowing syrup, and then the darkness would be flashing by and then I would be moving out and away, surrounded by the wailing roar and evil steel chuckling of a fast freight slashing through the night, hearing my whistle scream with the majestic cruelty of a stooping eagle and feeling the switches boom and clatter hollowly under me, and I would fall asleep still moving out and away, away and out.

—The rain is stopping slowly, trailing away across the

field, brushing the ground like long, dangling grey fingers. The tall grass creeps erect again, bobbing drunkenly, shedding its burden of water as a dog shakes himself dry after a swim. There are vicious little crosswinds in the wake of the storm, and they make the grass whip even more violently than the departing caress of the rain. The sky is splitting open above, black rainclouds pivoting sharply on a central point, allowing a sudden wide wedge of blue to appear. The overcast churns and tumbles and clots like wet heavy earth turned by a spade. The sky is now a crazy mosaic of mingled blue and grey. The wind picks up, chews at the edge of the tumbling wrack, spinning it to the fineness of cotton candy and then lashing it away. A broad shaft of sunlight falls from the dark undersides of the clouds, thrusting at the ground and drenching it in a golden cathedral glow, filled with shimmering green highlights. The effect is like that of light through a stained-glass window, and objects bathed in the light seem to glow very faintly from within, seem to be suddenly translated into dappled molten bronze. There is a gnarled, shaggy tree in the center of the pool of sunlight, and it is filled with wet, disgruntled birds, and the birds are hesitantly, cautiously, beginning to sing again—

And I remember wandering around in the woods as a boy and looking for nothing and finding everything and that clump of woods was magic and those rocks were a rustlers' fort and there were dinosaurs crashing through the brush just out of sight and everybody knew that there were dragons swimming in the sea just below the waves and an old glittery piece of Coke bottle was a magic jewel that could let you fly or make you invisible and everybody knew that you whistled twice and crossed your fingers when you walked by that deserted old house or something shuddery and scaly would get you and you argued about bang you're dead no I'm not and you had a keen gun that could endlessly dispatch all the icky monsters who hung out near the swing set in your backyard without ever running out of ammunition. And I remember that as a kid I was nuts about finding a magic cave and I used to think that there was a cave under every rock, and I would get a long stick to use as a lever and I would sweat and strain until I had managed to turn the rock over, and then when I didn't find any tunnel under the rock I would think that the tunnel was there but it was just filled in with dirt, and I would get a shovel and I would dig three or four feet down looking for the tunnel and the magic cave and then I would give up and go home for a dinner of beans and franks and brown bread. And I remember that once I did find a little cave hidden under a big rock and I couldn't believe it and I was scared and shocked and angry and I didn't want it to be there but it was and so I stuck my head inside it to look around because something wouldn't let me leave until I did and it was dark in there and hot and very still and the darkness seemed to be blinking at me and I thought I heard something rustling and moving and I got scared and I started to cry and I ran away and then I got a big stick and came back, still crying, and pushed and heaved at that rock until it thudded back over the cave and hid it forever. And I remember that the next day I went out again to hunt for a magic cave.

—The rain has stopped. A bird flaps wetly away from the tree and then settles back down onto an outside branch. The branch dips and sways with the bird's weight, its leaves heavy with rain. The tree steams in the sun, and a million raindrops become tiny jewels, microscopic prisms, gleaming and winking, loving and transfiguring the light even as it destroys them and they dissolve into invisible vapor puffs to be swirled into the air and absorbed by the waiting clouds above. The air is wet and clean and fresh; it seems to squeak as the tall grass saws through it and the wind runs its fingernails lightly along its surface. The day is squally and gusty after the storm, high shining overcast split by jagged ribbons of blue that look like aerial fjords. The bird preens and fluffs its feathers disgustedly, chattering and scolding at the rain, but keeping a tiny bright eye carefully cocked in case the storm should take offense at the liquid stream of insults and come roaring back. Between the tufts of grass the ground has turned to black mud, soggy as a sponge, puddled by tiny pools of steaming rainwater. There is an arm and a hand lying in the mud, close enough to make out the texture of the tattered fabric clothing the arm, so close that the upper arm fades up and past the viewpoint and into a huge featureless blur in the extreme corner of the field of vision. The arm is bent back at an unnatural angle and the stiff fingers are hooked into talons that seem to claw toward the grey sky—

And I remember a day in the sixth grade when we were struggling in the cloakroom with our coats and snow-encrusted overshoes and I couldn't get mine off because one of the snaps had frozen shut and Denny was talking about how his father was a jet pilot and he sure hoped the war wasn't over before he grew up because he wanted to kill some gooks like his daddy was doing and then later in the boys' room everybody was arguing about who had the biggest one and showing them and Denny could piss farther than anybody else. I remember that noon at recess we were playing kick the can and the can rolled down the side of the hill and we all went down after it and somebody said hey look and we found a place inside a bunch of bushes where the grass was all flattened down and broken and there were pages of a magazine scattered all over and Denny picked one up and spread it out and it was a picture of a girl with only a pair of pants on and everybody got real quiet and I could hear the girls chanting in the schoolyard as they jumped rope and kids yelling and everybody was scared and her eyes seemed to be looking back right out of the picture and somebody finally licked his lips and said what're those things stickin' out of her, ah, and he didn't know the word and one of the bigger kids said tits and he said yeah what're those things stickin' outta her tits and I couldn't say anything because I was so surprised to find out that girls had those little round brown things like we did except that hers were pointy and hard and made me tremble and Denny said hell I knew about that I've had hundreds of girls but he was licking nervously at his lips as he said it and he was breathing funny too. And I remember that afternoon I was sitting at my desk near the window and the sun was hot and I was being bathed in the rolling drone of our math class and I wasn't understanding any of it and listening to less. I remember that I knew I had to go to the bathroom but I didn't want to raise my hand because our math teacher was a girl with brown hair and eyeglasses and I was staring at the place where I knew her pointy brown things must be under her blouse and I was thinking about touching them to see what they felt like and that made me feel funny somehow and I thought that if I raised my hand she would be able to see into my head and she'd know and she'd tell everybody what I was thinking and then she'd get mad and punish me for thinking bad things and so I didn't say anything but I had to go real bad and if I looked real close I thought that I could see two extra little bulges in her blouse where her pointy things were pushing against the cloth and I started thinking about what it would feel like if she pushed them up against me and that made me feel even more funny and sort of hollow and sick inside and I couldn't wait any longer and I raised my hand and left the room but it was too late and I wet myself when I was still on the way to the boys' room and I didn't know what to do so I went back to the classroom with my pants all wet and smelly and the math teacher looked at me and said what did you do and I was scared and Denny yelled he pissed in his pants he pissed in his pants and I said I did not the water bubbler squirted me but Denny yelled he pissed in his pants he pissed in his pants and the math teacher got very mad and everybody was laughing and suddenly the kids in my class didn't have any faces but only laughing mouths and I wanted to curl up into a ball where nobody could get me and once I had seen my mother digging with a garden spade and turning over the wet dark earth and there was half of a worm mixed in with the dirt and it writhed and squirmed until the next shovelful covered it up.

—Most of the rain has boiled away, leaving only a few of the larger puddles that have gathered in the shallow depressions between grass clumps. The mud is slowly solidifying under the hot sun, hardening into ruts, miniature ridges and mountains and valleys. An ant appears at the edge of the field of vision, emerging warily from the roots of the tall grass, pushing its way free of the tangled jungle. The tall blades of grass tower over it, forming a tightly interwoven web and filtering the hot yellow sunlight into a dusky green half-light. The ant pauses at the edge of the muddy open space, reluctant to exchange the cool tunnel of the grass for the dangers of level ground. Slowly, the ant picks its way across the sticky mud, skirting a pebble half again as big as it is. The pebble is streaked with veins of darker rock and has a tiny flake of quartz embedded in it near the top. The elements have rounded it into a smooth oval, except for a dent on the far side that exposes its porous core. The ant finishes its cautious circumnavigation of the pebble and scurries slowly toward the arm, which lies across its path. With infinite patience, the ant begins to climb up the arm, slipping on the slick, mud-spattered fabric. The ant works its way down the arm to the wrist and stops, sampling the air. The ant stands among the bristly black hairs on the wrist, antennae vibrating. The big blue vein in the wrist can be seen under its tiny feet. The ant continues to walk up the wrist, pushing its way through the bristly hair, climbing onto the hand and walking purposefully through the hollow of the thumb. Slowly, it disappears around the knuckle of the first finger—

And I remember a day when I was in the first year of high school and my voice was changing and I was starting to grow hair in unusual places and I was sitting in English class and I wasn't paying too much attention even though I'm usually pretty good in English because I was in love with the girl who sat in front of me. I remember that she had long legs and soft brown hair and a laugh like a bell and the sun was coming in the window behind her and the sunlight made the downy hair on the back of her neck glow very faintly and I wanted to touch it with my fingertips and I wanted to undo the knot that held her hair to the top of her head and I wanted her hair to cascade down over my face soft against my skin and cover me and with the sunlight I could see the strap of her bra underneath her thin dress and I wanted to slide my fingers underneath it and unhook it and stroke her velvety skin. I remember that I could feel my body stirring and my mouth was dry and painful and the zipper of her dress was open a tiny bit at the top and I could see the tanned texture of her skin and see that she had a brown mole on her shoulder and my hand trembled with the urge to touch it and something about Shakespeare and when she turned her head to whisper to Denny across the row her eyes were deep and beautiful and I wanted to kiss them softly brush them lightly as a bird's wing and Hamlet was something or other and I caught a glimpse of her tongue darting wetly from between her lips and pressing against her white teeth and that was almost too much to bear and I wanted to kiss her lips very softly and then I wanted to crush them flat and then I wanted to bite them and sting them until she cried and I could comfort and soothe her and that frightened me because I didn't understand it and my thighs were tight and prickly and the blood pounded at the base of my throat and Elsinore something and the bell rang shrilly and I couldn't get up because all I could see was the fabric of her dress stretched taut over her hips as she stood up and I stared at her hips and her belly and her thighs as she walked away and wondered what her thing would look like and I was scared. I remember that I finally got up enough nerve to ask her for a date during recess and she looked at me incredulously for a second and then laughed, just laughed contemptuously and walked away without saying a word. I remember her laughter. And I remember wandering around town late that night heading aimlessly into nowhere trying to escape from the pressure and the emptiness and passing a car parked on a dark street corner just as the moon swung out from behind a cloud and there was light that danced and I could hear the freight trains booming far away and she was in the backseat with Denny and they were locked together and her skirt was hiked up and I could see the white flash of flesh all the way up her leg and he had his hand under her blouse on her breast and I could see his knuckles moving under the fabric and the freight train roared and clattered as it hit the switch and he was kissing her and biting her and she was kissing him back with her lips pressed tight against her teeth and her hair floating all around them like a cloud and the train was whispering away from town and then he was on top of her pressing her down and I felt like I was going to be sick and I started to vomit but stopped because I was afraid of the noise and she was moaning and making small low whimpering noises I'd never heard anyone make before and I had to run before the darkness crushed me and I didn't want to do that when I got home because I'd feel ashamed and disgusted afterward but I knew that I was going to have to because my stomach was heaving and my skin was on fire and I thought that my heart was going to explode. And I remember that I eventually got a date for the dance with Judy from my history class who was a nice girl although plain but all night long as I danced with her I could only see my first love moaning and writhing under Denny just as the worm had writhed under the thrust of the garden spade into the wet dark earth long ago and as I ran toward home that night I heard the train vanish into the night trailing a cruelly arrogant whistle behind it until it faded to a memory and there was nothing left.

—The ant reappears on the underside of the index finger, pauses, antennae flickering inquisitively, and then begins to walk back down the palm, following the deep groove known as the life line until it reaches the wrist. For a moment, it appears as if the ant will vanish into the space between the wrist and the frayed, bloodstained cuff of the shirt, but it changes its mind and slides back down the wrist to the ground on the far side. The ant struggles for a moment in the sticky mud, and then crawls determinedly off across the crusted ground. At the extreme edge of the field of vision, just before the blur that is the upper arm, there is the jagged, pebbly edge of a shellhole. Half over the lip of the shellhole, grossly out of proportion at this distance, is half of a large earthworm, partially buried by the freshly turned earth thrown up by an explosion. The ant pokes suspiciously at the worm—

And I remember the waiting room at the train station and the weight of my suitcase in my hand and the way the big iron voice rolled unintelligibly around the high ceiling as the stationmaster announced the incoming trains and cigar and cigarette smoke was thick in the air and the massive air-conditioning fan was laboring in vain to clear some of the choking fog away and the place reeked of urine and age and an old dog twitched and moaned in his ancient sleep as he curled close against an equally ancient radiator that hissed and panted and belched white jets of steam and I stood by the door and looked up and watched a blanket of heavy new snow settle down over the sleeping town with the ponderous invulnerability of a pregnant woman. I remember looking down into the train tunnel and out along the track to where the shining steel disappeared into darkness and I suddenly thought that it looked like a magic cave and then I wondered if I had thought that was supposed to be funny and I wanted to laugh only I wanted to cry too and so I could do neither and instead I tightened my arm around Judy's waist and pulled her closer against me and kissed the silken hollow of her throat and I could feel the sharp bone in her hip jabbing against mine and I didn't care because that was pain that was pleasure and I felt the gentle resilience of her breast suddenly against my rib cage and felt her arm tighten protectively around me and her fingernails bite sharply into my arm and I knew that she was trying not to cry and that if I said anything at all it would make her cry and there would be that sloppy scene we'd been trying to avoid and so I said nothing but only held her and kissed her lightly on the eyes and I knew that people were looking at us and snickering and I didn't give a damn and I knew that she wanted me and wanted me to stay and we both knew that I couldn't and all around us about ten other young men were going through similar tableaux with their girlfriends or folks and everybody was stern and pale and worried and trying to look unconcerned and casual and so many women were trying not to cry that the humidity in the station was trembling at the saturation point. I remember Denny standing near the door with a foot propped on his suitcase and he was flashing his too-white teeth and his too-wide smile and he reeked of cheap cologne as he told his small knot of admirers in an overly loud voice that he didn't give a damn if he went or not because he'd knocked up a broad and her old man was tryin' to put the screws on him and this was a good way to get outta town anyway and the government would protect him from the old man and he'd come back in a year or so on top of the world and the heat would be off and he could start collecting female scalps again and besides his father had been in and been a hero and he could do anything better than that old bastard and besides he hated those goddamned gooks and he was gonna get him a Commie see if he didn't. I remember that the train came quietly in then and that it still looked like a big iron beast although now it was a silent beast with no smoke or sparks but with magic still hidden inside it although I knew now that it might be a dark magic and then we had to climb inside and I was kissing Judy good-bye and telling her I loved her and she was kissing me and telling me she would wait for me and I don't know if we were telling the truth or even if we knew ourselves what the truth was and then Judy was crying openly and I was swallowed by the iron beast and we were roaring away from the town and snickering across the web of tracks and booming over the switches and I saw my old house flash by and I could see my old window and I almost imagined that I could see myself as a kid with my nose pressed against the window looking out and watching my older self roar by and neither of us suspecting that the other was there and neither ever working up enough nerve to watch the trains dance. And I remember that all during that long train ride I could hear Denny's raucous voice somewhere in the distance talking about how he couldn't wait to get to gookland and he'd heard that gook snatch was even better than nigger snatch and free too and he was gonna get him a Commie he couldn't wait to get him a goddamned Commie and as the train slashed across the wide fertile farmlands of the Midwest the last thing I knew before sleep that night was the wet smell of freshly turned earth.

—The ant noses the worm disdainfully and then passes out of the field of vision. The only movement now is the ripple of the tall grass and the flash of birds in the shaggy tree. The sky is clouding up again, thunderheads rumbling up over the horizon and rolling across the sky. Two large forms appear near the shaggy tree at the other extreme of the field of vision. The singing of the birds stops as if turned off by a switch. The two forms move about vaguely near the shaggy tree, rustling the grass. The angle of the field of vision gives a foreshortening effect, and it is difficult to make out just what the figures are. There is a sharp command, the human voice sounding strangely thin under the sighing of the wind. The two figures move away from the shaggy tree, pushing through the grass. They are medics; haggard, dirty soldiers with big red crosses painted on their helmets and armbands and several days' growth on their chins. They look tired, harried, scared and determined, and they are moving rapidly, half-crouching, searching for something on the ground and darting frequent wary glances back over their shoulders. As they approach they seem to grow larger and larger, elongating toward the sky as their movement shifts the perspective. They stop a few feet away and reach down, lifting up a body that has been hidden by the tall grass. It is Denny, the back of his head blown away, his eyes bulging horribly open. The medics lower Denny's body into the sheltering grass and bend over it, fumbling with something. They finally straighten, glance hurriedly about and move forward. The two grimy figures swell until they fill practically the entire field of vision, only random patches of sky and the ground underfoot visible around their bulk. The medics come to a stop about a foot away. The scarred, battered, mud-caked combat boot of the medic now dominates the scene, looking big as a mountain. From the combat boot, the medic's leg seems to stretch incredibly toward the sky, like a fatigue-swathed beanstalk, with just a suggestion of a head and a helmet floating somewhere at the top. The other medic cannot be seen at all now, having stepped over and out of the field of vision. His shallow breathing and occasional muttered obscenities can be heard. The first medic bends over, his huge hand seeming to leap down from the sky, and touches the arm, lifting the wrist and feeling for a pulse. The medic holds the wrist for a while and then sighs and lets it go. The wrist plops limply back into the cold sucking mud, splattering it. The medic's hand swells in the direction of the upper arm, and then fades momentarily out of the field of vision, although his wrist remains blurrily visible and his arm seems to stretch back like a highway into the middle distance. The medic tugs, and his hand comes back clutching a tarnished dog tag. Both of the medic's hands disappear forward out of the field of vision. Hands prying the jaw open, jamming the dog tag into the teeth, the metal cold and slimy against the tongue and gums, pressing the jaws firmly closed again, the dog tag feeling huge and immovable inside the mouth. The world is the medic's face now, looming like a scarred cliff inches away, his bloodshot twitching eyes as huge as moons, his mouth, hanging slackly open with exhaustion, as cavernous and bottomless as a magic cave to a little boy. The medic has halitosis, his breath filled with the richly corrupt smell of freshly turned earth. The medic stretches out two fingers which completely occupy the field of vision, blocking out even the sky. The medic's fingertips are the only things in the world now. They are stained and dirty and one has a white scar across the whorls. The medic's fingertips touch the eyelids and gently press down. And now there is nothing but darkness—

And I remember the way dawn would crack the eastern sky, the rosy blush slowly spreading and staining the black of night, chasing away the darkness, driving away the stars. And I remember the way a woman looks at you when she loves you, and the sound that a kitten makes when it is happy, and the way that snowflakes blur and melt against a warm windowpane in winter. I remember. I remember.

Barry N. Malzberg

Barry N. Malzberg is perhaps one of the most controversial writers ever to have entered the genre. Novels such as *Herovit's World, Guernica Night, Underlay, Galaxies, The Falling Astronauts, Beyond Apollo,* and *Revelations,* as well as collections such as *Final War and Other Fantasies* and *Down Here in the Dream Quarter,* were at the cutting edge of experimental science fiction in the 1970s. His intense, close-focus prose style, alienated characters, and dark apocalyptic vision were both attacked and lauded by critics and readers. In a retrospective of his work in *Twentieth Century Science Fiction Writers,* one critic writes that "Malzberg's obsessions, and those of his characters, expose the dark underbelly of the science-fiction mythos to the terrible light of art." He has edited a number of anthologies, including *Final Stage, Arena: Sports SF,* and *Graven Images,* with Edward L. Ferman; *Dark Sins, Dark Dreams: Crimes in SF* and *The End of Summer: Science Fiction in the Fifties,* with Bill Pronzini; and the mammoth *Arbor House Treasury of Horror and the Supernatural,* with Martin Harry Greenberg. He won the John W. Campbell Memorial Award for his novel *Beyond Apollo,* and his deeply felt but controversial history of science fiction in the 1980s, *The Engines of the Night,* was a Hugo award finalist in 1983. His latest novel, *The Remaking of Sigmund Freud,* was a Nebula award finalist in 1986. Malzberg lives with his wife, Joyce, and family in Teaneck, New Jersey.

The Queen of Lower Saigon

by

Barry N. Malzberg

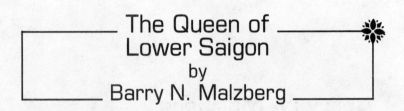

Begging pardon. Historical perspective so difficult when drenched in subjectivity, in the course of the moment. Begging your sincerest pardons, monsieurs and mesdames, obliged as I am to deal with the consequences of *fracture,* of utter dislocation, of that swarming leap from past to past, present to present which is heart of condition. I, the Queen of Lower Saigon, effortfully, effortfully to speak.

Here I am, presenting my case. Bombs bursting in air, American boys of all description come to plight their troth against me. All description but *one* description; they are confused, they are very much out of joint. Short-timers all, one year and out, up and over, still the circumstances get them, the hot flooding napalm, the *thought* of napalm, the sinister thud of bodies, the unraveling of the blood which is the war for them whether they are here or there, support personnel or, as they say, in Charlie's hives. "Fuck me," I advise them. "I am the Queen of Lower Saigon. Please to fuck me," solemnly rub that extension of self in and around until at last it is necessary, that is to say, it is inevitable that the napalm ignites, the hot, leaping fires. (Oh, a taste for metaphor, like a taste for humor, will take the Queen everywhere!) Over and out. Up and down. Fickee and fuckee. "I'm coming; I'm coming." But definitely, they are not going. There is no sign of their going, we will have to drive them out. Over and out.

To me, the Queen of Lower Saigon, they come. I know all of their blasted secrets, they utter their dirty little prayers, expel their wounded hearts into me. Of answers there are none but in and around, always, they will ask their questions. "Will it now? Will it end? Up and out? Over and in?"

In and over. Over and out. The slow, sucking, fragmentation wound of their incision.

Part One: The General Comes

"I don't do this ordinarily," the General said. "I know you don't believe that."

"Of course I believe that. Why shouldn't I believe it?" So small the energetic throb of his vitals. Huddled in the hooch, I waited for his appearance, waited for him to do it. But he is interested first in conversation. More and more, the Americans seek justification through their talk; it is not enough for them simply to evacuate and leave. They must bridge cultural gap, honored friends. They must make statement. "How old are you?" he wanted to know. I said in my heart, I said, what is it to them, to you, how old I am; I am ten thousand years old, I am the Queen of Lower Saigon, I am the Egyptians, the French, the British, the Grenadiers, I am the exiled armies of Ming. To him I said, "I am nineteen years old."

"So young," the General said. His hands investigated. They like us young. "Oh my," he said, a full field commander, "oh my, oh my."

I slid away from him, offered murmurs and apologies. "Tea?" I said. "Sake? A glass of wine?"

"No," he said, a full field commander, detailed from the Pentagon for this crucial assignment yet taking his pleasure in the field like all of his troops, policy decision that; to fuck like the troops with the Queen of Lower Saigon; enlisted man's nookie, noncom's tail, "that's not what I want. I just want to talk for a moment. I want to know you better."

All of them want to know me better. Ah, most elegant and attentive monsieurs and mesdames, my gathered audience, know how sincere the commitment in their quest; they not only wished to free us, to make us just like them, they sought to *know* us, to apprehend in their full American hearts the fullness of our own history. Never has there been such a task force.

"We must hurry," I said, "there is time for the knowing later."

"Why?" His eyes assumed a military insistence. "Why cannot we know each other now?"

"Because," I said, gathering the General to me, feeling his two-star prick with all of the force at my own command, "because this is a temporary action, an incursion of briefest mortality, this is merely an attempt to bring us to the level of managing our own defense and there is no time, no time, no time," feeling his urgent if diminished prick, guiding it into the center of me, feeling the slow, oozing sigh of penetration, closing my eyes against him, dragging him to attention, looking past and out of him so he could never see what all of *you* see, what you, oh, faithless monsieurs, have known from the outset, my indifference disguised—but only thinly, only thinly—as hatred. The never to be defeated, the indifferent who will live a thousand years. Grunting, he seeks, inch by inch, to force that indifference from me.

Part Two: The General Leaves

Later in the night, legs spread, alone in the hooch, I expel desire, feel my own deadly necessity sharpening like a knife in those depths, I think of all that has happened and all that will occur and of how caught, somewhere in that midway between history and possibility, I have reconstructed all of those ancient dreads of the abyss of the century; the heart, like the thighs, is a trip wire to fire tracers at their first stumbling loss of direction. I, the Queen of Lower Saigon, the first and insistent oracle of my race, haul their ashes over and again, general and corporal alike, hear their confessions blurted in climax over and again, and internalize secrets that I have not been able until this very moment to tell. Now at last I can tell them, surrounded by you in the high places and low, the attentive and quiet ladies and gents who will hear my confession as I have heard theirs, I find myself reaching toward a kind of summation which will lead you to understand as I came to understand during the time of the great and lost kings that there was no answer, no answer whatsoever, but from the slow and stunned looks upon your faces, from the shuffle of feet and the referral to the clutched notes in your hands I can see that you do not yet wish to comprehend this; you have come, in your faithful and characteristic fashion, for exposition, drama, climax, explanation, and it is hard to do this. I am not what I once was. None of us have been since the time of Tet.

"Inscrutable," he said to me, grabbing for his clothing, "all of you, damn it, inscrutable. Don't you know we're here to help you?" I said nothing. There was nothing to say. "You act as if we're the enemy but we're your friends," he said. I said nothing, not so much enmity, not so much inscrutability as a simple kind of mystification: What would he have of me? What did he want? The Queen of Lower Saigon is not, let me tell you my confessors, good on the metaphysics of the matter; crushing, crushing are the particularities.

Part Three: The Making of Fire

When the kings met in deep and sacred committee, they did not know with what they would emerge. That is the purpose of the committee; the need is to probe beyond the devices and the easy answers, part the shadows, open up the curtain of the night and know what truly lies beyond. And so they meshed in deep conferral for many days as the moon crawled across the landscape and the sighs of the drowning and defeated French arose from all of the bunkers, then at last they came from the secret place, the cavern of their consent, and they sent one of them in delegation to me, who said, "You will accept the surrender as the Queen; you will be for them what we cannot be, the symbol of their defeat."

"I cannot do this," I said. "There are many things of which I am capable but this is not one." How could I explain to him that he had utterly misjudged my own relation to the circumstance? But of course it was impossible to say this to my countryman; he had been hidden in the cavern for a long, long time and this decision, this outcome, was meant to be an honor. "I cannot do this for you," I said, but I was already weakening; all of my life I have moved in this way, from strength to weakness, confrontation to flight, certainty to doom; it has been my particular curse to see not only their certainty but their terror, not only their brutality but the pathos within. "How can I do this for you?" I said. "You are asking me to accept a surrender when we have not truly won. There is no triumph here, there is no cessation—there is merely continuance."

"That," he said, "that is the reason we wish you to accept that role, honored sister," and he bowed ceremonially, reached out his hands. "We see only in the harshest of colors, you see all the shades and greys of meaning in which we must live," and so then he dispatched me, there was no more convocation, no continuance of the dialogue, I went to Dien Bien Phu and I accepted from them the flower of defeat upon the sword, and then alone in the place they had left me I read the entrails and built a fire, I built a mighty fire which was enough to sear the landscape and in the fast and flickering flame I was however dimly able to perceive—

Part Four: Foreign Policy

—But it is not so easy, monsieurs and mesdames, it is to the timorous among you that I would now address myself, those spirits amongst you who would realize the cruel and indefinable position into which I have been thrust. There are among your number descendants of the kings and relatives of the peasants who find it impossible to see the complexities of the situation: "Kill, wreak an awful vengeance" I can hear you saying in your cracked and execrable French, your pidgin-illness, "Kill all the fuckface as they kill you," but it is not so easy to hear, not when one has heard their cries and confessions pelting across one in the night. "Oh mama," they would cry against me, "oh mama, oh mama," holding my breasts in their hands as if I were a real woman, not the Queen and if those breasts were the tits of the mother itself, "Oh mama," they would weep in the apex of their need, on the lip of climax, "Oh God, oh God," and I could see them then as I could so often see myself: they were nothing but victims illumined in the true and terrible fires of the night, *all* of us were victims—they to come, we to take, and as they would scramble inch by desperate inch through the wires of their need to at last spill out on me, I would see in the uneven flashes of the tracer fire the youth and cracked beauty of their faces, the broken children under their surfaces, and as they would spill and spill against me, I would find myself unable to hate them in their vulnerability and openness, rather it was *myself* that became the hated one for opening up, allowing them to pour out, being their receptacle and bearing so much witness to their pain—

Can you grasp any of this? Sitting there in what you would say is "judgment," asking the Queen of Lower Saigon to explain herself in this final and decreed court of all necessity, can you understand that witness is a kind of collaboration, that all policy is the policy of self and that there is no juncture, no division? There are the children of pain in their streets, the children of their expression underfoot, all of them, scrappling through the interstices of this place; it is not even a collaboration but a fusion—

I see impatience on your fine and wise faces. Enough of this, the elders among you are saying. It is not pity but circumstance which will drive us to the verdict; your appeals to the emotion will get you nowhere. You are a Queen, collaborator of Kings; you must be harsh and true, like Turandot thou must not break, oh unruptured vessel.

Part Five: The General Receives

In the morning after Tet there is much confusion and running in the streets; everything seems to have turned, but in the afternoon the General himself sends emissaries for me, they drag me from the hooch, call me a dink goddess, brace me as if in an abattoir and drag me to the stockade, where I am hurled with stunning force and abruptness and left to my own thoughts for a while. The skies are streaked with Tet; the stink of the land is in my nostrils—it is not the flesh this time but the land itself which I apprehend. I think the General will not come for a long time or he will not come at all, but then he does: he comes to my cell and leans his face against the bars and says, "Whore, bitch, cunt!" and other things which I cannot, having only an uncertain command of English, remember and then he slaps me and then he is gone. Alone, alone in the stockade of the dreaded but long-sought

Americanos I sink to the stone floor, the stain of his fingers high on my cheek, bleeding, bleeding and I think that this will be the end, then, this is the end of the Queen, the war will go on and the fickee-fuckee will go on but they will cry their words and needs to someone other than me and oh brothers and sisters, I think that it is done for me then but no, there are other plans, other possibilities. In the night, the committee comes; they emerge in my cell and they say, "More. There will be more."

"I cannot take any more. I have seen what I can, conveyed all that I must. There is nothing more left."

"Oh no, oh no," it is pointed out to me, "it is now only truly to begin."

And then they are gone, and when the General returns with key in hand and more dreadful purpose in his eyes, there is absolutely nothing for me to do but to take as it is given. Given as it is received. Received as it is taken. That is our mission and honor and it is as it has always been.

Part Six: The Mystery Revealed

The Queen of Lower Saigon is a figment of the General's imagination. If the war had gone the way that the General knew it should, if things had happened as he was trained to believe that they would, her construction would not have been an inevitability; the General would have enjoyed an honorable retirement, perhaps a second (even a third) career. Because of the severe and dislocating, terrifying and embarrassing, events of Tet and thereafter, however, permanently shattering the General's cultivated belief in the rigor of dreams and the permanence of foreign policy, the General was forced to create an imaginary Queen of Lower Saigon (there is *no* Upper Saigon in the General's estimation) in order to explain the disasters of the outcome, the corruption of the troops, the slow and final unraveling of the Great Society of Vietnam. The General was *driven* to this end; it was not easy for him to do this nor, strictly speaking, voluntary; as a servant of the people and career military officer, he had no alternative other than to seek this outside solution.

The Queen fucked his troops, she dispensed drugs, she

whispered dreadful improprieties into their vulnerable and innocent ears and extracted from them secrets of maneuvers; she gave all of these secrets to the committee of elders who had appointed her to the position. The committee conferred amongst themselves and gave the information to field commanders who set terrible traps, exploding mines, trip wires and tracers, disarming our troops of their own weaponry and element of surprise. The Queen of Lower Saigon did all of this, the General believes. He sincerely believes this to be the case and has constructed her in his own mind to say nothing of the principle of fictive address; over and again the Queen delivers justification to a court of nations, who will judge her most severely for her conduct, who will return to the General his commission and career and make him forty again and in the field, this damned, damnable, accursed, wretched war, one which can be fought rationally and won with honor.

Part Seven: The Mystery Concealed

Ah, monsieurs and mesdames, I confess it to you now, I give unto you the ultimate: there is no General, there is no stockade, there is no vengeance for Tet, there is no victimization of the Queen. There is, help us, only the Queen herself, her palms extended, addressing all of you in her own voice and pleading for mercy. It was necessary for me to invent the General, to create the concept of the General in order to atone for my own weakness and lack of spirit; I fucked the troops, I consorted with the enemy, I absorbed not only their semen but spirit, but it was for pity, for *pietà* that I did this. Now, in the rubble of our defeat, our victory, which was merely a poised version of disaster, I am filled with shame, I am filled with humility and weakness; not willing to believe, oh auditors, oh Elders and judges, that I could do such a thing, I have invented the General to excuse me for my acts. How can I face such knowledge, how can I deal with such outcome?

Oh, the children, the children are among us, mesdames, some are living and many are dead, they run the streets and cry for scraps, they are spurned by many and loved by none and they are my legacy, my gift to you, what I have done: I, the Queen of no absolution—

It is *my* weakness, my knowledge, that has caused this to happen and so, unable to know this, I have created for you a General for you to hate but there is no General, there is no General but the Queen and, oh my lords, and ah my ladies, I beg you now to grant me absolution, grant me *pietà*, grant me death, grant me an end to thought—

Part Eight: To Love Forever

"I had a dream," he said, shuddering against her. He felt the scream as it had been torn from him. "Oh, I had a dream." I must not scream again, he thought. I must not.

"Quiet," the girl said. "Oh, quiet, American." And in her language, began to pray again.

Dennis Etchison

Since his first story was published in 1961, Dennis Etchison has been quietly expanding the boundaries of dark fantasy with his subtle, incisive, and chilling tales. Karl Edward Wagner has called him "that rarest of genre writers: an original visionary." He has written several screenplays, including *Halloween IV*, and has done novelizations of *The Fog* and, under the pseudonym Jack Martin, *Halloween II, Halloween III,* and *Videodrome.* His story "The Dark Country," published in 1981, won both the World Fantasy Award and the British Fantasy Award. He has, to date, published three short story collections, *The Dark Country*, *Red Dreams,* and *The Blood Kiss*, and a novel, *Darkside*. He is also the editor of *Masters of Darkness* and *Cutting Edge*. He lives in Los Angeles, California.

Deathtracks

by

Dennis Etchison

ANNOUNCER: Hey, let's go into this apartment and help this housewife take a shower!

ASSISTANT: Rad!

ANNOUNCER: Excuse me, ma'am!

HOUSEWIFE: Eeek!
ANNOUNCER: It's okay, I'm the New Season Man!
HOUSEWIFE: You—you came right through my TV!
ANNOUNCER: That's because there's no stopping good news! Have you heard about New Season Body Creamer? It's guaranteed better than your old-fashioned soap product, cleaner than water on the air! It's—
ASSISTANT: Really rad!
HOUSEWIFE: Why, you're so right! Look at the way New Season's foaming away my dead, unwanted dermal cells! My world has a whole new complexion! My figure has a glossy new paisley shine! The kind that men . . .
ANNOUNCER: And women!
HOUSEWIFE: . . . love to touch!
ANNOUNCER: Plus the kids'll love it, too!
HOUSEWIFE: You bet they will! Wait till my husband gets up! Why, I'm going to spend the day spreading the good news all over our entire extended family! It's—
ANNOUNCER: It's a whole New Season!
HOUSEWIFE: A whole new reason! It's—
ASSISTANT: Absolutely RAD-I-CAL!

The young man fingered the edges of the pages with great care, almost as if they were razor blades. Then he removed his fingertips from the clipboard and tapped them along the luminous crease in his pants, one, two, three, four, five, four, three, two, one, stages of flexion about to become a silent drumroll of boredom. With his other hand he checked his watch, clicked his pen and smoothed the top sheet of the questionnaire, circling the paper in a cursive, impatient holding pattern.

Across the room another man thumbed a remote-control device until the TV voices became silvery whispers, like ants crawling over aluminum foil.

"Wait, Bob." On the other side of the darkening living room a woman stirred in her bean-bag chair, her hair shining under the black light. "It's time for *The Fuzzy Family*."

The man, her husband, shifted his buttocks in his own bean-bag chair and yawned. The chair's Styrofoam filling crunched like cornflakes under his weight. "Saw this one before," he said. "Besides, there's no laughtrack. They use three cameras and a live audience, remember?"

"But it might be, you know, boosted," said the woman. "Oh, what do they call it?"

"Technically augmented?" offered the young man.

They both looked at him, as though they had forgotten he was in their home.

The young man forced an unnatural, professional smile. In the black light his teeth shone too brightly.

"Right," said the man. "Not *The Fuzzy Family*, though. I filtered out a track last night. It's all new. I'm sure."

The young man was confused. He had the inescapable feeling that they were skipping (or was it simply that he was missing?) every third or fourth sentence. *I'm sure*. Sure of what? That this particular TV show had been taped before an all-live audience? How could he be sure? And why would anyone care enough about such a minor technical point to bother to find out? Such things weren't supposed to matter to the blissed-out masses. Certainly not to AmiDex survey families. Unless . . .

Could he be that lucky?

The questionnaire might not take very long, after all.

This one, he thought, has got to work in the industry.

He checked the computer stats at the top of the questionnaire: MORRISON, ROBERT, AGE 54, UNEMPLOYED. Used to work in the industry, then. A TV cameraman, a technician of some kind, maybe for a local station? There had been so many layoffs in the last few months, with QUBE and Teletext and all the new cable licenses wearing away at the traditional network share. And any connection, past or present, would automatically disqualify this household. Hope sprang up in his breast like an accidental porno broadcast in the middle of *Sermonette*.

He flicked his pen rapidly between cramped fingers and glanced up, eager to be out of here and home to his own video cassettes. Not to mention, say, a Bob's Big Boy hamburger, heavy relish, hold the onions and add avocado, to be picked up on the way?

"I've been sent here to ask you about last month's Viewing Log," he began. "When one doesn't come back in the mail, we do a routine follow-up. It may have been lost by the post office. I see here that your phone's been disconnected. Is that right?''

He waited while the man used the remote selector. On-screen, silent excerpts of this hour's programming blipped by channel by channel: reruns of *Cop City*, the syndicated version of *The Cackle Factory*, the mindless *Make Me Happy, The World as We Know It, T.H.U.G.S.*, even a repeat of that PBS documentary on Teddy Roosevelt, *A Man, a Plan, a Canal, Panama*, and the umpteenth replay of *Mork and Mindy*, this the infamous last episode that had got the series canceled, wherein Mindy is convinced she's carrying Mork's alien child and nearly OD's on a homeopathic remedy of Humphrey's Eleven Tablets and blackstrap molasses. Still he waited.

''There really isn't much I need to know.'' He put on a friendly, stupid, shit-eating grin, hoping it would show in the purple light and then afraid that it would. ''What you watch is your own business, naturally. AmiDex isn't interested in influencing your viewing habits. If we did, I guess that would undermine the statistical integrity of our sample, wouldn't it?''

Morrison and his wife continued to stare into their flickering twelve-inch Sony portable.

If they're so into it, I wonder why they don't have a bigger set, one of those new picture-frame projection units from Mad Man Muntz, for example? I don't even see a Betamax. What was Morrison talking about when he said he'd taped *The Fuzzy Family*? The man had said that, hadn't he?

It was becoming difficult to concentrate.

Probably it was the black light, that and the old Day-Glow posters, the random clicking of the beaded curtains. Where did they get it all? Sitting in their living room was like being in a time machine, a playback of some Hollywood Sam Katzman or Albert Zugsmith version of the sixties; he almost expected Jack Nicholson or Luana Anders to show up. Except that the artifacts seemed to be genuine, and in mint condition. There were things he had never seen before, not even in catalogues. His parents would know. It all must have been saved out of some weird prescience, in anticipation of the current run on psychedelic nostalgia. It would cost a fortune to find practically *any* original black-light posters, however primitive. The one in the corner, for instance, "Ship of Peace," mounted next to "Ass Id" and an original Crumb "Keep on Truckin' " from the Print Mint in San Francisco, had been offered on the KCET auction just last week for $450, he remembered.

He tried again.

"Do you have your Viewing Log handy?" Expectantly he paused a beat. "Or did you—misplace it?"

"It won't tell you anything," said the man.

"We watch a lot of oldies," said the woman.

The young man pinched his eyes shut for a moment to clear his head. "I know what you mean," he said, hoping to put them at ease. "I can't get enough of *The Honeymooners*, myself. That Norton." He added a conspiratorial chuckle. "Sometimes I think they get better with age. They don't make 'em like that anymore. But, you know, the local affiliates would be very interested to know that you're watching."

"Not that old," said the woman. "We like the ones from the sixties. And some of the new shows, too, if—"

Morrison inclined his head toward her, so that the young man could not see, and mouthed what may have been a warning to his wife.

Suddenly and for reasons he could not name, the young man felt that he ought to be out of here.

He shook his wrist, pretending that his collector's item Nixon-Agnew watch was stuck. "What time is it getting to be?" Incredibly, he noticed that his watch had indeed stopped. Or had he merely lost track of the time? The hands read a quarter to six. Where had they been the last time he looked? "I really should finish up and get going. You're my last interview of the day. You folks must be about ready for dinner."

"Not so soon," said the woman. "It's almost time for *The Uncle Jerry Show*."

That's a surprise, he thought. It's only been on for one season.

"Ah, that's a new show, isn't it?" he said, again feeling that he had missed something. "It's only been on for—"

Abruptly the man got up from his bean-bag chair and crossed the room.

He opened a cabinet, revealing a stack of shipment cartons

from the Columbia Record Club. The young man made out the titles of a few loose albums, "greatest hits" collections from groups which, he imagined, had long since disbanded. Wedged into the cabinet, next to the records, was a state-of-the-art audio frequency equalizer with graduated slide controls covering several octaves. This was patched into a small black accessory amplifier box, the kind that are sold for the purpose of connecting a TV set to an existing home stereo system. Morrison leaned over and punched a sequence of preset buttons, and without further warning a great hissing filled the room.

"This way we don't miss anything," said the wife.

The young man looked around. Two enormous Voice-of-the-Theatre speakers, so large they seemed part of the walls, had sputtered to life on either side of the narrow room. But as yet there was no sound other than the unfathomable, rolling hiss of spurious signal-to-noise output, the kind of distortion he had heard once when he set his FM receiver between stations and turned the volume up all the way.

Once the program began, he knew, the sound would be deafening.

"So," he said hurriedly, "why don't we wrap this up, so I can leave you two to enjoy your evening? All I need are the answers to a couple of quick questions, and I'll be on my way."

Morrison slumped back into place, expelling a rush of air from his bean-bag chair, and thumbed the remote channel selector to a blank station. A pointillist pattern of salt-and-pepper interference swarmed the twelve-inch screen. He pushed up the volume in anticipation, so as not to miss a word of *The Uncle Jerry Show* when the time came to switch channels again, eyed a clock on the wall over the Sony—there was a clock, after all, if only one knew where to look amid the glowing clutter—and half-turned to his visitor. The clock read ten minutes to six.

"What are *you* waiting to hear?" asked Morrison.

"Yes," said his wife, "why don't you tell us?"

The young man lowered his eyes to his clipboard, seeking the briefest possible explanation, but saw only the luminescence of white shag carpeting through his transparent vinyl chair—another collector's item. He felt uneasy circulation twitching his weary legs, and could not help but notice the way the inflated chair seemed to be throbbing with each pulse.

"Well," trying one more time, noting that it was coming up on nine minutes to six and still counting, "your names were picked by AmiDex demographics. Purely at random. You represent twelve thousand other viewers in this area. What you watch at any given hour determines the rating points for each network."

There, that was simple enough, wasn't it? No need to go into the per-minute price of sponsor ad time buys based on the overnight share, sweeps week, the competing services each selling its own brand of accuracy. Eight and a half minutes to go.

"The system isn't perfect, but it's the best way we have so far of—"

"You want to know why we watch what we watch, don't you?"

"Oh no, of course not! That's really no business of ours. We don't care. But we do need to tabulate viewing records, and when yours wasn't returned—"

"Let's talk to him," said the woman. "He might be able to help."

"He's too young, can't you see that, Jenny?"

"I beg your pardon?" said the young man.

"It's been such a long time," said the woman, rising with a *whoosh* from her chair and stepping in front of her husband. "We can try."

The man got slowly to his feet, his arms and torso long and phosphorescent in the peculiar mix of ultraviolet and television light. He towered there, considering. Then he took a step closer.

The young man was aware of his own clothing unsticking from the inflated vinyl, crackling slightly, a quick seam of blue static shimmering away across the back of the chair; of the snow pattern churning on the untuned screen, the color tube shifting hues under the black light, turning to gray, then brightening in the darkness, locking on an electric blue, and holding.

Morrison seemed to undergo a subtle transformation as details previously masked by shadow now came into focus. It was more than his voice, his words. It was the full size of him, no longer young but still strong, on his feet and braced in an unexpectedly powerful stance. It was the configuration of his head in silhouette, the haunted pallor of the skin, stretched taut, the large, luminous whites of the eyes, burning like radium. It was all these things and more. It was the reality of him, no longer a statistic but a man, clear and unavoidable at last.

The young man faced Morrison and his wife. The palms of his hands were sweating coldly. He put aside the questionnaire.

Six minutes to six.

"I'll put down that you—you declined to participate. How's that? No questions asked."

He made ready to leave.

"It's been such a long time," said Mrs. Morrison again.

Mr. Morrison laughed shortly, a descending scale ending in a bitter, metallic echo that cut through the hissing. "I'll bet it's all crazy to you, isn't it? This *stuff*."

"No, not at all. Some of these pieces are priceless. I recognized that right away."

"Are they?"

"Sure," said the young man. "If you don't mind my saying so, it reminds me of my brother Jack's room. He threw out most of his underground newspapers, posters, that sort of thing when he got drafted. It was back in the sixties—I can barely remember it. If only he'd realized. Nobody saved anything. That's why it's all so valuable now."

"We did," said Mrs. Morrison.

"So I see."

They seemed to want to talk, after all—lonely, perhaps—so he found himself ignoring the static and actually making an effort to prolong his exit. A couple of minutes more wouldn't hurt. They're not so bad, the Morrisons, he thought. I can see that now.

"Well, I envy you. I went through a Marvel Comics phase when I was a kid. Those are worth a bundle now, too. My mother burned them all when I went away to college, of course. It's the same principle. But if I could go back in a time machine . . ." He shook his head and allowed an unforced smile to show through.

"These were our son's things," said Mrs. Morrison.

"Oh?" Could be I remind them of their son. I guess I should be honored.

"Our son, David," said Mr. Morrison.

"I see." There was an awkward pause. The young man felt vaguely embarrassed. "It's nice of him to let you hold his collection. You've got quite an investment here."

The minute hand of the clock on the wall ground through its cycle, pressing forward in the rush of white noise from the speakers.

"David Morrison." Her voice sounded hopeful. "You've heard the name?"

David Morrison, David Morrison. Curious. Yes, he could almost remember something, a magazine cover or . . .

"It was a long time ago. He—our son—was the last American boy to be killed in Vietnam."

It was four minutes to six and he didn't know what to say.

"When it happened, we didn't know what to think," said Mrs. Morrison. "We talked to people like us. Mostly they wanted to pretend it never happened."

"They didn't understand, either," said Mr. Morrison.

"So we read everything. The magazines, books. We listened to the news commentators. It was terribly confusing. We finally decided even they didn't know any more than we did about what went on over there, or why."

"What was it to them? Another story for *The Six O'Clock News*, right, Jenny?"

Mrs. Morrison drew a deep, pained breath. Her eyes fluttered as she spoke, the television screen at her back lost in a grainy storm of deep blue snow. "Finally the day came for me to clear David's room. . . ."

"Please," said the young man, "you don't have to explain."

But she went ahead with it, a story she had gone over so many times she might have been recalling another life. Her eyes opened. They were dry and startlingly clear.

It was three minutes to six.

"I started packing David's belongings. Then it occurred to us that *he* might have known the reason. So we went through his papers and so forth, even his record albums, searching. So much of it seemed strange, in another language, practically from another planet. But we trusted that the answer would be revealed to us in time."

"We're still living with it," said Morrison. "It's with us when we get up in the morning, when we give up at night. Sometimes I think I see a clue there, the way *he* would have seen it, but then I lose the thread and we're back where we started.

"We tried watching the old reruns, hoping they had something to tell. But they were empty. It was like nothing important was going on in this country back then."

"Tell him about the tracks, Bob."

"I'm getting to it. . . . Anyway, we waited. I let my job go, and we were living off our savings. It wasn't much. It's almost used up by now. But we had to have the answer. *Why?* Nothing was worth a damn, otherwise. . . .

"Then, a few months ago, there was this article in *TV GUIDE*. About the television programs, the way they make them. They take the tracks—the audience reactions, follow? —and use them over and over. Did you know that?"

"I—I had heard . . ."

"Well, it's true. They take pieces of old soundtracks, mix them in, a big laugh here, some talk there—it's all taped inside a machine, an audience machine. The tapes go all the way back. I've broken 'em down and compared. Half the time you can hear the same folks laughing from twenty, twenty-five years ago. *And from the sixties*. That's the part that got to me. So I rigged a way to filter out everything—dialogue, music—except for the audience, the track."

"Why, he probably knows all about that. Don't you, young man?"

"A lot of them, the audience, are gone now. It doesn't matter. They're on tape. It's recycled, 'canned' they call it. It's all the same to TV. Point is, this is the only way left for us to get through, or them to us. To make contact. To listen, eavesdrop, you might say, on what folks were doing and thinking and commenting on and laughing over back then.

"I can't call 'em up on the phone, or take a poll, or stop people on the street, 'cause they'd only act like nothing happened. Today, it's all passed on. Don't ask me how, but it has.

"They're passed on now, too, so many of 'em."

"Like the boys," said Mrs. Morrison softly, so that her voice was all but lost in the hiss of the swirling blue vortex.

"So many beautiful boys, the ones who would talk now, if only they could."

"Like the ones on the tracks," said Mr. Morrison.

"Like the ones who never came home," said his wife. *"Dead now, all dead, and never coming back."*

One minute to six.

"Not yet," he said aloud, frightened by his own voice.

As Mr. Morrison cranked up the gain and turned back to his set, the young man hurried out. As Mrs. Morrison opened her ears and closed her eyes to all but the laughtrack that rang out around her, he tried in vain to think of a way to reduce it all to a few simple marks in a now pointless language on sheets of printed paper. And as the Morrisons listened for the approving bursts of laughter and murmuring and applause, separated out of an otherwise meaningless echo from the past, he closed the door behind him, leaving them as he had found them. He began to walk faster, and finally to run.

The questionnaire crumpled and dropped from his hand.

Jack, I loved you, did you know that? You were my brother. I didn't understand, either. No one did. There was no time. But I told you, didn't I? Didn't *I?*

He passed other isolated houses on the block, ghostly living rooms turning to flickering beacons of cobalt blue against the night. The voices from within were television voices, muffled and anonymous and impossible to decipher unless one were to listen too closely, more closely than life itself would seem to want to permit, to the exclusion of all else, as to the falling of a single blade of grass or the unseen whisper of an approaching scythe. And it rang out around him then, too, through the trees and into the sky and the cold stars, the sound of the muttering and the laughter, the restless chorus of the dead, spreading rapidly away from him across the city and the world.

Ronald Anthony Cross

Ronald Anthony Cross has published stories in a variety of books and magazines in this country, England, and Germany, including *Isaac Asimov's Science Fiction Magazine, New Worlds, The Berkley Showcase, Orbit, Das Fest Des Heiligen Dionysos, Kopernikus, Other Worlds, Future Pastimes, Last Wave, Far Frontiers,* and *Universe.* His novelette "The Dolls: a Tragic Romance" was a Nebula award finalist. He lives in Santa Monica, California, with his wife and son.

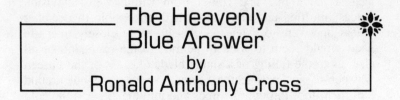

The Heavenly Blue Answer

by

Ronald Anthony Cross

I

He tried not to think of it at all. He wasn't interested in trying to come to terms with it. Just forget it. But sometimes they wouldn't let you forget it. Like when he opened the papers to the movie section, just going to a movie, and there is this ridiculous stud with muscles popping out all over him holding some kind of fancy gun with a big knobby head on it, from which was spraying—you guess. Talk about phallic. This dude had been pumping up until his muscles were like iron. Only they weren't iron, no, looks were deceiving, and one little piece of metal from one of those fucking AK-47s would deflate him like a balloon, forever. Big, tough, muscle-bound stud punches out Cong, right?

Only that wasn't the way it was at all. Nobody gave a shit about muscle, or manliness, and it was the little ones you worried about, not the big ones. The skinny little ones who could scurry into cracks in the walls like cockroaches, or hide in trees like snakes.

Which is one reason that the Cong were so fucking bad, because they were all the right size for fighting in a jungle.

Shit. He didn't want to think about it, but there it was. It sprang forth fully grown from his mind, like Athena from the mind of Zeus.

The same scene. Always the same, over and over again. Always happening now.

Edge of a deserted jungle village. Side of a river. They have spent the night here. There is argument as to whether they should wade out downriver to evade snipers (might be mined), or go out along the bank to evade the mines and run into sniper fire.

Meanwhile, Little Jim was seated on an oil drum, smoking a jay, watching Oogie fiddling around with one of his crazy Rube Goldberg traps. It wasn't that Little Jimmy was so little, but Big Jimmy was so big, right? So Little Jimmy he was.

And the argument about the river versus the riverbank didn't involve them. Let the brass fight it out. Fuck it. Whatever they chose was bound to be wrong. Because we're never getting out, right? It had dawned on him about a week ago (or was that only yesterday?), and it did not come from reason, or from anything at all. It was just some sort of goddamn wonderful divine revelation. It came along with its twin realization. This is real. Really real! All these guys are really dead. The bullets really kill you. Everything else is a dream. In the cruel light of this reality, "you ain't getting out" is another reality you simply live. It doesn't matter if it's true or not. You just ain't getting out. Fuck it. Fuck everything.

He sucked on the joint, strong grass. Like everything in 'Nam, too strong, too weird.

Like Oogie here, building his weird little booby trap. Well—big booby trap. Happy as could be, working away like a busy little beaver. Whistling. What kind of reality was he living?

As far as Little Jim could tell, the plan was this—or something like it.

Fu-gas. First Oogie had mixed the gasoline and soap together, sort of creating his own version of napalm. Stirring it and stirring it to get just the right consistency. There's a thermite grenade in front of the gas barrel, and a stick of dynamite underneath.

Oogie maintained that you had to use a No. 2 cap on the thermite and No. 4 on the dynamite. Little Jim had heard many arguments over that one. The dynamite is supposed to push the gas up and the thermite ignites it. Everything in a big circle is burnt to a crisp.

"Oogie, you crazy little bastard, one of these days you're going to blow yourself away." Little Jim got up and nervously moved back another fifty yards (out of range?).

Oogie looks up and grins his crazy grin. "Better me than them," he shouts. Laughs insanely. Turns back to his work.

Little Jim is trying to figure out what stage Oogie is working at, when it all happens. All at once. No matter how many times he has to live it all over again, he can't ever sort it out into a logical chain of events. Newton's laws don't work in 'Nam.

There is a popping noise: that came first. Of that he is certain. Almost certain. Sniper!

Then either the sniper hits Oogie and he accidentally somehow sets off the trap, or the sniper's bullets set it off, or even possibly, Oogie—crazy to start with—hears the sniper fire and flips out and deliberately just says fuck it and blows himself up. Maybe that's the reality he was living.

And Little Jim can dig that. Why not? Maybe there's just so much you can take, and—what was it Oogie had shouted? "Better me than them"? Famous last words. Had he really said that or was Little Jim's munged-up mind just making it up? Working overtime to bring Newton's laws to the jungle.

Anyhow. *Pop. Pop. Pop.* Oogie is hit (pretty sure of that). Then Oogie's booby trap goes off. Even at over fifty yards away, Little Jim is too close to this incredible homemade bomb to emerge unscathed. He is, in fact, both mentally and physically scathed.

For a moment, loud, loud noise and a blaze of light and heat that obliterates thought. Then silence and hot burning sensations on his cheeks and arms. Then ears ringing and his thoughts squirming around like fucking worms, and suddenly he can hear.

Everyone is shouting, including himself. For some reason he hears himself shouting "Oogie, you little fart, I'll kill your ass for this," while others are shouting about the sniper. "He's here, no, no, there, no—those trees over there," like a fucking silly magic trick.

And now all of a sudden everyone is firing everything they've got at once, all directions.

It is not so much that they are shooting at Charlie, as it is that they are responding to Oogie's crazy explosion in some kind of primitive ritual. It's the Fu-gas bomb that's thrown them over the edge. And here, in the middle of it all, this is clear to him, though later logic will enter in and confuse the issue. ("You were shooting at a sniper, Corporal? One sniper? All that ammo for one sniper?")

Because now everyone was firing off everything they had, in all directions at once, and shouting at the same time.

Little Jim was popping away with his M-16 into the nearest trees, and of course most everyone was blowing away the treetops with M-16s, but also machine guns were rattling away, grenade launchers were launching, and now—mortar fire.

For a long time everyone just fired away, using up, he guessed, maybe thousands of good old U.S. dollars' worth of ammunition on one little Cong tree snake—poisonous variety.

Then, gradually, everyone pulled themselves back into the area of consciousness we call control, until finally only one M-16 was still coughing. It stopped.

They all waited there in silence, sweating. Some were now in the river, some sharing the village foxholes with the corpses (Cong or whatever) which had been there since who knows when, and some were in huts. Some, like Little Jim, were just standing around.

"We must have blown away half the fuckin' jungle,"

someone shouts. Somebody laughs at that, but it is not fun laughter.

"Shit, we must have got him," someone else shouts.

Silence. Nobody moves. Then, *pop—pop—pop*. From somewhere. Anywhere. From little guy in trees, AK-47 sends message: Hello American pig. Find me if you can. Ha ha.

Everyone is firing into the trees again, and Little Jim notices a strange thing now. Several guys are down. Hit hard. And one of them is Big Jim. No longer Little Jim, he thinks insanely, now I'm just plain Jim. This thought fills him with weird brief elation. Which is here. Gone.

But there is no more room for fear. This is what flipped out means, he is saying to himself, when he sees something, someone coming out of one of the huts.

He aims the M-16 at the old man's belly. Vietnamese? Viet Cong? Outer space? Siamese if you please? his crazy mind is singing.

And the old man, empty hands (who cares at this point?), long scraggly grey beard and big, big brown eyes (the better to see you with), holding out empty hands (empty, full, who cares now?). Says, in English. In fucking English says, "I . . . am . . ." And just as he is saying this, holding out his hands, empty hands. Just as he is getting to the good part. The part that Little Jim (now just plain Jim) has got to hear, Jim's finger, independent of Jim's mind and body and philosophy and morality, just sort of squeezes off the trigger and blows him away. Then and there. Now. Always now.

But there is another kind of now. And in that less immediate yet coexistent now, Little Jim, who was no longer Little Jim or even Jim, but a man who worked away the days as a computer programmer everyone called James, closed the movie section of the newspaper with the macho stud super Vietnam vet fearlessly blowing away the Cong or whoever it was nowadays, and thought, No, it wasn't like that.

II

And so he lived in two nows—the one which was always right there, always the same, and the other one, which while being the reality that everyone else had agreed upon, was nevertheless somehow more distant and less realistic than the one frozen in his mind. There was not a day that went by without his asking himself, what had the old man been trying to say? "I am"—what?

In fact, now that he thought of it, perhaps he could make a case for three worlds. Because the America he left to go fight in Vietnam was not at all the America he came back to. Had it been the dream of his youth he had left behind, or an actual place? He could no longer be quite certain of anything.

In his memories it was bright and clean and simple. The bad guys wore duck-butt haircuts so you could distinguish them. There were good girls and bad ones, and you could tell them at a glance. No problem. Everything was like that. Simple. Straightforward.

Then there was the America he had come back to. Whoever it was said you can't go home again, James understood what he meant. It just plain wasn't there.

What was there was some strange cross between the America he had left and—surprise—Vietnam. America had become, in his absence, somehow Orientalized. Weird kids in orange robes danced in the streets chanting Hindu mantras, and everywhere he looked, restaurants advertised food from China, Japan—sure—but now India, Thailand, Korea, and yes—Vietnam. Every neighborhood was littered with karate and kung fu and Thai boxing schools. Schoolkids fought like Japanese soldiers, and his brother's wife, Jeanie, now served occasional (once a week) vegetarian meals, strangely Oriental in their nature.

Oriental concepts like guru, mantra, karma, and sushi were commonplace knowledge in every household. But even more alarming than that, and at the same time more subtle, was a sort of melting of the borders, of all the borders, so that everything ran together. Yes, that was it. That was what, to him, was the essence of Orientalism. This was all brought home to him, in a grand tragic style, by a trip to Disneyland.

James had been coerced into a family outing with his brother and his wife and their two kids.

For the family, it had been a success. His brother, Bob, felt that they had succeeded in cheering James up. But this was because James, who really could not bear to let the family down, knew enough to behave in a more manic manner. Crack more jokes, talk more, smile more often: he was aware of his brother and his sister-in-law constantly monitoring his expressions, and he could feel them both begin to relax as the day wore on. A family success.

"See, I know it's corny, James, but it's true," Bob told him. "It's the simple things that make life livable. A job. Kids. A wife. But mainly kids. It's through kids that you really get the most out of everything. They're like—like somehow being born again. Hell, I can't explain it, but I know it. It's what you've got to do, Jimmy, believe me." To James's surprise, upon staring into his brother Bob's eyes, he had found there tears. He really wanted to help. The whole family did. How had James ever managed to misunderstand this simple fact?

"I believe you, Bobbie, but I can't," he had said. "Not yet."

Bob seemed satisfied with the answer. Jeanie seemed satisfied. The kids were satisfied.

But for James the whole trip was a disaster. He remembered a visit to Disneyland when he was a kid: the first time.

It had gleamed. It had been so clear and clean and fresh and new. The sidewalks, in his memory, were clean enough to eat off of, for who would have thought of throwing trash on the ground in California in those days, let alone on the hallowed ground of Disneyland?

But, most important of all, the people were as clean as the park. And there was a certain uniformity about the dress, the hairstyles, that added—what was it?—a sense of style to the overall picture.

All of that was gone forever. Now the streets and sidewalks of the park were liberally sprinkled with trash and spilled food and drink. James had watched small children throw dirty napkins on the ground under the approving glances of their parents. He had watched the parents throw empty cartons on the sidewalks under the approving glances of their children. It seemed to James that everything in the park had faded, diminished, and become tainted.

And worst of all, the people. My God, there was no sense of style left in America anymore. But more than that: there was a flaunting, screaming insanity; people actually deliberately dressed like lunatics. Fully grown men with dazed marijuana expressions, dressed in crazy hats, some wearing loud garish shirts, some wearing undershirts—some not bothering to wear any shirts at all. Fully grown men wearing earrings and shorts. Older, grey-haired men in blaring, striped track costumes. And the women. Jesus, he didn't even want to think about that.

But when he contrasted all this in his mind with the pictures of the Disneyland he had visited when it was new, he had been more than merely shocked. He had been horrified. Because it was obviously not just Disneyland. No, it was his whole world. He had noticed it, of course, but it had taken this trip to Disneyland, the sanctuary of his ordered youth, to drive it home to him in its entirety: America's psyche was disintegrating, rather along the lines of one gigantic hebephrenic breakdown.

Suddenly he had to break away from his brother. Be alone with whatever it was that was throbbing and pounding inside his head.

"Bathroom," he mumbled. "Meet you at Peter Pan's in a few minutes."

And coming out of the bathroom and around the corner of the building, suddenly, impossibly, there it was. Again. Now.

The clearing. Crazy Oogie was working on his booby trap, humming, whistling to himself.

"Well, well, Little Jimmy, you can't bring America to 'Nam, but you bring 'Nam to America, am I right, man? I mean, who's invading who, here? Ha ha."

His laughter, as always, was totally manic. And he looked ridiculous, as always, in that stupid cowboy hat he was wearing.

"Should wear a helmet," Little Jim muttered, for what must have been the thousandth time.

Oogie laughed again. "Don't make no matter," he said. "Ain't going to make it. Ain't none of us going to make it out of here, Jimmy."

"But I made it."

"Wrong." Oogie laughed. "Here you is."

And he was, of course, right. Here Jim was.

I'll never get out, James thought, as he looked around him, not without terror, but yet not without—what?—interest, no, stronger than that.

Because, it was different from what he would have thought insanity would be like. More lucid. More simple.

It wasn't that Disneyland wasn't here. It was. And it wasn't as if the world of his mind had taken the place of his objective world. No, they were both sort of blended together. And he was aware, for instance, that he was not actually talking to Oogie. And he was aware of the tourists sporting mouse ears whom he almost bumped into, and he was quite aware that he was flipping out. The beginning of the end, he thought, not without terror, but then again, not without relief.

And then, just as suddenly as the vision had come, it was gone. No 'Nam, just Disneyland, but a Disneyland that was not so different from 'Nam as it once had been, and would never be again.

The beginning of the end. The trip was followed by such a fit of depression that he simply could not return to work: he called in sick. The beginning of the end, because, of course, he knew that now that the 'Nam in his mind had got out and mixed with the real world, it would do so again. And again. Until?

That night in bed, far from sleep, but so, so weary, he listened to Oogie babbling to him from the corner of his room, still working away, as always.

"I think it's the old man, you know? An ancient curse, right?" Laughs his crazy laugh. "The Vietnamese disease, right?" Laughs again. Suddenly turns serious and looks down into the Fu-gas he's stirring. "I still can't figure what went wrong, you know? It all happened so fast. Maybe I used the wrong-sized caps after all, or maybe I just flipped out and set the fuckin' thing off. Who the fuck knows? It all happened so fast."

And James finally dropped off to sleep to the sound of Oogie crying into his barrel of Fu-gas, stirring away. Working on his trap.

And dreamed. The old man. "I am"—squeezed the trigger. "I am"—squeezed the trigger. "What?" James shouts, "I am what?"

"I am," the old man says in English, and again James tries, but cannot keep from squeezing that trigger.

III

James has not been outside for two days, knows he must go outside, and so he manages to do so.

Vietnam is in the streets. Oh, it's L.A., all right. But Vietnam is here, too. And, here, he sees a flash of jungle. The clearing over there. He is fighting hard to get his mind back inside of his head, and out of the streets, but even as he is fighting to do it, he wonders if it really is the thing to do. All day long he wanders up and down the sidewalks, going nowhere. Just struggling, looking, and he is well aware that he is now talking to Oogie out loud. Mumbling to himself and stumbling along.

And what is so amazing is that he is not alone. Not even close to alone! The streets of L.A. are full of mumbling, stumbling burnouts, living out the lives from inside their heads out there on the sidewalks. Dirty. Crazy. Falling down un-drunks. Way beyond him. Experts at insanity.

Jesus Christ, he thought, it couldn't ever have been like this. What the fuck is this, anyway?

"Get a shopping cart from a grocery store," an old lady was telling him. "They're magic. They're what make me so beautiful. . . . Hell, look at that bitch. She used to be as big as a house. Now look at her. And that little fart used to be . . ."

A slender man whose age would have been impossible to guess, bolted by them in running shorts and shoes, obviously running home from work like James used to run home from school when he was a little kid. The runner paid no attention to the old lady's story, or curse or whatever it was, and James's consciousness followed him as he darted across the street, expertly dodging cars, the angry drivers of which seemed to James to be deliberately aiming at him. In a few moments he was gone, but somehow the incident had left James feeling a little better.

James wandered on, leaving the old lady cursing and mumbling, and next passed through the territory of a skinny black man who wore his hair in long intricately woven strings, Rastafarian style.

They each seemed to have staked out their own little plot of sidewalk, and somehow each lunatic operated within his or her own territory and respected thc boundaries. Home, sweet home!

And late that night, James found his way home, through the L.A. streets and the Vietnam jungle, to his apartment. Where he spent the night talking to Oogie and dozing off, from time to time. When he slept, he dreamed of the old man.

The next day was a warm smoggy day in the jungle. James was out on the sidewalks early, laughing and mumbling to himself with the best of them.

Yes, the jungle was here to stay now. He was sure of that. He would never force it all back into his head again. It was too big for that.

And at the same time, there was a kind of ecstasy to it. Once he stopped struggling with it, and just let go—why, hell—all that clutter and trash and weirdness had its own beauty.

He sat down on the curb and just looked at things for a while.

Objects glowed in the blazing sunlight. Broken glass was particularly ornamental. "Everything is God," the crazy Rastafarian had shouted at him. Sure. Why not?

As he sat there, an old man with a white beard wandered over and, seemingly reading his mind, stumbled and fell off the curb onto his hands and knees. "Shit!" he shouted. "But what a beauty."

James saw that he was alluding to a Coke bottle in the gutter.

Now the old man turned to James, his face transfixed with joy.

"See," he held out the bottle. "Blue heaven. Goddamn." He tilted the bottle up to the sun and peered directly into the mouth of it. A sticky syrup ran down out of it, into his eye, and down his cheek.

In spite of his revulsion, James was intrigued. "What do you see in there?" he said.

"I see everything in there," the old man said. "It's my blue heaven. I see every answer to every question. I see God. I see myself. Here, have a look."

James swallowed and held the bottle up to the sun and peered into it.

Blue fractured and sparkled into other blues, and there was

something he could almost see . . . but couldn't quite, and yet . . . Suddenly he was looking through dazzling blue light, and shimmering heat waves, into the dark cool interior of the hut. The old Vietnamese was holding out his hands. "I," he said. James's finger tried to squeeze on the trigger at the same time as James was struggling against that. "Am," the old man said. James fought desperately to hold himself back, but couldn't, and then, from the sky, like the voice of God, he heard the voice of another old man, from another world. "It's the answer to everything. Just everything. You can do it," the voice said.

And suddenly it was true. This time he did not have to squeeze the trigger, and at last the old Vietnamese man was able to finish his sentence:

"You. I am you."

James dropped the Coke bottle in the street, and began to weep.

"See, it didn't break," the old man sitting next to him on the curb said. "It's a miracle. They almost never break."

James was weeping in huge gasping sobs. Holding nothing back now. And was it his imagination, or did the old burnout actually pat him on the back and mumble, "The war is over, son," before he wandered off, shouting to himself?

And now emotion was pouring out of James, blasting out of his body like Oogie's fucking booby-trap explosion, and he wasn't even crying so much anymore as just plain howling, releasing everything all at once, clouds of pain and confusion and remorse and . . . just everything.

Later, when he came out of it, it was afternoon again. He felt so empty that for a moment he couldn't even remember who he was. But that was okay. Then he looked down, and there the blue Coke bottle lay in the street, near the curb. Still glittering. Still unbroken. A miracle. James smiled, but it was a weary smile.

I've got to get some sleep, he thought, if I'm going to make it to work tomorrow. And so he stood up, and began to thread his way methodically through the incredible crazy late afternoon L.A. pedestrian traffic. Back home.

Bruce McAllister

Bruce McAllister published his first story, "The Faces Outside," in *Worlds of If* in 1963, and since then he has produced a small but highly respected body of work. Many of his short stories have been selected for various *Year's Best* anthologies, and *Humanity Prime,* his only novel to date, was published in 1971 as one of the original "Ace Specials" edited by Terry Carr. McAllister was the managing editor of Harry Harrison and Brian Aldiss's *Year's Best* anthology series and also associate editor of the *West Coast Poetry Review.* Since 1974 he has been the director of the writing program at the University of Redlands in Southern California. McAllister is currently working on a revised edition of *Humanity Prime* and on several new novel projects. The unsettling story that follows is the heart of a novel in progress.

Dream Baby

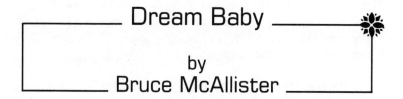

by
Bruce McAllister

Dream Baby, got me dreamin' sweet dreams
The whole day through.
Dream Baby, got me dreamin' sweet dreams
The night time too.

—Cindy Walker

I don't know whether I was for or against the war when I went. I joined and became a nurse to help. Isn't that why everyone becomes a nurse? We're told it's a good thing, like being a teacher or a mother. What they don't tell us is that sometimes you can't help.

Our principal gets on the PA one day and tells us how all these boys across the country are going over there for us and getting killed or maimed. Then he tells us that Tony Fischetti and this other kid are dead, killed in action, Purple Hearts and everything. A lot of the girls start crying. I'm crying. I call the Army and tell them my grades are pretty good, I want to go to nursing school and then 'Nam. They say fine, they'll pay for it but I'm obligated if they do. I say it's what I want. I don't know if any other girls from school did it. I really didn't care. I just thought somebody ought to.

I go down and sign up and my dad gets mad. He says I just want to be a whore or a lesbian, because that's what people will think if I go. I say, "Is that what you and Mom think?" He almost hits me. Parents are like that. What other people think is more important than what they think, but you can't tell them that.

I never saw a nurse in 'Nam who was a whore and I only

saw one or two who might have been butch. But that's how people thought, back here in the States.

I grew up in Long Beach, California, a sailor town. Sometimes I forget that. Sometimes I forget I wore my hair in a flip and liked miniskirts and black pumps. Sometimes all I can remember is the hospitals.

I got stationed at Cam Ranh Bay, at the 23rd Medevac, for two months, then the 118th Field General in Saigon, then back to the 23rd. They weren't supposed to move you around like that, but I got moved. That kind of thing happened all the time. Things just weren't done by the book. At the 23rd we were put in a bunch of huts. It was right by the hospital compound, and we had the Navy on one side of us and the Air Force on the other side. We could hear the mortars all night and the next day we'd get to see what they'd done.

It began to get to me after about a week. That's all it took. The big medevac choppers would land and the gurneys would come in. We were the ones who tried to keep them alive, and if they didn't die on us, we'd send them on.

We'd be covered with blood and urine and everything else. We'd have a boy with no arms or no legs, or maybe his legs would be lying beside him on the gurney. We'd have guys with no faces. We'd have stomachs you could hold in your hands. We'd be slapping ringers and plasma into them. We'd have sump pumps going to get the secretions and blood out of them. We'd do this all day, day in and day out.

You'd put them in bags if they didn't make it. You'd change dressings on stumps, and you had this deal with the corpsmen that every fourth day you'd clean the latrines for them if they'd change the dressings. They knew what it was like.

They'd bring in a boy with beautiful brown eyes and you'd just have a chance to look at him, to get a chest cut-down started for a subclavian catheter. He'd say, "Ma'am, am I all right?" and in forty seconds he'd be gone. He'd say "Oh, no" and he'd be gone. His blood would pool on the gurney right through the packs. Some wounds are so bad you can't even plug them. The person just drains away.

You wanted to help but you couldn't. All you could do was watch.

When the dreams started, I thought I was going crazy. It was about the fourth week and I couldn't sleep. I'd close my eyes and think of trip wires. I'd think my bras and everything else had trip wires. I'd be on the john and hear a sound and think that someone was trip-wiring the latch so I'd lose my hands and face when I tried to leave.

I'd dream about wounds, different kinds, and then the next day there would be the wounds I'd dreamed about. I thought it was just coincidence. I'd seen a lot of wounds by then. Everyone was having nightmares. I'd dream about a sucking chest wound and a guy trying to scream, though he couldn't, and the next day I'd have to suck out a chest and listen to a guy try to scream. I didn't think much about it. I couldn't sleep. That was the important thing. I knew I was going to go crazy if I couldn't sleep.

Sometimes the dreams would have all the details. They'd bring in a guy that looked like someone had taken an icepick to his arms. His arms looked like frankfurters with holes punched in them. That's what shrapnel looks like. You puff up and the bleeding stops. We all knew he was going to die. You can't live through something like that. The system won't take it. He knew he was going to die, but he wasn't making a sound. His face had little holes in it, around his cheeks, and it looked like a catcher's mitt. He had the most beautiful blue eyes, like glass. You know, like that dog, the weimer-something. I'd start shaking because he was in one of my dreams—those holes and his face and eyes. I'd shake for hours, but you couldn't tell anybody about dreams like that.

The guy would die. There wasn't anything I could do.

I didn't understand it. I didn't see a reason for the dreams. They just made it worse.

It got so I didn't want to go to sleep because I didn't want to have them. I didn't want to wake up and have to worry about the dreams all day, wondering if they were going to happen. I didn't want to have to shake all day, wondering.

I'd have this dream about a kid with a bad head wound and a phone call, and the next day they'd wheel in some kid who'd lost a lot of skull and brain and scalp, and the underlying brain would be infected. Then the word would get around that his father, who was a full-bird colonel stationed in Okie, had called and the kid's mother and father would be coming to see him. We all hoped he died before they got there, and he did.

I'd had a dream about him. I'd even dreamed that we wanted him to die before his mom and dad got there, and he did, in the dream he did.

When he died I started screaming and this corpsman who'd been around for a week or two took me by the arm and got me to the john. I'd gotten sick but he held me like my mom would have and all I could do was think what a mess I was, how could he hold me when I was such a mess? I started crying and couldn't stop. I knew everyone thought I was crazy, but I couldn't stop.

After that things got worse. I'd see more than just a face or the wounds. I'd see where the guy lived, where his hometown was and who was going to cry for him if he died. I didn't understand it at first—I didn't even know it was happening. I'd just get pictures, like before, in the dream and they'd bring this guy in the next day or the day after that, and if he could talk, I'd find out that what I'd seen was true. This guy would be dying and not saying a thing and I'd remember him from the dream and I'd say, "You look like a Georgia boy to me." If the morphine was working and he could talk, he'd say, "Who told you that, Lieutenant? All us brothers ain't from Georgia."

I'd make up something, like his voice or a good guess, and if I'd seen other things in the dream—like his girl or wife or mother—I'd tell him about those, too. He wouldn't ask how I knew because it didn't matter. How could it matter? He knew he was dying. They always know. I'd talk to him like I'd known him my whole life and he'd be gone in an hour, or by morning.

I had this dream about a commando type, dressed in tiger cammies, nobody saying a thing about him in the compound—spook stuff, Ibex, MAC SOG, something like that—and I could see his girlfriend in Australia. She had hair just like mine and her eyes were a little like mine and she loved him. She was going out with another guy that night, but she loved him, I could tell. In the dream they brought him into ER with the bottom half of him blown away.

The next morning, first thing, they wheeled this guy in and it was the dream all over again. He was blown apart from the waist down. He was delirious and trying to talk but his jaw wouldn't work. He had tiger cammies on and we cut them off. I was the one who got him and everyone knew he wasn't going to make it. As soon as I saw him I started shaking. I didn't want to see him, I didn't want to look at him. You really don't know what it's like, seeing someone like that and knowing. I didn't want him to die. I never wanted any of them to die.

I said, "Your girl in Australia loves you—she really does." He looked at me and his eyes had that look you get when morphine isn't enough. I could tell he thought I looked like her. He couldn't even see my hair under the cap and he knew I looked like her.

He grabbed my arm and his jaw started slipping and I knew what he wanted me to do. I always knew. I told him about her long black hair and the beaches in Australia and what the people were like there and what there was to do.

He thought I was going to stop talking, so he kept squeezing my arm. I told him what he and his girlfriend had done on a beach outside Melbourne, their favorite beach, and what they'd had to drink that night.

And then—this was the first time I'd done it with anyone—I told him what I'd do for him if I was his girlfriend and we were back in Australia. I said, "I'd wash you real good in the shower. I'd turn the lights down low and I'd put on some nice music. Then, if you were a little slow, I'd help you."

It was what his girlfriend always did, I knew that. It wasn't hard to say.

I kept talking, he kept holding my arm, and then he coded on me. They always did. I had a couple of minutes or hours and then they always coded on me, just like in the dreams.

I got good at it. The pictures got better and I could tell them what they wanted to hear and that made it easier. It wasn't just faces and burns and stumps, it was things about them. I'd tell them what their girlfriends and wives would do if they were here. Sometimes it was sexual, sometimes it wasn't. Sometimes I'd just ruffle their hair with my hand and tell them what Colorado looked like in summer, or what the last Doors concert they'd been to was like, or what you could do after dark in Newark.

I start crying in the big room one day and this corpsman takes me by the arm and the next thing I know I'm sitting on the john and he's got a needle in his hand, a 2% solution. He doesn't want to see me hurting so much. I tell him no. Why, I don't know. Every week or so I'd walk into the john and find somebody with a needle in their arm, but it wasn't for me, I thought. People weren't supposed to do that kind of thing. Junkies on the Pike back home did it—we all knew that—but not doctors and medics and nurses. It wasn't right, I told myself.

I didn't start until a couple of weeks later.

There's this guy I want to tell you about. Steve—his name was Steve.

I come in one morning to the big ER room shaking so hard I can't even put my cap on and thinking I should've gotten a needle already, and there's this guy sitting over by a curtain. He's in cammies, his head's wrapped and he's sitting up real straight. I can barely stand up, but here's this guy looking like he's hurting, so I say, "You want to lie down?"

He turns slowly to look at me and I don't believe it. I know this guy from a dream, but I don't see the dream clearly. Here's this guy sitting in a chair in front of me unattended, like he could walk away any second, but I've had a dream about him, so I know he's going to die.

He says he's okay, he's just here to see a buddy. But I'm not listening. I know everything about him. I know about his girlfriend and where he's from and how his mom and dad didn't raise him, but all I can think about is, he's going to die. I'm thinking about the supply room and needles and how it wouldn't take much to get it all over with.

I say, "Cathy misses you, Steve. She wishes you could go to the Branding Iron in Merced tonight, because that band you like is playing. She's done something to her apartment and she wants to show it to you."

He looks at me for a long time and his eyes aren't like the others. I don't want to look back at him. I can see him anyway—in the dream. He's real young. He's got a nice body, good shoulders, and he's got curly blond hair under those clean bandages. He's got eyelashes like a girl, and I see him laughing. He laughs every chance he gets, I know.

Very quietly he says, "What's your name?"

I guess I tell him, because he says, "Can you tell me what she looks like, Mary?"

Everything's wrong. The guy doesn't sound like he's going to die. He's looking at me like he understands.

I say something like "She's tall." I say, "She's got blond hair," but I can barely think.

Very gently he says, "What are her eyes like?"

I don't know. I'm shaking so hard I can barely talk, I can barely remember the dream.

Suddenly I'm talking. "They're green. She wears a lot of mascara, but she's got dark eyebrows, so she isn't really a blond, is she."

He laughs and I jump. "No, she isn't," he says and he's smiling. He takes my hand in his. I'm shaking badly but I let him, like I do the others. I don't say a word.

I'm holding it in. I'm scared to death. I'm cold-turkeying and I'm letting him hold my hand because he's going to die. But it's not true. I dreamed about him, but in the dream he didn't die. I know that now.

He squeezes my hand like we've known each other a long time and he says, "Do you do this for all of them?"

I don't say a thing.

Real quietly he says, "A lot of guys die on you, don't they, Mary."

I can't help it—I start crying. I want to tell him. I want to tell someone, so I do.

When I'm finished he doesn't say something stupid, he doesn't walk away. He doesn't code on me. He starts to tell me a story and I don't understand at first.

There's this G-2 reconnaissance over the border, he says. The insertion's smooth and I'm point, I'm always point. We're humping across paddy dikes like grunts and we hit this treeline. This is a black op, nobody's supposed to know we're here, but somebody does. All of a sudden the goddamn trees are full of Charlie ching-ching snipers. The whole world turns blue—just for me, I mean, it turns blue—and everything starts moving real slow. I can see the first AK rounds coming at me and I step aside nicely just like that, like always.

The world always turns blue like that when he needs it to, he says. That's why they make him point every goddamn time, why they keep using him on special ops to take out infrastructure or long-range recon for intel. Because the world turns blue. And how he's been called in twice to talk about what he's going to do after this war and how they want him to be a killer, he says. The records will say he died in this war and they'll give him a new identity. He doesn't have family, they say. He'll be one of their killers wherever they need him. Because everything turns blue. I don't believe what I'm hearing. It's like a movie, like that *Manchurian Candidate* thing, and I can't believe it. They don't care about how he does it, he says. They never do. It can be the world turning blue or voices in your head or some grabass feeling in your gut, or, if you want, it can be God or the Devil with horns or Little Green Martians—it doesn't matter to them what you believe. As long as it works, as long as you keep coming back from missions, that's all they care about. He told them no, but they keep on asking. Sometimes he thinks they'll kill his girlfriend just so he won't have anything to come back to in the States. They do that kind of thing, he says. I can't believe it.

So everything's turning blue, he says, and I'm floating up out of my body over this rice paddy, these goddamn ching-ching snipers are darker blue, and when I come back down I'm moving through this nice blue world and I know where they are, and I get every goddamn one of them in their trees.

But it doesn't matter, he says. There's this light-weapons sergeant, a guy they called the Dogman, who's crazy and barks like a dog and makes everyone laugh even if they're bleeding, even if their guts are hanging out. He scares the VC when he barks. He humps his share and the men love him.

When the world turns blue, the Dogman's in cover, everything's fine, but then he rubbernecks, the sonuvabitch rubbernecks for the closest ching-ching—he didn't have to, he just didn't have to—and takes a round high. I don't see the back of his head explode, so I think he's still alive. I go for him where he's hanging half out of the treeline, half in a canal full of stinking rice water. I try to get his body out of the line of fire, but Charlie puts the next round right in under my arm. I'm holding the Dogman and the round goes in right under my arm, a fucking heart shot. I can feel it come in. It's for me. Everything goes slow and blue and I jerk a little—I don't even know I'm doing it—and the round slides right in under me and into him. They never get *me*. The fucking world turns blue and everything goes slow and they never get *me*.

I can always save myself, he says—his name is Steve and he's not smiling now—but I can't save *them*. What's it worth? What's it worth if you stay alive and everybody you care about is dead? Even if you get what *they* want.

I know what he means. I know now why he's sitting on a chair nearly crying, I know where the body is, which curtain it's behind, how close it's been all this time. I remember the dream now.

Nobody likes to die alone, Steve says. Just like he said it in the dream.

He stays and we talk. We talk about the dreams and his blue world, and we talk about what we're going to do when we get out of this place and back to the Big PX, all the fun we're going to have. He starts to tell me about other guys he knows, guys like him that his people are interested in, but then he stops and I see he's looking past me. I turn around.

There's this guy in civvies at the end of the hallway, just standing there, looking at us. Then he nods at Steve and Steve says, "I got to go."

Real fast I say, "See you at nineteen hundred hours."

He's looking at the guy down the hallway. "Yeah, sure," he says.

When I get off he's there. I haven't thought about a needle all day and it shows. We get a bite to eat and talk some more, and that's that. My roommate says I can have the room for a couple of hours, but I'm a mess. I'm shaking so bad I can't even think about having a good time with this guy. He looks at me like he knows this, and says his head hurts and we ought to get some sleep.

He gives me a hug. That's it.

The same guy in civvies is waiting for him and they walk away together on Phan Hao Street.

* * *

The next day he's gone. I tell myself maybe he was standing down for a couple of days and had to get back, but that doesn't help. I know lots of guys who traveled around in-country AWOL without getting into trouble. What could they do to you? Send you to 'Nam?

I thought maybe he'd call in a couple of days, or write. Later I thought maybe he'd gotten killed, maybe let himself get killed. I really didn't know what to think, but I thought about him a lot.

Ten days later I get transferred. I don't even get orders cut, I don't even get in-country travel paper. No one will tell me a thing—the head nurse, the CO, nobody.

I get scared because I think they're shipping me back to the States because of the smack or the dreams—they've found out about the dreams—and I'm going to be in some VA hospital the rest of my life. That's what I think.

All they'll tell me is that I'm supposed to be at the strip at 0600 hours tomorrow, fatigues and no ID.

I get a needle that night and I barely make it.

This Huey comes in real fast and low and I get dust in my eyes from the prop wash. A guy with a clipboard about twenty yards away signals me and I get on. There's no one there to say good-bye and I never see the 23rd again.

The Huey's empty except for these two pilots who never turn around and this doorgunner who's hanging outside and this other guy who's sitting back with me on the canvas. I think maybe he's the one who's going to explain things, but he just stares for a while and doesn't say a thing. He's a sergeant, a Ranger, I think.

It's supposed to be dangerous to fly at night in Indian Country, I know, but we fly at night. We stop twice and I know we're in Indian Country. This one guy gets off, another guy gets on, and then two more. They seem to know each other and they start laughing. They try to get me to talk. One guy says, "You a Donut Dolly?" and another guy says, "Hell, no, asshole, she's Army, can't you tell? She's got the thousand yards." The third guys says to me, "Don't mind him, ma'am. They don't raise 'em right in Mississippi." They're trying to be nice, but I don't want in.

I don't want to sleep either. But my head's tipped back against the steel and I keep waking up, trying to remember whether I've dreamed about people dying, but I can't. I fall asleep once for a long time and when I wake up I can remember death, but I can't see the faces.

I wake up once and there's automatic weapon fire somewhere below us and maybe the slick gets hit once or twice. Another time I wake up and the three guys are talking quietly, real serious, but I'm hurting from no needle and I don't even listen.

When the rotors change I wake up. It's first light and cool and we're coming in on this big clearing, everything misty and beautiful. It's triple-canopy jungle I've never seen before and I know we're so far from Cam Ranh Bay or Saigon it doesn't matter. I don't see anything that looks like a medevac, just this clearing, like a staging area. There are a lot of guys walking around, a lot of machinery, but it doesn't look like regular Army. It looks like something you hear about but aren't supposed to see, and I'm shaking like a baby.

When we hit the LZ the three guys don't even know I exist and I barely get out of the slick on my own. I can't see because of the wash and suddenly this Green Beanie medic I've never seen before—this captain—has me by the arm and he's taking me somewhere. I tell myself I'm not going back to the Big PX, I'm not going to some VA hospital for the rest of my life, that this is the guy I'm going to be assigned to—they need a nurse out here or something.

I'm not thinking straight. Special Forces medics don't have nurses.

I'm looking around me and I don't believe what I'm seeing. There's bunkers and M-60 emplacements and Montagnard guards on the perimeter and all this beautiful red earth. There's every kind of jungle fatigue and cammie you can think of—stripes and spots and black pajamas like Charlie and everything else. I see Special Forces enlisted everywhere and I know this isn't some little A-camp. I see a dozen guys in real clean fatigues who don't walk like soldiers walk. I see a Special Forces major and he's arguing with one of them.

The captain who's got me by the arm isn't saying a thing. He takes me to this little bunker that's got mosquito netting and a big canvas flap over the front and he puts me inside. It's got a cot. He tells me to lie down and I do. He says, "The CO wants you to get some sleep, Lieutenant. Someone will come by with something in a little while." The way he says it I know he knows about the needles.

I don't know how long I'm in the bunker before someone comes, but I'm in lousy shape. This guy in civvies gives me something to take with a little paper cup and I go ahead and do it. I'm not going to fight it the shape I'm in. I dream, and keep dreaming, and in some of the dreams someone comes by with a glass of water and I take more pills. I can't wake up. All I can do is sleep but I'm not really sleeping and I'm having these dreams that aren't really dreams. Once or twice I hear myself screaming, it hurts so much, and then I dream about a little paper cup and more pills.

When I come out of it I'm not shaking. I know it's not supposed to be this quick, that what they gave me isn't what people are getting in programs back in the States, and I get scared again. Who are these guys?

I sit in the little bunker all day eating ham-and-mother-fuckers from C-rat cans and I tell myself that Steve had something to do with it. I'm scared but it's nice not to be shaking. It's nice not to be thinking about a needle all the time.

The next morning I hear all this noise and I realize we're leaving, the whole camp is leaving. I can hear this noise like a hundred slicks outside and I get up and look through the flap. I've never seen so many choppers. They've got Chinooks and Hueys and Cobras and Loaches and a Skycrane for the SeaBee machines and they're dusting off and dropping in and dusting off again. I've never seen anything like it. I keep looking for Steve. I keep trying to remember the dreams I had while I was out all those days and I can't.

Finally the Green Beanie medic comes back. He doesn't say a word. He just takes me to the LZ and we wait until a slick drops in. All these tiger stripes pile in with us but no one says a thing. No one's joking. I don't understand it. We aren't being hit, we're just moving, but no one's joking.

We set up in a highlands valley northwest of where we'd been, where the jungle is thicker but it's not triple canopy. There's this same beautiful mist and I wonder if we're in some other country, Laos or Cambodia.

They have my bunker dug in about an hour and I'm in it about thirty minutes before this guy appears. I've been looking for Steve, wondering why I haven't seen him, and feeling pretty good about myself. It's nice not to be shaking, to get the monkey off my back, and I'm ready to thank *somebody*.

This guy opens the flap. He stands there for a moment and there's something familiar about him. He's about thirty and he's in real clean fatigues. He's got MD written all over him—but the kind that never gets any blood on him. I think of VA hospitals, psychiatric wards, and I get scared again.

"How are you feeling, Lieutenant?"

"Fine," I say, but I'm not smiling. I know this guy from the dreams—the little paper cups and pills—and I don't like what I'm feeling.

"Glad to hear it. Remarkable drug, isn't it, Lieutenant?"

I nod. Nothing he says surprises me.

"Someone wants to see you, Lieutenant."

I get up, dreading it. I know he's not talking about Steve.

They've got all the bunkers dug and he takes me to what has to be the CP. There isn't a guy inside who isn't in real clean fatigues. There are three or four guys who have the same look this guy has—MDs that don't ever get their hands dirty—and intel types pointing at maps and pushing things around on a couple of sand-table mock-ups. There's this one guy with his back turned and everyone else keeps checking in with him.

He's tall. He's got a full head of hair but it's going gray. He doesn't even have to turn around and I know.

It's the guy in civvies at the end of the hallway at the 23rd, the guy that walked away with Steve on Phan Hao Street.

He turns around and I don't give him eye contact. He looks at me, smiles, and starts over. There are two guys trailing him and he's got this smile that's supposed to be charming.

"How are you feeling, Lieutenant?" he says.

"Everybody keeps asking me that," I say, and I wonder why I'm being so brave.

"That's because we're interested in you, Lieutenant," he says. He's got this jungle outfit on with gorgeous creases and some canvas jungle boots that breathe nicely. He looks like an ad from a catalog but I know he's no joke, he's no pogue lifer. He's wearing this stuff because he likes it, that's all. He could wear anything he wanted to because he's not military, but he's the CO of this operation, which means he's fighting a war I don't know a thing about.

He tells me he's got some things to straighten out first, but that if I go back to my little bunker he'll be there in an hour. He asks me if I want anything to eat. When I say sure, he tells the MD type to get me something from the mess.

I go back. I wait. When he comes, he's got a file in his hand and there's a young guy with him who's got a cold six-pack of Coke in his hand. I can tell they're cold because the cans are sweating. I can't believe it. We're out here in the middle of nowhere, we're probably not even supposed to be here, and they're bringing me cold Coke.

When the young guy leaves, the CO sits on the edge of the cot and I sit on the other and he says, "Would you like one, Lieutenant?"

I say, "Yes, sir," and he pops the top with a church key. He doesn't take one himself and suddenly I wish I hadn't said yes. I'm thinking of old movies where Jap officers offer their prisoners a cigarette so they'll owe them one. There's not even any place to put the can down, so I hold it between my hands.

"I'm not sure where to begin, Lieutenant," he says, "but let me assure you you're here because you belong here." He says it gently, real softly, but it gives me a funny feeling. "You're an officer and you've been in-country for some time. I don't need to tell you that we're a very special kind of operation here. What I do need to tell you is that you're one of three hundred we've identified so far in this war. Do you understand?"

I say, "No, sir."

"I think you do, but you're not sure, right? You've accepted your difference—your gift, your curse, your talent, whatever you would like to call it—but you can't as easily accept the fact that so many others might have the same thing, am I right, Mary—may I call you Mary?''

I don't like the way he says it but I say yes.

''We've identified three hundred like you, Mary. That's what I'm saying.''

I stare at him. I don't know whether to believe him.

''I'm only sorry, Mary, that you came to our attention so late. Being alone with a gift like yours isn't easy, I'm sure, and finding a community of those who share it—the same gift, the same curse—is essential if the problems that always accompany it are to be worked out successfully, am I correct?''

''Yes.''

''We might have lost you, Mary, if Lieutenant Balsam hadn't found you. He almost didn't make the trip, for reasons that will be obvious later. If he hadn't met you, Mary, I'm afraid your hospital would have sent you back to the States for drug abuse if not for what they perceived as an increasingly dysfunctional neurosis. Does this surprise you?''

I say it doesn't.

''I didn't think so. You're a smart girl, Mary.''

The voice is gentle, but it's not.

He waits and I don't know what he's waiting for.

I say, ''Thank you for whatever it was that—''

''No need to thank us, Mary. Were that particular drug available back home right now, it wouldn't seem like such a gift, would it?''

He's right. He's the kind who's always right and I don't like the feeling.

''Anyway, thanks,'' I say. I'm wondering where Steve is.

''You're probably wondering where Lieutenant Balsam is, Mary.''

I don't bother to nod this time.

''He'll be back in a few days. We have a policy here of not discussing missions—even in the ranks—and as commanding officer I like to set a good example. You can understand, I'm sure.'' He smiles again and for the first time I see the crow's-feet around his eyes, and how straight his teeth are, and how there are little capillaries broken on his cheeks.

He looks at the Coke in my hands and smiles. Then he

opens the file he has. "If we were doing this the right way, Mary, we would get together in a nice air-conditioned building back in the States and go over all of this together, but we're not in any position to do that, are we?

"I don't know how much you've gathered about your gift, Mary, but people who study such things have their own way of talking. They would call yours a 'TPC hybrid with traumatic neurosis, dissociative features.' " He smiled. "That's not as bad as it sounds. It's quite normal. The human psyche always responds to special gifts like yours, and neurosis is simply a mechanism for doing just that. We wouldn't be human if it didn't, would we?"

"No, we wouldn't."

He's smiling at me and I know what he wants me to feel. I feel like a little girl sitting on a chair, being good, listening, and liking it, and that is what he wants.

"Those same people, Mary, would call your dreams 'spontaneous anecdotal material' and your talent a 'REM-state precognition or clairvoyance.' They're not very helpful words. They're the words of people who've never experienced it themselves. Only you, Mary, know what it really feels like inside. Am I right?"

I remember liking how that felt—*only you*. I needed to feel that, and he knew I needed to.

"Not all three hundred are dreamers like you, of course. Some are what those same people would call 'kinetic phenomena generators.' Some are 'tactility-triggered remoters' or 'OBE clears.' Some leave their bodies in a firefight and acquire information that could not be acquired in ordinary ways, which tells us that their talent is indeed authentic. Others see auras when their comrades are about to die, and if they can get those auras to disappear, their friends will live. Others experience only a vague visceral sensation, a gut feeling which tells them where mines and trip wires are. They know, for example, when a crossbow trap will fire and this allows them to knock away the arrows before they can hurt them. Still others receive pictures, like waking dreams, of what will happen in the next minute, hour, or day in combat.

"With very few exceptions, Mary, none of these individuals experienced anything like this as civilians. These episodes are the consequence of combat, of the metabolic and psychological anomalies which life-and-death conditions seem to generate.''

He looks at me and his voice changes now, as if on cue. He wants me to feel what he is feeling, and I do, I do. I can't look away from him and I know this is why he is CO.

''It is almost impossible to reproduce them in a laboratory, Mary, and so these remarkable talents remain mere ancedotes, events that happen once or twice within a lifetime—to a brother, a mother, a friend, a fellow soldier in a war. A boy is killed on Kwajalein in 1944. That same night his mother dreams of his death. She has never before dreamed such a dream, and the dream is too accurate to be mere coincidence. He dies. She never has a dream like it again. A reporter for a major newspaper looks out the terminal window at the Boeing 707 he is about to board. He has flown a hundred times before, enjoys air travel, and has no reason to be anxious today. As he looks through the window the plane explodes before his very eyes. He can hear the sound ringing in his ears and the sirens rising in the distance; he can feel the heat of the ignited fuel on his face. Then he blinks. The jet is as it was before—no fire, no sirens, no explosion. He is shaking—he has never experienced anything like this in his life. He does not board the plane, and the next day he hears that its fuel tanks exploded, on the ground, in another city, killing ninety. The man never has such a vision again. He enjoys air travel in the months, and years, ahead, and will die of cardiac arrest on a tennis court twenty years later. You can see the difficulty we have, Mary.''

''Yes,'' I say quietly, moved by what he's said.

''But our difficulty doesn't mean that your dreams are any less real, Mary. It doesn't mean that what you and the three hundred like you in this small theater of war are experiencing isn't real.''

''Yes,'' I say.

He gets up.

''I am going to have one of my colleagues interview you, if that's all right. He will ask you questions about your dreams and he will record what you say. The tapes will remain in my care, so there isn't any need to worry, Mary.''

I nod.

''I hope that you will view your stay here as deserved

R&R, and as a chance to make contact with others who understand what it is like. For paperwork's sake, I've assigned you to Golf Team. You met three of its members on your flight in, I believe. You may write to your parents as long as you make reference to a medevac unit in Pleiku rather than to our actual operation here. Is that clear?"

He smiles like a friend would, and makes his voice as gentle as he can. "I'm going to leave the rest of the Coke. And a church key. Do I have your permission?" He grins. It's a joke, I realize. I'm supposed to smile. When I do, he smiles back and I know he knows everything, he knows himself, he knows me, what I think of him, what I've been thinking every minute he's been here.

It scares me that he knows.

His name is Bucannon.

The man that came was one of the other MD types from the tent. He asked and I answered. The question that took the longest was "What were your dreams like? Be as specific as possible both about the dream content and its relationship to reality—that is, how accurate the dream was as a predictor of what happened. Describe how the dreams and their relationship to reality (i.e., their accuracy) affected you both psychologically and physically (e.g., sleeplessness, nightmares, inability to concentrate, anxiety, depression, uncontrollable rages, suicidal thoughts, drug abuse)."

It took us six hours and six tapes.

We finished after dark.

I did what I was supposed to do. I hung around Golf Team. There were six guys, this lieutenant named Pagano, who was in charge, and this demo sergeant named Christabel, who was their "talent." He was, I found out, an "OBE clairvoyant with EEG anomalies," which meant that in a firefight he could leave his body just like Steve could. He could leave his body, look back at himself—that's what it felt like—and see how everyone else was doing and maybe save someone's ass. They were a good team. They hadn't lost anybody yet, and they loved to tease this sergeant every chance they got.

We talked about Saigon and what you could get on the

black market. We talked about missions, even though we weren't supposed to. The three guys from the slick even got me to talk about the dreams, I was feeling that good, and when I heard they were going out on another mission at 0300 hours the next morning, without the sergeant—some little mission they didn't need him on—I didn't think anything about it.

I woke up in my bunker that night screaming because two of the guys from the slick were dead. I saw them dying out in the jungle, I saw how they died, and suddenly I knew what it was all about, why Bucannon wanted me here.

He came by the bunker at first light. I was still crying. He knelt down beside me and put his hand on my forehead. He made his voice gentle. He said, "What was your dream about, Mary?"

I wouldn't tell him. "You've got to call them back," I said.

"I can't, Mary," he said. "We've lost contact."

He was lying I found out later: he could have called them back—no one was dead yet—but I didn't know that then. So I went ahead and told him about the two I'd dreamed about, the one from Mississippi and the one who'd thought I was a Donut Dolly. He took notes. I was a mess, crying and sweaty, and he pushed the hair away from my forehead and said he would do what he could.

I didn't want him to touch me, but I didn't stop him. I didn't stop him.

I didn't leave the bunker for a long time. I couldn't.

No one told me the two guys were dead. No one had to. It was the right kind of dream, just like before. But this time I'd *known* them. I'd met them. I'd laughed with them in the daylight and when they died I wasn't there, it wasn't on some gurney in a room somewhere. It was different.

It was starting up again, I told myself.

I didn't get out of the cot until noon. I was thinking about needles, that was all.

He comes by again at about 1900 hours, just walks in and says, "Why don't you have some dinner, Mary. You must be hungry."

I go to the mess they've thrown together in one of the big bunkers. I think the guys are going to know about the screaming, but all they do is look at me like I'm the only woman in the camp, that's all, and that's okay.

Suddenly I see Steve. He's sitting with three other guys and I get this feeling he doesn't want to see me, that if he did he'd have come looking for me already, and I should turn around and leave. But one of the guys is saying something to him and Steve is turning and I know I'm wrong. He's been waiting for me. He's wearing cammies and they're dirty—he hasn't been back long—and I can tell by the way he gets up and comes toward me he wants to see me.

We go outside and stand where no one can hear us. He says, "Jesus, I'm sorry." I'm not sure what he means.

"Are you okay?" I say, but he doesn't answer.

He's saying, "I wasn't the one who told him about the dreams, Mary, I swear it. All I did was ask for a couple hours' layover to see you, but he doesn't like that—he doesn't like 'variables.' When he gets me back to camp, he has you checked out. The hospital says something about dreams and how crazy you're acting, and he puts it together. He's smart, Mary. He's real smart—"

I tell him to shut up, it isn't his fault, and I'd rather be here than back in the States in some VA program or ward. But he's not listening. "He's got you here for a reason, Mary. He's got all of us here for a reason and if I hadn't asked for those hours he wouldn't know you existed—"

I get mad. I tell him I don't want to hear any more about it, it isn't his fault.

"Okay," he says finally. "Okay." He gives me a smile because he knows I want it. "Want to meet the guys on the team?" he says. "We just got extracted—"

I say sure. We go back in. He gets me some food and then introduces me. They're dirty and tired but they're not complaining. They're still too high off the mission to eat and won't crash for another couple of hours yet. There's an SF medic with the team, and two Navy SEALs because there's a riverine aspect to the mission, and a guy named Moburg, a Marine sniper out of Quantico. Steve's their CO and all I can think about is how young he is. They're all so young.

It turns out Moburg's a talent, too, but it's "anticipatory

subliminal''—it only helps him target hits and doesn't help anyone else much. But he's a damn good sniper because of it, they tell me.

The guys give me food from their trays and for the first time that day I'm feeling hungry. I'm eating with guys that are real and alive and I'm really hungry.

Then I notice Steve isn't talking. He's got that same look on his face. I turn around.

Bucannon's in the doorway, looking at us. The other guys haven't seen him, they're still talking and laughing—being raunchy.

Bucannon is looking at us and he's smiling, and I get a chill down my spine like cold water because I know—all of a sudden I know—why I'm sitting here, who wants it this way.

I get up fast. Steve doesn't understand. He says something. I don't answer him, I don't even hear him. I keep going. He's behind me and he wants to know if I'm feeling okay, but I don't want to look back at him, I don't want to look at any of the guys with him, because that's what Bucannon wants.

He's going to send them out again, I tell myself. They just got back, they're tired, and he's going to send them out again, so I can dream about them.

I'm not going to go to sleep, I tell myself. I walk the perimeter until they tell me I can't do that anymore, it's too dangerous. Steve follows me and I start screaming at him, but I'm not making any sense. He watches me for a while and then someone comes to get him, and I know he's being told he's got to take his team out again. I ask for some Benzedrine from the Green Beanie medic who brings me aspirin when I want it but he says he can't, that word has come down that he can't. I try writing a letter to my parents but it's 0400 hours and I'm going crazy trying to stay awake because I haven't had more than four hours' sleep for a couple of nights and my body temperature's dropping on the diurnal.

I ask for some beer and they get it for me. I ask for some scotch. They give it to me and I think I've won. I never go to sleep on booze, but Bucannon doesn't know that. I'll stay awake and I won't dream.

But it knocks me out like a light, and I have a dream. One of the guys at the table, one of the two SEALs, is floating down a river. The blood is like a woman's hair streaming out from his head. I don't dream about Steve, just about this SEAL who's floating down a river. It's early in the mission. Somehow I know that.

I don't wake up screaming, because of what they put in the booze. I remember it as soon as I wake up, when I can't do anything about it.

Bucannon comes in at first light. He doesn't say, "If you don't help us, you're going back to Saigon or back to the States with a Section Eight." Instead he comes in and kneels down beside me like some goddamn priest and he says, "I know this is painful, Mary, but I'm sure you can understand."

I say, "Get the hell out of here, motherfucker."

It's like he hasn't heard. He says, "It would help us to know the details of any dream you had last night, Mary."

"You'll let him die anyway," I say.

"I'm sorry, Mary," he says, "but he's already dead. We've received word on one confirmed KIA in Echo Team. All we're interested in is the details of the dream and an approximate time, Mary." He hesitates. "I think he would want you to tell us. I think he would want to feel that it was not in vain, don't you."

He stands up at last.

"I'm going to leave some paper and writing utensils for you. I can understand what you're going through, more than you might imagine, Mary, and I believe that if you give it some thought—if you think about men like Steve and what your dreams could mean to them—you will write down the details of your dream last night."

I scream something at him. When he's gone I cry for a while. Then I go ahead and write down what he wants. I don't know what else to do.

I don't go to the mess. Bucannon has food brought to my bunker but I don't eat it.

I ask the Green Beanie medic where Steve is. Is he back yet? He says he can't tell me. I ask him to send a message to Steve for me. He says he can't do that. I tell him he's a straight-leg ass-kisser and ought to have his jump wings shoved, but this doesn't faze him at all. Any other place, I say, you'd be what you were supposed to be—Special Forces and a damn good medic—but Bucannon's got you, doesn't he. He doesn't say a thing.

I stay awake all that night. I ask for coffee and I get it. I bum more coffee off two sentries and drink that, too. I can't believe he's letting me have it. Steve's team is going to be back soon, I tell myself—they're a strike force, not a Lurp—and if I don't sleep, I can't dream.

I do it again the next night and it's easier. I can't believe it's this easy. I keep moving around. I get coffee and I find this sentry who likes to play poker and we play all night. I tell him I'm a talent and will know if someone's trying to come through the wire on us, sapper or whatever, so we can play cards and not worry. He's pure new-guy and he believes me.

Steve'll be back tomorrow, I tell myself. I'm starting to see things and I'm not thinking clearly, but I'm not going to crash. I'm not going to crash until Steve is back. I'm not going to dream about Steve.

At about 0700 hours the next morning we get mortared. The slicks inside the perimeter start revving up, the Skycrane starts hooking its cats and Rome plows, and the whole camp starts to dust off. I hear radios, more slicks and Skycranes being called in. If the NVA had a battalion, they'd be overrunning us, I tell myself, so it's got to be a lot less—company, platoon—and they're just harassing us, but word has come down from somebody that we're supposed to move.

Mortars are whistling in and someone to one side of me says "Incoming—fuck it!" Then I hear this other sound. It's like flies but real loud. It's like this weird whispering. It's a goddamn flechette round, I realize, spraying stuff, and I don't understand. I can hear it, but it's like a memory, a flashback. Everybody's running around me and I'm just standing there and someone's screaming. It's me screaming. I've got flechettes all through me—my chest, my face. I'm torn to pieces. I'm dying. But I'm running toward the slick, the one that's right over there, ready to dust off. Someone's calling to me, screaming at me, and I'm running, but I'm not. I'm on the ground. I'm on the jungle floor with these flechettes in me and I've got a name, a nickname, Kicker, and I'm thinking of a town in Wyoming, near the Montana border, where everybody rides pickup trucks with shotgun racks and waves to everybody else, I grew up there, there's a rodeo every spring with a county fair and I'm thinking about a girl with braids, I'm thinking how I'm going to die here in the middle of this jungle, how we're on some recondo that no one cares about, how Charlie doesn't have flechette rounds, how Bucannon never makes mistakes.

I'm running and screaming and when I get to the slick the Green Beanie medic grabs me, two other guys grab me and haul me in. I look up. It's Bucannon's slick. He's on the radio. I'm lying on a pile of files right beside him and we're up over the jungle now, we're taking the camp somewhere else, where it can start up all over again.

I look at Bucannon. I think he's going to turn any minute and say, "Which ones, Mary? Which ones died from the flechette?" He doesn't.

I look down and see he's put some paper and three pencils beside me on the floor. I can't stand it. I start crying.

I sleep maybe for twenty minutes and have two dreams. Two other guys died out there somewhere with flechettes in them. Two more guys on Steve's team died and I didn't even meet them.

I look up. Bucannon's smiling at me.

"It happened, didn't it, Mary?" he says gently. "It happened in the daylight this time, didn't it?"

At the new camp I stayed awake another night, but it was hard and it didn't make any difference. It probably made it worse. It happened three more times the next day and all sorts of guys saw me. I knew someone would tell Steve. I knew Steve's team was still out there—Echo hadn't come in when the rocketing started—but that he was okay. I'm lying on the ground screaming and crying with shrapnel going through me, my legs are gone, my left eyeball is hanging out on my cheek, and there are pieces of me all over the guy next to me, but I'm not Steve, and that's what matters.

The third time, an AK round goes through my neck so I can't even scream. I fall down and can't get up. Someone kneels down next to me and I think it's Bucannon and I try to hit him. I'm trying to scream even though I can't, but it's not Bucannon, it's one of the guys who was sitting with Steve in the mess. They're back, they're back, I think to myself, but I'm trying to tell this guy that I'm dying, that there's this medic somewhere out there under a beautiful rubber tree who's trying to pull me through, but I'm not going to make it, I'm going to die on him, and he's going to remember it his whole life, wake up in the night crying years later and his wife won't understand.

I want to say, "Tell Steve I've got to get out of here," but I can't. My throat's gone. I'm going out under some rubber tree a hundred klicks away in the middle of Laos, where we're not supposed to be, and I can't say a thing.

This guy who shared his ham-and-motherfuckers with me in the mess, this guy is looking down on me and I think, Oh my God, I'm going to dream about him some night, some day, I'm going to dream about him and because I do he's going to die.

He doesn't say a thing.

He's the one that comes to get me in my hooch two days later when they try to bust me out.

They give me something pretty strong. By the time they come I'm getting the waking dreams, sure, but I'm not screaming anymore. I'm here but I'm not. I'm all these other places, I'm walking into an Arclight, B-52 bombers, my ears are bleeding, I'm the closest man when a big Chinese claymore goes off, my arm's hanging by a string, I'm dying in all these other places and I don't even know I've taken their pills. I'm like a doll when Steve and this guy and three others come, and the guards let them. I'm smiling like an idiot and saying, "Thank you very much," something stupid some USO type would say, and I've got someone holding me up so I don't fall on my face.

There's this Jolly Green Giant out in front of us. It's dawn and everything's beautiful and this chopper is gorgeous. It's Air Force. It's crazy. There are these guys I've never seen before. They've got black berets and they're neat and clean, and they're not Army. I think, Air Commandos! I'm giggling. They're Air Force. They're dandies. They're going to save the day like John Wayne at Iwo Jima. I feel a bullet go through my arm, then another through my leg, and the back of my head blows off, but I don't scream. I just feel the feelings, the ones you feel right before you die—but I don't scream. The Air Force is going to save me. That's funny. I tell myself how Steve had friends in the Air Commandos and how they took him around once in-country for a whole damn week, AWOL, yeah, but maybe it isn't true, maybe I'm dreaming it. I'm still giggling. I'm still saying, "Thank you very much."

We're out maybe fifty klicks and I don't know where we're heading. I don't care. Even if I cared I wouldn't know how far out "safe" was. I hear Steve's voice in the cockpit and a bunch of guys are laughing, so I think *safe*. They've busted me out because Steve cares and now we're *safe*. I'm still saying "Thank you" and some guy is saying "You're welcome, baby," and people are laughing and that feels good. If they're all laughing, no one got hurt, I know. If they're all laughing, we're safe. Thank you. Thank you very much.

Then something starts happening in the cockpit. I can't hear with all the wind. Someone says "Shit." Someone says "Cobra." Someone else says "Jesus Christ what the hell." I look out the roaring doorway and I see two black gunships. They're like nothing I've never seen before. No one's laughing. I'm saying "Thank you very much" but no one's laughing.

I find out later there was one behind us, one in front, and one above. They were beautiful. They reared up like snakes when they hit you. They had M-134 Miniguns that could put a round on every square centimeter of a football field within seconds. They had fifty-two white phosphorous rockets apiece and Martin-Marietta laser-guided Copperhead howitzer rounds. They had laser designators and Forward-Looking Infrared Sensors. They were nightblack, no insignias of any kind. They were model AH-1G-X and they didn't belong to any regular branch of the military back then. You wouldn't see them until the end of the war.

I remember thinking that there were only two of us with talent on that slick, why couldn't he let us go? Why couldn't he just let us go?

* * *

I tried to think of all the things he could do to us, but he didn't do a thing. He didn't have to.

I didn't see Steve for a long time. I went ahead and tried to sleep at night because it was better that way. If I was going to have the dreams, it was better that way. It didn't make me so crazy. I wasn't like a doll someone had to hold up.

I went ahead and wrote the dreams down in a little notebook Bucannon gave me, and I talked to him. I showed him I really wanted to understand, how I wanted to help, because it was easier on everybody this way. He didn't act surprised, and I didn't think he would. He'd always known. Maybe he hadn't known about the guys in the black berets, but he'd known that Steve would try it. He'd known I'd stay awake. He'd known the dreams would move to daylight, from "interrupted REM-state," if I stayed awake. And he'd known he'd get us back.

We talked about how my dreams were changing. I was having them much earlier than "events in real time," he said. The same thing had probably been happening back in ER, he said, but I hadn't known it. The talent was getting stronger, he said, though I couldn't control it yet. I didn't need the "focal stimulus," he said, "the physical correlative." I didn't need to meet people to have the dreams.

"When are we going to do it?" I finally said.

He knew what I meant. He said we didn't want to rush into it, how acting prematurely was worse than not understanding it, how the "fixity of the future" was something no one yet understood, and we didn't want to take a chance on stopping the dreams by trying to tamper with the future.

"It won't stop the dreams," I said. "Even if we kept a death from happening, it wouldn't stop the dreams."

He never listened. He wanted them to die. He wanted to take notes on how they died and how my dreams matched their dying, and he wasn't going to call anyone back until he was ready to.

"This isn't war, Mary," he told me one day. "This is a kind of science and it has its own rules. You'll have to trust me, Mary."

He pushed the hair out of my eyes, because I was crying. He wanted to touch me. I know that now.

* * *

I tried to get messages out. I tried to figure out who I'd dreamed about. I'd wake up in the middle of the night and try to talk to anybody I could and figure it out. I'd say, "Do you know a guy who's got red hair and is from Alabama?" I'd say, "Do you know an RTO who's short and can't listen to anything except Jefferson Airplane?" Sometimes it would take too long. Sometimes I'd never find out who it was, but if I did, I'd try to get a message out to him. Sometimes he'd already gone out and I'd still try to get someone to send him a message—but that just wasn't done.

I found out later Bucannon got them all. People said yeah, sure, they'd see that the message got to the guy, but Bucannon always got them. He told people to say yes when I asked. He knew. He always knew.

I didn't have a dream about Steve and that was the important thing.

When I finally dreamed that Steve died, that it took more guys in uniforms than you'd think possible—with more weapons than you'd think they'd ever need—in a river valley awfully far away, I didn't tell Bucannon about it. I didn't tell him how Steve was twitching on the red earth up North, his body doing its best to dodge the rounds even though there were just too many of them, twitching and twitching, even after his body wasn't alive anymore.

I cried for a while and then stopped. I wanted to feel something but I couldn't.

I didn't ask for pills or booze and I didn't stay awake the next two nights scared about dreaming it again. There was something I needed to do.

I didn't know how long I had. I didn't know whether Steve's team—the one in the dream—had already gone out or not. I didn't know a thing, but I kept thinking about what Bucannon had said, the "fixity," how maybe the future couldn't be changed, how even if Bucannon hadn't intercepted those messages something else would have kept the future the way it was and those guys would have died anyway.

I found the Green Beanie medic who'd taken me to my hooch that first day. I sat down with him in the mess. One of Bucannon's types was watching us but I sat down anyway. I said, "Has Steve Balsam been sent out yet?" And he said, "I'm not supposed to say, Lieutenant. You know that."

"Yes, Captain, I do know that. I also know that because you took me to my little bunker that day I will probably dream about your death before it happens, if it happens here. I also know that if I tell the people running this project about it, they won't do a thing, even though they know how accurate my dreams are, just like they know how accurate Steve Balsam is, and Blakely, and Corigiollo, and the others, but they won't do a thing about it." I waited. He didn't blink. He was listening.

"I'm in a position, Captain, to let someone know when I have a dream about them. Do you understand?"

He stared at me.

"Yes," he said.

I said, "Has Steve Balsam been sent out yet?"

"No, he hasn't."

"Do you know anything about the mission he is about to go out on?"

He didn't say a thing for a moment. Then he said, "Red Dikes."

"I don't understand, Captain."

He didn't want to have to explain—it made him mad to have to. He looked at the MD type by the door and then he looked back at me.

"You can take out the Red Dikes with a one-K nuclear device, Lieutenant. Everyone knows this. If you do, Hanoi drowns and the North is down. Balsam's team is a twelve-man night insertion beyond the DMZ with special MAC V ordnance from a carrier in the South China Sea. All twelve are talents. Is the picture clear enough, Lieutenant?"

I didn't say a thing. I just looked at him.

Finally I said, "It's a suicide mission, isn't it. The device won't even be real. It's one of Bucannon's ideas—he wants to see how they perform, that's all. They'll never use a nuclear device in Southeast Asia and you know that as well as I do, Captain."

"You never know, Lieutenant."

"Yes, you do." I said it slowly so he would understand.

He looked away.

"When is the team leaving?"

He wouldn't answer anymore. The MD typc looked like he was going to walk toward us.

"Captain?" I said.

"Thirty-eight hours. That's what they're saying."

I leaned over.

"Captain," I said. "You know the shape I was in when I got here. I need it again. I need enough of it to get me through a week of this place or I'm not going to make it. You know where to get it. I'll need it tonight."

As I walked by the MD type at the door I wondered how he was going to die, how long it was going to take, and who would do it.

I killed Bucannon the only way I knew how.

I started screaming at first light and when he came to my bunker, I was crying. I told him I'd had a dream about him. I told him I dreamed that his own men, guys in cammies and all of them talents, had killed him, they had killed him because he wasn't using a nurse's dreams to keep their friends alive, because he had my dreams but wasn't doing anything with them, and all their friends were dying.

I looked in his eyes and I told him how scared I was because they killed her too, they killed the nurse who was helping him too.

I told him how big the 9-millimeter holes looked in his fatigues, and how something else was used on his face and stomach, some smaller caliber. I told him how they got him dusted off soon as they could and got him on a sump pump and IV as soon as he hit Saigon, but it just wasn't enough, how he choked to death on his own fluids.

He didn't believe me.

"Was Lieutenant Balsam there?" he asked.

I said no, he wasn't, trying not to cry. I didn't know why, but he wasn't, I said.

His eyes changed. He was staring at me now.

He said, "When will this happen, Mary?"

I said I didn't know—not for a couple of days at least, but I couldn't be sure, how could I be sure? It felt like four, maybe five, days, but I couldn't be sure. I was crying again.

This is what made him believe me in the end.

He knew it would never happen if Steve were there—but if Steve was gone, if the men waited until Steve was gone?

Steve would be gone in a couple of days and there was no way that this nurse, scared and crying, could know this.

He moved me to his bunker and had someone hang canvas to make a hooch for me inside his. He doubled the guards and changed the guards and doubled them again, but I knew he didn't think it was going to happen until Steve left.

I cried that night. He came to my hooch. He said, "Don't be frightened, Mary. No one's going to hurt you. No one's going to hurt anyone."

But he wasn't sure. He hadn't tried to stop a dream from coming true—even though I'd asked him to—and he didn't know whether he could or not.

I told him I wanted him to hold me, someone to hold me. I told him I wanted him to touch my forehead the way he did, to push my hair back the way he did.

At first he didn't understand, but he did it.

I told him I wanted someone to make love to me tonight, because it hadn't happened in so long, not with Steve, not with anyone. He said he understood and that if he'd only known he could have made things easier on me.

He was quiet. He made sure the flaps on my hooch were tight and he undressed in the dark. I held his hand just like I'd held the hands of the others, back in Cam Ranh Bay. I remembered the dream, the real one where I killed him, how I'd held his hand while he got undressed, just like this.

Even in the dark I could see how pale he was and this was like the dream too. He seemed to glow in the dark even though there wasn't any light. I took off my clothes, too. I told him I wanted to do something special for him. He said fine, but we couldn't make much noise. I said there wouldn't be any noise. I told him to lie down on his stomach on the cot. I sounded excited. I even laughed. I told him it was called "around the world" and I liked it best with the man on his stomach. He did what I told him and I kneeled down and lay over him.

I jammed the needle with the morphine into his jugular and when he struggled I held him down with my own weight.

No one came for a long time.

When they did, I was crying and they couldn't get my hand from the needle.

Steve's team wasn't sent. The dreams stopped, just the way Bucannon thought they would. Because I killed a man to keep another alive, the dreams stopped. I tell myself now this was what it was all about. I was supposed to keep someone from dying—that's why the dreams began—and when I did, they could stop, they could finally stop. Bucannon would understand it.

"There is no talent like yours, Mary, that does not operate out of the psychological needs of the individual," he would have said. "You dreamed of death in the hope of stopping it. We both knew that, didn't we. When you killed me to save another, it could end, the dreams could stop, your gift could return to the darkness where it had lain for a million years—so unneeded in civilization, in times of peace, in the humdrum existence of teenagers in Long Beach, California, where fathers believed their daughters to be whores or lesbians if they went to war to keep others alive. Am I right, Mary?"

This is what he would have said.

They could have killed me. They could have taken me out into the jungle and killed me. They could have given me a frontal and put me in a military hospital like the man in '46 who had evidence that Roosevelt knew about the Japanese attack on Pearl. The agency Bucannon had worked for could have sent word down to have me pushed from a chopper on the way back to Saigon, or had me given an overdose, or assigned me to some black op I'd never come back from. They were a lot things they could have done, and they didn't.

They didn't because of what Steve and the others did. They told them you'll have to kill us all if you kill her or hurt her in any way. They told them you can't send her to jail, you can send her to a hospital but not for long, and you can't fuck with her head, or there will be stories in the press and court trials and a bigger mess than My Lai ever was.

It was seventy-six talents who were saying this, so the agency listened.

Steve told me about it the first time he came. I'm here for

a year, that's all. There are ten other women in this wing and we get along—it's like a club. They leave us alone.

Steve comes to see me once a month. He's married—to the same one in Merced—and they've got a baby now, but he gets the money to fly down somehow and he tells me she doesn't mind.

He says the world hasn't turned blue since he got back, except maybe twice, real fast, on freeways in central California. He says he hasn't floated out of his body except once, when Cathy was having the baby and it started to come out wrong. It's fading away, he says, and he says it with a laugh, with those big eyelashes and those great shoulders.

Some of the others come, too, to see if I'm okay. Most of them got out as soon as they could. They send me packages and bring me things. We talk about the mess this country is in, and we talk about getting together, right after I get out. I don't know if they mean it. I don't know if we should. I tell Steve it's over, we're back in the Big PX and we don't need it anymore—Bucannon was right—and maybe we shouldn't get together.

He shakes his head. He gives me a look and I give him a look and we both know we should have used the room that night in Cam Ranh Bay, when we had the chance.

"You never know," he says, grinning. "You never know when the baby might wake up."

That's the way he talks these days, now that he's a father. "You never know when the baby might wake up."

To D.A., J.P., J.S., A.W. and all the others who went in our stead; and to Linda Van Devanter, Gayle Smith and unnamed sisters for their courage and inspiration in the pages of Nam: An Oral History, Home Before Morning *and* Everything We Had.

Afterword to "Dream Baby"

It was not the editors' intention to include afterwords to the stories, but we think that the following warrants making the exception to the rule. McAllister writes:

> "Dream Baby" is based on four years of interviews and correspondence with a dozen vets ranging from privates through seasoned NCOs to intelligence officers, all of whom had "spontaneous anecdotal ESP experiences" in 'Nam which they felt helped keep them alive. There isn't an ESP "talent" in the story that doesn't come from a vet interviewed or corresponded with; the plan to blow the Red Dikes was an actual contingency plan; and the CIA did try to recruit a light weapons specialist who, because of what he experienced as ESP, kept coming back from missions untouched. The point, very simply, is that the Vietnam War, even now, isn't what it seemed. . . .

Susan Casper

Susan Casper sold her first story, "Spring Fingered Jack," to Charles L. Grant's anthology *Fears* in 1983. Since then her work has appeared in *The Magazine of Fantasy & Science Fiction, Isaac Asimov's Science Fiction Magazine, Playboy, Shadows, Amazing, Midnight*'s, and *Whispers*. She is coediting an anthology with Gardner Dozois entitled *Jack the Ripper*, forthcoming from Tor Books, and is working on her first novel, tentatively entitled *The Red Carnival*. She lives in Philadelphia, and is currently serving on the 1986 Nebula award jury.

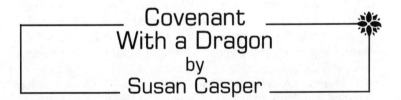

Covenant With a Dragon

by

Susan Casper

She reached for him. It was not unusual for Richard to feel her hand slipping through the covers in that hazy time between sleep and wakefulness, a gentle touch to see if he, too, was awake and wanting, and knowing this, he feigned sleep. She made no attempt to wake him, merely rested her fingers against his thigh for just a moment and then slowly moved them away. As soon as her hand was gone he was sorry that he hadn't responded. He disliked disappointing her even in small ways, but he just couldn't bring himself to make love to her this morning. Carol had not been the woman he'd been dreaming of in the sultry heat of that lonely summer.

Too many times in the last few weeks he had given in to the temptation and held Carol in his arms pretending that she was Thot. It never worked very well. The textures were wrong—skin and hair—and the scent. Carol was candy sweet compared to Thot's heady musk. Besides, Carol was his wife. Even if she never guessed, and he wondered sometimes if she might not already know, it wasn't right to use her as a substitute for long-dead dreams. Thot had been too much on his mind of late. More than she had been through all the last decade. More than she had when he first returned home. He had no idea why.

He reached up and clutched the little carving of a dragon that always hung on a leather thong around his neck. The memories came. Romantic ones at first—sweetly scented flowers, gentle heat, the laughter he shared with Thot as she gave him the carving and tried to convince him that it would help keep him safe—but he made an effort of will and slowly the reality began to penetrate. For the first time in a long time he saw the squalid house, ruined by war, invaded by insects. He could hear the baby cry and once again felt a desperate desire to go and comfort her . . . to assure her that things would be all right when he knew that there was no such assurance. The pain in his leg throbbed as he searched the debris while his world crumbled and hope collapsed within him. He grasped the dragon, holding it tightly in his fist, and allowed the pain to ease slowly away.

"Honey, are you okay? It's getting late." Carol's voice startled him back to reality. He noted the look of concern on her face and forced himself to smile.

"Of course I am," he said. He pounced, grabbing her suddenly by the shoulders and forcing her back against the pillows. "One for you," he said, kissing her cheek, "and one for Godzilla" he added, bending to kiss the barely noticeable bulge of her abdomen. He rolled out of the bed and began to get dressed. "Remember, Pop's coming home from the hospital tonight, so we're eating at Dom and Marie's."

He said good-bye to his son and went out into the early

morning breeze. His brother Joey had often offered to pick him up with the truck on his way back from the food distribution center, but it was so beautiful in the mornings before the worst of the day's weather hit, and only a handful of people on the streets. Besides, it wasn't such a long walk.

The market was already a busy place when he got there. Angelina Lo Patto was emptying a bucket of ice into her display window, for the squid and porgies and filets of bluefish, cod, and flounder to rest on. Outside her store were barrels of live crabs and buckets of mussels and clams. Several of the butchers were laying out bright red cuts of meat delivered fresh from the slaughterhouse around the corner, and the poultry men were stacking crates of squawking birds and frantically scrabbling rabbits waiting to be selected for their moment of glory. Mrs. Ly, an elderly Vietnamese woman who was the newest vendor in his block of the market, had just let herself out of her son's station wagon to begin setting up her card table across the street.

Joey was late with the truck. There were no crates to be pried open, no oranges to tumble out onto the dusty gray planks of his rickety stand, no onions to rustle their brown paper skins in the cool morning breeze. He lit a cigarette and leaned back against the cool bricks of the spice store to wait. Across the street, Mrs. Ly's son piled boxes on the sidewalk so that the children with him could unpack their goodies onto the table. There were always groups of children around Mrs. Ly's stand in the mornings. So many, that he had been unable to keep himself from asking her once if they were all hers. How she had laughed. Two were her grandchildren, the rest belonged to the other families who shared the rented house with her. All came to help from time to time, and Richie loved to watch them as they stopped to play, got in each other's way, and occasionally broke some of the merchandise. When that happened, Mrs. Ly would cuff the offender soundly, yelling all the while in short, unintelligible, singsong bursts. Most of the children were very young, but today there was an older girl with them, wearing one of those purple balloon coats that had been the rage a year or so ago. She worked with her back to him, setting out rows of cheap, cut-glass bud vases, her hair swaying back and forth against the violet nylon as she moved. Thot had not been much older than that when he had first seen her, leaning over a small, magnetic chessboard behind the HQ. She had been so pathetically eager to learn to play the game, so charmingly anxious to improve her English that he had felt compelled to ask her father if he could give her lessons. He had never meant to become more than her teacher.

The girl in the purple coat reminded him of Thot; though she was of bigger build, she had the same delicateness of movement, as though the very air around her was made of crystal that she might shatter with an ungraceful move. Slowly, she turned and fixed on Richie a sad-eyed stare that made his chest ache and sent his cigarette rolling across the sidewalk in a flash of sparks. What was there about that face? It was not Thot's face. Only the child's eyes were Oriental. The rest of her features were very European. And yet . . .

"Well, are you gonna help or what?" Joey asked, punching Richie gently on the arm.

"Huh? Help what?"

"What the hell do you *think* I'm talking about?" Joey said disgustedly. "We gotta unload."

Richie looked into Joey's face, which was a younger mirror of his own. Vinnie, Dom, Joey, himself, Pop . . . there was no denying the relationship. All had the same squared-off jaw, that thin upper lip balanced against a much fuller lower one, a straight nose with slightly flared nostrils. Even the kids, Vinnie's four, Dom's three, and his own son, Jason, had that same Augustino face, looking more like sisters and brothers than cousins. He glanced back across the street in time to catch one more look at the girl as she followed the other children into the waiting car. Nose, mouth, chin . . . except for the eyes, she had the same face. His heart lurched. Without a word to his brother, he started across the street.

"Richie!"

He stopped and changed gears, noticing his brother through a haze of fog. It wasn't possible. He had checked it out very carefully. Thot and Mia were *both* dead.

"Okay, I don't need to work today if you don't," Joey said, tossing a crate of lettuce back on the ground.

"The hell you don't," Richie said, and grabbing the nearest crate, he began to pry open one of the wooden slats. He threw himself into the work, but thoughts of the child nagged at him all through the early morning chores. There were few customers on the streets as yet; if he was going to talk to Mrs. Ly, there would be no better time. "Joey, I'm takin' a break," he called back over his shoulder.

"Good morning, Augustino," Mrs. Ly said, pronouncing his name as if it were four separate words.

"That girl," he said, without greeting. "That girl in the purple coat who was helping you unload this morning—who is she?"

"Very pretty, that one, but much too young for you." Mrs. Ly laughed.

"How old is she?" Richie asked, and something about his expression took the smile off of her face. She looked him over carefully, and then as if she too noticed something for the first time, she nodded gravely.

"The child was orphaned very young. We cannot be certain of her true age. None of her relatives have ever claimed her. Her age of record is fifteen. She may be younger, but not much. Some of these mixed-blood children tend to be a little bit bigger."

His temples throbbed and his neck ached, the dragon felt like a lead weight on its thong. Fourteen . . . She could be fourteen. "Tell me whatever you know about her? Or her family? How did you happen to find her . . . ?"

"Slow down, Augustino. This is not the place or time. We will talk later. You come back to my house for lunch. My daughter makes *bahn cuon*. . . . It is very good," she said.

He nodded. "When?" he asked.

"My daughter-in-law comes to watch the stand at twelve. We can go then," she said and turned to face her first customer of the morning.

The day dragged slowly, with just enough business to keep his mind from wandering completely out of the present, though he felt much more comfortable with his daydreams. He found it hard to keep the resentment out of his voice when some old lady would interrupt him by paying for her purchases. Joey was little help. Periodically, Richie looked up to see if Mrs. Ly's relief had come yet. What would she be able to tell him? Was there any way that he could know for sure. He touched the dragon through the thin cotton cloth of his T-shirt.

At exactly twelve-thirty Mrs. Ly's daughter-in-law turned onto 9th Street and the old woman nodded to him from across the street.

Richie followed the old lady through the crowds and stalls of the market until she turned down a tiny row-house-lined street. All the while, his mind flooded with the memory of a tiny baby pressed briefly into his arms. For a long time he had hoped and searched, and then he had searched without hope until the word came back that they were dead. Now he could feel the warmth of hope radiate in his chest, right under the dragon; he could almost believe that the carving itself was glowing with its own warmth and sending the heat throughout his body.

They stopped in front of a shabby-looking brick house on Christian Street that would have been too small even for *one* large family. Mrs. Ly led him up the weatherworn stairs and through the aluminum screen door into a living room crammed with worn furniture and knickknacks. It was a noisy home. Voices came from every room, along with the cry of babies, and the high-pitched giggle and chatter of small children too young to be out playing on their own. But beneath the clutter of a house stuffed with more people than it was ever designed to hold, he could see that the place was spotlessly clean. Mrs. Ly left him seated on the sofa and went into the kitchen. He heard a long exchange of rapid-fire Vietnamese. It had never really sounded like a language to him, and he wished now that he had taken the trouble to learn it from Thot, as she had learned English from him. Whatever Mrs. Ly had said, a parade of people came out of the kitchen, passed quickly through the living room and up the stairway. One young woman smiled and nodded in Richie's direction, the other two completely ignored him. Mrs. Ly then motioned for Richie to follow her.

They ate first, with only occasional, polite bursts of conversation about business. The food was good, but the smell of boiling cabbage that hung about the kitchen made it difficult for him to eat. Mrs. Ly finished first and waited patiently while he popped the last bite into his mouth. "Now, Augustino," she said at last, "tell me why you want to know about this child."

He told her what he could about himself and Thot, about

the child they had had together, revealing more with his eyes and the tone of his voice about just how lost he had been when he had been forced to return home without them—about the painful readjustment to the life he had left.

She did not interrupt his speech. When he finished she took his hand and said, "Augustino, I am sorry. No one can give you the information you seek. The child herself knows nothing of her past. She was an orphan, a street child, when she was found. Phen Ngo worked for my husband many years ago in Saigon. Her own children were both killed in the war. It was said that single women with children were given preference in leaving the country, so she and the child adopted each other. This way it worked out better for both of them.

"As for the child's name, she has used many. She was content to take the name of Phen Ngo's oldest girl. And while it does seem likely that her father was an American soldier, there were so *many* soldiers there fifteen years ago, so many mixed-blood children left behind . . . This resemblance you see, it could be coincidence. You will never be more sure than you are at this moment. Is this enough for you? You must think about this thing carefully. Remember, it has been fourteen years."

Richie flipped a finger under the thong around his neck and tugged out the dragon. It felt warm and alive in his hand. "Thot gave me this," he said. "The child has one also."

Mrs. Ly studied the carving. "Lynn has such a thing," she said slowly, "but even that means very little. Such carvings are not uncommon in my country. Many have them."

"I think I might be her father," he said at last.

"You must not *think*. You must be certain in your heart. More than that, you must make a decision as to what you will do about it. The child is not unhappy here. This is a better life than the one she knew before. If you decide that she is your child, will you take her away? It will be very hard for her. She does not speak your language, she does not know your ways.

"And *your* family, Augustino. Will they be as eager to welcome this child that may or may not be yours?" She stared at him for a long time. "We will go back to work now. You must talk with your wife. You must talk with your brothers and your parents. When you are sure, then you can come back . . . if you still want to."

All the way home that night, Richie tried to think up ways of telling Carol. There didn't seem to be any way to avoid hurting her, but she was so damned maternal that—once she got over the shock—she would have no problem accepting the girl. Then, when he had Carol on his side, they could stand together against anything his family had to offer.

He was nervous when he entered the house, anxious to tell her and have done with it, but she was busy helping Jason with his day-camp project. Then Marge Braunstein called and Carol settled in for a nice long chat. He didn't get her alone until she was seated at the vanity getting ready to put on her evening's makeup. "Carol, I have something very important to talk to you about," he said.

"Go ahead," she said, brushing a thin dark line above the lashes on her upper eyelid.

"It's about when I was in 'Nam," he said, "and it's kind of hard for me to talk about. I know I never told you much about what went on over there, or why I stopped writing to you. It was very good of you, sweetheart, not to push me about things until I was ready, but now there's a reason why you have to know. So, please, be patient with me for a few minutes. You see, there was this girl—"

"Oh, spare me, Richie. True confessions . . . just what I need," she said angrily, blinking back a tear. "Did it ever occur to you to wonder *why* I never asked you about all this? Did you really think it was my overwhelming patience, or maybe that I just didn't care? I never thought that you were celibate the whole two years that you didn't write. I didn't ask because I didn't want to know about 'this girl.' As long as you didn't say anything, I could convince myself that it wasn't anything serious, that it was only because I wasn't around. Then it wasn't so bad. But now . . . now you're going to tell me that you were ready to throw me over for one of *them*, aren't you? Tonight; when I have to go over your brother's house and play sweet adoring wife for your whole family." She slammed her hairbrush down on the vanity and stood up, her face tight and red-streaked with tears.

"You know, it wouldn't have been so bad back when we were kids and I had all those romantic notions of what *they* were like, but now . . . Now that I see them every day, sitting out in front of their foul-smelling apartments with their tight little monkey asses, gabbing together like a flock of turkeys, grabbing free this and free that off the government while decent people have to work their asses off to get anything." She stood over him breathing heavily for a moment, then turned and walked out of the room.

He stared after her, shaking with rage. How dare she betray him like this. For the first time since they had been married, he wanted to hit her. But in a moment the feeling left him and he found himself strangely empty and lost. There was nothing left to do. This woman would *never* accept the child. He reached for his dragon and felt its warmth burning there beneath his cotton shirt, but this time it gave him no comfort. What good was it? It was a part of his past, like Thot, like the girl . . . like the woman he had thought he was married to. He would have to put it all behind him and get on with his life. He reached for the dragon and tugged it off, rubbing the back of his neck raw on the thong before it finally parted. He slipped the tiny carving from the leather string and stared at it in his palm. It, too, had betrayed him. He took a deep breath and threw the dragon across the room.

"Darling," Carol whispered. He turned to see her standing in the doorway, looking much more controlled. "I'm sorry, honey. I know you didn't tell me just to hurt me. I know you're not that kind of person. There had to be a reason. Whatever it is, I want to help. Has she turned up in Philly? Is that it? Is she trying to hurt you, now, after all these years? Whatever it is, I'll stand by you," she said. She walked toward him with her hand outstretched to soothe him, but he couldn't bear to let her touch him. Not just yet. He brushed past her.

"I'll meet you at Dom's," he said.

Even a walk through his beloved South Philly streets didn't seem to be much help. The problem, as it unfolded in his mind, seemed to be an endless maze from which there was no exit. His parents would be worse than Carol. What a fuss they had made when Dom had started dating that Jewish girl.

He sat on an empty step for a while to watch a group of girls playing rope, until tears came to his eyes, then forced himself to move on. Guilt and worry were a terrible load on his mind. He began to feel as if he were being followed.

Stalked, rather, like a deer during hunting season. But a look over his shoulder told him what he already knew—there was nobody there.

Dom's house was alive and crackling with the casual tension that overlaid most family gatherings. Poppa, the undisputed king of the castle, being thoroughly patronized by his sons. The women always found some excuse to go off together, leaving Mama in the kitchen by herself. Only Richie stood aloof, watching it all with mixed emotions. The children took their turns going to grandpa for their little tokens of affection—he would like to see Mia as part of that group. And yet, seeing how ill the old man was, how much he had aged in the last few weeks, Richie wondered if he had the right to disturb the old man's peace.

Carol went to bed as soon as they got home, but he couldn't bring himself to get that close to her. He stayed downstairs, awake most of the night, trying to concentrate on a movie. He awoke in the morning to find himself crumpled into the unopened recliner. Everything ached. The cut on his neck burned unbearably and the long-healed injury of his leg throbbed almost as badly as it had when the bone was broken. He could hear no signs of movement from upstairs, though his watch told him that it was an hour past their usual wake-up time. How could they sleep so long in this muggy and stifling heat? Summer seemed to have crept up on them during the night. He rubbed his gritty eyeballs and went about the painful business of disentangling himself from the chair.

The world wobbled. Noise; the nerve-wrenching noise of grinding metal and rock, human voices shrieking, shouting, glass shattering, desks, typewriters, chairs being flung against the walls. Heat, and the bitter smell of burning wood and flesh. Reaching out for something, anything solid, and his leg, almost with a will of its own, twisting in the opposite direction. A dull thump; an incredible burst of pain that momentarily took his vision, his arms working, vainly trying to pull himself out. Dust closed his eyes and choked his nose and throat. The endless hours that seemed like years waiting for anything, even death, to free him from the pain.

His leg ached so badly that he almost didn't make it up the stairs, and his hands shook as he fumbled with the shower knobs. He'd read enough to know about flashbacks without ever having one before—but it had been so real that he had trouble placing himself in the present. His dragon, his only comfort during that long time waiting for rescue and the months in the hospital that followed, was gone. He couldn't remember what he'd done with it. He sank down until he was seated in the tub and let the stinging water wash away his tears.

He didn't bother to towel off after his shower, allowing the air to cool him as it dried. The day was so humid that this didn't work very well, sweat replacing the water before he ever reached the point of being dry. He limped into the bedroom and lay down on top of the sheet. Carol reached out for him and he took her hand, grateful for the warmth and companionship. She murmured sleepily and rolled into his arms. He held her tightly.

"Richie, are you . . . ?" He placed a finger over her lips and she bit back the words. It was Carol in his arms, her short blond curls cushioning his shoulder from the weight of her head. This time he tried to picture Thot but found that he could not do it. This was the way it was supposed to be and yet it wasn't right. It was as though a piece of himself were missing. Without knowing why, he was afraid.

For a long time they lay there, without moving. The door opened and Jason stuck his head into the room.

"Good morning, Daddy," he said. Richie lifted his arms and the child crawled into bed. Richie clasped him tightly. What was the matter with him? He was a man of riches, his family surrounding him with love. How could he let a thing that had happened almost fifteen years ago—a thing that had not entered his thoughts in many years—shake his faith in that? He kissed his wife and his son, each on the top of the head, and forced himself to dress.

The heat, dreadful for April when the day started, soared to temperatures that would have been bad in the dog days of August. Air currents moved down 9th Street, but they were not cooling breezes. To Richie it felt more as if some giant, foul creature were breathing down his neck. So real was the image that he found himself continually looking over his shoulder, expecting to see . . . he wasn't sure what. Nothing there but the heavy, invisible heat. And as the day wore on, bright scarlet fruit turned brown and rich greens darkened and shriveled, until the whole market began to take on the sickly, sweet rotting smell of the jungle.

Only a very few people picked their way through the stalls, as if the unseasonal heat had made most folks afraid to venture out of the cool shade or away from their air-conditioning.

Once Mrs. Ly looked up and smiled at him from across the street, but he turned his head away, unable to answer with a smile of his own. He couldn't shake the feeling that something actually *was* coming, and he knew that whatever it was, it would be coming from that direction. He could almost make it out when he looked down the little street that entered 9th Street from the east, right next to her stand. A vague white mist rolling down the street.

"You all right?" Joey asked.

"I'll manage," he answered coldly. "Heat's so bad I almost feel like I'm seeing things," he added half under his breath. He rubbed his eyes to clear the hallucination, and yet when he looked back it seemed even more detailed—a great white mass, visible, and yet so transparent that he could clearly see the street behind it.

Two old ladies came by, followed by a younger woman with children. Richie's mouth was so dry that he couldn't even wait on them. He grabbed one of his own overripe peaches and sucked the sickly-sweet juice to clear his throat, but by the time he had finished, Joey had already taken care of them. "Why don't you go home, Richie," Joey said when he had finished with the customers.

"I'm okay," Richie shouted, his fists knotted, amazing himself with the force of his anger. He had to take a deep breath and calm himself down. Slowly, he would turn his head and look across the street. He would force himself to see it the way it really was, the way it rationally had to be. Slowly, he turned his head and raised his eyelids.

It was still there. Perhaps even a little more solid than it had been before. A white and terrible thing that seemed to be taking the shape of a giant beast.

Richie whirled around and pounded his fist on the stand, shattering an overripe cantaloupe into an explosion of orange pulp. He pulled off his fruit-stained T-shirt and wiped his face and neck with the damp material. "You're right, kid. Maybe I should go home," he said.

All the way home Richie paused at every corner to see if he was being followed, but if the creature was behind him, it was far enough away that he couldn't see it.

Carol must have been staring out the window, for she greeted him at the door with a look that he could have sworn was furtive and nervous. "Guess who came to see me today?" she said before she even kissed his cheek in greeting. The thought passed briefly through his mind that she was having an affair. He limped up to the top step to see his father sitting on the sofa.

"Hi, Pop," he said, but his disappointment amazed him. How convenient it would have been to find out she was cheating on him. How easy it would have made everything.

He made an effort not to limp as he entered the house, though the leg was hurting so badly that he was beginning to wonder if he hadn't reinjured it. "What brings you to see my wife in the middle of the day? Should I be jealous?"

"Ah, if it weren't for your mother . . ." the old man said.

"Honey, I have to pick up a few things for dinner. Pop, if you'll excuse me?" So *that* was the setup. Carol had asked Pop to come over and have a talk with him, and she was afraid that Richie would be angry. Well, far from it. Richie was glad to have a chance to speak to his father alone.

"Carol's worried about me?" Richie asked the moment she was out the door.

His father nodded. "And not just Carol. Your mother and I are a little worried, too. She says you've been acting funny."

"Acting funny?" Richie asked, raising his voice, feeling the old rage boil back up in him.

"Slow down, son." Frank Augustino patted him gently on the arm. "She's only concerned for your welfare. Your mother and I saw it, too, last night. Moody, short-tempered, staring into space, your mind a million miles away. Son, this isn't like you. What's bothering you?"

Richie wanted to tell him. While there were things they had never discussed, he had never actually lied to his father. Besides, he wanted the old man to take charge and make everything better—the way he had when Richie was a boy, but Pop was so sick. The heat alone was dangerous for a man in his state of health, and if he took the news badly . . .

"It's nothing, Pop," he said at last. He tried to keep his hands from trembling where his father could see, but the feeling was back. That same feeling of being watched, stalked, that he'd had all afternoon. Something was *out* there, just beyond his range of vision . . . just outside the window. He wanted to go and look and yet he knew that it was the worst thing that he could do. Looking at it, acknowledging its existence, seemed to give it form and substance—as if it were his own willingness to give it power over him that *gave* it that power.

"Richie?"

He wouldn't look. He wouldn't even think about it. He tried to find something that he could concentrate on.

"Richie, look at you. How can you tell me there's nothing wrong?"

"Damn it, Pop. It's nothing. I can handle it." He heard a noise. A low bass rumble that could have been a roar. He had to look. He got up and crossed to the window, forgetting to hide his limp.

It was there, outside the window, just as he knew that it would be. A great white beast, no longer featureless, and so familiar that he knew that if he could just lift the veils of gauze from his mind, he would know just what to do about it. He felt a moan escape his lips—and the next thing he knew, his father was at his side, helping him back to the sofa, the sick old man taking most of Richie's weight on his shoulders.

"Richard, if there's something wrong, you can't just ignore it and hope that it goes away. You can't just say, 'I can handle it.' You're a husband and a father. You have responsibilities. If you let your problems get out of hand—if something should happen to you—who will be there to take care of your wife and your children? Your mother and I won't be around much longer. Your brothers are barely supporting their own families. Think about Jason growing up without a father's guiding hand. Think about the coming baby who would never really even *know* you. It is a terrible thing for a child to grow up without a father."

Richie looked up, startled by his father's phrase, and his

eye caught a shape at the window. It was visible, now, from where he sat, and its form was quite distinct. Scales scalloping down its back, red eyes that seemed to glow from within, snakelike white tendrils curling from the sides of its awful mouth . . . It might have been his own little dragon grown to mammoth size, except for a large yellow stain down its side. It stood outside in the street, so motionless that it might still have been carved of bone, and yet he could tell that the eyes were watching him, the ears taking in everything that he had to say. *His* dragon. He had forsaken it, and now it had turned on him. He didn't know if he could win it back, but he knew that he had to try.

"Pop, listen!" Richie said with sudden urgency. "There *is* a problem, but I have to tell you something about my life in 'Nam for you to understand.

"When I was stationed at headquarters, I worked with a local translator, a man named Pai Som Trinh. You know me, Pop. I was never one for hanging around the bars, chasing hookers and getting drunk, yet there wasn't much else for a man to do in his spare time. This man and his family sort of took me in. I missed you all so much, it was like having a second family. Anyway, Som had a daughter named Thot. She wanted to learn to speak English and she wanted to learn to play chess and she wanted to know all about America. I thought it would be fun to teach her. She was such a cute little kid. And then one day I realized she wasn't a kid anymore. I never meant to fall in love with her—there was her father, and there was Carol—but things just happened." He paused, trying to decide what kind of look it was that flitted briefly over his father's face.

"Things got pretty desperate after a while. Both of her parents were killed, and she was pregnant. I really wanted to marry her, to bring her and the child home with me when I came, but in the Army there was a lot of red tape involved in that sort of thing.

"I only saw the baby once. All leaves were canceled, and then we were bombed and I wound up in the hospital. When I finally got out, I tried to find them, but they were gone. I got word later that they were dead."

"All this you never told us?"

"I'm sorry, Pop. At first I couldn't bear to talk about it;

later there didn't seem to be any point. Carol was willing to forgive my long silence without asking questions and I found that I still had feelings for her. Why hurt her? I squeezed myself back into my old life and tried to pick up the pieces."

"And what has this to do with now? Have you found this woman again?" Pop asked.

"No. Thot is dead. I accepted that a long time ago, or I never would have married Carol. But I think I've found my child. I know I have. My daughter." The old man's eyes were closed; Richie could read nothing from his expression. "She's living right here in Philly—not more than five blocks from here—with a family of refugees. Pop, you should see her. She's a beautiful child with her mother's eyes and hair, but the rest of her face is pure Augustino."

"I can see why you've been so troubled. Does the child know that you're her father? Is she asking you for anything? What do you plan to do about it?"

"I wanted to tell her, but Carol . . ." He spat his wife's name bitterly. "How could she have become so prejudiced without my even knowing? Now I don't know what to do."

"You told Carol?"

"No, I didn't tell her about the girl. Not yet. Not after the reaction I got from telling her about Thot." Richie sighed and watched his father expectantly.

"How could you keep such a secret from your wife?" The elder Augustino sighed and shook his head. "Son, this is not an easy thing for me to say, but I think it would be best if we just kept this between ourselves. Best for everyone. I know that your mother and I raised you with a strong sense of family responsibility, but, I think you are being very selfish to want to bring that child here. You think you would be helping her, but she is almost grown. Her ways are not your ways. And could you really ask Carol to take in another woman's child, the child of a woman you had been prepared to leave her for? She would have to be a saint . . ." The old man kept on talking, but Richie was no longer listening. He had tried his best and he had failed.

And Thot's dragon was still standing outside the window. Listening . . . Watching . . . Waiting until the moment was right . . . His leg throbbed, his mind was slow and foggy and the heat was almost unbearable, and Richie wasn't even sure he cared about anything anymore.

"Oh, Pop," he said weakly. "A moment ago you said it was a terrible thing for a child to grow up without a father. Now you tell me it's in my daughter's best interest to forget her."

"In some cases—"

"Please. I don't want to hear it anymore. Just go home, will you?" Without waiting for an answer, Richie got up and pulled himself up the stairs, leaning most of his weight on the banister. He was so tired. Much too tired to fight anymore. But even now, with everything against him, there was one final answer. One quick way to stop all of the pain and make everything right again. He reached up on the closet shelf and brought down a beat-up pink shoebox. With trembling hands he cleared away a stack of old photographs and greeting cards and pulled out his gun. It was an old .38 police special that Carol had bought for him to keep at the stand, but which he never remembered to take. He fished out the box of bullets and with gentle, almost loving fingers, he rolled out the cylinder and pressed a bullet into every chamber. Then he laid the gun down on the neat white bedspread and dropped to his knees on the floor.

Silently, he prayed. He said a prayer for his own redemption, for the future of those he left behind. He prayed that Jason would not be the one to find him. He prayed for the unborn child, but his father's words continued to haunt his prayers. It *was* a terrible thing for a child to grow up without a father, and he would be leaving three of them. But that left him no answer at all. Unless . . .

He wished that his mind would clear, that he could think things *out*. Yet even through the mist that shrouded his thoughts, he could see only one solution. He would have to take them all with him. No child left behind to suffer. God would open his waiting arms and take them all to his bosom.

He could not remember the walk to Mrs. Ly's house, the pause to sit and rest his leg on almost every block, or the fear of the thing that stalked behind him—so strong that he dared not even look around. Fear that it would get him before he could finish his work. Before he knocked he made an effort to straighten up, brushing his hair back from his face and tugging at his clothes. The man who answered the door did not speak English, but soon Mrs. Ly appeared behind him.

Her eyes widened for a moment and then she lowered her eyelids, nodding, and backed up to usher him inside. She barked out a strange word and a plump, dour-looking woman got up from the sofa and ran upstairs. If there were other people in the room, Richie failed to notice them.

"I've come for my daughter," he said. "I want her to meet my wife and son."

"Augustino, it is getting late. I cannot go with you and you will need a translator."

He shook his head. "Mrs. Ly, I hope you understand. This is a very delicate matter. It cannot be done with strangers present. I won't take very long."

"You are certain then that she is your child?"

"Mrs. Ly, I don't have any doubts."

Mrs. Ly sighed. "I think you may be right. Wait for just a moment, please." She shouted something into the other room and a moment later the girl appeared in the doorway.

"I want her with me," he said, his voice hoarse and dry. "It is a terrible thing for a child to be without a father." He took the child's hand and led her out the door.

The ease with which they let the girl go—and with someone who was practically a stranger—strengthened his belief that what he was doing was right. They cared nothing for her. She was just another mouth to feed, cast in with them by chains of circumstance.

They walked in silence. At first she would giggle when he stopped on someone's stoop to rest, but after the first few times it appeared to make her nervous. He quickened the pace in spite of the pain and heat, and did not stop again. When they got to the house, her expression changed and he could tell that she was frightened. She reached for something under her blouse. It was a gesture he knew quite well. The dragon. Mrs. Ly had said that she had one. It would have to go. Nothing could interfere with his plan.

He moved behind her and swept the hair from the back of her neck. A silver chain gleamed against her pale skin. He undid the clasp and jerked it free of her clutching fingers, holding it high against her efforts to reclaim it. It was a tiny carved dragon, much like his own, except for a slight discoloration along one side. A yellow stain on the flank.

He froze. Then, slowly, he turned to look at the creature he knew was standing behind him. It was no longer still. It roared at him silently, pawing the air . . . a yellow discoloration matching the one on the carving he held in his hand. *Her* dragon!

Suddenly, there was hope. The child was jumping up and down, reaching for her necklace, but he couldn't let her have it back. Not yet. He grabbed her by the wrist and made her sit down on the front steps, then motioned for her to wait.

Carol was seated on the sofa. There was a book across her knees, but he could tell that she hadn't been reading. Used tissues littered the top of the cocktail table and dark mascara streaks soiled her eyes.

"Wait here," he shouted. "And whatever you do, don't come upstairs."

The dragon was still behind him. He could feel its breath on his back as he crossed the living room and forced his way painfully up the stairs. He wondered that the house didn't collapse under its ponderous weight as it mounted the stairs behind him.

Even knowing that such measures were a waste of time, he limped across the hall as fast as his useless leg permitted and slammed the bedroom door behind him.

It was here. It *had* to be. He remembered it quite clearly now, like a moment spotlighted in time. He had taken the dragon off and thrown it against the window; had heard the tiny click as it hit the glass and bounced off into the cushioning draperies. He felt along the edge of the windowsill, ran his hand along the baseboard below—he even shook the drapes several times. No dragon . . . And he was running out of time.

"Richie! What is going on?" Carol was standing in the doorway. And the dragon was right behind her. Its terrible mouth opened, exposing a lash of bright red tongue. He watched her turn to follow his gaze, shrug, and turn around again.

"You don't see it, do you?" he asked almost calmly.

"Richie, what *are* you talking about?" She took a few steps into the room. Jason was right behind her.

"The dragon," he said, moving to interpose himself between them and the creature.

"This?" she asked, holding a small carved dragon on her outstretched palm. Gingerly, he reached out to touch it and felt its vitality like a spark running through his fingers. He took it in his hand. Instantly, he felt its power surging through him, easing his pain and lifting the clouds from his mind.

But the dragon was still there in the hallway, and now it was starting to move toward the bedroom door. Richie brushed past Carol and Jason out into the hallway and shut the door behind him, ignoring Carol's questions, her worried tears.

The dragon was walking toward him, its hot breath burning through his body. He looked toward the stairs on one side, the doorway to Jason's room on the other. He backed into Jason's doorway and laid the child's carving down on the dark gray carpet. His own dragon he kissed once for luck and laid it down too, facing the other. Then, like a miracle, he noticed a cloud of steam on the stairs, billowing and growing until it solidified into a creature very much like the first one.

The hallway was tiny, but walls seemed to be no problem for them. They circled each other tentatively. Two great paws raised, they probed at each other. And then they lunged. Two impossible creatures locked in battle, their bodies rearing on hind legs until he could no longer see their heads. And then they fell, rolling over through the banister, rolling down the stairs. He followed, unable to tear his eyes away.

They rolled, two distinct forms, across the living room floor. Then, suddenly, an even stranger thing happened. They stood, facing each other, paws raised and flailing, and yet, Richard realized, they were no longer fighting. They began to merge, sinking each into the other like one creature falling into a mirror. They slowly came together until there was only one great white dragon that thinned and faded even as he watched, until there was nothing left but a thin white mist . . . and then even that was gone.

He turned and saw Carol standing at the top of the stairs, her face a tortured mask of worry. He climbed the stairs and placed a comforting arm around her shoulder. "Carol, there's something I have to tell you," he said softly. He knew he would have to hurry because his child was waiting outside, and it was starting to rain.

Lewis Shiner

Lewis Shiner has been quickly gaining a reputation as one of the hottest new writers of the 1980s on the strength of his well-received first novel, *Frontera,* and a handful of stories, such as "Twilight Time," "Mystery Train," "Till Human Voices Wake Us," "Deserted Cities of the Heart," and the short but powerful story that follows. Shiner's fiction has appeared in *The Magazine of Fantasy & Science Fiction, Omni, Oui,* and *Isaac Asimov's Science Fiction Magazine*, among others. He served on the Nebula award jury in 1984.

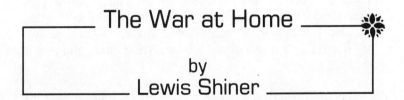

The War at Home

by
Lewis Shiner

Ten of us in the back of a Huey, assholes clenched like fists, C rations turned to snow cones in our bellies. Tracers float up at us, swollen, sizzling with orange light, like one dud firecracker after another. Ahead of us the gunships pound Landing Zone Dog with everything they have—flex guns, rockets, and .50-calibers—while the artillery screams overhead and the Air Force A1-Es strafe the clearing into kindling.

We hover over the LZ in the sudden phosphorous dawn of a flare, screaming, "Land, motherfucker, land!" while the tracers close in, the shell of the copter ticking like a clock as the thumb-sized rounds go through her, ripping the steel like paper, spattering somebody's brains across the aft bulkhead.

Then falling into the knee-high grass, the air humming with bullets and stinking of swamp ooze and gasoline and human shit and blood. Spinning wildly, my finger jamming down the trigger of the M-16, not caring anymore where the bullets go.

And waking up in my own bed, Clare beside me, shaking me, hissing, "Wake up, wake up for Christ's sake."

I sat up, the taste of it still in my lungs, hands twitching with berserker frenzy. " 'M okay," I mumbled. "Nightmare. I was back in 'Nam."

"What?"

"Flashback," I said. "The war."

"What are you talking about? You weren't in the war."

I looked at my hands and remembered. It was true. I'd never even been in the Army, never set foot in Vietnam.

Three months earlier we'd been shooting an *Eyewitness News* series on Vietnamese refugees. His name was Nguyen Ky Duk, a former ARVN colonel, now a fry cook at Jack In The Box. "You killed my country," he said. "All of you. Americans, French, Japanese. Like you would kill a dog because you thought it might have, you know, rabies. Just kill it and throw it in a ditch. It was a living thing, and now it is dead."

The afternoon of the massacre we got raw footage over the wire. About a dozen of us crowded the monitor and stared at the shattered windows of the Safeway, the mounds of cartridges, the bloodstains and the puddles of congealing food.

"What was it he said?"

"Something about 'gooks.' 'You're all fucking gooks, just like the others, and now I'll kill you, too,' something like that."

"But he wasn't in 'Nam. They talked to his wife."

"So why'd he do it?"

"He was a gun nut. Black market shit, like that M-16 he had. Camo clothes, the whole nine yards. A nut."

I walked down the hall, past the lines of potted ferns and bamboo, and bought a Coke from the machine. I could still remember the dream, the feel of the M-16 in my hands, the rage, the fear.

"Like it?" Clare asked. She turned slowly, the loose folds of her black cotton pajamas fluttering, her face hidden by the conical straw hat.

"No," I said. "I don't know. It makes me feel weird."

"It's fashion," she said. "Fashion's supposed to make you feel weird."

I walked away from her, through the sliding glass door and into the backyard. The grass had grown a foot or more without my noticing, and strange plants had come up between the flowers, suffocating them in sharp fronds and broad green leaves.

"Did you go?"

"No," I said. "I was 1-Y. Underweight, if you can believe that." But in fact I was losing weight again, the muscles turning stringy under sallow skin.

"Me either. My dad got a shrink to write me a letter. I did the marches, Washington and all that. But you know something? I feel weird about not going. Kind of guilty, somehow. Even though we shouldn't ever have been there, even though we were burning villages and fragging our own guys. I feel like . . . I don't know. Like I missed something. Something important."

"Maybe not," I said. Through cracked glass I could see the sunset thickening the trees.

"What do you mean?"

I shrugged. I wasn't sure myself. "Maybe it's not too late," I said.

I walk through the haunted streets of my town, sweltering in the January heat. The jungle arches over me; children's voices in the distance chatter in their weird pidgin Vietnamese. The TV station is a crumbling ruin and none of us feel comfortable there any longer. We work now in a thatched hut with a mimeo machine.

The air is humid, fragrant with anticipation. Soon the planes will come and it will begin in earnest.

John Kessel

The winner of the prestigious Nebula award for his novella "Another Orphan," which was also a finalist for the Hugo award, John Kessel has earned a reputation as a serious and important writer. He sold his first story in 1975, and since then his work has appeared in *The Magazine of Fantasy & Science Fiction, Isaac Asimov's Science Fiction Magazine, Galileo, New Dimensions, Twilight Zone,* and *The Berkley Showcase.* He lives with his wife, graphic designer Sue Hall, in Raleigh, North Carolina, and is an assistant professor of American literature and creative writing at North Carolina State University. His first novel *Freedom Beach*—a fascinating, surrealistic depiction of a place where memory is all but lost—was coauthored with James Patrick Kelly and published in 1985.

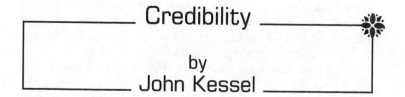

Credibility

by

John Kessel

"Point eight!" Harry had to shout to be heard over the keening whine that filled the lab even though they were separated from the engine by the wall of the test chamber. On the monitor screen the propeller was a haze, a pale orange disk. The thickness of the disk decreased as the blades pivoted; the velocity of the tips of the prop was approaching Mach 2. It looked, Wesley thought, as if you could reach out and touch it, and it would be soft, yielding with some resistance, like a good pillow. If you leaned your cheek against it, it would be cool and dry. But that was crazy. Lean your cheek against the prop and your head would explode into a mist of blood and minced bone.

"That's enough," Wes said. Harry looked at him through his wire-rimmed glasses as if he had not quite heard; Bob Eliott and Stan Curtis were so intent on the board that they didn't respond at all. Wes reached abruptly past them and cut the power. "Enough," he repeated. As the whine of the engine faded, the whine of a guitar blasting out of the lab stereo rushed back. The song was old, yet familiar: Wes suddenly recognized it as Hendrix. "Let me stand next to your fire." The noise was irritating. The others stared at him, waiting for him to explain why he had aborted the test.

"We all know it works," he snapped at Harry. "We're just wasting fuel."

It was a good enough reason: the turboprop had passed six hundred hours of lab tests without notable problems. The stall/flutter qualities were excellent. Fuel efficiency was fifteen percent higher than that of the Pratt and Whitney. Still, what he'd told them was not the truth. The truth was that Wes just could not stand watching it anymore; it had been whirling in his mind long before they had ever built it, so that the engine itself was only a shadow of the idea that had formed in him years before. Maybe that was why he wanted it stopped: he needed a rest, he needed to stop whirling himself so that he could come to his own center. But he had at least another day of spinning to do.

Eliott was making a show of turning off the monitor, the VCR and the other instruments. Curtis looked at the clock, leaned against the board and lit a cigarette. Wes had worked hard creating the right atmosphere for the men to get the work done; he had gone against his own moods countless times in the effort to be agreeable. He was a good manager. Now, when they were close enough to success that he could feel it, all of a sudden he was getting edgy.

Harry turned to him. "So what now?"

Wes forced calm into his voice. "I think we ought to send everybody home. Do you want to meet Burdock?" he asked Curtis. Curtis took a drag on his cigarette; with his curly red hair, lean face and Western shirts he looked like the Marlboro man. The kind of white man who baited black men until they went crazy.

Before he could answer, Harry broke in. "The point is, Wes, that Burdock will want to meet him."

"He has all the specs he needs."

"He's not here to see specs. He's here to see us. He's not going to advise that they invest deep money on the basis of specs."

Wes looked at the blank monitor screen. "All right. Bob, Stan, see if you can find something to do until this guy shows up. You've done all you can. So let's impress him this afternoon."

Eliott was concentrating on the board. Curtis looked at Wes coolly, and again Wes cursed himself for losing control. There was no easy recovery; the best he could do was to act as if there was nothing to recover from. Let Curtis guess what Wesley was thinking without Wes giving him any more reason to know.

"Harry, let's talk." Wes headed for the door and Harry followed, out of the lab and across the dusty concrete toward the Quonset hut office that crouched against the side of the hangar. It was one of those June days that reminded you how bad it was going to be in mid-August: a hundred degrees, hard sunlight like standing at ground zero beneath an airburst. It was a wonder that their shadows weren't imprinted on the apron. Wes had bought the space at Rawdon Field cheap when he started Purcell Aviation. Back then it had been just Wes and Harry, but now there were two other engineers, three technicians, a secretary and the prototype engine that might make them all rich. All out of Wes's brain. It was no wonder that he got preoccupied sometimes.

Wes grimaced when he saw Harry's battered green Volvo baking in the sun beside the office. "Is your air-conditioning working?" he asked.

Harry shrugged. "More or less. It's not that important."

Wes had a sinking feeling in his gut. "We should have rented a limo."

"No. You've got to understand these VC types, Wes."

"VC?"

Harry laughed. "Sorry. Wrong VC. I mean the venture capitalists. Though sometimes I'm not sure there's much difference."

"This guy Burdock's going to sweat his ass off in your Volvo."

"No problem. He wants to know that we need the money. When he gets a load of my car, he'll be sure we need it. Believe me, a limo would be a mistake, Wes. If you try to act rich, they get suspicious—they figure you must not be able to deliver the goods if you have to put on a show. At dinner, you let them pick up the tab, because that lets them think they're in the driver's seat. And they are."

Wes gritted his teeth. Didn't Harry understand that that was the whole problem? Wes stared at him. Harry bounced ahead, full of nervous energy, and yanked open the side door to the hangar.

Inside, Wes paused to look over the plane. Harry stood beside him, fidgeting. They had already mounted one of the meter-and-a-half turboprops in the left wing engine cowling; the eight curving blades looked like fat tangerine sections. If they ever were used commercially, they would probably mount them in the tail, as pushers, to keep the noise down—even though it would cut fuel efficiency. That didn't matter now. Wes had had the refurbished RB-26 painted bright red, his favorite color. He could see his and Harry's reflections in the polished fuselage, stretched taller by its curved surface: a tall thin black man and a tall thin Jew, tinted red.

"Hey, I almost forgot," said Harry. "This could help us. Molly told me that Burdock was in Vietnam back in the sixties. He talks about it all the time, she says."

Wes stared at his reflection, reached out to touch it. The hand of the distorted reflection reached out to meet his. He ran his fingertips along the metal. "No kidding," he said, keeping his voice under tight control. "When was he there?"

"I don't know—'67, '68. This is the thing: we show Burdock the layout and he looks around, but what he's really here to do is scope you and me out."

Harry was tiresome when he got going. But it was more than his hectoring that was twisting a knot in Wes's stomach. "I know that," Wes said.

Harry looked annoyed; he turned his back to the plane. "All I'm saying is that you should use this Vietnam connection. You're both vets. You're both black. That could make a difference."

"Yeah, yeah," Wes said. He drew his hand back and rubbed it on his trousers. "My stomach is acting up. I'll be in my office. When you going to pick him up?"

Harry looked at his watch, broke into one of his looks of mock horror. "Right now. Are you ready?"

"I will be."

Harry left and Wes retreated to the bathroom next to his office. He took two Alka-Seltzers. Watching the tablets fizz in the crusted glass he kept on the sink, he had a sudden, vivid memory of eighteen years before. He'd been a freshman at RPI, a scared black kid from Rochester who had never been away from his mother for more than a day in his entire life. At his first beer blast he drank so much he spent half the night puking into the dorm toilet. His roommate, a Jewish kid from Port Washington, told him to quit moaning and gave him some Alka-Seltzers. Wes didn't know that you had to dissolve them in water first. He'd swallowed them, and heaved his guts out for the next half hour.

He had felt like a fool. He had wanted to go home. But his mother was making up rooms at the Ramada Inn and working a second job evenings to keep him in school. So he stayed. He never let anyone know how naïve he was.

Looking into the mirror now, Wes saw the sweat standing out on his forehead. He ran some cold water into the basin and splashed it into his face. His reflection did not look so distorted as the one in the plane, but, watching his brown eyes shot with red, he thought about that scared kid and knew that most images were illusions.

The lie had started simply enough. It was remarkable how many things that came to rule your life began so simply. They might have been the matter of a half hour some afternoon except they touched some nerve deep inside you that went back to who knew where—to the womb, probably, or the coded DNA threaded like a secret message in each of your cells. And there you were, caught.

Wesley had graduated from Benjamin Franklin High School in 1966. At that time nobody in high school took the Vietnam protests seriously—maybe in Berkeley they did, but not in Rochester. Some of Wesley's friends had even enlisted. Shit, they were going to be drafted anyway. Wes considered it briefly, except he got accepted to fulfill a minority quota in aeronautical engineering at Rensselaer Polytechnic. Rensselaer was full of grade grinds, but even so, by the end of his sophomore year everybody was talking about the war, the Tet offensive, the big troop shipments, Johnson abdicating, King and Kennedy. Although Wesley was no radical, he got caught up in the protests, the rallies, the strikes. People seemed to be paying more attention to blacks then. It was as if the white world—the left and the right, the students and the faculty, the administration and the administrated—had suddenly discovered that it needed Wesley; a black man gave your position a legitimacy that it wouldn't have otherwise. Wes remembered meeting a couple of white women who styled themselves as radicals back when making it with a "spade" was a badge of cool. At some level Wes suspected they were hypocrites, but he was confused, too. He wanted them to like him. He wanted to get laid as much as the next twenty-year-old. "Let me stand next to your fire." Sure. They all liked Hendrix and Sly and the Temps. They liked Wes, too.

When he thought about the black men his own age who were dying in Vietnam, it was only to pity them, and maybe to scorn them a little for not realizing that they were walking into a meat grinder. Most of the time he was more worried about keeping his marks up. When the lottery started he pulled number 194, just high enough so that he was able to wait until December, abandon his student deferment, take his chance for two weeks and escape the pool of eligibles because he was not picked by the year's end. After graduating he got one of the last jobs available with Grumman before the collapse in demand for engineers when NASA cut back after the moon landings. He voted for Dick Gregory in 1972, knowing McGovern was going to lose and not caring much.

And the war was over. Wesley felt a twinge of something that felt like conscience when the POWs were released and there was a lot of talk about the plight of the vets. It was like a delayed reaction. Too many brothers had fought and died for him to keep ignoring their side of it, yet he could not exactly make himself feel that he was wrong for not going over there and dying—black men killing yellow men for the white man. Still, they had taken it and he had not. For the first time in his life he felt guilty because he had been spared one of the ordeals of being black. Except he *was* black. Something was wrong.

He didn't realize how much was wrong until he cut his heel one day on a broken bottle in his backyard. For a week he was limping around the office. When one of the new draftsmen asked him how he'd hurt himself, out of Wesley's mouth popped, "Vietnam."

He did not know why he said it, but he remembered it. When his mother died in 1975, Wes quit Grumman and moved to Wichita. He was a blank slate to everybody west of the Mississippi, so just for curiosity's sake, when people asked if he had served in Vietnam, he simply said, "Yeah. I was there for ten months."

It didn't seem like much. He didn't owe them the truth anyway. But in saying it he had opened the floodgates, and the deluge washed over him. At first idly but then with increasing interest he started reading about the war, every book he could find. He bought a VCR in 1977 and got hold of videotapes of TV documentaries. He made friends with a sound engineer at the local ABC affiliate and got some dupes made from the network's news-tape library. Within a year he was sitting up in front of the tube nights until well after midnight, then stumbling to bed bleary-eyed to dream about firefights and napalmed villages and young Hispanic soldiers with their legs blown off by claymore mines. He studied the army command structure in Southeast Asia. He talked to vets at McConnell Air Force Base. He settled on the 196th Light Infantry, and on the period of 1967 and 1968, when the 196th was assigned to Task Force Oregon in Quang Ngai Province. If he had been drafted right out of high school, it was a good bet that that was where he would have ended up.

From the research it was a small step to concocting a history for himself. It was so easy he was not even sure when it went from idea to action. In order to obtain some of the documents he wanted to look at, he found it easier to claim he was a member of the 196th than to explain why someone who had never been there would take such an interest. After he started telling lies, he found it easier to tell more than to admit the truth. Then he had to invent more lies to support the ones he had started with. He had to refine them, come up with the corroborating details that would make the fiction entirely credible even to the experts.

"The 'Nam" was what the bloods called it. That was what Wes called it, too. He bought himself an M-16 through a weapons dealer on Hydraulic Avenue. He set up a shooting range on his farm outside Mt. Hope. On weekends he would dress up in his combat fatigues, strap on the ammunition belt, pouch, canteen and pack, stuff the earplugs into the case he carried in the left front pocket of his fatigue shirt, put on the helmet with its camouflage cover and crawl through the cottonwoods down by the Arkansas River, imagining himself one of thirteen scared black kids in Bravo Company, humping into the hills above Thanh Phuoc, walking into an L-shaped ambush like ducks in a shooting gallery just so they could call down an air strike and napalm Charlie into barbecue. Southern Kansas in August was as hot as the 'Nam, but not as humid. So he went down to Guatemala one summer for a vacation. He said he was going to see the Mayan ruins at Tikal, but instead he spent two weeks in a godforsaken hut in the jungle, attacked by insects and dehydrated from lack of potable water, trying to imagine that he was in the boonies of Quang Ngai, scared shitless, under fire.

He was scared. But it was the wrong kind of scared, because at some level it was fun. That was the problem—it was not supposed to be fun. The frustration bred some anger, and it felt good. He sheltered the anger like a seed flame in a rainstorm, hoping it would grow into a blaze that might warm him. He got real good with the M-16. Then he asked around, carefully, under a phony name (by now he had learned to do all his research through a post office box, under phony names—William Dietrich, Walter Bucknell, Sam Esperanza, T. D. Walsh—Wes had a lot of names; he was a whole platoon all by himself). From a dealer in Las Vegas he bought an M-60 machine gun. "The Pig." He learned to shoot it, to haul its twenty-four pounds and a full pack without drag-assing around or tripping on the ammo belt. When you pulled the trigger on the Pig it was like someone was punching you in the gut with a jackhammer. You had to lean on it just to keep it from leaping up in your hands and spraying the treetops, and it took real skill to hit what you were aiming at. But if Wes was going to be a vet, he would be a vet who had done something hard. Not just a regular grunt, but the guy who carried the firepower for the platoon, the man who was the target for the VC in any ambush because he carried the only weapon with enough range to make a dent in Charlie without picking him out in the jungle.

Learning to be a soldier was hard. He had to do it on his own, without the support of an army. He had to use his wits, his imagination, more than any of the brothers who had shipped over had had to, he told himself. But he knew all along that he had never really stood up to fire. What he was doing was a game—an elaborate game, but still a game, and that knowledge wore at him. Learning to be a soldier was easy after all. Lying was easy. Living with it was the hard part.

But no one seemed to want the truth, anyway. By the early eighties the whole country was busy burying the truth in a sediment of lies that rapidly solidified into the bedrock of received opinion. That the war had been a noble effort. That the U.S. had been there at the request of a democracy, to protect it against Communism. That America would have won if the army had not been held back by a timid government and a bunch of disloyal agitators back home. There were a hundred other half truths, outright fabrications, sudden and convenient bouts of amnesia. Wes's lie fit right in. His was small, human-sized. After a while it fit him well, like the fatigues, so that he almost forgot he was wearing it. When, in 1983, he managed to bribe a Spec 4 in the Pentagon to falsify some records for him, placing Wes in Bravo Company, 196th Light Infantry, from May 1967 to March 1968, it was more like correcting a mistake than lying.

In the meantime his career had prospered. He was a talented engineer. He loved engineering. On a drafting table, in a computer simulation, on a test stand there were no lies and no colors. Only the numbers, the performance and the tolerance of the metals counted, and though it was a tricky game to control those things, at least you had a chance. Wes was always a good engineer. Seeing someone make a reality out of something that had started as nothing more than a vague notion in his mind was an inexpressible pleasure to him. It made Wes feel as if there was a place for him in the world after all. So he did good work for McDonnell-Douglas, and when he quit them he did good work as a consultant.

It was away from the drafting table that the lies set in. It wasn't enough to be a good engineer—you had to be a politician. You had to get yourself listened to or else you might as well not exist. Wes learned what it took. By the eighties there were a few businesses willing to hire a black entrepreneur. Wes could spot a racist a mile off, and he used their racism against them. The best kinds were the sincere ones, the ones who pretended not to even notice he was black. Whenever he saw that, he knew he had them. He would give them a few meetings, then mention something about the 'Nam and watch their guilt level double. He let them indulge their fantasies that they had a black friend. He could imagine them undressing at night in their bedrooms, fat men telling their dull wives, "That Wes Purcell, he's okay. He's not looking for a free ride. He respects us."

He knew that he got work from some people simply because he was black, and he shoved it back into their faces by doing an impeccable job, on time and under budget, so that their condescension might rot inside them and fester, and he could simply smile and act businesslike and know that he was a better man than they. But they didn't fester. They didn't even look uncomfortable. For all he could tell their consciences were bland and milk-white as mashed potatoes. They had never been in the war, either. On weekends he would drive out to Mt. Hope and fire the Pig until his shoulders ached and the ringing in his head drove away all other sound and his hands blistered from holding the barrel. He would rip a hole in his plywood target big enough to walk through, and then he would walk through it. Then he would haul another sheet out of the barn, nail it up to the four-by-fours and shoot a hole in that one, too. After three or four sheets of plywood he would feel okay.

Eventually he didn't need Vietnam so much, but by then it was too late. By the time he met Harry and set up Purcell

Aviation to try to develop the turboprop, he was well enough known in veterans' circles that there was no way he could escape. He declined to talk about his war experiences. People thought he was either modest or burdened, and it only served to increase their respect for him. As a successful black businessman, he was caught between the expectations of whites that he spoke for other blacks, and those of blacks that he had obligations to them. The fact was that he did feel some obligation at the same time he chafed under it. So he served on a couple of committees, but he kept a low profile. He lived alone. A few women took an interest in him but he never married. He imagined what they said: that he was carrying too many scars from the war, and would never marry. That he had been in love with a Vietnamese whore in Saigon and she had not escaped when the city fell in 1975. That he would never forget the war.

And now he was going to have to face this Burdock, yet another black man who had been in the 'Nam for real. Wes had met all comers so far without defeat; he was the heavyweight champion of misleading appearances. The odds were against Burdock's having been in Quang Ngai in 1967 anyway. But Wes's house of cards had gotten stacked pretty high during the last ten years.

"I like this setup, Wesley," Burdock said. "It's small, and you can't do as much as you'd like, maybe, but being your own boss must have its own rewards."

Burdock was maybe forty, not much older than Wes, but unlike Wes he had let himself go to fat. He smelled. His breath was like a trash fire and he had a bad smoker's cough. Under the fluorescent lights, his high brown forehead glistened. His white shirtfront sagged comfortably over his belt, his eyes were bright behind steel-rimmed glasses, his broad face was placid. One corner of his mouth, beneath a moustache, quirked higher than the other, making him look as if he were going to deliver a sarcastic comment at any moment. There was a false heartiness about the man that set Wes's teeth on edge. He kept wondering if Burdock was serious or merely testing them. And for once Harry seemed to be leaving all the talking to him.

"Being the boss is okay," Wes said. "To tell you the

truth, I'm more interested now in seeing the prop put into production. How long do you think it will be before we can expect a decision from Aerodyne?"

Burdock settled heavily into one of the armchairs across from Wes's desk. Harry headed for the cabinet where they kept their meager bar. He had stocked up on some pricey booze; apparently his desire to look needy did not extend to the alcohol budget.

"Hard to say. Let me ask you, Wes: what are you after with all this? I mean, suppose your machine goes into production on every aircraft in America. What will that mean to you?"

Harry looked over his shoulder. "Drink?" he asked.

"Absolutely," said Burdock. "Scotch on the rocks." Wes nodded.

"It means we'll be rich," Wes said. He smiled.

Burdock's sardonic expression was unchanged. "Does the money matter that much to you? What you going to do with it?"

"Money doesn't matter to Wes," Harry interrupted. He came over with two glasses of Chivas and gave one to each of them. Wes sat down behind the desk, near the air conditioner, trying to get away from the smell of Burdock.

"Money isn't the real reason," Wes agreed. "It's just the way you keep score. If Aerodyne comes through, that just tells me that my design work is good. It means strangers are willing to bet big money on my work."

"Not just on your work, Wesley," Burdock said. "On the whole concept. On Harry, and on these other men you've got working for you. There are a dozen firms working on engines like yours. So if Aerodyne bets, they're betting mostly on you."

"Maybe that's what I want."

"That's the line to take." Burdock gulped at the scotch as if it were the water of life. "We might have to stand you up in front of some of the men in New York. They'll want to get their tip right from the horse's mouth before they lay down a bet."

"You know more about that than we do," Harry said.

Burdock started to speak, but instead burst into a racking, tubercular cough, ragged with phlegm. Wes half expected him to cough up a wad of bloody sputum and spit it on the carpet. But Burdock seemed unfazed. "Three quarters of this business is making a good impression," he said, drawing a shallow breath. "You got to learn to lie like a nigger, and smile."

Harry laughed nervously. Wes forced another smile. Burdock grinned with half his mouth, a twisted smile at once savage and vastly amused. Wes suddenly realized that the crooked expression was not just habit—Burdock's face was disfigured. The nerve on that side of his mouth was permanently frozen.

"You've played that game, Wesley?" Burdock asked.

Before Wes could answer Burdock started coughing again. The man's lungs must be rotting away. Yet instead of feeling sorry for him, Wes was repulsed. It was as if there was something bogus about Burdock, as if his ill health were some ruse to put them off guard, an appeal for sympathy from a man who did not need their sympathy. He waited impatiently for the fit to end.

With a wheeze, Burdock finally caught his breath. "Have you?" he repeated.

Wes told himself to relax. "Sure. Sometimes. I don't usually go out on the limb and say so."

"I always go out on the limb. You can see farther from out there." Burdock laughed out loud. The laugh turned into another cough. This time, even before he had stopped he produced a silver case from his pocket and took from it a ludicrously oversized cigar. He lit it with the lighter from Wes's desk, leaned back and exhaled a cloud of smoke. "In 'Nam, the guys who played it safe were the ones that came back in body bags. You're caught in an ambush, the only way out is to charge them head-on."

Wes got out of his chair and went for the liquor cabinet. He would survive this if he kept his head and if Harry kept his mouth shut. Tomorrow he would go out to the farm and load up the Pig. "How about a refill?"

"Absolutely."

Harry stood up. "If you'll excuse me, I'll call Alice and tell her where to meet us for dinner." He left the office. Wes tried not to look relieved. Burdock heaved himself out of the chair and ambled over to the window, poisoning the breeze from the air conditioner.

When Wes approached him with two more glasses of Chivas, Burdock was looking across the airfield toward the old control tower. He tasted the scotch, smacked his lips. Even over the sound of the air conditioner Wes imagined he could hear the man's clogged lungs laboring. The cigar's tip glowed as smoke was sucked from it into the vent. "Remember the war?" Burdock asked. "The sky was full of helicopters, planes—too full. They burned the old JP-4 like there was no tomorrow. It wasn't so long ago."

Wes sipped carefully at his scotch. "I remember."

"Thank God somebody does. I don't need another one of these all-American boys." He leaned on the "boys."

Wes said nothing. The twisted mouth made it hard for Wes to judge whether the man was as skeptical as he appeared.

Burdock poked a thick forefinger into Wes's ribs. "Men like us, Wesley, the way things are made, we should be against the system. That's the way you'd expect a proud man to go. We fight all our lives. But the Man's too strong. So we go underground, we tell lies. We make up our whole lives for them."

Wes's stomach revolved. He had the sudden, absurd thought that Burdock could read his mind, and for an instant he wanted to throw down his glass and run out of the room. Burdock raised one eyebrow. It was enough to turn the lazy face into a devil's mask. A fat, lazy devil.

"You were in the war, Wesley," Burdock said, turning to the desk. He picked up the Purple Heart Wes kept there, ran the pink pad of his thumb over the silk ribbon, the wooden frame.

"I don't talk about it."

"Why not?" Burdock licked his lips. "Don't get me wrong—I'm not trying to bust you, brother. I was there, too. The experience of my life. If I hadn't gone to Vietnam, I would have been just another dumb nigger. Lots of us died. But I came back and now it's over."

"I just don't like to talk about it."

"So why the certificate on the wall and the medal on the desk?"

"That's for business. It's not for me."

The half smile teased Wes. It made him angry, and that dulled his fear. Who was this black bastard to give him a hard time with his phony shit about the Man? "Vietnam ruined guys. It didn't make them better."

"Depends on the man. Lots of guys came back lazy, looking for an excuse. There's a million men looking for an excuse. Look at these Lebanon Marines. The papers shed the tears like Niagara Falls. Hell, those Marines didn't have to spend months sweating in the jungle, worrying about getting killed before it finally happened. They bought it while they were asleep, clean as a schoolmarm's privates. What was there to complain about?"

"They died for no reason. It was stupid."

"Vietnam wasn't? You take your chances. It's a war, not a pig pickin'."

Wes finished his drink and went over to the cabinet for another. Burdock didn't know shit about Wes. The panic he had felt a moment before was just edginess. He poured a good three fingers of scotch. Something was working in him. He felt reckless, and he wanted to spit in the eye of this fat blowhard.

"I don't agree with you. Are you telling me that because men get killed in any war, then it's okay? 'Nam was a lot tougher than that. If the brass didn't lie to the men, maybe you'd be right. But what grunt ever knew why the hell he was fighting? In Vietnam, what unit ever got sent out to the boonies with a sensible strategy? They were just meat for the grinder."

"All I'm saying, Wesley, is that you got to expect bullshit from the Man. You got to expect lies. You just feed it back to them. That's what they want to hear."

Lies. Just like that the fear was back again. But for some reason Wes felt suicidally strong. "I don't care what they think."

Burdock looked amused. "So you are against the motherfucking system after all, Wesley. Good."

Wes stared at him. The cigar was out.

"I was wondering whether I ought to back this idea with Aerodyne. Your work looks good in the lab, but I wasn't sure about your guts. You didn't strike me as a man who could make up his mind. But now you got some credibility."

"What are you talking about?"

"Credibility. Business runs on it. Trying to swing a deal without credibility is like trying to run one of these engines without fuel."

"Are you saying—"

Burdock talked over him. "Why do you think they fought the fucking war? To kill VC? To save South Vietnam? Credibility! They couldn't use the Bomb against the Reds, and so the only way they could show the Russians and Chinese that America wasn't pussy was to feed those soldiers into the 'Nam."

"Bull. Look at what they did in Southeast Asia after we left. They ran over the place. We were there to prevent that."

Burdock gave him that half smile, eyes as cold as if he were examining a fly caught in his screen door, waiting for it to pause long enough for him to squash it. "Wesley, you're my man. You got the party line down pat. You were made to stand in front of the VC."

Wes felt like he was choking. He took a drink. "What?"

"The venture capitalists, Wes," Burdock explained patiently. "You'll make a good impression. You'll put it over. Look: when you're living in prison, how do you keep from getting buttfucked? You kick some ass whenever you have to, and people know not to fuck with you. Even the Man knows that. You maintain your credibility."

"Sure," Wes said weakly. He loosened his tie.

"It's like when you're humping the Pig. You seen the guys who get handed the fucking Pig and you know they can't handle it. They walk along, and all they're thinking about is how they're the target. It's like they got a big bull's-eye on their chest, and if there's an ambush, they're going to get it first. They're not thinking offense, they're thinking defense. They're looking to run before there's any reason to run. So they get shot the first time there's a firefight, or else they're on their face in the mud while the brothers are getting killed around them.

"You remember Bo. If Sarge hadn't taken the Pig away from him after two days and given it to you, we wouldn't be here sucking this booze today. Everybody in the unit knew it; it didn't take any brains to tell."

Wes stared at him. The steel glasses glinted in the sunlight shooting through the window. They shone so brightly that Wes was blinded. It was as if Burdock were becoming larger, expanding to fill the room. His smell was everywhere. It was a nightmare. Burdock would grow until he got to the point of crushing Wes, and then Wes would wake up in the bedroom of the Mt. Hope farm, sweating, on the damp sheets, a hot Kansas breeze wafting the gauze curtains. In the town, white people would be going about their business. Black people would be working for them. Wes would lie there, breathing slowly, under no kind of compulsion at all—free.

Burdock flopped back into an armchair. The nightmare wasn't over yet. He squinted up at Wes. "Now you remember me. I wondered how long it would take you. Now we're solid, Wesley. Bloods. Don't worry about what I tell Aerodyne." He reached out the brown hand holding his empty glass. "Refill?"

Wes took the glass. He handled it gingerly, as if it might explode. He forced himself to speak slowly. "Sure I remember. But I thought we were talking business."

"Business? I am talking business, Wes. I'm talking about balls, and that's business. The minute I recognized you I realized that you were a man I could work with. You've got credibility. You proved that a long time ago. You only need to prove it once with me. It's like being saved. Once you been saved then you're washed in the Blood. Doesn't mean you can't fuck up. But it means the Man listens when it comes time for you to explain."

Wes poured Burdock another glass of scotch. He felt himself moving in slow motion, a scuba diver, deep underwater. Running out of air. He had to hold himself tightly to keep from screaming. His mind worked furiously. Burdock was lying. He couldn't possibly remember Wes. If he was lying, it must be some kind of test. Either he expected Wes to crack and admit he had never been in the war, or he expected Wes to brass it out.

Or maybe Burdock had mistaken Wes for a guy who really was in the 'Nam, in the 196th. Maybe Harry had said something to him and when Burdock met Wes he just filled Wes into the blank in his memory. Christ, it was eighteen years ago. Who remembered what happened when they were twenty?

Or else Burdock was pretending to know Wes because *he* was lying, too. Because he had never been in Vietnam either. Maybe a little offense was the best defense.

"How's the wound?" Wes asked, handing him the glass. He stepped back to get out of the range of Burdock's body odor, but it didn't work. "Ever bother you?"

Burdock touched the twisted corner of his mouth. He started to speak and instead started coughing again. It took him a full minute to catch his breath, and when he did his face was an unpleasant liver color. "This? Hardly know it's there. Dead nerve never grows back, you know."

"You think about it very often?"

"Almost never. All that stuff about how the vets can't ever forget, how it haunts them—bull. You know it, I know it. The ones who claim they can't are just looking for excuses."

"I don't know about that."

Burdock's smile was a sneer. "You don't? Well, could be. I'm not saying I don't remember. I remember humping along the Song Tram, it was about a million degrees out and Willie Estivez talking to himself with dysentery 'cause he'd lost his fat rats and started drinking the river water."

"He was pretty sick," Wes said leadenly.

"Sick? He crapped his pants till he bled. You had a piss-poor attitude, Wesley. Too long in the boonies. That night Handjob sent us out to check on some noise he heard in the brush and you got pissed and started firing at nothing, and we ran back and told them we'd got jumped by Charlie. And the time in that ambush on the hillside you fired the Pig so long the barrel fell off and you almost shot the Spook when he tried to get you to let up long enough for him to put on the new one?"

At that Burdock started hacking again, looking as if he might die right there in Wes's office. That would be one way out. But Wes knew it was fantasy. He felt nauseated, helpless.

If Burdock felt ill, he wasn't letting it stop him. "Maybe you got more to remember than me, Wesley," he gasped. "Some guys got more twisted than others. Remember Duc Tan? Pinned in that break for sixteen hours? Then when we got out you plugged that girl in the love-hole with your bayonet. Lordy. I guess I might remember that, too.''

Wes sat down in the other armchair. He didn't say anything.

''Still got the trophy box? I remember when Sarge tried to take it away from you during R & R when he found you with Madame Whoopie in that hooch in Chu Lai, you had it open next to the bed and were trying some stuff out on her. Stank to high heaven. I wouldn't talk about that either, if I was you. That's smart.''

Wes tried to catch his breath, but all he inhaled was a lungful of sulfurous air. Sometime during his monologue Burdock had let out an enormous, silent fart. Wes leaned on the chair's arm and put his palm over his mouth and nose.

''And how we were all brothers then. The guys come in from all over the States but after six months in the boonies there's no more black and white. You're all going to die or live and the only way you're gonna live is to stick together. And then you come back Stateside and it's business as usual. The Man is in charge, and you're Mr. Black Boy. Yes, sir. I wouldn't want to remember that either. Too much irony.''

Burdock relit his cigar, talking between puffs. ''Hate irony.'' Puff. ''Kills people.'' Puff.

''Stop it,'' Wes said, and he was surprised at the steadiness in his voice.

Burdock's face was round and open. ''Stop what?''

''I never did those things.''

''Don't worry. I know when to keep my mouth shut.''

''Stop it!'' Wes gripped his glass until his hand shook, spilling scotch on his trousers. He was amazed that he wasn't screaming. ''You know I wasn't there.''

''Wasn't there?'' Burdock raised his eyebrow, and it was like pulling the lever on a trapdoor. ''What are you talking about? Where did you get this Purple Heart, then?'' Burdock waved his cigar at the desk.

''I bought it. I bought the certificate, too. I made it up, you son of a bitch!''

''If you weren't there, Wesley, then how come I remember you?''

Wes stood up, shaking. ''Because you weren't there, either!''

''Keep it down, Wesley. Don't say something you're gonna

want to take back later." Burdock puffed the cigar, coughed a little. "If you like, I'll mail you my discharge papers. 'Langston H. Burdock' it says up top."

"You're not Burdock."

"Langston H. Burdock." He flapped a hand at Wes. "In the flesh. Go ahead, touch me."

Wes recoiled. "You're crazy."

"Doesn't that just burn you up, Wesley, the way they say that about all us vets?"

The door opened and Harry came in. "Sorry I took so long. All set. She'll meet us at the Buttonwood at seven. You guys get it all figured out?"

Wes stared at Harry as if he had fallen out of the sky. He turned and carefully set his glass down on the desk. Langston H. Burdock got up, smiling. "We were just talking over old times. Did you know Wes and me were in the same unit in Vietnam?"

"No kidding! I thought you might be."

"Yep. Wes here was something special. I bet he never talks about it."

"Not much."

"Modest." Burdock looked at Wes. "Doesn't pay to be too modest, Wes."

"People wouldn't believe half of it."

"I hear you." Burdock set his glass down on the desk, beside Wes's. "Well, let's eat."

As they left the office, Burdock brushed against Wes's arm. It was a light, quick contact, so slight as to be incidental. But it wasn't. It felt as if Burdock had smeared shit on him. Harry was ahead of them, on the way to the car.

"Harry," Wes called to him, shuddering. "You take Mr. Burdock with you. I want to check something. I'll catch up with you."

Harry looked at him. Wes could tell he was worried that Wes had said something to queer the deal. "You'll be late."

"I'll be there," Wes insisted. He saw that Harry was mad.

"Okay, Wes," Harry said grimly.

Burdock stopped. "Wesley, pleased to meet you. Pleased to talk over old times. There's more we should talk about."

Wes stared at Burdock, and for the first time saw that the expression on the twisted face could be read as pain. Burdock had two faces. It was like a drawing Wes had seen once that from one angle looked like a young girl, and from another like a withered hag. Did it hurt to look like that? But no—in another instant the impression was gone, and Wes saw written there only sardonic amusement. Burdock wasn't sick at all. He was in his prime. "But I'll be around for a while," he said. "We'll see a lot of each other."

"No," said Wes quietly. I can't, he thought. Then he realized that he couldn't smell Burdock anymore.

Burdock smiled with both sides of his mouth then.

After he watched them climb into the Volvo, Wes crossed the apron to the lab. It was still stiflingly hot. The brutal sun was setting. He felt so exhausted. His mind was like a lump of hot wax, melting; his face felt flushed and his forehead burned. The bloods in the 'Nam must have felt this hot as they stumbled through the boonies, waiting for their time to run out. The short-timers—the ones who were going home soon—they were the most nervous. Wes did not feel nervous at all.

In the lab, he powered up the board and turned on the prop. On the screen it began to revolve, slowly at first, so that you could count the individual blades—but in a second they were a blur. The pitch of the engine's whine rose to a high keen, then stayed there. Whirling, whirling. He remembered when it had been just an idea, a very good idea. How hard it had been to make it real. The problem he had had to solve was that when the engine got going too fast, the stresses on the blades became too much for the metal, and the prop would tear itself apart. But he had solved that problem. So far his design had withstood every test. Wes checked the board one more time to see that everything was normal, then opened the door to the test chamber.

Harlan Ellison

He has won more awards in the field of imaginative literature than any other living writer: at the 1986 World Convention he was awarded his eighth and a half Hugo for "Paladin of the Lost Hour." He has also been awarded three Nebulas; the Edgar Allan Poe Award of the Mystery Writers of America; two Jupiter awards; Grammy and Emmy nominations; the Silver Pen for journalism awarded by P.E.N.; the Milford Award for Lifetime Excellence in Editing; three-time winner of the Writers Guild of America award for Most Outstanding Teleplay. He has been called "the modern Lewis Carroll" by the *Los Angeles Times*, and the *Washington Post* has referred to him as "one of the great living American short story writers." In more than thirty years of steady work, he has produced forty-two books, more than twelve hundred stories, articles, essays, critical reviews, film and television scripts—and in the bargain has emerged as a media celebrity (including one notable 9-page assessment by *People* magazine that dwelled with morbid fascination on his extraordinary private life). He conceived and edited *Dangerous Visions* and *Again, Dangerous Visions*—considered the seminal anthologies of original writing in the field—and *Medea: Harlan's World*. Among his best-known titles are *Spider Kiss, Strange Wine, Deathbird Stories, Love Ain't Nothing But Sex Misspelled, I Have No Mouth & I Must Scream, Shatterday, Stalking The Nightmare, Ellison Wonderland* and *No Doors, No Windows*. Equally well-known for his non-fiction, in such volumes as *The Glass Teat* and *The Other Glass Teat*,

Memos From Purgatory, An Edge in My Voice and the forthcoming *Harlan Ellison's Watching* he has commented with passion and uncommon insight on subjects ranging from juvenile delinquency to social unrest, television and motion pictures to the evils of censorship. His most recent publication is the massive 1000+ page compilation of his best and most widely-ranging work over thirty-five years as *The Essential Ellison.*

Basilisk

by
Harlan Ellison

What though the Moor the basilisk has slain
And pinned him lifeless to the sandy plain,
Up through the spear the subtle venom flies.
The hand imbibes it, and the victor dies.
—Lucan, *Pharsalia*
(Marcus Annaeus Lucanus,
A.D. 39–65)

Returning from a night patrol beyond the perimeter of the firebase, Lance Corporal Vernon Lestig fell into a trail trap set by hostiles. He was bringing up the rear, covering the patrol's withdrawal from recently overrun sector eight, when he fell too far behind and lost the bush track. Though he had no way of knowing he was paralleling the patrol's trail, thirty yards off their left flank, he kept moving forward hoping to intersect them. He did not see the pungi stakes set at cruel angles, frosted with poison, tilted for top-point efficiency, sharpened to infinity.

Two set close together penetrated the barricade of his boot; the first piercing the arch and his weight driving it up and out to emerge just below the anklebone, still inside the boot; the other ripping through the sole and splintering against the fibula above the heel, without breaking the skin.

Every circuit shorted out, every light bulb blew, every vacuum imploded, snakes shed their skins, wagon wheels creaked, plate-glass windows shattered, dentist drills ratcheted across nerve ends, vomit burned tracks up through throats, hymens were torn, fingernails bent double dragged down blackboards, water came to a boil; lava. Nova pain. Lestig's heart stopped, lubbed, began again, stuttered; his brain went dead refusing to accept the load; all senses came to full stop; he staggered sidewise with his untouched left foot, pulling one of the pungi stakes out of the ground, and was unconscious even during the single movement; and fainted, simply directly fainted with the pain.

This was happening: great black gap-mawed beast padding through outer darkness toward him. On a horizonless journey through myth, coming toward the moment *before* the piercing of flesh. Lizard dragon beast with eyes of oil-slick pools, ultraviolet death colors smoking in their depths. Corded silk-flowing muscles sliding beneath the black hairless hide, trained sprinter from a lost land, smoothest movements of choreographed power. The never-sleeping guardian of the faith, now gentlestepping down through mists of potent barriers erected to separate men from their masters.

In that moment before the boot touched the bamboo spike, the basilisk passed through the final veils of confounding time and space and dimension and thought, to assume palpable shape in the forest world of Vernon Lestig. And in the translation was changed, altered wonderfully. The black, thick and oily hide of the deathbreath dragon beast shimmered, heat lightning across flat prairie land, golden flashes seen spattering beyond mountain peaks, and the great creature was a thousand colored. Green diamonds burned up from the skin of the basilisk, the deadly million eyes of a nameless god. Rubies gorged with the water-thin blood of insects sealed in amber from the dawn of time pulsed there. Golden jewels changing from instant to instant, shape and scent and hue . . . they were there in the tapestry mosaic of the skin picture. A delicate, subtle, gaudy flashmaze kaleidoscope of flesh, taut over massive muscled threats.

The basilisk was in the world.

And Lestig had yet to experience his pain.

The creature lifted a satin-padded paw and laid it against the points of the pungi stakes. Slowly, the basilisk relaxed and the stakes pierced the rough sensitive blackmoon shapes of the pads. Dark, steaming serum flowed down over the stakes, mingling with the Oriental poison. The basilisk withdrew its paw and the twin wounds healed in an instant, closed over and were gone.

Were gone. Bunching of muscles, a leap into air, a caldron roiling of dark air, and the basilisk sprang up into nothing and was gone. Was gone.

As the moment came to an exhalation of end, and Vernon Lestig walked onto the pungi stakes.

It is a well-known fact that one whose blood slakes the thirst of the *vrykolakas*, the vampire, himself becomes one of the drinkers of darkness, becomes a celebrant of the master deity, becomes himself possessed of the powers of the disciples of that deity.

The basilisk had not come from the vampires, nor were his powers those of the blood drinkers. It was not by chance that the basilisk's master had sent him to recruit Lance Corporal Vernon Lestig. There is an order to the darkside universe.

He fought consciousness, as if on some cellular level he knew what pain awaited him with the return of his senses. But the red tide washed higher, swallowed more and more of his deliquescent body, and finally the pain thundered in from the blood-sea, broke in a long, curling comber and coenesthesia was upon him totally. He screamed and the scream went on and on for a long time, till they came back to him and gave him an injection of something that thinned the pain, and he lost contact with the chaos that had been his right foot.

When he came back again, it was dark and at first he thought it was night; but when he opened his eyes it was still dark. His right foot itched mercilessly. He went back to sleep, no coma, sleep.

When he came back again, it was still night and he opened his eyes and he realized he was blind. He felt straw under his left hand and knew he was on a pallet and knew he had been captured; and then he started to cry because he knew, without even reaching down to find out, that they had amputated his foot. Perhaps his entire leg. He cried about not being able to run down in the car for a pint of half-and-half just before dinner; he cried about not being able to go out to a movie without people trying not to see what had happened to him; he cried about Teresa and what she would have to decide now; he cried about the way clothes would look on him; he cried about the things he would have to say every time; he cried about shoes; and so many other things. He cursed his parents and his patrol and the hostiles and the men who had sent him here and he wanted, wished, prayed desperately that any one of them could change places with him. And when he was long finished crying, and simply wanted to die, they came for him, and took him to a hooch where they began questioning him. In the night. The night he carried with him.

They were an ancient people, with a heritage of enslavement, and so for them anguish had less meaning than the thinnest whisper of crimson cloud high above a desert planet of the farthest star in the sky. But they knew the uses to which anguish could be put, and for them there was no evil in doing so: for a people with a heritage of enslavement, evil is a concept of those who forged the shackles, not those who wore them. In the name of freedom, no monstrousness is too great.

So they tortured Lestig, and he told them what they wanted to know. Every scrap of information he knew. Locations and movements and plans and defenses and the troop strength and the sophistication of armaments and the nature of his mission and rumors he'd picked up and his name and his rank and every serial number he could think of, and the street address of his home in Kansas, and the sequence of his driver's license, and his gas credit card number and the telephone number of Teresa. He told them everything.

As if it were a reward for having held nothing back, a gummed gold star placed beside his chalked name on a blackboard in a kindergarten schoolroom, his eyesight began to come back slightly. Flickering, through a haze of gray; just enough light permitted through to show him shapes, the change from daylight to darkness; and it grew stronger, till he could actually *see* for whole minutes at a time . . . then blindness again. His sight came and went, and when they realized he could see them, they resumed the interrogations on a more strenuous level. But he had nothing left to tell; he had emptied himself.

But they kept at him. They threatened to hammer bamboo slivers into his damaged eyeballs. They hung him up on a shoulder-high wooden wall, his arms behind him, circulation cut off, weight pulling the arms from their shoulder sockets, and they beat him across the belly with lengths of bamboo, with bojitsu sticks. He could not even cry any more. They had given him no food and no water and he could not manufacture tears. But his breath came in deep, husking spasms from his chest, and one of the interrogators made the mistake of stepping forward to grab Lestig's head by the hair, yanking it up, leaning in close to ask another question, and Lestig—falling falling—exhaled deeply, struggling to live; and there was that breath, and a terrible thing happened.

When the reconnaissance patrol from the firebase actualized control of the hostile command position, when the Huey choppers dropped into the clearing, they advised Supermart HQ that every hostile but one in the immediate area was dead, that a Marine lance corporal named Lestig, Vernon C. 526-90-5416, had been found lying unconscious on the dirt floor of a hooch containing the bodies of nine enemy officers who had died horribly, most peculiarly, sickeningly, you've gotta see what this place looks like, HQ, jesus you ain't gonna believe what it smells like in here, you gotta see what these slopes look like, it musta been some terrible disease that could of done this kinda thing to 'em, the new lieutenant got really sick an' puked and what do you want us to do with the one guy that crawled off into the bushes before *it* got him, his face is melting, and the troops're scared shitless and . . .

And they pulled the recon group out immediately and sent in the Intelligence section, who sealed the area with Top Security, and they found out from the one with the rotting face—just before he died—that Lestig had talked, and they medevacked Lestig back to a field hospital and then to Saigon and then to Tokyo and then to San Diego and they decided to court-martial him for treason and conspiring with the enemy, and the case made the papers big, and the court-martial was held behind closed doors and after a long time Lestig emerged with an honorable and they paid him off for the loss of his foot and the blindness and he went back to the hospital for eleven months and in a way regained his sight, though he had to wear smoked glasses.

And then he went home to Kansas.

* * *

Between Syracuse and Garden City, sitting close to the coach window, staring out through the film of roadbed filth, Lestig watched the ghost image of the train he rode superimposed over flatland Kansas slipping past outside. The mud-swollen Arkansas River was a thick, brown underline to the horizon.

"Hey, you Corporal Lestig?"

Vernon Lestig refocused his eyes and saw the wraith in the window. He turned and the sandwich butcher with his tray of candy bars, soft drinks, ham&cheeses on white or rye, newspapers and *Reader's Digest*s, suspended from his chest by a strap around the neck, was looking at him.

"No thanks," Lestig said, refusing the merchandise.

"No, hey, really, aren't you that Corporal Lestig—" He uncurled a newspaper from the roll in the tray and opened it quickly. "Yeah, sure, here you are. See?"

Lestig had seen most of the newspaper coverage, but this was local, Wichita. He fumbled for change. "How much?"

"Ten cents." There was a surprised look on the butcher's face, but it washed down into a smile as he said, understanding it, "You been out of touch in the service, didn't even remember what a paper cost, huh?"

Lestig gave him two nickels and turned abruptly to the window, folding the paper back. He read the article. It was a stone. There was a note referring to an editorial, and he turned to that page and read it. People were outraged, it said. Enough secret trials, it said. We must face up to our war crimes, it said. The effrontery of the military and the government, it said. Coddling, even ennobling traitors and killers, it said. He let the newspaper slide out of his hands. It clung to his lap for a moment then fell apart to the floor.

"I didn't say it before, but they should of shot you, you want *my* opinion!" The butcher said it, going fast, fast through the aisle, coming back the other way, gaining the end of the car and gone. Lestig did not turn around. Even wearing the smoked glasses to protect his damaged eyes, he could see too clearly. He thought about the months of blindness, and wondered again what had happened in that hooch, and considered how much better off he might be if he were *still* blind.

The Rock Island Line was a mighty good road, the Rock

Island Line was the way to go. To go home. The land outside dimmed for him, as things frequently dimmed, as though the repairwork to his eyes was only temporary, a reserve generator cut in from time to time to sustain the power-feed to his vision, and dimming as the drain drank too deep. Then light seeped back in and he could see again. But there was a mist over his eyes, over the land.

Somewhere else, through another mist, a great beast sat haunchback, dripping chromatic fire from jeweled hide, nibbling at something soft in its paw, talons extended from around blackmoon pads. Watching, breathing, waiting for Lestig's vision to clear.

He had rented the car in Wichita, and driven back the sixty-five miles to Grafton. The Rock Island Line no longer stopped there. Passenger trains were almost a thing of the past in Kansas.

Lestig drove silently. No radio sounds accompanied him. He did not hum, he did not cough, he drove with his eyes straight ahead, not seeing the hills and valleys through which he passed, features of the land that gave the lie to the myth of totally flat Kansas. He drove like a man who, had he the power of images, thought of himself as a turtle drawn straight to the salt sea.

He paralleled the belt of sand hills on the south side of the Arkansas, turned off Route 96 at Elmer, below Hutchinson, due south onto 17. He had not driven these roads in three years, but then, neither had he swum or ridden a bicycle in all that time. Once learned, there was no forgetting.

Or Teresa.

Or home. No forgetting.

Or the hooch.

Or the smell of it. No forgetting.

He crossed the North Fork at the western tip of Cheney Reservoir and turned west off 17 above Pretty Prairie. He pulled into Grafton just before dusk, the immense running sore of the sun draining itself off behind the hills. The deserted buildings of the zinc mine—closed now for twelve years—stood against the sky like black fingers of a giant hand opened and raised behind the nearest hill.

He drove once around the town mall, the Soldiers and

Sailors Monument and the crumbling band shell its only ornaments. There was an American flag flying at half-mast from the City Hall. And another from the Post Office.

It was getting dark. He turned on his headlights. The mist over his eyes was strangely reassuring, as if it separated him from a land at once familiar and alien.

The stores on Fitch Street were closed, but the Utopia Theater's marquee was flashing and a small crowd was gathered waiting for the ticket booth to open. He slowed to see if he recognized anyone, and people stared back at him. A teenaged boy he didn't know pointed and then turned to his friends. In the rearview mirror Lestig saw two of them leave the queue and head for the candy shop beside the movie house. He drove through the business section and headed for his home.

He stepped on the headlight brightener but it did little to dissipate the dimness through which he marked his progress. Had he been a man of images, he might have fantasized that he now saw the world through the eyes of some special beast. But he was not a man of images.

The house in which his family had lived for sixteen years was empty.

There was a realtor's FOR SALE sign on the unmowed front lawn. Gramas and buffalo grass were taking over. Someone had taken a chain saw to the oak tree that had grown in the front yard. When it had fallen, the top branches had torn away part of the side porch of the house.

He forced an entrance through the coal chute at the rear of the house, and through the sooty remains of his vision he searched every room, both upstairs and down. It was slow work: he walked with an aluminum crutch.

They had left hurriedly, mother and father and Neola. Coat hangers clumped together in the closets like frightened creatures huddling for comfort. Empty cartons from a market littered the kitchen floor and in one of them a tea cup without a handle lay upside down. The fireplace flue had been left open and rain had reduced the ashes in the grate to a black paste. Mold grew in an open jar of blackberry preserves left on a kitchen cabinet shelf. There was dust.

He was touching the ripped shade hanging in a living room window when he saw the headlights of the cars turning into the driveway. Three of them pulled in, bumper to bumper.

Two more slewed in at the curb, their headlights flooding the living room with a dim glow. Doors slammed.

Lestig crutched back and to the side.

Hard-lined shapes moved in front of the headlights, seemed to be grouping, talking. One of them moved away from the pack and an arm came up, and something shone for a moment in the light, then a Stillson wrench came crashing through the front window in an explosion of glass.

"Lestig, you motherfuckin' bastard, come on out of there!"

He moved awkwardly but silently through the living room, into the kitchen and down the basement stairs. He was careful opening the coal chute window from the bin, and through the narrow slit he saw someone moving out there. They were all around the house. Coal shifted under his foot.

He let the window fall back smoothly and turned to go back upstairs. He didn't want to be trapped in the basement. From upstairs he heard the sounds of windows being smashed.

He took the stairs clumsily, clinging to the banister, his crutch useless, but moved quickly through the house and climbed the stairs to the upper floor. The top porch doorway was in what had been his parents' room; he unlocked and opened it. The screen door was hanging off at an angle, leaning against the outer wall by one hinge. He stepped out onto the porch, careful to avoid any places where the falling tree had weakened the structure. He looked down, back flat to the wall, but could see no one. He crutched to the railing, dropped the aluminum prop into the darkness, climbed over and began shinnying down one of the porch posts, clinging tightly with his thighs, as he had when he'd been a small boy, sneaking out to play after he'd been sent to bed.

It happened so quickly, he had no idea, even later, what had actually transpired. Before his foot touched the ground, someone grabbed him from behind. He fought to stay on the post, like a monkey on a stick, and even tried to kick out with his good foot; but he was pulled loose from the post and thrown down violently. He tried to roll, but he came up against a mulberry bush. Then he tried to dummyup, fold into a bundle, but a foot caught him in the side and he fell over onto his back. His smoked glasses fell off, and through the sooty fog he could just make out someone dropping down to sit on his chest, something thick and long being raised above the head of the shape . . . he strained to see . . . strained . . .

And then the shape screamed, and the weapon fell out of the hand and both hands clawed at the head, and the someone staggered to its feet and stumbled away, crashing through the mulberry bushes, still screaming.

Lestig fumbled around and found his glasses, pushed them onto his face. He was lying on the aluminum crutch. He got to his foot with the aid of the prop, like a skier righting himself after a spill.

He limped away behind the house next door, circled and came up on the empty cars still headed-in at the curb, their headlights splashing the house with dirty light. He slid in behind the wheel, saw it was a stick shift and knew with one foot he could not manage it. He slid out, moved to the second car, saw it was an automatic, and quietly opened the door. He slid behind the wheel and turned the key hard. The car thrummed to life and a mass of shapes erupted from the side of the house.

But he was gone before they reached the street.

He sat in the darkness, he sat in the sooty fog that obscured his sight, he sat in the stolen car. Outside Teresa's home. Not the house in which she'd lived when he'd left three years ago, but in the house of the man she'd married six months before, when Lestig's name had been first splashed across newspaper front pages.

He had driven to her parents' home, but it had been dark. He could not—or would not—break in to wait, but there had been a note taped to the mailbox advising the mailman to forward all letters addressed to Teresa McCausland to this house.

He drummed the steering wheel with his fingers. His right leg ached from the fall. His shirtsleeve had been ripped and his left forearm bore a long, shallow gash from the mulberry bush. But it had stopped bleeding.

Finally, he crawled out of the car, dropped his shoulder into the crutch's padded curve, and rolled like a man with sea legs, up to the front door.

The white plastic button in the baroque backing was lit by a tiny nameplate bearing the word HOWARD. He pressed the button and a chime sounded somewhere on the other side of the door.

She answered the door wearing blue denim shorts and a man's white shirt, buttondown and frayed; a husband's castoff.

"Vern . . ." Her voice cut off the sentence before she could say *oh* or *what are you* or *they said* or *no!*

"Can I come in?"

"Go away, Vern. My husband's—"

A voice from inside called, "Who is it, Terry?"

"Please go away," she whispered.

"I want to know where Mom and Dad and Neola went."

"Terry?"

"I can't talk to you . . . go away!"

"What the hell's going on around here, I *have* to know."

"Terry? Someone there?"

"Good-bye, Vern. I'm . . ." She slammed the door and did not say the word *sorry*.

He turned to go. Somewhere great corded muscles flexed, a serpentine throat lifted, talons flashed against the stars. His vision fogged, cleared for a moment, and in that moment rage sluiced through him. He turned back to the door, and leaned against the wall and banged on the frame with the crutch.

There was the sound of movement from inside, he heard Teresa arguing, pleading, trying to stop someone from going to answer the noise, but a second later the door flew open and Gary Howard stood in the doorway, older and thicker across the shoulders and angrier than Lestig had remembered him from senior year in high school, the last time they'd seen each other. The annoyance look of expecting Bible salesman, heart fund solicitor, Girl Scout cookie dealer, evening doorbell prankster changed into a smirk.

Howard leaned against the jamb, folded his arms across his chest so the off-tackle pectorals bunched against his Sherwood green tank top.

"Evening, Vern. When'd you get back?"

Lestig straightened, crutch jammed back into armpit. "I want to talk to Terry."

"Didn't know just when you'd come rolling in, Vern, but we knew you'd show. How was the war, old buddy?"

"You going to let me talk to her?"

"Nothing's stopping her, old buddy. My wife is a free agent when it comes to talking to ex-boyfriends. My *wife*, that is. You get the word . . . old buddy?"

"Terry?" He leaned forward and yelled past Howard.

Gary Howard smiled a ladies' choice dance smile and put one hand flat against Lestig's chest. "Don't make a nuisance of yourself, Vern."

"I'm talking to her, Howard. Right now, even if I have to go through you."

Howard straightened, hand still flat against Lestig's chest. "You miserable cowardly sonofabitch," he said, very gently, and shoved. Lestig flailed backward, the crutch going out from under him, and he tumbled off the front step.

Howard looked down at him, and the president of the senior class smile vanished. "Don't come back, Vern. The next time I'll punch out your fucking heart."

The door slammed and there were voices inside. High voices, and then the sound of Howard slapping her.

Lestig crawled to the crutch, and using the wall stood up. He thought of breaking in through the door, but he was Lestig, track . . . once . . . and Howard had been football. Still was. Would be, on Sunday afternoons with the children he'd made on cool Saturday nights in a bed with Teresa.

He went back to the car and sat in the darkness. He didn't know he'd been sitting there for some time, till the shadow moved up to the window and his head came around sharply.

"Vern . . . ?"

"You'd better go back in. I don't want to cause you any more trouble."

"He's upstairs doing some sales reports. He got a very nice job as a salesman for Shoop Motors when he got out of the Air Force. We live nice, Vern. He's really very good to me . . . . Oh, Vern . . . . why? Why'd you *do* it?"

"You'd better go back in."

"I waited, God you *know* I waited, Vern. But then all that terrible thing happened . . . . Vern, why did you *do* it?"

"Come on, Terry. I'm tired, leave me alone."

"The whole town, Vern. They were so ashamed. There were reporters and TV people, they came in and talked to *every*one. Your mother and father, Neola, they couldn't stay here any more."

"Where are they, Terry?"

"They moved away, Vern. Kansas City, I think."

"Oh, Jesus."

"Neola's living closer."

"Where?"

"She doesn't want you to know, Vern. I think she got married. I know she changed her name . . . Lestig isn't such a good name around here any more."

"I've got to talk to her, Terry. Please. You've got to tell me where she is."

"I can't, Vern. I promised."

"Then call her. Do you have her number? Can you get in touch with her?"

"Yes, I think so. Oh, Vern . . ."

"Call her. Tell her I'll stay here in town till I can talk to her. Tonight. Please, Terry!"

She stood silently. Then said, "All right, Vern. Do you want her to meet you at your house?"

He thought of the hard-lined shapes in the glare of headlamps, and of the thing that had run screaming as he lay beside the mulberry bush. "No. Tell her I'll meet her in the church."

"St. Matthew's?"

"No. The Harvest Baptist."

"But it's closed, it has been for years."

"I know. It closed down before I left. I know a way in. She'll remember. Tell her I'll be waiting."

Light erupted through the front door, and Teresa Howard's face came up as she stared across the roof of the stolen car. She didn't even say goodbye, but her hand touched his face, cool and quick; and she ran back.

Knowing it was time once again to travel, the dragonbreath deathbeast eased sinuously to its feet and began treading down carefully through the fogs of limitless forevers. A soft, expectant purring came from its throat, and its terrible eyes burned with joy.

He was lying full out in one of the pews when the loose boards in the vestry wall creaked, and Lestig knew she had come. He sat up, wiping sleep from his fogged eyes, and replaced the smoked glasses. Somehow, they helped.

She came through the darkness in the aisle in front of the altar, and stopped. "Vernon?"

"I'm here, Sis."

She came toward the pew, but stopped three rows away. "Why did you come back?"

His mouth was dry. He would have liked a beer. "Where else should I have gone?"

"Haven't you made enough trouble for Mom and Dad and me?"

He wanted to say things about his right foot and his eyesight, left somewhere in Southeast Asia. But even the light smear of skin he could see in the darkness told him her face was older, wearier, changed, and he could not do that to her.

"It was terrible, Vernon. Terrible. They came and talked to us and they wouldn't let us alone. And they set up television cameras and made movies of the house and we couldn't even go out. And when they went away the people from town came, and they were even worse, oh God, Vern, you can't believe what they did. One night they came to break things, and they cut down the tree and Dad tried to stop them and they beat him up so bad, Vern. You should have seen him. It would have made you cry, Vern."

And he thought of his foot.

"We went away, Vern. We had to. We hoped—" She stopped.

"You hoped I'd be convicted and shot or sent away."

She said nothing.

He thought of the hooch and the smell.

"Okay, Sis. I understand."

"I'm sorry, Vernon. I'm really sorry, dear. But why did you do this to us? Why?"

He didn't answer for a long time, and finally she came to him, and put her arms around him and kissed his neck, and then she slipped away in the darkness and the wall boards creaked, and he was alone.

He sat there in the pew, thinking nothing. He stared at the shadows till his eyes played him tricks and he thought he saw little speckles of light dancing. Then the light glimmers changed and coalesced and turned red and he seemed to be staring first into a mirror, and then into the eyes of some monstrous creature, and his head hurt and his eyes burned . . . .

And the church changed, melted, swam before his eyes and he fought for breath, and pulled at his throat, and the church re-formed and he was in the hooch again; they were questioning him.

He was crawling.

Crawling across a dirt floor, pulling himself forward with his fingers leaving flesh-furrows in the earth, trying to crawl away from them.

"Crawl! Crawl and perhaps we will let you live!"

He crawled and their legs were at his eye level, and he tried to reach up to touch one of them, and they hit him. Again and again. But the pain was not the worst of it. The monkey cage where they kept him boxed for endless days and nights. Too small to stand, too narrow to lie down, open to the rain, open to the insects that came and nested in the raw stump of his leg, and laid their eggs, and the itching that sent lilliputian arrows up into his side, and the light that hung from jerry-rigged wires through the trees, the light that never went out, day or night, and no sleep, and the questions, the endless questions . . . and he crawled . . . God how he crawled . . . if he could have crawled around the world on both bloody hands and one foot, scouring away the knees of his pants, he would have crawled, just to sleep, just to stop the arrows of pain . . . he would have crawled to the center of the earth and drunk the menstrual blood of the planet . . . for only a time of quiet, a straightening of his legs, a little sleep . . .

Why did you do this to us, why?

Because I'm a human being and I'm weak and no one should be expected to be able to take it. Because I'm a man and not a book of rules that says I have to take it. Because I was in a place without sleep and I didn't want to be there and there was no one to save me. Because I wanted to live.

He heard boards creaking.

He blinked his eyes and sat silently and listened, and there was movement in the church. He reached for his smoked glasses, but they were out of reach, and he reached farther and the crutch slid away from the pew seat and dropped with a crash. Then they were on him.

Whether it was the same bunch he never knew.

They came for him and vaulted the pews and smashed into him before he could use whatever it was he'd used on the kid at the house, the kid who lay on a table in the City Hall, covered with a sheet through which green stains and odd rotting smells oozed.

They jumped him and beat him, and he flailed up through the mass of bodies and was staring directly into a wild-eyed mandrill face, and he *looked* at him.

Looked at him. As the deathbeast struck.

The man screamed, clawed at his face, and his face came away in handfuls, the rotting flesh dripping off his fingers. He fell back, carrying two others with him, and Lestig suddenly remembered what had happened in the hooch, remembered breathing and looking and here in this house of a God gone away he spun on them, one by one, and he breathed deeply and exhaled in their faces and stared at them across the evil night wasteland of another universe, and they shrieked and died and he was all alone once more. The others, coming through the vestry wall, having followed Neola, having been telephoned by Gary Howard, who had beaten the information from his wife, the others stopped and turned and ran . . .

So that only Lestig, brother to the basilisk, who was itself the servant of a nameless dark one far away, only Lestig was left standing amid the twisted body shapes of things that had been men.

Stood alone, felt the power and the fury pulsing in him, felt his eyes glowing, felt the death that lay on his tongue, deep in his throat, the wind death in his lungs. And knew night had finally fallen.

They had roadblocked the only two roads out of town. Then they took eight-cell battery flashlights and Coleman lanterns and cave-crawling lamps, and some of them who had worked the zinc mine years before, they donned their miner's helmets with the lights on them, and they even wound rags around clubs and dipped them in kerosene and lit them, and they went out searching for the filthy traitor who had killed their sons and husbands and brothers, and not one of them laughed at the scene of crowd lights moving through the town, like something from an old film. A film of hunting the monster. They did not draw the parallel, for had they drawn the parallel, they would still never have laughed.

And they searched through the night, but did not find him.

And when the dawn came up and they doused their lamps, and the parking lights replaced headlights on the caravans of cars that ringed the town, they still had not found him. And finally they gathered in the mall, to decide what to do.

And he was there.

He stood on the Soldiers and Sailors Monument high above them, where he had huddled all through the night, at the feet of a World War I doughboy with his arm upraised and a Springfield in his fist. He was there, and the symbolism did not escape them.

"Pull him down!" someone shouted. And they surged toward the marble-and-bronze monument.

Vernon Lestig stood watching them come toward him, and seemed unconcerned at the rifles and clubs and war-souvenir Lugers coming toward him.

The first man to scale the plinth was Gary Howard, with the broken-field cheers of the crowd smile on his face. Lestig's eyes widened behind the smoked glasses, and very casually he removed them, and he *looked* at the big, many-toothed car salesman.

The crowd screamed in one voice and the forward rush was halted as the still-smoking body of Teresa's husband fell back on them, arms flung out wide, torso twisted.

In the rear, they tried to run. He cut them down. The crowd stopped. One man tried to raise a revolver to kill him, but he dropped, his face burned away, smoking pustules of ruined flesh where his eyes had been.

They stopped. Frozen in a world of muscles that trembled, of running energy with no place to go.

"I'll show you!" he yelled. "I'll show you what it's like! You want to know, so I'll show you!"

Then he breathed, and men died. Then he looked and others fell. Then he said, very quietly, so they would hear him: "It's easy, till it happens. You never know, patriots! You live all the time and you say one thing or another, all your rules about what it takes to be brave, but you never *know*, till that one time when you find out. *I* found out, it's not so easy. Now *you'll* find out."

He pointed to the ground.

"Get down on your knees and crawl, patriots! Crawl to me

and maybe I'll let you live. Get down like animals and crawl on your bellies to me."

There was a shout from the crowd; and the man died.

"*Crawl, I said!* Crawl to me!"

Here and there in the crowd people dropped from sight. At the rear a woman tried to run away and he burned her out and the husk fell, and all around her, within sight of the wisps of smoke from her face, people fell to their knees. Then entire groups dropped; then one whole side of the mob went down. Then they were all on their knees.

"Crawl! Crawl, brave ones, crawl nice my people! Crawl and learn it's better to *live*, any way at all, to stay alive, because you're human! Crawl and you'll understand your slogans are shit, your rules are for others! Crawl for your goddamned lives and you'll understand! *Crawl!*"

And they crawled. They crept forward on hands and knees, across the grass, across cement and mud and the branches of small bushes, across the dirt. They crawled toward him.

And far away, through mists of darkness, the Helmet-Headed One sat on his throne, high above all, with the basilisk at his feet, and he smiled.

"Crawl, God damn you!"

But he did not know the name of the God he served.

"Crawl!"

And in the middle of the mob, a woman who had hung a gold star in her front window, crawled across a .32 Police Positive, and her hand touched it, and she folded her fingers around it, and suddenly she raised up and screamed, "For Kennyyyyy . . . !" and she fired.

The bullet smashed Lestig's collarbone and he spun sidewise, up against the Yank's puttees, and he tried to regain his stance but the crutch had fallen, and now the crowd was on its feet and firing . . . and firing . . .

They buried the body in an unmarked grave, and no one talked of it. And far away, on a high throne, tickling the sleek hide of the basilisk that reclined at his feet like a faithful mastiff, even the Armed One did not speak of it. There was no need to speak of it. Lestig was gone, but that was to have been expected.

The weapon had been deactivated, but Mars, the Eternal

One, the God Who Never Dies, the Lord of Futures, Warden of the Dark Places, Ever-Potent Scion of Conflict, Master of Men, Mars sat content.

The recruiting had gone well. Power to the people.

Brian Aldiss

The best-selling British author Brian Aldiss is a major figure in the science fiction genre and in the literary world at large. His work has always defied categorization, for he never seems to repeat himself. He shocked, influenced, and expanded the field with his surrealistic anti-novel *Report on Probability A*, and his Joycean tour de force *Barefoot in the Head*, and then went on to write the gothic *Frankenstein Unbound*, the elegant and lyrical *The Malacia Tapestry*, and the acclaimed *Helliconia* trilogy, his most recent work. This last effort is comparable only to Gene Wolfe's *Book of the New Sun* tetralogy, and its place of honor in science fiction is virtually assured. Other novels include the classic *The Long Afternoon of Earth*, *The Dark Light Years*, *Greybeard*, *The Eighty-Minute Hour*, *An Island Called Moreau*, *Enemies of the System*, and *Cryptozoic!*, and the best-selling mainstream novels *The Hand-Reared Boy* and *Soldier Erect; or, Further Adventures of the Hand-Reared Boy*. Some of his non-science fiction novels are *The Brightfount Diaries*, *Brothers of the Head*, *A Rude Awakening*, and *Life in the West*. The critic Douglas Barbour has written that Aldiss's short stories are "creating an *oeuvre* which for breadth of vision and variety of formal experimentation is unmatched in the genre." His stories can be found in various collections, such as *Space, Time, and Nathaniel*; *Galaxies Like Grains of Sand*; *Starswarm*; *Who Can Replace a Man?*; *New Arrivals, Old Encounters*; *The Airs of Earth*; *The*

Saliva Tree and Other Strange Growths; Last Orders; and *Seasons in Flight.* Aldiss has also made his influence felt as an editor. In collaboration with Harry Harrison, he edited, among others, nine volumes of *Best SF*; nine volumes of *The Year's Best Science Fiction*; the seminal *Hell's Cartographers: Some Personal Histories of Science Fiction Writers*; the short-lived but excellent journal *SF Horizons; Decade: the 1940's; Decade: the 1950's; Decade: the 1960's*; *The Astounding-Analog Reader*; and *Nebula Award Stories 2*. He is also the editor of many other anthologies, including *The Penguin Science Fiction Omnibus, Best Fantasy Stories, Introducing SF, All About Venus, Evil Earths, Space Opera, Space Odysseys, Galactic Empires,* and *Perilous Planets.* Aldiss has also been a reviewer for *The Times Literary Supplement* and literary editor of *The Oxford Mail.* His nonfiction works include *The Shape of Further Things: Speculations on Change, Science Fiction Art, This World and Nearer Ones: Essays Exploring the Familiar*, and the newly published *Year Spree: the Trillion History of Science Fiction.* He has also written a play, *Distant Encounters*, which was produced in London in 1978, and a book of verse, entitled *Pile: Petals from St. Klaed's Computer*. He is a recipient of the Hugo award, the Nebula award, the Ditmar award, the British Science Fiction Award, the James Blish Award for excellence in SF criticism, Cometa d'Argento, Prix Jules Verne, and the Pilgrim Award. He lives with his family in an Edwardian mansion in Boars Hill, to the south of the city of Oxford.

In World War II, Aldiss saw action against the Japanese Army in Burma.

My Country 'Tis Not Only of Thee

by

Brian Aldiss

The little lieutenant from Chicago said, "Remember, guys, the folk in the South are on our side. We're fighting for them. You can exploit 'em but you mustn't shoot 'em. Don't go getting no wrong ideas."

Huddled together, the troops laughed.

Lieutenants had been saying things like that for many years. Troops had been laughing like that for many years. At thirty-five thousand feet, when you are heading for action in an alien land way across the wide ocean, you laugh. It helps with the nerves.

People get hurt looking after Democracy.

From outside the craft, the scene must have appeared beautiful. The big troop carriers look so good with their heavy bellies and stub wings. As the planes came down toward a landing through the blue evening air, cloud layers floated up to meet them, layers burnished with gold. No sign, no whisper, of the catastrophe being played out below.

Nor was there in the troop carriers much sign of the sense of purpose, the vision, which had involved the American people in this distant struggle.

As the planes entered the cloud layer, the troops inside the heavy bellies fell silent. A lid was coming down on them. The thick moisture beyond the ports made the distance to the U.S. almost tangible.

Then we were through the cloud.

Little could be seen. The sun was obscured. All below us was shadow.

We altered course, sinking. Suddenly the ground was close, dark, without detail. It promised nothing, said nothing, was silent under an ancient sense of outrage.

As we came in to land, a brief glimpse of ocean, with sun split wide like a spilt egg between cloud curtain and horizon. Tension, no speech. Smooth landing.

Amazing silence as the jets cut. Muzak: "Everything's Coming Up Roses" for reassurance. By the look on some of the guys' faces, they were expecting to be fired on straight away. The approach and touchdown lights died. The glow around the perimeter indicated we were on a large base.

An officer in a jeep was waiting for me. The troops moved off under shouted orders. They became anonymous, war statistics. I remembered that eleven percent of all our casualties were killed without actual combat, killed in enemy booby traps: just part of the price of involvement in someone else's civil war. At least I was not infantry.

The jeep drove me around to the far side of the air base. A helicopter gunship was waiting, big and clumsy, floodlights trained on its camouflaged flank. The lights turned the evening to total darkness. I inhaled before stepping aboard, trying to orient myself after several hours of dislocating flight. All I could smell was ozone and gasoline.

Two men searched me without interest or hope. I was then free to greet a tall hollow-chested man with greying hair cut short. He had a leathery countenance, thick eyebrows, and a belligerent jaw. Half-moon spectacles gave him a curiously mild look, despite contraindications.

"My name is Gratinelli. I'm in Intelligence. You are James Lambard?"

When I said I was, he wanted to see my identification. Then he relaxed.

"Okay, Jim, take a seat right here. We'll be airborne soonest. Welcome to the war zone. We know you're special and we're glad you came over. You were born here, I understand?"

He must have known. He had seen my papers. He must have heard by my accent. He just wanted to hear it for himself.

"Okay, Jim. That's great. We're going to see to it that your mission is made as safe as can be."

He intended reassurance. I found him creepy. When he smiled, he showed a gold-capped tooth. My feelings were still ruffled from the journey. I felt it as a snub that an ally—that's what I was—should have been made to travel with infantry in a troop carrier when on a special mission. The gold tooth might have been planted just to annoy me.

The gunship lifted almost at once. Gratinelli told me to relax. We were flying ten miles along the coast to an R & R base where I would be properly briefed.

"You won't come across any VCs in this area."

Since I had no small talk, Gratinelli, speaking above the roar of the engines, gave me a lecture on how the war was necessary to defend the Free World. An expenditure of firepower was the only effective argument the enemy understood. And in fact the war would have been won at least a year ago had it not been for the suppport coming in to the North from outside. He let the word "outside" linger like a threat between us.

When I said nothing, he eyed me, I thought, with hostility, and began on another tack.

"Also, we would have less difficulty if the goddamned slimeys—I mean, sorry, I mean the South—was not so corrupt. Corruption is everywhere. You probably heard the president's speech. We are pledged to win not only a military victory over here, but a moral victory against hunger, disease, and despair. Vast quantities of matériel have been airlifted into your country, Mr. Lambard. We have increased food relief for the countryside as well as the towns. Vehicles, machinery to build highways." He ticked the items off on his thumb. "Pharmaceutical factories, steel plants, garbage trucks. A massive aid program. What happens? They all disappear. Just vanish. Might as well pour the money down the sink."

"Too bad," I said.

"*Too bad . . .*" he echoed, scornfully. "Widespread corruption. We're after the hearts and minds of these people. What do we get? This shit."

I sat with my hands on my knees, avoiding his gaze.

The helicopter sank onto its landing pad. Brilliant lights showed round us. A reluctance to leave the machine overwhelmed me, so sure was I that I was on the fringe of some humiliating experience; although his condemnation was couched in familiar terms, it remained oppressive. Gratinelli gestured impatiently. I climbed out with him close behind me.

As we got into a waiting jeep, he said, "You're assigned to the Metro. Quite a comfortable hotel, if old-fashioned. Get a night's rest, and the men who will escort you on your mission will be round at eight in the morning. Be ready for them." He gave me an Army pass.

"Where are we, exactly?"

"The troops call this Sugar City. It's where they come for R & R." He gave a dry laugh, showing the gold-capped tooth again.

The Metro proved to be a large hotel almost on the waterfront. Its grand crumbling facade stretched upward into the night, seemingly without termination, since a garish neon sign with kicking dancing girls over the main foyer dazzled the eyes, making the darkness darker.

I slung my pack over one shoulder and jumped on to the pavement. The jeep bore Gratinelli away into the night.

A crowd of GIs, garishly dressed local girls, and kids swarmed about the steps of the Metro. Youths roared about on Hondas, miraculously avoiding running into anyone. Beggars and vendors were everywhere. A boy tried to sell me a watch. All along the front by the Metro were hotel signs, dance signs, bar signs, massage signs. American music blared, pops competing with bluegrass, country, jazz. I stood there in a mood of dull amazement before pushing through the crowd and entering the hotel.

The foyer was as disorderly as the front.

Military police were on duty, too busy with girls to take any notice of new arrivals. Couples were coming and going everywhere. Raucous laughter sounded from a lounge bar, where a sailor could be glimpsed, dancing on a table. Going up in the elevator after I had checked in, I pushed among men kissing and feeling girls who could scarcely have been more than thirteen.

My room was at the back, small, uninviting. I sat on the bed. The whole hotel pulsed with its transitory life like a coral reef. A painful anguish seized me. Anything was better than solitude, trapped in one cell of this labyrinth. I had to get a girl myself.

She was young and said her name was Velvet. I picked her up in the foyer. Rather, she chose me. She generally worked with a friend, but the friend was ill tonight. She opened her legs and invited me in.

Afterward, as she washed herself, she did not wish to talk.

She knew very little, but she said a general had told her that Sugar City's population of a half million had swollen to three million since the Americans had arrived. Surrounding the central area was a city of refugees and derelicts from the war farther north. Velvet grew spiteful when I questioned her further. I let her go.

After a restless night, I rose and showered. I watched the TV intermittently while I dressed and drank a cup of coffee. There were only American stations, run by local U.S. Armed Forces Networks. The news concerned the capture of a VC general, Tom Scargill, apparently the most brilliant general fighting for the North. There was also a one-minute burst of hate for the IRA, fighting against the South, and responsible for blowing up a U.S. naval frigate in Plymouth harbor, with the loss of nine lives. The Irish government was being denounced by Washington for supporting the IRA.

These news items were perfunctorily done. An incest case in San Antonio got more coverage. There were old cartoons and the customary pap, shoveled out in the usual half-joking American way, all interspersed by items from home: how rain persisted in the Detroit area and a high-pressure ridge was stable over Seattle and the Pacific Northwest.

In came my two American escorts. One went straight over and switched off the television without invitation.

"Sure thing, American wealth and technology allows us our own little enclaves over here," one of them said, in answer to a comment I made. "You don't expect us to exist on their standard of living, for god's sake. The local culture has nothing to offer."

"A thousand years of history?"

"Forget history. This dump is falling apart at the seams. If you want my personal opinion, we should hand it over to the VCs. But the U.S. always honors its treaties. Worse luck."

At that they both laughed. The men were in their early twenties. Solid energetic young men with pale heavy faces. Hair short, uniform casual. One wore a big cowboy hat. Both were army officers and carried revolvers. One of them had the Stars and Stripes tattooed on his biceps. They told me their names were Pedro and Len. Pedro was the one with the cowboy hat and the tattoo. Their manner toward me was a mixture of friendliness and insult; I was familiar with it from my years in Florida.

We ate a quick breakfast in the hotel dining room. The windows looked out across the sea. The sun shone as if disaster never happened. With the tide out, the beach glittered in the sunlight.

Already there were guys about, soldiers on R & R, stumbling along, clutching girls. Pedro and Len made a hearty breakfast of pancakes with sausages and hash browns. They complained about the quality of the food as they devoured it. It was better back home. I drank coffee, listening to their contempt.

"You despise this place," I said to the one who had last spoken. He was Len.

"No offense, Jim, but what else? Look, we have to be over here putting things to rights. We don't have to like it. See, I'm well informed on the general picture. The country was divided, North and South. It's poor up North, real poor, so they turned to Communism. These sons of bitches will not stay put in the North. They keep infiltrating across the frontier. It's like a contagion, and the slimeys in the South just don't have the motivation to kill the VCs in any wholehearted way."

"We try to slam a little spirit into them," Pedro said. He smiled a lot more than his partner. "Like you know why they are called VCs? Because their leader is a Southerner. He got started in a town called Ventnor on an island out in that ocean there." He pointed through the window with his fork. "VC stands for Ventnor Commies. Maybe you know. Somehow the name stuck—nostalgia, maybe. But when the U.S. weighed in, one of the first things we did was take out Ventnor and the island, so that at least the South was safe in our hands. I suppose you saw that on TV back in Florida, but I was here on my first tour of duty and I saw it happen. It's history. You feel proud to be part of history."

He gave a drum roll with two heavy fingers on the edge of the table.

"History," Len said thoughtfully. "Give me Atlanta, Georgia, every time. Stuff history. History is for heroes."

"What do I have to do?" I asked, when they finally got to the coffee and cigarette stage. They sized me up and Pedro gave a secret smile.

"You went to school at a place called Christ Church College. That right?"

"Not a school. University. A college at a university. What about it?"

"Okay." He exaggerated his patience. "You went to university at a place called Christ Church College?"

"Just called Christ Church. It is a college but it is just called Christ Church. That's the tradition."

Smiling even more heavily, Pedro slammed his fist to the table. "Don't give me that slimey shit. From now on it's Christ Church College, okay? Let's be clear, okay?"

"The foundation dates back to the time of Henry VIII. You can't simply change things overnight that—"

He interrupted with another bang on the table. "Listen, we don't have to take crap, Lambard. Just so you know this dump we're talking about, that's enough. Screw history. How long were you there?"

"Three years. The statutory period."

"Three years. So you would remember your way around?"

"Of course. If the college is still intact."

"Jesus. Henry the Eighth," Len said, belatedly. "You slimeys really are a caution. Didn't he have seven or eight wives?"

Ignoring him, Pedro said, "The VCs have got a VIP locked up in Christ Church College. We want that guy. He is valuable to both sides and we need him. You are going to help us. Understand?"

"Who is this guy? A secret agent?"

"There won't be much danger. The less you know, the better," Pedro said. He stubbed out his cigarette forcefully, as if illustrating his point.

"Who is he?"

"Code name Hawk," Len said. "We need him, okay? Let's move. We're going to get you into local clothing and then we'll hit the trail. It isn't going to be dangerous."

They had both told me that. It did not make me feel happier. Nor did the underlying assumption that because of my nationality I must be a coward. I followed them from the dining room.

* * *

We took a route north from Sugar City. I could see for the first time what had become of the land in which I had been born.

The disaster which had overtaken it had been twofold.

First, during the eighties, high rates of unemployment, an indifferent government, and inner-city decay, coupled with inevitable problems of racism, had led to demonstrations and ferocious rioting in the North, that part of the country worst hit by the poverty trap. The rioting was met by increasingly repressive measures from a police force once renowned throughout the world for its restraint. Several pitched battles were fought, notably in Leeds, Liverpool, and Sheffield. Liverpool had become the HQ of a rebel army, supplied with war matériel coming from the country's traditional enemies in the Marxist camp. As the news bulletin I had seen admitted, the IRA was also active. There are always many who wish to see society destroyed.

In the nineties, decline was rapid. Police were defeated at the Battle of Warrington, with three hundred of them mowed down by machine-gun fire. The government in the affluent South decided to divide the country, leaving the North to its own increasingly antiestablishment devices. Despite trails of refugees wending north and south, a wall—the infamous Cotswold Wall, for many miles little more than a few strands of barbed wire—marked a physical division between the two halves of the country.

Secondly, the USA had moved to the aid of its ancient democratic ally, the land from which so many of its own traditions, legal and cultural, had come. Many voices urged the president not to take such a step. The parallels with the Vietnam War, still a scar in many minds, were stressed. But the military argued that all that was needed was an increased presence. American bases had to be defended. There were treaty obligations through NATO. And there was, as there had been in World War II, strategic value to an island lying off the coast of a Europe also undergoing a series of violent disruptions in many major cities. So a presence was maintained, and increased. Pressure induces counterpressure. Islam insurgency was added to Marxist strength in the North. Infiltration into the South continued. Month by month, the American presence in the South was increased. There was no pulling back.

"We're after the hearts and minds of these people," Gratinelli had said, echoing his president's words. But those in the South, in the old capital of London, had seen the corruption that American wealth brought in its wake. They watched hungrily as Skycranes flew in meat and beer for the daily barbecues behind defended U.S. enclaves. They became sucked into the dirty trades that black marketeering brings. About the U.S. bases grew tatty tinsel towns constructed from waste, the nonbiodegradables of plastic packing cases and wrappings from which brothels, cafés, bars, dope shops and the rest could be constructed. Goods and equipment from the base made their way through the wire in a steady stream, paying for services which a ruined country readily supplies. And every weekend, the casualties—the men with AIDS and the new quick-syph and chancres and hepatitis cases with dirty needles and the poisoned and the maimed who had driven drunkenly off the winding local roads—every weekend, these casualties were shipped back to the States on special hospital flights, or flown to secret recovery bases in the Mediterranean, away from the investigative eye of reporters. The States itself was torn apart by this new overseas war.

The route from the south coast northward ran over downland. Apart from a few encampments, the country looked much as ever. Not many people were about. Those who walked the road froze as we went by. The sight of a U.S. uniform was enough to stop them in their tracks. They knew GIs fired at moving targets, in a war where they could not tell one side from the other.

Over the downs, toward the outskirts of London, change was more apparent. Sprawling shantytowns had gone up. By Purley, these makeshift quarters were visible on either side. The road became fenced and roofed with electrified fencing, so that civilians could not interfere with troop movements. Beyond the fencing people stood, looking into the road, sullen, unmoving. They were in the main the people who had fled from the North and found no shelter, no trust, in the homes of relations.

"Slimeys! Lost the gift of movement," Pedro said. I thought I disliked him more than Len. It was something to do with his sunny smile.

Our vehicle and the two vehicles escorting us were halted at a barrier. Our credentials were checked. Someone had blown up a lorry a mile ahead and the road was blocked. We were sent on a detour.

So we drove through the heart of London.

Everywhere was stamped the insignia of decay. No building had been maintained. Paint had come near no dwelling in the last fifteen years. Gutters and roofs had not been repaired. Many of the streets we drove through were boarded up, perhaps by the military to facilitate their movements. As we drove along Millbank, burnt-out buildings confronted us on either side of the Thames. Military traffic could be seen patrolling on the river.

Some of the famous landmarks had gone.

The House of Commons, that individual Gothic building, had disappeared, and Big Ben along with it. The entire structure had been bought by a consortium of billionaires, and shipped stone by stone to Arizona, where, with the aid of computers, it had been assembled just as before, to stand on the lip of the Grand Canyon, an object of reverence and curiosity for the tourist trade. It housed an unrivaled collection of old pinball machines.

"We got to many of the old art treasures before the VCs ruined them," Len said. "The entire contents of the National Gallery are now safe in an annex of the Smithsonian, as maybe you heard. Worth zillions. Zillions." He repeated the word with satisfaction.

The Stars and Stripes flew over Buckingham Palace, dominating the Union Jack. An immense battery of tanks and weaponry was drawn up in front of the palace. There were no tourists, no guards in scarlet uniforms and bearskins.

"That's where we have your royal family, Jim," Len said. "They're safe as long as they are there, and we take good care of them."

Pedro laughed. "Imagine, the Canadians wanted to take them over. Some chance . . ."

We drove on, to stop for a break in a new barracks area in Hyde Park. Then through Paddington to the Oxford road.

Paddington was in ruins. The whole area had been reduced to rubble. The IRA had been at work. Later, a wide road had been bulldozed through the rubble. Again, the local population was kept off the road by electrified fencing. Behind the fencing, clusters of stalls had been set up. I saw men and women climbing over piles of bricks to see what trade was to be had. All were thin and crudely dressed. As our cars went by they froze.

I noted that Len and Pedro kept carbines ready in case of trouble, but there was none.

Vegetation had sprung up among the ruins. Beds of a pink flower, rose-bay willow herb, created a little beauty among the blackened debris.

Driving up the Thames Valley was no longer the pleasant experience it had been when I had first gone to the University of Oxford. Here were more indicators of the disaster which had overtaken my country. Whole towns evacuated, prison camps set up, immense fortifications, airfields, mobile guns on the move, convoys, once a wood on fire. The only moving figures we saw were Americans. They were everywhere: marching, directing the traffic, swarming over vehicles, drinking. Old Glory hung everywhere, limp in the mild afternoon sun. I was in an occupied country.

Before Henley, we had to detour to avoid a pitched battle. The U.S. forces, perhaps out of contempt for the opposition, were careless. They commanded heavy armor but not vigilance. The average GI had no stomach for defending Europe. So the guerrillas from the North, with a few well-placed mines, were often able to raid camps for supplies or capture whole convoys.

Three Tomcats screamed overhead, cannons blazing. The noise went straight through to the very fibers of being.

"Give it to the bastards!" Len shouted after them. He went into a story about how he had been on a patrol outside Norwich when one of the men triggered an IRA mine of the kind known as a Jumping Jenny. When a boot touched a concealed prong, the mine jumped a meter in the air before exploding. Len's friends were reduced to an area of raw shredded meat around the spot, with red tissue and white bone splinters sprayed everywhere. Len was lucky. He had just skipped behind a big tree to urinate. He was the only one to survive. Len seemed more friendly after he had told me this.

"I'm sorry about your friends."

"Forget it."

I remembered when I had first gone up to Oxford, to Christ Church, that most beautiful of colleges. The start of my first academic year. Oxford seemed to me a peaceful and civilized place. True, there was much talk of the country's economy declining, with manufacturing industry closing down; and there were strikes and the occasional riot. Troop movements increased, along with demonstrations. But none of it touched Oxford. Oxford had been there since the thirteenth century. It was impossible to imagine its green lawns besmirched, its welcoming libraries looted. Wrapped up in our own little lives, we had not taken alarm.

But my father had. My father ran a successful chain of trendy clothes stores, some in high streets, some within department stores. He often visited his shops in the North.

At the Glasgow store, he received a threatening letter. Someone did not approve of the way the profits of the branch went south. My father ignored the letter. On his next visit, he was attacked by three men in a side street when returning to his hotel. He carried an illegally purchased British Army revolver. As the men came up, he drew the gun and fired. One man fell. Panic seized my father. As the other two froze, he shot them too. I remember his return home in a state of shock.

The incident changed our lives. My father became a haunted man. He saw the civil war coming, sold up the clothes chain and our house, and took us over to live in the States, in Florida, where many other English were settling. I managed to get a porter's job on the local air base.

In Florida we are the poor whites. Why are we so unpopular? Because the war is unpopular. American viewers are tired of seeing their boys being blown up outside Leicester and Stow-on-the-Wold. Escalating costs, escalating deaths: for these we are in some way responsible.

I believe it. We are responsible. We didn't care enough in the good years. We didn't care when millions of people went on the scrap pile of unemployment. We thought all the American talk about Democracy and Eternal Vigilance was crap. So it may be. But we tried to live without Democracy and Eternal Vigilance and it finished us. Throughout the eighties our divided society had ceased to believe in the idea of equal rights for the individual.

Oxford was only a few miles south of the Cotswold Wall. Big U.S. air bases lay nearby, together with a store of missiles and nuclear weapons—so far unused but kept perpetually on the ready for the next stage of the war, which many saw as inevitable. Infiltration from the North was constant. Both sides saw that when London was blotted out, Oxford would make a suitable second capital for government. Hitler had had the same idea long ago, refraining from bombing the ancient city in consequence.

Now it was less privileged. Evidence of damage was clear, as we studied the city through binoculars from the adjacent hill. I wondered as I viewed it, Did you teach us aright?

Pedro and Len gave me a casual briefing. By now I had the two of them separate and distinct. Their manner was basically sullen, perhaps of a cultivated sullenness in order to keep me in my place but more likely an attitude fostered by their resentment at being here at all. But Len, I now perceived, was the stronger of the two. He was a stolid individual, even likable in a way. His cold, deliberate manner was part of his approach to life—a life which, from various hints he let fall, seemed to have been spent surviving in the tougher districts of Atlanta, Georgia. He did not like England, but to Len it was merely an extension of back-street existence.

In some curious way, Len—neither he nor Pedro would reveal their surnames—wanted to secure my liking. He explained to me with care that the U.S. was in my country legally, in response to treaty obligations and the obligation of a long-standing relationship between our two nations.

Pedro laughed when he heard this. I did not laugh.

Pedro was from Detroit. His real name was Peter, but his wife was Mexican. Watching him as we traveled—for my life might depend on understanding the two officers—I saw his nervousness. His sullen manner hid fear. He took his cues from Len and tried to imitate his manners. He was a minor academic in civilian life, now trying to be one of the bunch. Perhaps his tattoo was another of his bids to be thought something other than he was; he had acquired it in Sugar City. As he saw that Len and I were reaching a kind of tacit understanding, Pedro became more personally edgy.

Our vehicles were drawn up in what had been the garden

of a private house. The house had been hastily fortified at one time, since it commanded a good view of Oxford. It was now deserted, with that woebegone look of a building for whom maintenance is a forgotten word. Sycamore seedlings sprouted in its gutters. Its roof sagged and there were damp stains on its stuccoed walls.

With friendly insults, the soldiers dispersed themselves about the garden, negligently keeping watch. Lighting cigarettes, they adopted casual poses. The radio operator took messages back and forth between the officers and his set. Why was it all like a play? I asked myself. Had Americans so far embraced unreality that they did not believe in death?

The three vehicles were drawn up on what had once been lawn.

We looked over shaggy hedges of lonicera and laurel toward the old city.

"There's Christ Church," I said. "You can see Tom Tower." The famous tower gleamed in the afternoon sun. Something seemed to flutter in my throat as I stared at it. I was looking back at the peaceful past we had lost, which could never return.

The Cumnor Hills to the west of Oxford were yellow, not with autumn but with Agent Orange defoliant. Near at hand, the trees were blighted and woebegone. It was as if we stood on the edge of a bowl of rotting salad.

As we stared, tracer bullets came spanging through the hedge just to the left of us. They hit the side of the house behind us and went ricocheting off into space. We dropped immediately, faces in early summer buttercups.

My first experience of being under fire was immensely exciting. I was not frightened. Rather, it occurred to me that the experience was right and just. Everything that had gone before had prepared me for being shot at in my own native land.

Pedro retrieved his cowboy hat. He jumped up and was peering through cover. There was nothing to be seen. He thrust his fists into his pockets.

"Some bastards got the approaches covered," he muttered.

"All those towers down there make great snipers' posts," Len said. He was very calm. He looked at me almost with approval, one eyebrow raised, as if to say, See what we're up against?

Shivering fits began inside me, although I remained unfrightened. I hid them as best I could, wishing I were back in bed with Velvet, her arms about me.

The two officers lit a joint and shared it between them.

Sheltered by hedge, our backs against the wall of the house, they gave me the rest of my orders, one sitting one side of me, one the other.

Half of Oxford was in enemy hands—that is, held by the North. The South, after initial resistance, had accepted the situation. Separated only by no-go areas, the two sides lived in truce together, thus proving the American hypothesis that both were rotten with Communism. It was left to the States to stir things up in the old city and awaken British fighting spirit now and again.

"We go get Hawk as soon as we get the signal over the air," Pedro said, leaning his head against the wall behind and inhaling deeply.

"When do we get the signal?"

He shrugged. Neither he nor Len answered me. Pedro's smile had become a grimace. I could not look at him. The soldiers were reappearing from various hiding places, sheepishly lighting up fresh cigarettes.

No more shots sounded. Perhaps the firing had been random. We sat mute.

After a while, Len rose and went across to the radio operator. Pedro followed. Opening his hand, Len took over the operator's headphones.

He stood tethered to the vehicle by the headphones.

"No decision," he said finally to Pedro. They lit another joint. When it grew dark, Len kicked in the door of the house. We established occupancy, taking the radio with us. Screens were put up against the window of a downstairs room. There was no electricity, but a battery light was lit.

After a while, we ate sausage and beans from self-heating cans, followed by ice cream and coffee.

Consultations with the men were intermittent. Although they were there to protect us, the arrangements appeared casual. A machine gun was mounted in the grounds of the house, and a sentry posted. Pedro and Len brought out collapsible beds. I slept beside them, rolled in a khaki army blanket.

* * *

Toward dawn, I was awakened by their boots on the bare floor and their subdued voices. The other men were in the room, and all were in a state of suppressed excitement. I propped myself on one elbow.

"Get up, Jim," Len said. "We're on the move."

"What is it?"

"Signal came through, that's all. Get up."

They were looking at each other from under eyebrows, with pleased, eager expressions. I was excluded from their circle of quiet triumph.

"Operation Hawk," Pedro said, with relish. He shaved with a cordless razor.

Dawn was seeping from behind the blackout. I peered round the screen. The garden was grey, with a discarded look, as if it were an old indoor film set. Nothing moved there. Everything had gone away.

One of the drivers hustled in with a canister of coffee and mugs. We drank standing up. Still the Americans talked in low voices full of expectation, their occasional glances in my direction excluding me from their secrets.

We pissed in the garden before climbing into the vehicles. As we rolled forward, Pedro opened up a bag and passed me a revolver. He grinned at me without showing his teeth.

"Stick this in your pocket. Listen to orders. We're aiming to halt before we hit this college of yours, okay? You're to go on on foot. You're an ordinary civilian. Remember, the college is in the hands of the VC, so you say you are from the North. Get inside, ask for a job. Hawk is kept in an upstairs room, so Intelligence says. Get him out of there. We'll be outside to give you support."

"How do I do that? How do I get him out?"

"We'll be outside with the cars. The quick getaway. First, you bring him out. He's in the bursary, according to our Intelligence."

I found myself waving my hands at him.

"Who is this Hawk? What's his real name? This is crazy!"

Len leaned forward and said, reassuringly, "He's no one. We need him, Lambard, and we trust you." Here he gripped my knee to steady my resolve. "We'd join you, happen we didn't look so American."

That being undeniable, I sat tight as we bumped down the neglected road, trying to rehearse what I might do. After all, I was going to be among my own people, in my own college. Although I had been out of touch with events, except as reflected through the distorting lens of American TV, I could rely on my native wits to see me through.

The revolver helped my courage. The memory of my father's bravery in killing three attacking Northerners put spirit into me.

As we rolled into the town, past a checkpoint set up by the forces of the South, a dull roar like that of an earthquake filled the air. Like the roar of an earthquake, it seemed to come from all sides at once.

Overhead in the pale blue sky planes were flying. Pedro pointed upward with the muzzle of a carbine and let out a cheer. The planes moved steadily, lines of them, high, heading westward.

At the bridge over the Isis called Folly Bridge stood another checkpoint. Here our small convoy stopped; the vehicles were backed into a concealing side lane. Christ Church loomed on the rise a short way ahead. The venerable foundation made an ornamental kind of fortress. The flag of the North, the Red Rose, flew from its towers.

People I passed in the street harbored a skulking look, a tendency to hide their chins behind their shoulders. The old and the very young were represented only. Several carried boxes or bore bundles of sticks. Most of the women walked with dogs. Their clothes were neutral in color, their eyes downcast but mobile in their set faces. I thought, They scarcely look English.

A woman with an old tartan rug over her shoulders went to the great gate of Christ Church, under Tom Tower. She carried a basket of goods, possibly laundry, her manner anxious. Someone opened the door set in the gate and she slipped through.

Momentarily uncertain, I paused, glancing round. Len was following, some way back down the street. He made no gesture when he saw me looking at him. I went ahead under the shadow of the portal and knocked on the worn door.

When the door opened, I explained to the eye presenting itself that I was looking for work. A porter dragged the door wider and admitted me. I was immediately seized. Two men in camouflage jackets pinned me to the inside of the great gate. They searched me roughly. My revolver was removed from my pocket.

I stood with my face pressed to the rough timber, listening as one of the men examined the weapon. "No firing pin," he said, contemptuously. I heard my revolver thrown into a nearby bin. They both laughed and stood back.

They let me go without question, motioning me away.

What had been a spacious quadrangle—Mercury—was now filled with sheds containing the vehicles of mobile units, battered lorries and Land-Rovers. Under the cloisters surrounding Mercury, stalls had been established—to sell what I could not see. People were coming and going, mainly young men in a kind of uniform and young women scantily dressed. A sense of unreality possessed me as I witnessed this degradation of a revered seat of learning. It might all have been a strange charade enacted for my benefit, a parable of folly.

To add to the feeling of unreality, planes were still droning overhead on their westward path. The sky was now full of them. Nobody in the quad was paying them any attention.

A few people were casting glances in my direction. The influence of American propaganda caused me in part to regard the VC as enemies; yet, since I had not been personally involved in the civil war, I felt in part that they were merely fellow countrymen. All the same, I began to walk as if with innocent purpose toward where the bursar's office had been situated in my day.

Discreet windows which had once been closed were now thrown wantonly open. Glass was missing in many cases. Trousers, skirts, long johns, hung over the sills to dry. I reached a stone staircase and ascended to the upper level. Looking back, I saw that one of the soldiers who had frisked me was following me.

This decided me to act fast. I would enter the bursar's office and ask for work. Perhaps I should demand to join the VC. Perhaps I should reveal that I was an old student of Christ Church. Perhaps there would be some clue as to who or where Hawk was.

The door still bore a small brass plate saying BURSAR.

I knocked and went in.

An elderly man, very square, sat with arms folded against the window. Nearer at hand was a tough black sergeant in a red beret and green uniform, pointing a submachine gun at me. In that frozen moment, I heard the planes still passing overhead, wave after wave. The Red Rose hung over the stone fireplace.

I turned too late. The soldier who had been following me ran up and stuck a gun into my spine. I did as I was told, moving reluctantly into the room. The door was slammed behind us. The three men regarded me with satisfaction.

The man in the window came over to inspect me. He had an immense expanse of face, most of it whiskered or wrinkled, with a great nose and a mouth that remained slightly open, as if he was about to bite. He scrutinized me unblinkingly, almost as if I were a piece of furniture.

"Papers," he said, holding out a hand.

"Are you Hawk?"

"Papers."

I handed them over.

"James Malcolm Lambard. Good. Sit in that chair."

I did as I was told and the tension in the room eased.

"Your father, Arthur Lambard, is a war criminal."

"My father is dead. And he was certainly no criminal."

"His name remains registered as a war criminal with the government of the North. Three deaths to answer. His anti-Communist activities are well known."

Terrible confusion ran through me. Among the old college photographs and engravings on the wall was a portrait of Lenin. It disoriented me.

"There's been a misunderstanding," I said. "I have come just to meet a man called Hawk."

"We'll be sending you to a prisoner-of-war camp near Bootle, Lambard. A tribunal will try you and adjudge your classification. There is no Hawk. It's a code name. Once you step into Christ Church with a revolver with no firing pin and ask for Hawk, you are delivered. Like a parcel."

He was turning away as he spoke, throwing my papers on his desk and motioning to the armed men to march me off. I jumped up. Before I could take a step toward him, I was seized roughly and held.

"This is all crazy. I've done nothing wrong. Let me go at once." I shouted madly until the sergeant punched me in the ribs.

"You're cooperating with the American enemy." The man at the window spoke without looking round at me.

"But if I understand you, you are cooperating with them, too."

"Not cooperation. It's an arrangement on a war footing." He turned round to me as if suddenly pleased and said, "We collect little men like you, Lambard. The Yanks are happy to hand you over. When we get enough of you we exchange you for a big name the Yanks are holding. There's another war going on—a diplomatic war—and it looks good for both sides if we exchange a few bodies we don't need. The United Nations approves of that sort of thing. Keeps the Third World quiet. You may be part of a deal for our General Scargill, held by the Yanks. Just behave yourself, you'll be okay."

As the guards led me from the room, I shouted, "I thought you people hated the Yanks. You're in league with them."

He had returned to the window, to stand looking out at the planes overhead, and did not reply. The door slammed.

As they led me away, the black sergeant said, "You want to keep your mouth shut, mate, or you'll be in trouble. 'Course we hate the bloody Yanks, but the real enemy's the South. The Yanks'll have to go away in the end, same as they did in Vietnam. Pack up and go."

"They'll never go. They believe they have a duty to this country. They still have a vision of saving the world."

We came out into Mercury. Armed vehicles were revving up. I could see other prisoners, a dejected bunch, standing handcuffed behind a lorry.

The sergeant gave me a push from behind. "Saving the world from what? That persistence of vision will ruin them—and us. You know nothing, Lambard. You bloody chose to clear off—into their camp. The Yanks will overreach themselves, like they did before. Then the U.S. public'll get pissed off of the whole shooting match. They won't want to know about Europe—will they?—won't want to stump up the taxes necessary to save the world."

A fit of trembling made me weak. I staggered, and the

stone buildings seemed to whirl about me. I fought not only to keep my balance but to fend off the extent of my betrayal.

"They saved the world before . . . Europe . . . World War II . . ."

His hand was tight round my arm, steadying me and shaking me at the same time. His big face came close to mine.

"They're too stinking rich to go through that stuff again. Too stinking rich. Now stop blowing your mouth and move it."

"Listen . . . when I get back . . . if I'm exchanged . . . I'm going to tell this whole rotten Hawk story to the world. Then you'll—"

He hit me with his fist in the stomach, so that I doubled up, gasping for breath. So much fury at the injustice of things rose in me that it burst out as hot tears, springing from my eyes to the stones below my feet.

The sergeant straightened me up, saying quite gently, "Who's going to believe what you say? No one will listen—on our side, or on their side. You're discredited, Lambard. Now, come on, move it, man."

His words were lazily delivered, without malice, and he stood there a moment while I got my breath back, thinking there was rough justice in what the sergeant said. Much had been discredited by war—not I alone. The planes still roared overhead.

"Saving the world for Democracy, shit!" he said, and laughed.

I said nothing. He was producing a chit and signing me over. As a corporal took me into custody, the sergeant said, almost pityingly, "You're dumb, Lambard. What price their latest move? Didn't the Yanks tell you before they sold you down the river? They're reenacting Cambodia now."

Seeing that I didn't immediately take his meaning, he said, "Washington has just decided to attack the IRA direct. The loonies have begun the strategic bombing of Ireland. A neutral country . . ."

Raising my eyes, I saw the long-range bombers crossing a sky that was now a clear hard blue.

As we prisoners were herded into the waiting trucks, loudspeakers round the quadrangle blared forth the martial noise of the national anthem, "There'll Always Be North England."

Joe Haldeman

Joe Haldeman was drafted in 1967 and fought in the Central Highlands of Vietnam as a combat engineer, where he was seriously wounded in action. He was awarded the Purple Heart and returned home in 1969. It is not surprising that the war has informed and influenced his fiction, notably the fine early novel *War Year*, a realistic account of a young draftee's tour of duty in Vietnam, and his award-winning science fiction novel *The Forever War*, considered to be one of the landmark books of the 1970s. In a letter to the critic Joan Gordon, Haldeman writes that *The Forever War* operates on a "metaphysical level as a discussion of Vietnam, war, and its effect on American society." The novel—a frightening depiction of a thousand-year war fought by soldiers who are alienated from their own time and culture because of time dislocations caused by faster-than-light travel—won the Hugo, Nebula, and Ditmar awards as the best science fiction novel of 1975. He took another Hugo in 1977 for his short story "Tricentennial," which can be found in his collection *Infinite Dreams*; he is also the author of the collection *Dealing in Futures*. In 1983 he won the Rhysling Award for best science fiction poem of the year. Among his other novels are *Mindbridge, All My Sins Remembered, There Is No Darkness* (with his brother, the science fiction writer Jack C. Haldeman II), *Worlds, Worlds Apart*, and most recently *Tool of the Trade*. He has edited the anthologies *Study War No More, Cosmic Laughter*, and

Nebula Stories Seventeen. He is currently working on four novels and a nonfiction book, which are "in various stages of incompletion." He is a visiting professor in the writing department of the Massachusetts Institute of Technology, and he and his wife, Gay, live in Gainesville, Florida, and in Cambridge, Massachusetts.

In the April 1986 issue of *Isaac Asimov's Science Fiction Magazine*, Haldeman writes: "The march of technology may affect the gruesome details of war, what device kills you and how well and how fast it works, but the fictionally important parts don't change. Pain, confusion, fear, heroism, cowardice; all are the same from Homer to Hemingway, from dumb rocks to smart bombs."

DX

by
Joe Haldeman

So every night
You build a little house

You dig a hole
and cover it with
logs

Cover with logs
with sandbags
against the
shrapnel weather

A house you
sleep beside
and hope not
to enter

Some nights you wake
to noise and light
and metal singing

Roll out of the bag
and into the house
   with all the scorpions
   centipedes   roaches
but no bullets flying inside it

Most nights
you just sleep

deep sleep
and dreamless
mostly
from labor

This night was just sleep.

In the morning
you unbuild the house

hours of work
again
for nothing

Kick the logs away
pour out the sandbags
into the hole

Roll up the sandbags
for the next night's bit
of rural urban renewal

Eat some cold bad food
Clean your weapon
Drink instant coffee
from a can

Check the tape on
the grenades;
check the pins.
Inspect ammo clips
(Clean the top
rounds with
illegal
gasoline.)

Most carefully
repack the demolition
bag: blasting caps
TNT   plastic   time fuse
det cord—

ten kilograms of fragile
most instant
death

Then shoulder the heavy rucksack
Secure your weapons and tools
and follow the other primates
into the jungle watching the trees

walk silently
as possible
through the green
watching the ground

Don't get too close
to the man in front of you

This is good advice:
don't let the enemy
have two targets.

Remember that: don't get too close to any man.

Only a fool, or an officer,
doesn't grab the ground high-pitched
at the first shot rattle
of M-16s
even if it's rather distant
louder
Russian rifles
answer
even if it's
a couple of klicks away manly chug
of heavy
God knows which way they're shooting machine
guns

grenade's
flat
bang
Like fools, or officers,
we get up off the ground and move

All that metal
flying through
the air—
and do we move away
from it?

no

We make haste
in the wrong direction

like fools or officers
we head for the
action

making lots of noise now
who cares now

but careful not to bunch up

Remember: don't get too close to any man.

It's over before we get there.
The enemy, not fools
(perhaps lacking officers)
went in the proper direction.

As we approach
the abandoned enemy camp
a bit of impolite and
(perhaps to you)
incomprehensible
dialogue greets us:

"You wanna get some
X-Rays down here?
Charlie left
a motherfuckin'
DX pile
behind."

TERMS:

X-Rays are engineers,
demolition men,
us.

Charlie is the enemy.

"DX" means destroy;
A DX pile is a collection
of explosives that are no longer
trustworthy. When you leave
the camp finally, you
put a long fuse on the DX pile, and
blow it up.

(Both "motherfucker" and "DX"
are technical terms that can serve as
polite euphemisms:

"Private,		"Private,
you wanna	instead	kill
DX that	of	that
motherfucker?"		man.")

We'd been lucky.
No shooting.
Just a pile of
explosive
leftovers
to dispose of.

And we'd done it before.

It was quite a pile,
though,
taller than a man

enough to kill
everybody
with some left over

all

artillery shells
mortar rounds
satchel charges
rifle grenades

festooned with
chains of
fifty-caliber
ammunition

The major wouldn't
let us
evacuate his troops
then put a long fuse on the pile

We had to stand there
nervous
and guard it

no

They'd been working hard
first they get lunch and a nap
then we can move them out
and we can blow it.

(we liked his "we")

We didn't know
it was wired for sound

it was booby-trapped

Remember: don't get too close to any man:

Don't know that Farmer
has an actual farm waiting
back in Alabama

and

Don't know that
Crowder
has new grandbabies
and is headed
for retirement
when he gets home

and don't know that Doc
was a basketball champ
in his black high school
and really did want
to be a doctor

Because they all are
one short beep
of a radio detonator
away
from
a sound
so loud
you don't
hear it
really

grey smoke

blood

It just hits you like a car.

everywhere blood
and screaming

Doc
both his long legs
blown off
dies quickly

Sergeant Crowder
separated from one
foot
is unconscious
or stoic

Farmer had his belly spilled
but lived long enough to shout
"Professor?
Where'd they get you?" and

since I didn't have
enough breath
for a complete catalog

(foot shins knees
thigh groin genitals
arm ear scalp
and disposition)

I settled for "the balls."

Oh my God
Farmer said
then he died

Two days later
I woke up in a dirty hospital
(sewed up like Frankenstein's charge)
woke up in time
to see Crowder leave
with a sheet over his eyes

and so it was over

in a way

the whole squad DX
but me

there is nothing for it
there is nothing you can take for it

they are names on a wall now
they are compost in Arlington
and somehow   I am not

but give me this

There are three other universes, like this:

In one,   Farmer curses the rain
wrestles his tractor through the mud
curses the bank that owns it
and sometimes remembers
that he alone survived

In another   Crowder tells grown grandchildren
for the hundredth time
over a late-night whiskey
his one war story
that beats the others all to hell

In the third   Doc stands over a bloody patient
steady hand   healing knife
and sometimes he recalls
blood years past   and sometimes
remembers   to be glad to be alive;

in these worlds
I am dead

and at peace.

Further Reading

This list of books and stories is by no means comprehensive. It is, rather, a personal and thus idiosyncratic selection. We have included genre as well as nongenre subject material, which we hope may be of interest.

Novels and Collections

Anderson, Robert A. *Cooks & Bakers*. New York: Avon, 1982.

Dodge, Ed. *Dau*. New York: Macmillan, 1984; Berkley, 1984.

Durden, Charles. *No Bugles, No Drums*. New York: Viking Press, 1976; Charter, 1978.

Eastlake, William. *The Bamboo Bed*. New York: Avon, 1985.

Greenberg, Martin H., and Augustus R. Norton, eds. *Touring Nam: The Vietnam War Reader*. New York: William Morrow, 1985.

Haldeman, Joe. *War Year*. New York: Holt, Rinehart and Winston, 1972; Pocket Books, 1978.

——. *The Forever War*. New York: St. Martin's Press, 1974.

Hasford, Gustav. *The Short-Timers*. New York: Harper & Row, 1979; Bantam, 1980.

Hempstone, Smith. *A Tract of Time*. Boston: Houghton Mifflin, 1966.

Karlin, Wayne *et al.*, eds. *Free Fire Zone*. New York: McGraw-Hill, 1973.

Klinkowitz, Jerome, and John Somer, eds. *Writing Under Fire: Stories of the Vietnam War*. New York: Delta, 1978.

Kovic, Ron. *Born on the Fourth of July*. New York: McGraw-Hill, 1976; Pocket Books, 1977.

Mayer, Tom. *The Weary Falcon*. Boston: Houghton Mifflin, 1971.

Moorcock, Michael. *My Experiences in the Third World War*. London: Savoy Books, 1980.

Morrell, David. *First Blood*. New York: M. Evans and Company, 1972; Fawcett Crest, 1973; Ballantine, 1982.

Nelson, Charles. *The Boy Who Picked the Bullets Up*. New York: William Morrow, 1981; Avon, 1982.

O'Brien, Tim. *Going After Cacciato*. New York: Delacorte, 1978; Delta, 1979; Dell Laurel, 1980.

——. *If I Die in a Combat Zone: Box Me Up and Ship Me Home*. New York: Delacorte, 1973.

Pelfrey, William. *The Big V*. New York: Liveright, 1972; Avon, 1984.

Pratt, John Clark. *The Laotian Fragments*. New York: Viking Press, 1974.

Roth, Robert. *Sand in the Wind*. Boston: Little, Brown, 1973. New York: Pinnacle, 1974.

Rubin, Jonathan. *The Barking Deer*. New York: George Braziller, 1974; Avon, 1982.

Sack, John. *M*. New York: Avon, 1985.

Sloan, James Park. *War Games*. New York: Houghton Mifflin, 1971; Avon, 1973.

Smith, Steven Philip. *American Boys*. New York: G. P. Putnam's Sons, 1975; Avon, 1984.

Suddick, Tom. *A Few Good Men*. New York: Avon, 1978.

Thacker, Jada. *Finally, the Pawn*. New York: Avon, 1986.

Walsh, Patricia L. *Forever Sad the Hearts*. New York: Avon 1982.

Webb, James. *Fields of Fire*. Englewood Cliffs, N.J.: Prentice-Hall, 1978. New York: Bantam, 1979.

Short Stories

Algren, Nelson. ''What Country Do You Think You're In?'' *The Last Carousel*.

Baber, Asa. ''How I Got Screwed and Almost Tattooed, by Huck Finn.'' *Tranquility Base, and Other Stories*.

Bambara, Toni Cade. ''The Sea Birds Are Still Alive.'' *The Sea Birds Are Still Alive*.

Beal, M. F. ''Survival.'' *The Fact of Fiction*.

Belanger, Charles A. ''Once Upon a Time When It Was Night.'' *Angels in My Oven*.

Boyle, Kay. ''You Don't Have to Be a Member of the Congregation.'' *Little Victories, Big Defeats*.

Brunner, John. ''The Inception of the Epoch of Mrs. Bedonebyasyoudid.'' *From This Day Forward*.

Carper, Charles. ''The Land of the Free.'' *Story: The Yearbook of Discovery/1969*.

Carr, Jess. ''A Flicker of the Torch.'' *A Creature Was Stirring, and Other Stories*.

Chatain, Robert. ''On the Perimeter.'' *New American Review*, no. 13.

——. ''The Appointment.'' *Ship Ride Down the Spring Branch, and Other Stories*.

Ch'en, Ying-chen. "A Rose in June." *Born of the Same Roots*.

Cohan, Stanley. "I'm Sorry, Mr. Griggs." *A Special Kind of Crime*.

Dann, Jack. "Among the Mountains." *Timetipping*.

Dawson, Fielding. "The Triangle on the Jungle Wall." *Krazy Kat/The Unveiling & Other Stories*.

De Grazia, Emilio. "Brothers of the Tiger." *Likely Stories*.

Deighton, Len. "First Base." *Eleven Declarations of War*.

Dempsey, Hank. "The Defensive Bomber." *Nova 3*.

Dick, Philip K. "Faith of Our Fathers." *Dangerous Visions*.

Domini, John. "Over 4000 Square Miles." *Bedlam*.

Drake, David A. "The Dancer in the Flames." *Whispers IV*.

Dwan, Kevin. "War Chips." *Intro 6*.

Eastlake, William. "The Biggest Thing Since Custer." *Fifty Years of the American Short Story*, vol. 1.

Ellison, Harlan. "Night of Black Glass." *Stalking the Nightmare*.

Epstein, Leslie. "Lessons." *The Steinway Quintet, Plus Four*.

Ferlinghetti, Lawrence. "Where Is Vietnam?" *New Directions in Prose and Poetry* 19.

Ferry, James. "Dancing Ducks and Talking Anus." *The Best American Short Stories, 1982*.

Fowler, Karen Joy. "The Lake Was Full of Artificial Things." *Isaac Asimov's Science Fiction Magazine*, October 1985.

Geller, Ruth. "Pat's Friend Norm." *Pictures From the Past, and Other Stories*.

Gerald, John Bart. "Walking Wounded." *The Best American Short Stories, 1969*.

Gibson, Margaret. "All Over Now." *Considering Her Condition*.

Grant, Charles L. "Come Dance With Me on My Pony's Grave." *The Magazine of Fantasy & Science Fiction*, July 1973.

Grau, Shirley Ann. "Homecoming." *The Wild Shifting West.*

Grinstead, David. "A Day in Operations." *The Fact of Fiction.*

Haldeman, Joe. "Counterpoint." *Infinite Dreams.*

Hannah, Barry. "Midnight and I'm Not Famous Yet." *Airships.*

Hasford, Gustav. "The Short-Timers" (excerpt). *Yesterday's Tomorrows.*

Heinemann, Larry. "The First Clean Fact." *The Best American Short Stories, 1980.*

Hoch, Edward D. "The Nine Eels of Madame Wu." *A Special Kind of Crime.*

Huddle, David. "Rosie Baby." *A Dream With No Stump Roots in It.*

——. "The Interrogation of the Prisoner Bung by Mister Hawkins and Sergeant Tree." *A Dream With No Stump Roots in It.*

Ireland, David. "The Wild Colonial Boy." *Winter's Tales 25.*

Jacobs, Harvey. "The Negotiators." *Writing Under Fire: Stories of the Vietnam War.*

Jorgensen, Erik. "Typhoon." *Angels in My Oven.*

Jose, Nicolas. "Outstretched Wings and Orient Light." *The Possession of Amber.*

Just, Ward. "The Congressman Who Loved Flaubert." *The Congressman Who Loved Flaubert, and Other Washington Stories.*

——. "Journal of a Plague Year." *Honor, Power, Riches, Fame, and the Love of Women.*

Kaplan, Johanna. "Dragon Lady." *Other People's Lives.*

Kelly, F. J. "The Vietnam Circle." *Alfred Hitchcock's Tales to Fill You With Fear and Trembling.*

Kerr, Blaine. "Rapture." *Jumping-Off Place.*

Kolpacoff, Victor. "The Room." *New American Review,* no. 1.

Koons, George. "Extra Man." *Angels in My Oven.*

Kumin, Maxine. "The Missing Person." *The Best American Short Stories, 1979.*

——. "These Gifts." *Why Can't We Live Together Like Civilized Human Beings?*

Malzberg, Barry N. "Final War." *Final War and Other Fantasies.*

Masur, Harold Q. "Dead Game." *Alfred Hitchcock Presents: Stories That Go Bump in the Night.*

McCluskey, John A. "John Henry's Home." *The Best American Short Stories, 1976.*

Menzies, H. N. "About, March!" *Festival, and Other Stories.*

Metcalfe, Barry. "Black Cat." *The Oxford Book of New Zealand Writing Since 1945.*

Meyer, Mike. "Klein's Wedding." *The Story Workshop Reader.*

Moorcock, Michael. "Crossing into Cambodia." *Light Years and Dark.*

Oates, Joyce Carol. "Out of Place." *The Seduction and Other Stories.*

O'Brien, Tim. "The Ghost Soldiers." *Great Esquire Fiction.*

——. "Going After Cacciato." *The Best American Short Stories, 1977.*

——. "Night March." *Prize Stories, 1976: The O. Henry Awards.*

——. "Speaking of Courage." *Massachusetts Review*, Summer 1976.

Pancake, Breeze D'J. "The Honored Dead." *The Stories of Breeze D'J Pancake*.

Parker, Thomas. "Troop Withdrawal." *The Fact of Fiction*.

Prager, Emily. "The Lincoln-Pruitt, Anti-Rape Device: Momoirs of the Woman's Combat Army in Vietnam." *A Visit From the Footbinder, and Other Stories*.

Rasco, Judith. "Soldier, Soldier." *Yours, and Mine*.

Richie, Mary. "Hunt and Destroy." *The Fact of Fiction*.

Robinson, Spider. "Unnatural Causes." *Callahan's Crosstime Saloon*.

Ryman, Geoff. "The Unconquered Country." *Interzone 4*.

Sang, Nguyen. "The Ivory Comb." *Fragments From a Lost Diary, and Other Stories*.

Sayles, John. "Tan." *The Anarchists' Convention*.

Schmidt, Warren. "A War Dream." *Believing Everything*.

Shepard, Lucius. "Salvador." *The Magazine of Fantasy & Science Fiction*, April 1984.

——. "R & R." *Isaac Asimov's Science Fiction Magazine*, April 1986.

——. "Fire Zone Emerald." *Playboy*, February 1986.

Sloan, James Park. "Vietnam No Big Deal." *Moral Fiction*.

Thacker, Julia. "A Civil Campaign." *New Directions in Prose and Poetry 44*.

Tiptree, James, Jr. "Beam Us Home." *Ten Thousand Light-Years From Home*.

Wolfe, Gene. "Feather Tigers." *The Island of Doctor Death and Other Stories and Other Stories*.

Wolfe, Tobias. "Wingfield." *Encounter*, July 1980.

Yates, Ethel M. "Seeds of Time." *Alabama Prize Stories 1970*.

Poetry

Ehrhart, W. D., ed. *Carrying the Darkness: American Indochina—The Poetry of the Vietnam War*. New York: Avon, 1985.

Nonfiction

Baker, Mark. *Nam*. New York: William Morrow, 1981

Byrd, Barthy. *Home Front: Women and Vietnam*. Berkeley: Shameless Hussy Press, 1986. [P.O. Box 3092, Berkeley, California 94703].

Caputo, Philip. *A Rumor of War*. New York: Holt, Rinehart and Winston, 1977.

Edelman, Bernard. *Dear America: Letters Home From Vietnam*. New York: Norton, 1985.

FitzGerald, Frances. *Fire in the Lake*. Boston: Little, Brown, 1972.

Gettleman, Marvin E., Jane Franklin, Marilyn Young, and H. Bruce Franklin. *Vietnam and America: A Documented History*. New York: Grove Press, 1985.

Giglia, Paul. *A Time for Heroes: Self-Help Handbook for Vietnam Veterans*. Buffalo, N.Y.: Perfect Press, 1983.

Goldman, Peter, and Tony Fuller. *Charlie Company: What Vietnam Did to Us*. New York: William Morrow, 1983; Ballantine, 1984.

Herr, Michael. *Dispatches*. New York: Alfred A. Knopf, 1968; Avon, 1978, 1980.

Karnow, Stanley. *Vietnam: A History*. New York: Viking Press, 1983; Penguin, 1984.

MacPherson, Myra. *Long Time Passing: Vietnam & the Haunted Generation*. New York: Doubleday, 1984; Signet, 1985.

Mailer, Norman. *The Armies of the Night*. New York: New American Library, 1968.

Polner, Murray. *No Victory Parades: The Return of the Vietnam Veteran*. New York: Holt, Rinehart and Winston, 1971.

Pratt, John Clark. *Vietnam Voices: Perspectives on the War Years, 1941–1982*. New York: Viking Press, 1984.

Robins, Christopher. *Air America*. New York: G. P. Putnam, 1979; Avon, 1985.

Salisbury, Harrison E. *Vietnam Reconsidered: Lessons From a War*. New York: Harper & Row, 1984.

Santoli, Al. *Everything We Had: An Oral History of the Vietnam War by Thirty-three American Soldiers Who Fought It*. New York: Random House, 1981; Ballantine, 1982.

——. *To Bear Any Burden: The Vietnam War and Its Aftermath in the Words of Americans and Southeast Asians*. E. P. Dutton, 1985.

Schurmann, Franz, Peter Dale Scott, and Reginald Zelnik. *The Politics of Escalation in Vietnam*. New York: Beacon Press, 1966; Fawcett Premier, 1966.

Starr, Paul. *The Discarded Army: Veterans After Vietnam*. New York: Charterhouse, 1973.

Wheeler, John. *Touched With Fire: The Future of the Vietnam Generation*. New York: Franklin Watts, 1984; Avon, 1985.

Articles

Boman, Bruce. "The Vietnam Veteran Ten Years On." *Australian & New Zealand Journal of Psychiatry*, September 1982.

Brown, Patti Coleen. "Legacies of a War: Treatment Considerations with Vietnam Veterans and Their Families." *Social Work*, July–August 1984.

Dewane, Claudia J. "Posttraumatic Stress Disorder in Medical Personnel in Vietnam." *Hospital & Community Psychiatry*, December 1984.

Foy, David W. *et al*. "Etiology of Posttraumatic Stress Disorder in Vietnam Veterans: Analysis of Premilitary, Military, and Combat Exposure Influences.'' *Journal of Consulting and Clinical Psychology*, February 1984.

Glover, Hillel. ''Guilt and Aggression in Vietnam Veterans.'' *American Journal of Social Psychiatry*, 1985, vol. 5.

Jurich, Anthony P. ''The Saigon of the Family's Mind: Family Therapy With Families of Vietnam Veterans.'' *Journal of Marital and Family Therapy*, October 1983.

Keane, Terence M. *et al.* ''Social Support in Vietnam Veterans With Posttraumatic Stress Disorder: A Comparative Analysis.'' *Journal of Consulting and Clinical Psychology*, February 1985.

Lund, Mary et al. ''The Combat Exposure Scale: A Systematic Assessment of Trauma in the Vietnam War.'' *Journal of Clinical Psychology*, November 1984.

Lynn, Edward J. ''Factitious Posttraumatic Stress Disorder: The Veteran Who Never Got to Vietnam.'' *Hospital & Community Psychiatry*, July 1984.

Malloy, Paul F. ''Validation of a Multimethod Assessment of Posttraumatic Stress Disorders in Vietnam Veterans.'' *Journal of Consulting and Clinical Psychology*, August 1983.

Pearce, Kathy A. ''A Study of Post Traumatic Stress Disorder in Vietnam Veterans.'' *Journal of Clinical Psychology*, January 1985.

Stretch, Robert H., James D. Vail, and Joseph Maloney. ''Posttraumatic Stress Disorder Among Army Nurse Corps Vietnam Veterans.'' *Journal of Consulting and Clinical Psychology*, October 1985.

U.S. Congress, House, Committee on Veterans' Affairs. *Readjustment Counseling Programs for Vietnam Veterans*, 97th Congress, 1982, 1st session, parts I, II. (Available from Superintendent of Documents, U.S. Government Printing Office, Washington, D.C. 20402.)

Glossary of Acronyms and Selected Terms

AFB: Air Force Base
AFVN: Armed Forces Vietnam Network, radio station
AID: Agency for International Development
AIT: Advanced Individual Training; specialized training, also referred to as Advanced Infantry Training
AK-47: Soviet-manufactured combat rifle, used by North Vietnamese and the NLF
AO: Area of Operations for a military unit
APC: Armored Personnel Carrier
ARVN: Army of the Republic of Vietnam; the South Vietnamese regular army
AWOL: Absent Without Leave
B-40 rocket: a shoulder-held rocket-propelled grenade launcher
BOQ: Bachelor Officer Quarters
CA: Combat Assault
CAS: Covert Action branch, Saigon office of the CIA
CHMAAG: Chief, Military Assistance Advisory Group
CI: Counterinsurgency
CIA: Central Intelligence Agency
CIB: Combat Infantryman's Badge; awarded to army infantrymen who had been under fire in a combat zone.
CIDG: Civilian Irregular Defense Group
CINCPAC: Commander in Chief, Pacific
Claymore: an antipersonnel mine
CO: Commanding Officer
CONUS: Continental U.S.
Corps: Military regions dividing Vietnam, as follows:
I Corps—the five northern provinces of South Vietnam
II Corps—the Central Highlands and Central Coastal area of South Vietnam

III Corps—the provinces immediately surrounding Saigon
IV Corps—the southern provinces of South Vietnam

COS: Chief of Station, CIA country team

CP: Command Post

CQ: Charge of Quarters; an officer officially in charge of a unit headquarters at night.

DEROS: Date of Expected Return from Overseas

DIA: Defense Intelligence Agency

DMZ: Demilitarized Zone; the area at the seventeenth parallel (17° North Latitude) which divided North and South Vietnam.

DOD: Department of Defense

DRV: Democratic Republic of Vietnam; North Vietnam

E and E: Escape and Evasion

EOD: Explosive Ordnance Disposal; specialists in disarming explosive devices

FAC: Forward Air Controller

FO: Forward Observer

FOA: Foreign Operations Administration

Green Berets: Special Forces Unit of the U.S. military, trained in guerrilla warfare and counterinsurgency

HM: Navy Hospital Corpsman; a medic

Hooch: a hut or simple dwelling

Hot LZ: a landing zone under enemy fire

ICA: International Cooperation Administration

ICC: International Control Commission for Vietnam and Laos

ICSC: International Commission for Supervision and Control in Vietnam

IDA: Institute for Defense Analysis

ISA: International Security Agency

JCS: Joint Chiefs of Staff

KIA: Killed in Action

Lao Dong: the Communist Party of Vietnam

LBJ: Long Binh Jail; a military stockade at Long Binh post; also, Lyndon Baines Johnson, the President

LCM: a medium-sized landing craft, used to transport troops ashore

LP: a listening post; a forward observation post of two or three men; also, an amphibious landing platform used by the infantry.

LRRP: Long Range Reconnaissance Patrol; a team of five to

seven men sent into the jungle to observe the enemy without making contact.

LST: troop landing ship

Lurp: the slang term for LRRP, derived from the pronunciation of the acronym

LZ: Landing Zone for helicopters

MAC SOG: Military Advisory Command Studies and Observations Group

MACV: Military Assistance Command, Vietnam; the U.S. Army military advisors in Vietnam.

M-14: wood-stock rifle used in the early portion of the Vietnam War

M-16: American standard-issue rifle after 1966

M-60: a lightweight machine gun used by U.S. forces in Vietnam

M-79: a single-barreled grenade launcher used by the infantry

MIA: Missing in Action

Montagnard: the aboriginal tribespeople inhabiting the hills and mountains of Central and Northern Vietnam

MP: Military Police

NCO: Noncommissioned Officer

NLF: National Liberation Front of South Vietnam

NSA: National Security Agency

NSC: National Security Council

NVA: North Vietnamese Army

NVN: Democratic People's Republic of Vietnam (North Vietnam)

OBE: Out-of-Body Experience

OP: Observation Post

Ops: Operations

OR: Operating Room

PAT: Political Action Team

PAV: People's Army of Vietnam

PAVN: People's Army of (North) Vietnam

Perimeter: outer limits of a military position

PFC: Private First Class

Point: the forward man or element on a combat mission

PRG: Provisional Revolutionary Government of South Vietnam

Psyops: Psychological operations

Psywar: Psychological warfare

PX: Post Exchange; military store

Ranger: a soldier especially trained for reconnaissance and combat missions

R & R: Rest and Relaxation; a three-to-seven-day leave from the combat zone

Recon: Reconnaissance

RPG: Rocket-propelled grenade

RTO: Radio and telephone operator

SeaBees: Navy construction engineers

SEAL: member of the Navy's Sea Air Land Special operations team, comparable to Army Green Berets

Short-timer: a soldier nearing the end of his tour in Vietnam.

SKS: Soviet semiautomatic rifle

SF: Special Forces; a unit of the U.S. military especially trained in guerrilla warfare and counterinsurgency; known as Green Berets because of their identifying headgear. The Special Forces were the first troops sent into Vietnam by President Kennedy in the early '60s.

Sp/5: Specialist Fifth Class; equivalent to a sergeant

Sp/4: Specialist Fourth Class; equivalent to a corporal

Tet: the lunar New Year; a Buddhist holiday

Tracer: a round of ammunition treated to glow or give off smoke

USAF: U.S. Air Force

USIA: U.S. Information Agency

USIS: U.S. Information Service

USOM: U.S. Operations Mission

VC: Viet Cong

Viet Cong: the South Vietnamese guerrilla forces in rebellion against the government of South Vietnam; the enemy. Originally the name was a term of derision used by the South Vietnamese government for the Lao Dong (the Vietnamese Communist Party)—Viet Cong loosely translates as "slaves" or "peasants."

Ville: a Vietnamese village

WIA: Wounded in Action

World: the United States

XO: Executive Officer

About the Editors

Jeanne Van Buren Dann has been a nurse for seventeen years. During her career she has been in charge of an intensive-care–coronary care unit and has also worked in the operating room. Currently she is pursuing an M.S.W. at the Nelson A. Rockefeller College of Public Affairs and Policy at SUNY Albany, and is planning a career in counseling disabled American veterans. She has recently sold her first story to *Omni*. She lives and works in Binghamton, New York.

Jack Dann is the author or editor of twenty-one books. Among his novels are *Junction*, *Starhiker*, and *The Man Who Melted*, which *The Washington Post Book World* compared to Ingmar Bergman's classic film *The Seventh Seal*. He is the editor of the anthology *Wandering Stars*, one of the most acclaimed anthologies of the 1970s, and several other well-known anthologies, such as *More Wandering Stars*. His short fiction has appeared in *Playboy*, *Penthouse*, *Omni*, and most of the leading science fiction magazines and anthologies. He has many times been a finalist for the Nebula award, and has also been a finalist for the World Fantasy Award and the British Science Fiction Award. Some of his stories are included in his collection *Timetipping*. His critical work has appeared in *The Washington Post*, *Starship*, *Nickelodeon*, *The Bulletin of the Science Fiction Writers of America*, *Empire*, *The Fiction Writers Handbook*, and other magazines and newspapers. His most recent book is the mainstream novel *Counting Coup*. Forthcoming are two more anthologies in the fantasy series, edited with Gardner Dozois. Dann is currently working on a historical fantasy novel about Leonardo da Vinci, tentatively entitled *Da Vinci Airborn*, and on several other novel and anthology projects. Dann lives with his family in Binghamton, New York.